THE

BLIND

SPOTS

ALSO BY THOMAS MULLEN

The Last Town on Earth
The Many Deaths of the Firefly Brothers
The Revisionists
Darktown
Lightning Men
Midnight Atlanta

The item should be returned or renewed
by the last date stamped below.

Dylid dychwelyd neu adnewyddu'r eitem erbyn
y dyddiad olaf sydd wedi'i stampio isod.

To renew visit / Adnewyddwch ar
www.newport.gov.uk/libraries

THE

THOMAS MULLEN

BLIND

SPOTS

abacus
books

ABACUS

First published in the United States in 2023 by Minotaur Books,
an imprint of St. Martin's Publishing Group
First published in Great Britain in 2023 by Sphere

1 3 5 7 9 10 8 6 4 2

A CIP catalogue record for this book
is available from the British Library.

Hardback ISBN 978-1-4087-1504-8
Trade Paperback ISBN 978-1-4087-1503-1

Printed and bound in Great Britain by
Clays Ltd, Elcograf S.p.A.

Papers used by Sphere are from well-managed forests
and other responsible sources.

Sphere
An imprint of
Little, Brown Book Group
Carmelite House
50 Victoria Embankment
London EC4Y 0DZ

An Hachette UK Company
www.hachette.co.uk

www.littlebrown.co.uk

For Jenny

PART ONE

VISIONS

CHAPTER 1

Owens still remembers what it was like to trust. Trust his eyes, his friends, his employer. Trust his own mind, the signals firing inside his brain, the response of his body to the world around him.

Trust is something you don't think about. When it exists, it's invisible.

Like gravity. When something you let go of falls to the ground, you might be annoyed but never surprised, because that's just how it works.

Until it stops working, and everything's floating in the air, and nothing makes sense.

And for the rest of your life—even if things get fixed later, even if the earth regains its gravitational pull and the world returns to "normal"—you will never again feel as certain as you once did, no matter how many things you see fall.

Owens sits in his squad car and he trusts what he sees. Because that's how it's supposed to work.

Beside him, Peterson only half stifles a belch. Salami breath, fragrant and thick.

In the back seat, Khouri too plays her role by shaking her head in disgust. Owens can't see behind himself, but he can *feel* her shaking her head; that's how well he knows her. She says, "Thanks, Jimmy."

"At least you can't smell it back there," Owens says.

"Oh, but I can."

They're parked in the River District, the deceptively picturesque name of this shithole. A river does indeed snake through here, somewhere. Not that anyone strolls along its banks or kayaks it or God forbid fishes out of it. Empty warehouses decay around them. Once upon a time this neighborhood was high on some developers' lists, inspiring fever dreams of gentrification and easy money from postindustrial urban redevelopment, but The Blinding put an end to such plans.

The few nightclubs in the area trade on their proximity to crime and danger. Adventurous young professionals come out to dance and party and get high, catch rides to their safer communities to fuck and cuddle and sleep. If something goes wrong for them here, they'll call for people like Owens to help out.

Years ago pranksters or artists or some combination had thrown paint in wild colors over many of the derelict buildings. Not so much graffiti as orgasms of color. Swatches of yellow here, orange there, violet. Formerly quiet, gray and brown surfaces now proclaiming themselves in loud hues. Owens isn't sure if it had been during the early stages of The Blinding, when everyone liked vibrant colors because that was about all people could see, or the early stages of the vidders, when people were so relieved to be able to "see" again that they threw colors everywhere. Clothing during those days was wild, neon or shiny and reflective, everyone reveling once again in the once-lost pleasures of sight.

Well, almost everyone.

Owens watches the street, looking for anything unusual. He sees the normal line of clubgoers waiting to get into Slade's, the bouncers checking IDs. Down the street, a pop-up ad on his display informs him that a run-down garage called Cranky Joe's is now offering specials on lithium and solar batteries. Another pop-up at sky level notes a temperature of 56 with a 5 mph southwesterly wind and a 60 percent chance of rain after midnight.

And the time, of course, in the info bar that always lingers at the lowest point of his field of vision, tells him it's 11:15 P.M. The fact that it is night is meaningless, visually, as Owens, like everyone else, sees equally well in darkness. A whole planet of vampire bats.

Except he misses sunlight. Glare. Even misses squinting.

Finally his phone buzzes in his pocket. He holds it to his ear. Dispatch gives the green light.

He kills the call and tells them, "Warrant went through. We're on for X-ray."

He adjusts a dial on his vidder, the small, 1-inch-diameter metal disc implanted on his right temple. On nearly everyone's right temple. The vidder relays radar, GPS, and every variety of visual data to his occipital lobe's visual cortex, compensating for his permanently blinded eyes.

"Bureaucratic nonsense," Peterson says. "Could have closed this case weeks ago if we'd had X-ray then."

"Right to privacy's a bitch," Khouri says. Unclear if she's agreeing or not.

The good news is that the powers that be within the municipal government, given the okay from a judge, are now transmitting code to Owens's vidder to unlock, temporarily, its ability to interpret even 3D radar that normal vision wouldn't be able to access.

In other words, to see through walls.

He focuses on the brick exterior of the club down the street. With his court-approved enhancement, he can now "see" through the brick wall of the old factory building. The ability is limited to a short range, but still, every time he's used it he's felt like a superhero, a god. Adrenaline spikes as he peruses the building's secrets.

"Full house, two guards inside the door," he tells them. "They're carrying." He aims his view upstairs, peels away one wall, then another. "That's our man on the second floor. Matches his heat readout."

Peterson touches his earpiece. "Your mike's good."

Owens opens the door.

"Good luck," Khouri blesses him.

Peterson translates: "Don't fuck up."

* * *

Christ Almighty, the bass. If pop music had leaned on the crutch of bass a bit too much back in the good ol' sighted days, things have gotten down to a whole new octave of heavy since The Blinding. When you lose a sense, the others crave extra stimulus. The introduction of vidders six years ago hasn't seemed to push music on a more trebly track. Owens's feet vibrate, his chest vibrates. He could have a heart attack in here and not know it until everything went black. Again.

Dance floors are mobbed, the bars three deep. Bartenders hustle yet disappoint. Despite the cold outside, the coat check girl must be busy, as some serious flesh is on display. Owens figures maybe 10 to 25 percent of the people here are on opsin, a derivation of X that's become a scourge in recent years. A drug that can make you hear colors and see music, at a time when eyes on their own don't work at all? Yes, please. Even his wife used to take it, when she thought he wouldn't notice, insisting it helped her see correctly. Like before.

Owens misses being young. Misses not knowing what's behind the curtain. The many curtains.

He hates being in crowds like this. When he was a teenager, a fire broke out at a nearby rock club, killing dozens. People had been crushed to death trying to squeeze out of the few doors they could find. Some of his friends had been there. They'd lived, but they were emotionally scarred. So even before earning his badge, he's always carried a certain amount of near-paranoia, the need to be aware of escape routes at all times.

So goddamn loud in here, he could say into his earpiece, *Abort, I'm blown, they're going to kill me, help,* and Peterson and Khouri might not hear a thing. So hopefully it won't come to that.

Four clubgoers (two male, two female) move from the main floor to a second, smaller dance room. No-bullshit bouncer approaches them. He looks displeased and points to the sign, "FOUR SENSES ONLY."

His mouth moves, but who can hear him? They read lips: "No vidders in this room."

The four kids wear the grins of people trying something illicit for the first time. Practically giggling as they walk to a small window and detach their vidders by rotating them until they come free. They hand them to the heavily mascaraed, Goth-dressed vidder-check girl, who tags and files them like so many jackets.

The four now-blind clubgoers get crazy on the Four Senses dance floor, ears working overtime, touch working double overtime, hands everywhere, caressing and tapping and rubbing, no one stopping, synapses afire. Damn near *everyone* in this room on something.

Owens takes the merest glimpse into that borderline orgy. Feels even older. Looks back at one of the bars, spots the undercover. Eye contact for less than a second.

He finds the bouncer he's been looking for, yells in the guy's ear. Deafness is a serious occupational hazard here. The bouncer nods, leads Owens to and then through a black door.

Back at the bar, the undercover's lips move. Tells her mike, and therefore Peterson, that Owens is in.

Owens stands in a large, loftlike living room on the second floor. Surprisingly swank, the furniture somehow both sleek and comfortable. Windows everywhere. As if it's just another rich guy's bachelor pad that happens to have an earthquake roaring beneath it.

Enter the man himself, Slade. Tall, long hair, phony smile. Many tattoos, the raised kind, evidence of a past searing of flesh. He wears a faux-metallic suit that (Owens's vidder informs him) reflects what little light exists in the room. Like everywhere else, the loft doesn't bother with electric lighting, as people don't require it anymore.

Handshake, no how's-life bullshit. Sits down and gets to business.

On the glass coffee table sits a tablet, which Slade picks up. He "reads" the display of numbers thanks to the tiny scanner in his vidder.

Owens sees no one else in the very large room. Which is weird.

Either it's a sign of inordinate trust, or Slade has plenty of men just outside.

"It's all transferred into the account, instantaneous," Owens explains. He scans the walls and perceives movement behind one of them. Tries not to be obvious about it.

Slade nods at the numbers, puts down the tablet. "You're good at this."

"Took more than a month to cover my tracks. C'mon, if we're gonna do this, I don't have all night."

Do this meaning move black-market firearms.

"All right, all right. My boy's getting it. Calm down."

Slade gets up to pour a drink. Owens stands, too, though he wasn't offered one.

"Sorry," Owens says. "It's not every night I do this."

"No shit."

Owens scans the walls again. Big dude on the other side of the near one. Not the bouncer from before. Someone new.

"What?" Slade's eyes scream *suspicion*. Owens was too obvious. His gut muscles constrict.

"Nothing. Lovely place."

Slade's expression like a human polygraph. Awaiting results. "I didn't know any better, I'd think you were looking through the walls."

Fuck.

Owens makes himself laugh. Tries to project calm. "That'd be cool."

Slade's polygraph going *beep beep beep*.

"Of course," Slade says, dead calm, "the only people who can do that are cops with warrants."

In the car, Khouri is silently cursing the fact that she forgot to bring her own headset and instead has to sit here dumb and clueless and staring at Peterson's fugly face awaiting signs.

Until Peterson's face falls and he looks sick and says, "He's blown. Let's go."

Car doors are thrown open, sidearms leap out of holsters.

Owens feigns mere annoyance. Keeps still, like he's prey that a predator won't spot without motion.

He says, "We've had this conversation, man."

Slade puts his glass on the bar. Moves his hands to his hips.

"If you were a cop with a warrant, you'd be able to tell if I had a gun in this jacket."

"Cut the paranoia, okay?"

Yet that's exactly what Owens does. Visually frisks Slade, the layers peeling away X-ray style. And yes, that would be a pistol in Slade's jacket.

They eye each other for a moment. Even though everyone's eyes are now sightless, and visual data is sent to their brains via devices, people still aim their gazes the way they always have, need a place within their visual field to focus their attention. Stare-downs, evil eyes, wicked looks—they all still exist.

Slade makes a motion like he's going to reach into his jacket. Owens backs up instinctively. Slade laughs, not drawing the gun, merely taking his empty hand back out.

"Damn, you looked scared!" Slade's laugh reaches a new pitch. Owens never liked guys with that high of a laugh. Too performative. Like they're laughing at themselves laughing at you. "You're no cop."

Owens exhales in relief but tries not to look like it. "Hilarious."

Shaking his head, he turns and scans the wall behind him. And that's when he sees it, that a man in that other room is picking up a large gun.

Coincidence or danger?

Tries to think.

While Owens is facing that way, he hears Slade un-holster a gun and say, "Keep your hands where I can see them."

Not coincidence. Shit.

Owens half turns, so he's profile to Slade, who's only three feet away and training a gun on him. He keeps his hands in front of him.

"There are a dozen cops entering this building right now," Owens says. Calm voice, just the facts. "Don't make this worse on yourself."

Also a fact: Slade could shoot him now and then try to escape.

Behind Owens, a door opens and in comes Nayles, Slade's deputy. Long dreads and braids, muscles that have muscles. He's brandishing an automatic rifle that would look massive in a mere mortal's hands.

"Cops at the front door," Nayles says.

Slade says, "Son of a bitch."

The good news is they don't shoot Owens. The bad news is Slade swings his gun into Owens's temple, square into his vidder. Hurts like hell.

Owens hits the floor. He sees a flash of black, then gray-screen pixelations. They seem to vibrate and thrum (or maybe that's just the pain?) but don't go away. As he begins to pull himself up he thinks, *Fuck fuck fuck.* His vidder's been damaged. He can't see.

He hears Slade say, "Upstairs."

Footsteps. Owens turns toward the sound and launches himself. Maybe lucky, maybe not, but he feels impact, wraps his arms around someone, tackles him to the ground.

Something heavy and metal lands on the ground too. The rifle. Which means he's tackled big Nayles. Footsteps recede, Slade escaping up the stairs.

Owens wrestles atop Nayles. He uses one hand to make sure he knows where Nayles's face is, then punches him with the other. Twice. The back of Nayles's head hits the floor both times, and he's out.

Lucky, hell yes.

Owens fiddles with his vidder, but he feels broken pieces and still can't see. Waste of time. He crawls on the ground, finds the rifle. One he isn't terribly familiar with. Has a thought, puts the rifle down. Crawls back to Nayles and searches him. *Voila*—a semiautomatic pistol.

Has to hope it's loaded. Flicks off the safety. Cocks it.

Assuming his mike wasn't damaged during the wrestling match, he says, "Jimmy, my vidder's out. I think Slade ran up to the top floor."

He stands unsteadily, reaching forward until he finds the wall. His hands trace it to the doorway.

The feeling vertiginous, familiar in all the worst ways. Wills himself forward: *Move now, experience awful flashbacks later.*

Hand on the railing, he climbs the first step.

Giving chase to an armed suspect while blind would rank high on anyone's list of Things Not to Do. Surely they covered this in officer training. But Owens was a rookie way back before The Blinding, when such concerns were unthinkable.

At the top of the stairs, he steps into an unfamiliar room, blind, with a gun in his hands. He focuses on his other senses.

Smell tells him damp, mortar dust, metal pipes. If the second floor was a warehouse space retrofitted as a trendy urban loft, the third floor seems to be the same, minus the retrofitting.

Sound. The music from the ground floor is slightly less loud up here. Sound waves and echoes tell him the walls are widely spaced and bare.

Touch. He reaches forward and finds a metal pipe. Heat. Pain. He pulls his scalded hand away and shakes it.

Taste. Acid in the back of his throat. Fear and energy and a metallic tang, along with a hunger for more.

He steps slowly, left hand out, and concentrates on putting his feet down silently. He realizes he got turned around in the stairway, he rushed, so he lost track of which direction he's now facing, his place within the geometry of the building. He's in a large rectangular room but unsure if he's near the long walls or the short ones.

His foot hits something, but his left hand tells him *Empty space.* A half wall, then. Brick up to his knees. He navigates around it.

This is a mistake.

Keeps hoping he'll hear footsteps pounding up the stairs, the cops in force. Where are they?

He hears Slade's voice.

"Get a car at the corner of 17th and Wilson, now." Talking to someone on a phone. Far enough away that he hasn't spotted Owens.

The darkness vast, impenetrable. It allows passage through it only grudgingly, and it takes more than it gives. The only thing Owens hates more than darkness is death, and of course the two are inextricably bound in his mind. The adrenaline and the chase are probably the only reason he isn't curled up in a ball, screaming.

That will come after, if he makes it that far.

Here are the things he cannot see, but will understand later, after the others reconstruct it for him:

Slade standing at a window, looking out at the scene below. Closer than Owens would have thought, his voice reflecting off the glass in a way that confuses Owens's ears. Maybe forty feet.

Slade turning and noticing Owens. Smiling at the blind cop. Aiming his gun at Owens.

Then a door opening behind Owens and to his right.

Owens turns his head at the sound but can't tell what's happening. One of Slade's goons, gun in hand. Slade puts a finger to his lips to shush the goon. The guy mouths *Cops* as if Slade wasn't already well fucking aware that his place was being stormed.

Slade can shoot one cop now, at least.

Except the shot that rings out doesn't come from his gun, or his associate's. The associate staggers and falls. Peterson takes his place in the doorway, gun first.

Peterson and Slade aim at each other, and fire, and miss, and duck.

* * *

Owens taking cover on the floor now, gunfire everywhere. His world darkness and deafening explosions. Mortar dust on his face and hands.

What he doesn't see:

The guy whom Peterson shot rising like a zombie. Kevlar vest. He tackles Peterson, puts him in a headlock. Peterson's gun falls.

Slade watching them, gun aimed, mentally debating how much he likes his accomplice and whether he should just fire at both of them.

Chooses leniency, for now. But creeps closer.

Peterson drives the other guy's head into a wall. The goon falls.

So Slade sneaks behind Peterson, puts an arm around his neck, a gun at his temple.

"You're my ticket out of here, cop."

Owens stands, not liking the sound of that. He points his weapon at the general area the sounds came from.

"Drop it!" Slade shouts. "I got your buddy right here! Drop it or I shoot him!"

Owens slowly steps toward them, gun first.

His POV dark gray, washed out. The pixelations have faded and now offer him the visual equivalent of white noise. Stone blind.

"Let him go. Don't be stupid."

He bumps into what might be a chair or an ironing board or a torture device and knocks it away. Listening carefully.

"*I'm* being stupid? You can't *see*, motherfucker."

"So keep talking."

Owens thinks Slade's face might look slightly nervous now. Foot scuffs. Slade is slowly moving toward a door, taking his captive with him. Another scuff, louder. Peterson probably doing that on purpose, aural bread crumbs.

Peterson says into his mike, "We're at the southwest corner—"

"Shut up or I'll shoot!" Slade sounding like someone who realizes he is no longer in control.

"You don't have to talk, Jimmy," Owens assures his partner. "I can hear him breathing."

Owens can also hear Slade purse his lips in hopes that it silences his breathing. His nostrils flare as a result, the breaths just as loud as before. Slade's panicked and his chest is heaving and all his muscles are tense as he tries to move the very large Peterson along with him, but he can't stop how loudly he's breathing.

Owens thinks they're maybe twenty feet away.

"Keep breathing, Slade. Keep breathing."

Of course, Peterson is breathing too.

Maybe Peterson's eyes have widened as he realizes what's happening. Maybe that's *Peterson* panting, out of breath from wrestling the goon a moment ago. The fear Owens senses—the hairs prickling along the back of his neck, the taste of the air and the smell of the sweat—maybe that's coming from his partner, not from Slade, and Owens has misjudged the situation badly.

He's only fifteen feet away. Close enough. Holding the gun at what he imagines to be the level of Slade's head, based on sound and proximity and his memory of the man's height. Taller than Peterson by at least three inches.

Or maybe only two? No, three.

He tells himself that if Slade moves his gun from Peterson's head and toward Owens, he'll hear Slade's sleeve rustle.

He's pretty sure Slade is holding his breath now.

"More to your left!" Peterson blurts just in time, and Owens fires.

He normally wouldn't trust a single bullet, but he's afraid to fire a second. Either he's right, or he's catastrophically, tragically wrong.

He hates the silence almost as much as the darkness. Two seconds, three . . .

Something lands on the ground. Gravity still works.

"*Fuck* you, Mark!" Peterson screams. Aghast, stunned, and so hyped up he sounds like he could punch through a wall. But not shot. "You can't *see*?!"

"Not a thing. But I imagine he looks pretty bad right now."

CHAPTER 2

Nothing quite like the stink of a nightclub after hours. Sweat, spilled booze, puked booze, old smoke. The ghost of a good time. Owens remembers his days as a young bartender, cleaning up. Except tonight, Slade's was evacuated and cleared out by the police, no cleaning allowed.

On one of the main dance floors, boxes and boxes of guns are laid out. Uniforms painstakingly unpack, inspect, and document them.

Not that Owens can see any of this.

Someone who sounds young is fiddling with Owens's vidder, adjusting it. Running cables to it and connecting to a mainframe.

"This is way beyond gunrunning. This is fitting an army."

That voice belongs to Captain Carlyle. Mid-fifties, African American, known to fire up a cigar after closing a big case. Came up via Vice and Homicide, like Owens. Now running Major Crimes.

"That better?" the tech asks Owens.

On cue, his POV granulizes from the blank gray to a pixelated, phantasmagoric array of colors in the form of tiny boxes, then crystallizes again into more or less accurate vision.

"Better," he tells the tech, "but still a little wonky."

"Takes a few seconds."

Owens turns his glitchy gaze to Carlyle as he says, "I suppose I should know that by now, seeing as how this is the *third time* I've been blinded on the job."

"Cool off," Carlyle says. He's wearing the same annoyed expression Owens had been visualizing him wearing. His hairline seems more receded, as if the poor man has grown more bald over the last few hours. Really, Owens just hadn't noticed till now.

Funny the things you don't see when you can see.

Khouri joins in. "These things are too vulnerable, Captain."

"Damn right," Peterson says. White-faced. In case Owens needed confirmation that he'd truly scared the shit out of his partner.

Vidders are mostly reliable devices. Long warranties, seldom needed. Instant firmware updates almost daily, fixing bugs people hadn't even noticed. That said, they weren't designed for the daily wrestling matches that highlight many cops' shifts. People who play contact sports can buy special protective guards for them, but cops find that they get in the way. Many beat cops do wear the guards as part of their uniforms, but most plainclothes don't. For an undercover like Owens, they're out of the question.

"Think I don't know that?" Carlyle snaps. "I've lost seven officers this year. I've petitioned the mayor, we've got the union lobbying EyeTech for improvements. What else do you want?"

Owens ventures, "I'd sooner get a black-market vidder than risk another—"

"I'm not hearing this." Carlyle shakes his head. "Surely no officer of mine would even consider violating the law by equipping himself with contraband eyewear."

The black-market devices are said to be more tamperproof, for reasons Owens doesn't understand. Also highly illegal, as they sometimes come with other bells and whistles.

Owens adjusts a dial on his vidder, futzing with the focus.

The captain stands before him and asks, "Everything crystal clear now?"

Owens almost never invites other cops to his apartment, because he can't stand the envy. It's not especially ostentatious, but it's a whole echelon above your typical blue-collar or government-salary residence. A two-bedroom, situated on the top, fourth floor of a new building. Windows all around, offering a view of a better neighborhood than most of his colleagues could possibly afford. The early sunrise pours in, bathing the living room and kitchen in yellow.

Also unusual for a cop: the walls are busy with original paintings and mixed-art collages, oil paints mixed with sand and dirt and stones and found objects. Kitchen utensils, swimming goggles, sunglasses painted or glued or shattered and stuck to backgrounds of fever-dream color. Their combined value staggering, when he thinks about it, but he tries not to.

Amira Quigley stands in the kitchenette, drinking her first of several coffees. Her post-shower hair wet at the base of her neck, due for a trim. Sunrise and she's dead tired, up half the night worrying about what Owens had told her. Learning that someone you love is alive and mostly unharmed should come as a relief, but instead she felt haunted by visions of all that almost happened.

A cop herself, she allows the fear to take hold only when she's at her place, or at his. Because at work, she tamps all those fears far, far down.

She worked a different shift, off at 7 P.M. A beat cop, yesterday she broke up two fights, one in a bar and one in an apartment. Terrified neighbors had phoned in that last one. Husband and wife both bloody when she got there, both hating her for interrupting. Both now in lockup, hating her even more.

She had been warned when she started: the job makes you absorb everyone's anger, everyone's sadness. The warnings had failed to dissuade her. This has been the only job she's ever thought about, for years. Twenty-six years old now, four years in. No matter what the veterans at the academy threw at her, she was ready. Growing up, she hadn't thought about being a cop; then came the moment, during the early days of The Blinding, when a tough female officer promised to find Amira's missing brother, Dante. Despite barely being able to see *herself*, despite the chaos in the streets, the cop told Amira's family she'd find him.

She proved herself right a few days later, though not in the way they had hoped. She found his body, helped them ensure he had a proper burial. Despite Amira's grief and the shock of it all, she remembers thinking, *I want to be like her. I want to be that strong.*

After that, there was no other job she ever considered. She'd dropped out of college during The Blinding, as so many had, but when vidders were introduced she didn't go back, choosing the police academy instead.

When she joined the force and tried to find that cop and thank her once again, she learned the cop had eaten her gun months earlier.

She wishes she enjoyed the job more. She has the broad shoulders and the height, five-ten, and she can out-curl and out-bench many of the men she sizes up on her beat, but it's the internal pain that weighs on her.

The keypad beeps and Owens enters. Looks half dead.

"Hey," he exhales.

She hugs him. He seems to hold on extra long.

"You all right?" she asks.

He breaks it off, picks up her mug and sips her coffee. Makes a face. He's been up for more than twenty-four hours.

"Why am I drinking this?"

"This is probably the part when you start to realize how blinked out you are."

He looks at the mug. He regards his shaking hand dispassionately for a moment, as if it belongs to someone else. She takes the mug from him before he can drop it.

"You're okay. Just try to relax."

"Yeah. Sure." To calm his hands, he leans on the counter. "Nearly shot my partner, though."

"You've always wanted to shoot him."

He manages to smile, but barely.

"It just . . ."

"Makes you think about before?"

"Yes."

She holds him again, from behind. He turns and, eyes closed, traces her face with his fingers. Remembering that feeling of blindness, when all they had was touch.

CHAPTER 3

As cities go, it could be worse. Could be better, but people don't complain much. Because for a long time, it was much, much worse.

Seven years since The Blinding. The world had its share of troubles back then, sure, but even problems like wars and depressions fell into context, all life grinding to a halt as people began to realize, *Shit, my vision's funny.* Started gradually. Reports began in Indonesia, India, Australia. Optometrists and ophthalmologists became very busy indeed. "Extreme macular degeneration," the likes of which had never before been observed. Theories: it's a weird virus; it's something in the water; it's a new bioweapon unleashed by the Chinese or maybe the Russians; there's an atmospheric disturbance, climate change, an ozone hole, a parasite that itself must be invisible.

Started as minor news, a "Hey, that's weird" piece, random stories popping up in people's feeds. Then in less than a week the blinding (not yet capitalized) had blitzed across the Asian continent and over the Pacific to the Americas. Accelerated within every population, going from the initial, shockingly high 10 percent of Australians and 15 percent of Indians and then up to 75 percent of entire countries, then 90 percent.

In less than a month there wasn't a soul in those first countries who claimed to be unaffected.

Some people in Europe and Africa tried wearing swimming goggles at all times, but that didn't help. Entrepreneurs made quick fortunes hawking different types of sunglasses made from supposedly super-protective plastics, to no avail. Canceled flights, quarantines, closed borders: nothing worked. The crisis went global with frightening speed. Astronomers noted the recent close passage of certain asteroids and comets. Geiger counters were deployed, scientists of various stripes studying "invisible nuclear fallout." Chinese and Russian and American spy and military agencies insisted they weren't to blame; there was no death ray that someone forgot to turn off. Possibly a tipping point of wireless signals, maybe a subtle shift in Earth's rotation, or global warming releasing toxic gases from Antarctica, Siberia, the Arctic.

Such studies became increasingly difficult to conduct because *no one could fucking see.*

Officer Safiya Khouri has been on the force six years. Meaning she started as vidders were becoming commonplace and the unwieldy scaffolding of civic society was finally being reinforced after a year of hell.

She knows that the veteran cops, the ones who'd actually walked beats before—and, somehow, during—The Blinding look down on cops her age. Like she'd joined the Army right after the other side raised the white flag. So she puts up with their macho bullshit. She hears enough of their stories to agree that, *Yeah, I'm glad I wasn't in charge of anything back then. I was quite well consumed with trying to* survive, *trying to help my family survive.* The idea of being held responsible for enforcing safety, doing anything for anyone but yourself, was downright impossible to imagine.

So she never asks Owens or Peterson what it was like. Just waits to gather their random comments, half sentences. Assembles them over time to complete her Boschian internal portrait. She's glad she wasn't a cop then, but she's glad she's one now. Because that scaffolding of civic society remains very unwieldy indeed. An entire planet with PTSD.

She walks to headquarters at noon, sidewalks aswarm. Traffic passes near-silently, driverless e-cars drifting like ghosts. A pop-up informs her that the 12th Street ramp is closed due to construction today, and another offers her half off her favorite shawarma joint, as she hasn't been there in two weeks and it misses her.

She sees Peterson lumbering up the steps ahead of her.

"Jimmy." Khouri hurries after him. "Get any sleep?"

The bags under his eyes answer the question. As do the red lines in the eyes themselves. Even though eyes no longer function the way they once did, they retain some telltale signs. People still crave a place to focus within the vast visual field that their brain interprets, a way to orient themselves. Millions of years of evolution die hard. Most people still point their eyes toward the person they're addressing.

It's harder to read someone's emotions from their eyes than it used to be, tougher to detect deceit, but only slightly. People still look away if they're evasive. Reading body language becomes more important, feeling the other person's stiffness or relaxation, noting smell, detecting the subconscious hints, perceiving pheromones. Khouri took a course on this during officer training, thought it was bullshit, later changed her mind.

Point is, Peterson's sightless eyes still manage to convey *I am very, very tired.*

"Some," he admits.

Peterson is a large man. Clearly an ex-athlete, struggling to keep weight off his gut but still the proverbial kind of fellow you want on your side if you have to go through a door. Not the kind of guy you pitch softballs like *Are you okay?* Asking how he'd slept was as far as Khouri could imagine going. Usually it receives a bro-ish sexual response, so the lack this time means *Hell yes, he's beat.*

"Listen, I wanted to ask," Khouri says. Meaning, *Ask out here, away from anyone else. Away from Owens.* "Between you and me. How far away was he?"

Peterson pauses. "Not that far."

"He could have killed you."

"No shit."

He clearly does not want to discuss this. She presses.

"A shot like that is one in a million. Unless he had some kind of help."

"Yeah, they're called ears. Slade was panting like a hyena."

He moves toward the station again. As if he doesn't take this line of questioning seriously, but his body language screams *evasive,* which means he does.

In fact, it scares him.

She puts a hand on his shoulder to prevent his escape. "Come on, Jimmy. *You* want to take vidder-free target practice sometime?"

Peterson looks at her hand, which she removes. Then looks dead at her. "What are you trying to say?"

She's almost embarrassed to voice it aloud. Feels childish. But she's gone this far.

"You've heard the stories. What if he's one of *them*? What if he doesn't really need it?"

A few miles away, Amira drinks more coffee in Owens's kitchenette. She'd managed a bit more sleep after he came home, but she's groggy, her body confused. She's on 10-to-7 today, hoping for a calm shift. She checks herself in the mirror again.

Owens stumbles out of his room. Hair a mess.

He'd slept only a few hours. Not that his vidder is to blame—when people close their eyes now, the visual feed to their brain cuts out, so they see black, the way sleepers have since the dawn of time. Everyone's heard stories about the earliest vidders, the beta tests that sometimes failed to shut down when people closed their eyes. Those first subjects were thrilled to be able to see again but decidedly less thrilled to realize that even when they lay down and shut their eyes, it felt like they were staring at their ceilings.

So at least Owens doesn't have that problem, which was fixed years ago. Vidders even flash split seconds of black when people blink, to make it feel more like real vision.

Plenty of other things keep him up at night, though. Memories. Not visions so much as sounds, feelings.

He walks up to Amira and wraps his arms around her from behind. Kisses her neck.

"How come no one ever talks about the sexiness of a *woman* in uniform?"

She turns and kisses him back. Finally brings up the subject she's been excited about and worrying over. "So, have you thought any more about my proposition?"

He gets the wrong idea. "I seem to recall a number of propositions." Kisses her neck again. "Which one are we talking about?"

"The one about . . . real estate."

He still doesn't follow.

His hands are on her hips now. Her hands are on his hands as she says, "My lease ends in a month. Remember?"

He releases her. Backs up a step. She can already read the answer.

"Look, Amira . . . It's not that I don't want to. It's just—"

"That you don't want to." She turns and looks for her wallet on the counter.

A weighty silence. Owens could say something, but doesn't.

She turns around. "You're afraid that if I move in, suddenly I'm not going to want her paintings hanging there in the living room. Or the one in the hallway. Or the one over the *bed*."

He sighs. "We don't have to talk about—"

"Well, it hasn't stopped me from sleeping with you in that bed, has it? It sure hasn't stopped you."

"This isn't about Jeanie. All right?"

Her phone buzzes. She checks it, shoves it back in her pocket. "Fine. I'll renew my lease. See you at the station."

He feels empty as she leaves him there. He knows he played that wrong. Knows his emotions are wrong. Doesn't understand how he's supposed to act when he feels a way that someone else doesn't like, someone he cares about.

They've been seeing each other for about a year now, although the relationship has been gradual. Partly due to their incompatible schedules, and partly because . . . why, exactly? For the first few months they saw each other only once a week, and even now it's barely twice that. Her wanting to talk about the future is entirely understandable, yet still somehow he hadn't expected it.

He realizes she's called him out as a faker. And perhaps she's right.

He stares up at one of Jeanie's pieces, the one that hangs over the living room sofa. Various hues of red, with lines swirled into them by Jeanie's fingers.

As with so much of her work, he fears he never truly understood it.

CHAPTER 4

In the station that afternoon, cops in Major Crimes make light of what Owens did last night. They ask him why his aim wasn't better—how could he miss a big target like Peterson? *I woulda emptied my clip on the motherfucker!* Laughs all around.

These are men and women who confront the worst of humanity on a daily basis, and many of them, like him, were tasked with controlling the city during The Blinding, when they dealt with even worse. Gallows humor is a requirement for the maintenance of sanity.

Still, the jokes feel off to him. Like there's an undercurrent of judgment or fear, like they think what he did was wrong, or crazy, or both.

In the hallway, the laughs behind them now, Owens asks Peterson, "Seriously, you okay?"

"Just keep that gun holstered and I'll be fine." Peterson pats him on the shoulder. *No hard feelings.*

Owens hopes.

Peterson adds, "Carlyle isn't happy about how you handled it. I'm just saying."

"I got that impression."

"I'm not saying there's going to be an investigation about it or anything, but he asked me a whole lot of questions. And between you and me, I made you sound better than you deserved. I told him I dictated to you where to aim and everything."

"Which is kind of true."

"I'm just saying, so we have our stories straight. I gave you detailed directions and Slade wasn't moving. He held still, and *I* told *you* to fire. Got it?"

Owens stops. "We don't need to go that far with it."

"I think that we should." He means, *For your sake, Mark*. Jesus, now he feels even more guilty. First he put his partner in danger, now his partner is going to lie to protect him.

"Okay. Thank you."

"Sure. And if you ever do that again"—he claps Owens on the shoulder a second time, harder, and smiles—"I will fucking kill you."

"Owens!" a voice calls down the hallway.

Owens turns around and thinks, *Speaking of investigations.*

Enter Damien Winslow. Early fifties, suspiciously good suit, briefcase in hand (who but attorneys carry briefcases anymore?), gray hair cut military-short.

Owens curses under his breath. He waits as Winslow hurries over.

"Owens, we need to talk. Your hearing with the Truth Commission is tomorrow, remember?"

"Tell them I'm on a case."

Peterson backs up a few steps to give them space, but stays close enough to let Winslow know this will not be a private conversation. No attorney-client privilege here. Partners have each other's back, period.

"You've dodged this for weeks," Winslow says. "The Truth Commission will file a complaint if you—"

"Let them."

Winslow's shoulders slump. He turns to Peterson and asks, "Could you excuse us a minute?"

Peterson gives him the dead-eye stare. Which remains effective, especially from someone his size. He finally steps away, but not as far as Winslow had probably been hoping.

The Truth Commission into the Events of The Blinding is the

long-winded name for the various committees set up across the country, passed by Congress and signed into law by the new President. He glided into office partly by promising a more thorough investigation into not just how The Blinding had happened, but also into the alleged crimes and malfeasance committed by government officials and police during that chaotic time. His campaign argued that enough time had passed for the country to take a good hard look at itself and what it had become, to point out flaws in the system that had made the ordeal perhaps worse than it should have been, and to correct injustices that had helped some segments of society land on their feet much faster than others. Owens, like most cops who'd served during The Blinding, feels personally insulted by the Truth Commission's very existence.

Winslow lowers his voice and sidles attorney-client-close to Owens. "I'm on your side here. I've been appointed as your counsel, which means everything you—"

"I'm not on trial."

"I understand that. But the union made sure every cop would have counsel, to protect them from—"

Owens starts walking away, Peterson joining him.

"I have nothing to say to them," Owens says, loud enough for Winslow to hear.

"They have the power to suspend you," Winslow calls back.

At the end of the hallway, the two cops turn the corner. Winslow doesn't give chase.

"Fucking 'Truth Commission,'" Peterson nearly spits.

"When's yours?"

"Next month." After a beat, Peterson adds, "Maybe you should just get it over with. I know you didn't do anything wrong, man. Just sit through the bullshit and I'll buy you a beer afterwards."

Owens doesn't reply. His face a mask.

The last thing a cop could ever want is to be interrogated. They prefer it the other way around, like this:

Owens and Peterson sit at one side of the table, and on the other side is Nayles, sporting a black eye from his tussle with Owens at the club last night.

Nayles looks even larger yet in this tiny room. His neck is massive. More muscular than some men's arms. Owens realizes anew how unlikely it was that he punched this man out.

"We knew you boys were running guns," Owens says. "But let's just say the amount rather surprised us."

"I'm not talking," Nayles contradicts himself.

"Two hundred firearms," Peterson says. Then he echoes Carlyle's observation from last night. "That's not selling black-market weapons, that's outfitting a militia."

"Not talking."

During The Blinding, the Second Amendment was heavily altered by the passage of the Thirtieth, which put major restrictions on the possession of firearms and detailed what exactly a "well-regulated militia" should be and how it must operate. Given the chaos of those years, the existence of so many weapons in the hands of people who couldn't see became a rather enormous problem. The amendment had only so much impact at first, but it gave the police widespread powers to repossess many of the millions of firearms in circulation.

Most cops are thankful for the changes, as they're less likely to encounter perps who are strapped like they're ready to go to war. One of the downsides, as with all prohibitions, is that it's spawned an enormous black market for firearms. The Department had suspected Slade's crew for months before finally launching its sting.

Owens tries again to get Nayles to loosen his lips: "The good news is, you'll likely avoid jail. Guys get put to death for treason."

The poker face breaks. *"Treason?"*

"That's what you call it when someone tries to overthrow a government," Peterson explains.

"I don't know nothing about governments, man."

"You don't have to pass a civics test to be tried for treason," Owens replies.

"I help run a nightclub! I don't even know what you're talking about."

Owens keeps his face blank, his voice calm. "You and Slade thought you owned that side of the city. And you were tired of cops trying to take back the neighborhood. So you decided to fight us for it. You've been arming yourselves for months and selling to friendly crews all over town."

"This is . . ." Nayles shakes his head. "Where were you bastards during The Blinding, huh? Nowhere. I had a *kid*, goddamn it. He *starved to death*."

This is the point where cops might typically say boo-fucking-hoo, but they don't. Not about this.

They let Nayles continue. "Slade and his boys, they were the only ones helping people out. So hell yes I joined with him."

The only ones helping people out? That's not how Owens remembers the constant toil and stress of that time.

He says, "'Helping people out,' meaning hooking them on opsin so you'd have regular customers. Selling them guns at a markup. What a saint."

"Maybe things have gotten a little complicated lately. But back then? We were getting them their *food*. Their drinking water. Their medicine. We saved lives. Where were the cops? You were guarding the banks, blocking the grocery stores. Protecting big shots and kicking everyone else's asses. You two in particular."

Owens stands, this having outrun its usefulness. Peterson mirrors him.

"Yeah, fucking run," Nayles says to their backs. "Don't think I don't know what you really are."

CHAPTER 5

The two look the way academics and scientists have looked for generations, except of course for the lack of eyeglasses. No one wears them anymore, other than the occasional artist who digs the retro look.

Rumpled clothing, devoid of style. Not because they can't afford better—theirs is a lucrative field—but because they can't be bothered to care about such trivialities. Their gaze focused higher than mere fashion.

In his late fifties, white, Dr. Ray Jensen recently abandoned the comb-over and has accepted the fact that he's mostly bald. He wears one of the three tweed jackets he has worn on rotation for two decades. He nods as he sees his colleague, Dr. Madeleine Leila, walking toward the same subway station he is. Born to Ethiopian and English parents, she has long, dark hair, tinseled with gray and hanging thick around her shoulders.

Bio-Lux Technologies occupies one of the newest office towers in the city. They've both worked there for years, chased out of academia for various reasons, yet neither has fully adjusted to the sheer capitalist exuberance of their employer. The espresso machines and free gym, the yoga classes and evening lectures. They like it but distrust it, feeling somehow that the perks are beneath them, that they're being insulted by the bounty offered to them. Their jobs come with free parking spaces, yet they both take the train, preferring to save electricity by not owning cars.

"You worked late," Jensen says. It's past nine at night, and the sidewalks that would have been packed three hours ago are nearly empty.

"Yeah, crazy month. Guess I shouldn't be surprised that *you* were burning the midnight oil."

At the next intersection they pass a blind panhandler on the sidewalk. Unshaven, thin, no vidder on his temple. He wears a long gray tunic, New Testament chic. His eyes vacant as he extends a leaflet to them, which they decline.

"Seek Inner Sight, my friends. Join Reverend Miriam and reject the false images they force upon us."

Leila and Jensen shake their heads as they cross the street and enter Northwest Park, walking along an empty path shrouded by oak boughs.

"Rumor has it you're working on some secret project," she says.

She'd meant it to sound friendly, but he looks at her like she's been sneaking peeks at his diary. And in truth, maybe she'd let herself sound a little snide. With competitive colleagues like this, the line between banter and taunting is thin.

"Who says that?"

"No one. Never mind."

He looks at her for a silent moment. Then gazes ahead and keeps walking. They're walking beside each other still, but it's also like they're both walking alone.

She needs to break the awkward silence. He's the kind of antisocial person who could wallow in it, or not even notice it, but she's not.

"Look, Ray. For what it's worth, I think it's lousy how you were treated. I had nothing to do with it."

"Sure you didn't." He stops then, so she does too.

She tries to explain, "Just because I didn't agree with your findings doesn't mean I—"

"Of course you don't agree, because I'm just the old crank working on something no one else believes in. Fine. But I've got the data. I look forward to everyone's reactions when I finally prove it."

She feels bad, but believes he deserves it. She wouldn't ever want to sound ageist, but the fact is, she's noticed that people who had reached a certain point in their lives when The Blinding hit have never fully adjusted to the new reality. Not unlike that crazy street prophet they just passed, although Jensen would recoil at the comparison. He may be a scientist, but he can't seem to maintain the rational distancing necessary for good science. He distrusts everything in the viddered world, she can tell, wandering through this new life with palpable distaste. So his science is flawed, his experiments absurd, his conclusions comic.

She hadn't made any jokes about him. But she'd laughed when others did.

Surely he knew his job was on the line. But then again, the doomed tend not to pick up on clues terribly well.

She's trying to think of a polite way to end the conversation when she notices something strange in the distance. It's a dark form. *Quite* dark. The deepest black. She tries to focus, but it seems to resist her. Some glitch in her depth perception or color readout, or both.

"I'm sorry I brought it up," she says, her voice distracted.

Jensen seems to notice it too. His stride slows, as does hers.

The dark form is approaching them. It's close enough now that she can discern a few things, its basic shape. Legs that power it forward at a standard pace, arms that swing in time, a head. It's definitely a person.

But he or she is all dark. Completely blacked out from Leila's vision.

"Do you see that?" Jensen asks.

"Yes. I mean . . . no."

"Exactly."

They both touch their vidders, make minor adjustments. Nothing changes except that the surrounding world gets more or less blurry. The figure stays dark. It's as though the person has been scrubbed from their vidders by a censor. A human redaction.

Walking toward them.

Leila is conscious of a ringing in her ears that wasn't there before.

Maybe she's imagining it. The hairs on the back of her neck rise, and she shivers.

"Who are you?" Jensen asks when the figure stops before them, a mere five feet away.

She adjusts her vidder again, as if she can correct this. She can't even hear the person breathing. Maybe he's not really there.

"How . . . How are you doing that?" Leila asks.

One of the figure's arms lifts up until the hand is level with Jensen's head. Leila is just beginning to realize that the arm looks unusually long and strangely shaped, which must mean that it's holding something, when the world becomes impossibly loud.

Sound like a physical force, pushing her back. She nearly trips.

Jensen's response is more violent. His head snaps backward like it's trying to escape its tether to the rest of him. Some of it succeeds, a mass of red flying behind him.

Then he falls backward, and she sees the hole in his forehead, and it takes an amazingly long time for a brilliant biologist like Madeleine Leila to assemble these bits of data into an obvious conclusion: someone just shot Jensen in the head.

It shoots him again, twice.

She steps back again. The dark figure's long arm moves toward her. She's too stunned to scream, two steps behind a world that has permanently outpaced her. Wondering what that clicking sound is.

Again, a click.

The figure pulls its arm down and she realizes: its gun is jammed.

Leila turns and runs through the park. Screaming for help. Wondering why she had to work late, why this normally busy park could be so hauntingly empty at night.

She hears the figure giving chase.

"Help! Help me!"

Vidders have tricked people into thinking darkness doesn't exist anymore, that nights are as safe as day. She's read the studies, heard the experts discuss this new phenomenon. Reminding people that, yes, crime is still more common at night. Yes, women alone are at greater risk at night than at noon. Predators still exist, and even though they can't cloak themselves in darkness anymore, they prefer night, its relative lack of witnesses, the fact that in the evening victims are more tired and distracted or drunk and sloppy, easy prey.

Yet somehow this figure *has* cloaked itself in darkness.

She runs and runs, unsure whether she's in a nightmare or has become a cautionary tale to be cited for others.

This is the emptiest park on earth, it seems. She used to be fast, ran track in college, but she's out of shape.

She darts across the street. If any vehicle had been passing, she would have flagged it down, but no.

She sees a door, runs through it without thinking. It leads to a nearly empty parking garage. No one here. No security guard, no Good Samaritan, no random stranger.

She runs up the stairs. The more she's running, the longer she's alive, the more chance she has to lose him.

She slips. Lands hard on her hand. Might have broken her wrist, if it matters. She tries to climb to her feet, but he pushes her from behind. She hadn't realized he was that close. She lands hard again. Turns over, crawls backward, and she's staring right up at a completely black figure. This cannot be happening.

"Help me, someone! He has a gun!"

The figure seems to crouch before her. Again his arm is extended. Did he fix his gun? Does he have a knife? Leila keeps crawling backward, but she reaches the landing and the back of her head presses against the wall. Nowhere left to go.

The figure keeps coming, slowly. Enjoying this. She can tell, even without seeing him. Somehow she knows it's a him. She believes he is smiling. Hair all over her body is standing up right now.

He reaches forward and presses the gun into her forehead. It feels metallic and warm.

A hoarse whisper, male: "You can't see me at all, can you?"

She is too terrified to reply. Nearly hyperventilating. She realizes she wet herself at some point, smells her urine. Shakes her head *No.*

The barrel moves slightly when she does, but it stays pressed against her forehead.

Should she slap it away? Can she kick him down?

He whispers, "Then there's no reason to waste the bullet."

The arm retracts. For a second he is simply standing there. She will live.

He will let her live.

But no.

He leans over and extends his arm again. This time he . . . he pats her on the head. He takes a strand of her thick, curly hair and gently pulls it out, as if admiring it. She realizes he's showing off his ability not only to move through but also to interact with a world that cannot see him. She can see the strands of her hair, pulled out in front of her and pinched between two finger-shaped slivers of pure darkness.

The fingers release her hair, which cascades down into her face, partially covering her eyes.

"Goodbye, Dr. Leila."

The figure walks down the stairs, his steps echoing in the concrete stairway. She hears a door open, footsteps recede, and she realizes she is alone and alive.

CHAPTER 6

Owens hasn't seen Maxine Johnson in years. Just the sight of her, and the smell—same perfume as before—floods him with memories. Some good, sure, but funny how they're overpowered by all the bad.

They spend a few minutes catching up, and he finds he doesn't have much to report about himself. Day by day, the job can be fascinating. Step back when you're asked what's new with your life, though, and language fails.

Or maybe *you've* failed.

Maxine used to work at the Museum of Modern and Contemporary Art and has since become a private art dealer. One of the many professions he was amazed to hear still existed, back when he was with Jeanie. The fact that people (only some people, but still) can actually earn a living doing that. That there are people so awash with money that they can throw it at those few artists lucky enough to fall under their favor.

Jeanie had been so favored. Not that it brought her much happiness.

Maxine's hair had occasionally been bleached or dyed black in those days. Now that it's probably going gray, it is instead a vibrant, look-at-me-I'm-an-artist magenta. Her various bracelets clink and chime as she gesticulates. She is a symphony of tiny vibraphones.

"So," she says, gauging him. "You're really sure?"

"I've been thinking about it for a while now. It's time."

"This is . . . extremely generous."

He smiles ruefully. "A lot more generous than it would've been a few years ago. I looked up the appraised worth—it quadrupled after she died."

"That tends to be the way it works. I'm sorry, Mark."

Owens walks her down the hallway that leads to the bedroom, and he points at two of Jeanie's paintings.

"These two I'd like auctioned, to raise money for that kids' foundation she worked with." He walks back into the main room. "But the museum can have all the others."

"And you're sure you don't want anything for . . . ?"

"I'm not making money off her, Maxine." He puts his empty mug in the sink.

"I meant, do you want to keep any for yourself?"

He chooses three, in the study, that he will hold on to, but the rest she can take.

Silence hangs there as Maxine pirouettes back and forth, taking the pieces in. Owens is the only detective on earth who could charge admission to his apartment, if he so chose. Most museums wouldn't necessarily *kill* for a score like this, but they'd at least *contemplate* homicide, before deciding it was beneath them. Maybe.

"I just can't . . . see them, you know?" He confesses. Hates himself for it. "She was right. It isn't the same."

All those arguments and debates. The many times he coaxed Jeanie back from the cliff, metaphorically. Telling her she was overthinking things, that yes, it *was* still possible to create art in a world where everyone sees with machines. Then her replying that overthinking is precisely what artists do, they overthink and overfeel, it's like they have amplifiers hooked up to all their nerves, and sometimes this just felt so *wrong*, she feared she couldn't tolerate it anymore.

They talked in circles, getting nothing but dizzy.

She drank too much, maybe to dampen the overfeeling. So did he.

There was a lot he hadn't understood. How a man like him had landed with a mercurial artist, even *that* he hadn't fully understood.

A chance encounter, a frank conversation, mutual attraction. Opposites that weren't so opposite as they'd at first thought.

But what he hadn't realized was that, whenever he coaxed her back from that cliff and encouraged her to keep going, the cliff was less metaphorical than he'd realized. Jeanie was toeing an abyss, and he wouldn't always be able to keep her away from it.

"How are you otherwise?" Maxine asks.

"Same old. Fooling some people, fooled by the rest."

"And are you . . . with anyone?"

Maybe she's noticed one of Amira's jackets hanging by the door, maybe she's smelled her perfume or spotted something in the bathroom.

"Sort of."

"Good. Good for you."

"I mean, she's sweet, but it's not . . ." What *does* he mean? A second ago he felt he was betraying Jeanie. Now he feels like he's betraying Amira. No matter what he does, what he says, he is a terrible person.

They silently look at the paintings for a while.

"I think of her all the time still," Maxine says. "There's not a day I don't think of her. But to be surrounded by her work like this . . ." She shakes her head, marveling. "It's like she's here with us."

Owens shifts his gaze to the window, the city below. "She isn't."

Working Major Crimes means everything from complicated undercover-gun-trafficking busts to your run-of-the-mill homicide. Their new case seems too easy, and maybe it is, Captain Carlyle handing them the simplest possible murder after putting the complex weapons sting behind them.

They sit in another interrogation room, one less intimidating than the one they'd put Nayles in. This room is larger, the furniture not attack-proofed, considering they're talking to a smallish middle-aged woman—a cast on her right wrist, red tear streaks down her cheeks—who still seems in too much shock to stand unassisted.

Hasn't slept all night. On the verge of cracking—honestly, Owens is surprised she hasn't yet, surprised he's even needed for this.

"It was just a . . . a black mark," she tells them. "Like he'd been blotted out."

Owens had already been told she's been saying this, but he plays dumb. "You mean, you were having trouble with your vidder?"

"No, because we both saw it."

"'We,' meaning you and the victim?" Peterson asks.

She recoils at that word. Then nods.

Owens asks, "How do you know he saw the same thing you claim you did?"

"'Claim'?" She sounds more offended than afraid. An intelligent, successful scientist, annoyed at hearing her words questioned by plebeians like these. Still doesn't seem to realize how much trouble she's in.

Peterson explains, "Dr. Leila, all due respect, we hear this sort of thing a lot. Guy's caught buying drugs, other guy gets away. We ask him what his dealer looked like—*Oh, gee, my vidder was malfunctioning. Sorry, I never got a good look at him.*"

Her face reads *You two are morons.* "Why would I lie about this?"

Owens gives her the first, gentle jab. "You work for a lab that tests products for new sight technology. Maybe it's in your best interest to spread rumors that our vidders aren't working right, to goad us into buying the new models? Who knows?"

Still she acts more insulted than alarmed. "For God's sake, you can't think . . ."

The pause means she finally gets it. She'd placed her cast-less hand on the table but now she pulls it back, slowly, as if realizing too late she needs to cocoon herself in silence until a lawyer shows up.

Owens presses. "You were the last person to see Dr. Jensen alive. Dr. Jensen was something of a rival of yours, and—"

"He wasn't a 'rival,' he was more of a vexing colleague."

In truth, Owens has no idea of their relationship—they haven't done enough legwork yet, haven't interviewed their colleagues—but it seems a decent guess, and it clearly riles her.

Peterson spells it out: "Dr. Leila, the murder weapon was found near where officers found you. You claim someone else shot him at close range, but you can't describe that person." He shrugs, raises his eyebrows.

Tears in her eyes now. "You . . . You honestly think I . . . ?"

Owens completes the thought. "Think you shot your colleague, then ran away to hide, and ditched the weapon with you in the stairwell where the cops found you?"

"I . . . This is . . ."

They watch her unsympathetically as she cries. It's a difficult thing to do, but with practice it becomes easier. With enough practice, you're just wearing a mask and so is everyone else.

Backstage, meaning the hallway, Owens and Peterson confer.

"I don't know," Owens admits. "She's not acting guilty—she's acting scared."

"Scared is what rich people feel when they realize for the first time that they aren't going to get away with something. C'mon, he was shot at close range, so it was someone he trusted. She panicked and didn't ditch the weapon far enough away. Simple."

"But she'd shoot him in a park like that? Where there were maybe witnesses or security cameras?"

"Haven't found any witnesses yet. Or cameras."

"I'm just saying, if they work together, surely she could have found a better time to shoot him."

Peterson just shrugs again. His body projecting, *We've been handed a simple case, easy to close. Why would you question it?*

"Maybe we can find a real motive after we've talked to their colleagues," Owens says. "And the vidder glitch bothers me."

"Like I said, everyone tries it."

"Which is why a nerdy scientist like her should be able to come up with something better."

"Yeah, but the smart ones are the dumb ones." One of Peterson's mantras. Meaning: when solid citizens cross a line and commit a crime, they often haven't thought through the angles as well as a drug dealer or prostitute would have. Players in the system know how to play. Whereas financial analysts, programmers, professors— when something snaps and they kill their lover or rival or neighbor, they never cover their tracks as well as they thought they did.

"Let's not overthink this one, Mark."

"Just a little legwork first, okay? Humor me."

Peterson nods, *Whatever*, and heads to the restroom.

Sometimes Owens wonders whether he himself is a smart one or a dumb one.

CHAPTER 7

Late afternoon, the sun hiding. A slight brightness around some of the cirrus clouds to the southwest assures Owens that the sun is indeed there, somewhere.

He mentally prepares himself for what he still thinks of as traveling back through time.

Like many others, he often wonders what would have happened had The Blinding been instantaneous instead of simply very, very fast. He charted his own progress back when it happened. At that point, the epidemic (or plague, or catastrophe, or apocalypse) had been in the news for a couple weeks, so he noticed the first day that things looked just slightly *off*. Felt sick to his stomach that morning, terror in the base of his gut.

Jeanie didn't have it yet, but she would three days later.

Going from that first day until he was more or less functionally blind took forty-seven terrifying days. Then another four weeks when he went from barely seeing anything, just rough shapes and degrees of light, until he reached pure, total blindness. Nothing but darkness, no perception of light even when someone held a flashlight to his face.

Seventy-five days from 20/15 vision to zero. Eleven weeks of terror.

Followed by many weeks of worse.

The gradual deterioration at least gave people a fighting chance to prepare. Governments and police tried to put systems in place, retrofitted old contingency plans for pandemics and nuclear war. But even the most doomsday of such scenarios had assumed that survivors would be able to *see*.

The fact that everyone on earth experienced this terror together didn't make it any easier. If anything, the way that everyone fell apart in different ways made it worse.

He drives out of the city, beneath that glaucoma of clouds obscuring the sun. He passes the decrepit industrial corridor, still mostly vacant, then the spookily abandoned suburban subdivisions, many of them burned down during The Blinding. The population plummeted back then, with the violent competition for resources, the food riots, the water riots. Those who had vision the longest held power, as did those with firearms. A bleak and bloody time.

Traffic thins out as he reaches the exurbs. He leans back in his seat.

"Autopilot," he says. "News."

A 3D image of a male, Asian American newscaster appears to his right, just inside the windshield.

"New jobless reports are down slightly, the unemployment rate dropping to 14.5 percent. Myers Administration spokeswoman Rebecca Simmons welcomed the news and noted that this is one of the lowest figures since The Blinding. Some economists, however, have criticized the administration's decision to stop counting people who are both jobless and without vidders, saying that this artificially deflates the number. Next Friday a Sight Is a Right rally will be held—"

"Skip."

"The Myers Administration announced details about the National Day of Mourning, to occur on the seven-year anniversary of the start of The Great Blinding." He's not looking forward to that, but it's another part of the new President's attempt to "shed light" on The Blinding. Owens doesn't understand the point of a collective Day of Mourning when honestly everyone is still in mourning all the time—they hardly need a special day for it.

The newscaster moves on, telling him how the previous secretary of state—rumored to have profited greatly from shady real estate deals during The Blinding—is vowing to resist subpoenas and not testify before the Truth Commission. She's encouraging other members of the last administration to do the same. Then the newscaster's face vanishes and the car, in its digital "male" announcer voice, says, "Call coming."

"Answer."

Peterson's face appears on a monitor, 2D. He asks, "Where are you?"

"Visiting the crazies. Long overdue."

"You know they're not crazy, man. They just have a different outlook on this."

The comment surprises him. Every now and then Peterson reveals a softer side. "What's up?"

"Look, you can piss off Winslow all you want, but now he's bothering *me*."

Owens's Truth Commission testimony. "Sorry. I honestly forgot."

"Sure you did."

"If he asks again, tell him I'll do the deposition tomorrow. You find anything on Dr. Jensen?"

"No affairs or financial malfeasance. Some people at the office didn't like him, 'smartest guy in the room' thing. But nobody mad enough to kill him."

"Any luck on security cameras?"

"No. One outside the parking deck shows a male figure walking by at roughly that time, but he ain't holding a gun. And all you can see is dark hair—not a very clean visual."

"Figured."

"One more thing. Dr. Leila has a lawyer saying we have no right to hold her. We gotta charge her or release her."

"How long do we have?"

"Maybe twelve hours. So hurry home, partner."

"Trust me, I won't be out here any longer than necessary."

Sixty miles outside the city, he takes an exit and drives past former farmland gone wild. Generations ago this was all woods, then it was logged and the land was carved into farms, forced through painstaking labor to produce crops. And then generations later the family farms died and were replaced by corporate concerns or just went vacant.

Until The Blinding reworked the population and its needs. Most corporate farms now are entirely robot-run, and their number declined due to fewer people needing less food. When 10 percent of the planet perishes over a few awful years, the economy takes a while to reboot. Most farmers lost their land, some of them so poor now that they've established squatter camps, lawless areas everyone else avoids, where some of the inhabitants can't afford vidders. Luckily there are none out this way, though Owens has heard stories about some in the Midwest growing, banding together.

Another ten miles of nothingness and the woods thicken, no landmarks he remembers, until he sees the sign, "INNER SIGHT COMMUNE, All Are Welcome." As if that will get people to flock here.

He drives up a mild incline, at the top of which is the guard post and a retractable barrier that blocks the road. A young, uniformed security guard sits inside the post, an automatic rifle within reach.

Owens pulls to a stop and flashes his badge. "Thank God they still use guards who can see."

The commune's guard isn't himself a true believer, obviously. Young, racially mixed, medium-toned skin, military-short hair, and a vidder. He grins.

"Some of them want to stop, actually. They say it goes against their mission. Been thinking I should apply for the force, maybe. You got any openings?"

* * *

And here he is, back in time. Late eighteenth century, maybe early nineteenth. He remembers childhood field trips to colonial American villages, where oddball adult volunteers with too much free time wore period dress and tried to work Ye Old English into their lexicon to impress schoolchildren. Recalls blacksmith shops, apothecaries, mapmakers with their sextants and quills, woodworkers carving ship masts.

This place is like that, minus vision.

The parking lot sits immediately behind the guard shack, as nothing so modern as an electronic vehicle is allowed here. The trails are mostly gravel, though a few are only dirt. Gravel you can hear better.

From this rise in the earth he can see the series of small, utilitarian, concrete-and-metal dwellings dotting a field, surrounded by woods. Like a combination Sleepy Hollow and communist yurt. The worst elements of each. A serial killer would have a field day here, as would a totalitarian dictator.

In Owens's opinion, they already have the latter.

He passes a large garden. Crouched along the furrows are seven men and women, some wearing gloves as they work with their hands, others using shovels and spades and hoes. Owens wears the only vidder around. One of the gardeners, a short, thin man no more than twenty-five, hears Owens's steps on the gravel.

He looks up and says, "Welcome." Like he'd known Owens was a visitor and not a resident. How? His smell? His gait?

"Hello," Owens replies. Telling himself, *Be nice, stay polite.*

He carries a bouquet of flowers and feels self-conscious about it, which is ridiculous, as no one can see him. He could be naked and they wouldn't know. Or would they? Would they smell him more? Would they detect his shame?

He sees her now, a hundred yards to his right. Near where the woods begin. He's heard coyotes are rampant out here, and that even wolves have come back, reclaiming land that the depleted population has ceded to them. These people are so unsafe. Not just from the real wolves but the metaphoric ones, the gangs and vigilantes who prey on the weak for fun. That young rent-a-cop at the gate is useless.

She's wearing a sleeveless shirt and work pants, gardening like the others. She stops digging and turns her ear to the wind.

"Who's there?" Sarah asks.

"Look at those forearms. You doing all the work around here?"

He realizes with a pang that his first word was *look*, understands again that language dooms him to offend her even when he's trying to rebuild the bridge between them. At least she doesn't comment on it this time.

In fact, she smiles as she stands. Holds out a hand to find him. He takes it, holds it a moment, then they embrace. He kisses her forehead and hands her the bouquet.

He tells himself he only imagines the sparkle in her brown eyes.

"You brought tulips," she says.

How the hell? He can't even smell them.

"Happy birthday, Sis."

The sun still hides behind the clouds and now there's a breeze, but the autumn crispness feels delicious. The air cleaner out here, the scents of fresh earth, dry leaves, fallen walnuts. They walk on a trail that snakes into the woods and back out again. In a clearing Owens sees two dozen small dwellings, along with a few larger structures he figures for general stores or meeting rooms or reeducation brainwashing centers.

"You look good, Sarah." But he stares sadly at her vidderless temple, at her still eyes.

His sister is two years younger, a close enough age difference that they fought incessantly as kids. Then they bonded in their teen years, when other siblings drift apart. She's thinner than he's ever seen her, fit. He wasn't joking about her physique. And he still isn't used to her with short hair—not a flattering haircut, but that happens when your barber is blind.

"Thanks. I assume you look good, too."

"You could find out, you know."

She doesn't take the bait. Maybe he shouldn't have dangled it. He can't help himself.

This place breaks his heart.

As they walk, he notices a large building at the edge of the hill. Three stories tall, the size of a city high school. A spire at the top. It's easily the biggest structure he's ever seen at the commune. Nearly complete, though in need of a paint job. Maybe they won't bother.

"Some serious construction going on around here. That's an awfully big church."

"It's not a church, it's an enlightenment center. They do research, too. It's providing a lot of jobs around here."

"Research? Proving the existence of God?"

"Of Inner Sight."

"How's that research working out for you?"

She stops. "How's *yours* working out for *you*?"

He looks away, feeling guilty for the jab. Damn, he made it maybe three minutes.

"Why are you so bothered by the fact that some people can be guided by something other than your little electronic eyeballs and government-appointed watchdogs?"

He loathes the rhetoric. Hates it from the street-corner prophets, hates it when a random commenter on social media spews it. Hates it even more for its subtle effects on everyday conversations, how so many people (even those who wear vidders and owe so much to them) criticize the supposedly scary, all-seeing government and the evilly powerful tech corporations with their tentacles everywhere.

Please.

Owens is an employee of the government, technically, and he knows from experience that it is so very far from all-seeing. And he's had enough brushups with EyeTech employees to be less than impressed by those people, too.

The reality, he likes to say, is that organizations are comprised of people, and people are deeply flawed. That's it, end of conspiracy theory. You want a perfect government or perfect company, staff it with perfect people. Best of luck finding them.

He hates the anti-everything attitude, and he hates it most when it comes from his sister. But he doesn't want to argue with Sarah about it, so he says, "I'm sorry. Let's keep walking."

He takes her hand to guide her, but she shakes him off.

"I know this trail better than you know your apartment. I know there's a big rock two paces in front of me, I know there's a dip three paces ahead of that."

They walk in silence for a bit. She's right, walking confidently and with perfect posture. Most people here use canes or walking sticks, but some go without sometimes, as she's doing now. He's always found that disquieting.

In the distance, on a flat pitch of grass, he sees six acolytes drilling, fighting with wooden staffs. At first he thinks he's misconstruing due to the distance, but no, that's what they're doing: three pairs of them, wielding long staffs, go through martial arts–style moves, parrying and thrusting. They're slow at first, as would be expected, but soon they speed up their tempo. The tapping of the staffs like strikes against a tree. He wouldn't have thought something like this possible for the blind. Maybe they'd be better at defending themselves than he feared.

"I went to their grave on Tuesday," he tells her. "It would have been their forty-fifth anniversary."

"That was good of you."

"So how are things going with, um . . ."

"With Kendrick? The guy I've been with more than a year?"

"It's funny. People usually say 'the guy I'm seeing,' but of course—"

"I thought cops were supposed to be good with names."

"The good cops are."

She smiles again. The expression of a lovestruck teenager on the face of a thirty-three-year-old. "To answer your question, things with Kendrick are going very well. We've been talking about making things official. Getting married."

"Wow. How uncharacteristically traditional of you."

"Well, actually . . . we're expecting. So we decided—"

Owens stops. She doesn't notice, takes another step, so he puts a hand on her arm.

"Sarah."

"What?"

"You can't raise children. Not if you keep living like this."

"Why not? Plenty of people here have children."

They're near another garden, where three men are working. At the sound of Owens's and Sarah's raised voices, the men stop, listening to the exchange.

"How can you take care of a baby you can't see? And what are you going to do, force it to grow up blind? There are laws against that."

Yet another element of The Blinding that continues to elude scientists: babies born over the years since it started do possess some vision, a scant amount (as they always have), but it quickly fades.

"Those laws have been overturned in fifteen states."

"Not this one."

"Then we'll move to a more enlightened place. Damn it, Mark! Is this why you came here? To rehash all your old arguments?"

"It's not an old argument if you're talking about raising a blind child. I'm sorry I can't just stand around while my niece or nephew is brought up in The Darkness like some freak, but—"

She slaps him. Perfect aim.

He glares at her while she stares at the void between them.

"I choose to live an honest life. If you came here to talk me out of that, then I'd like you to leave."

Behind her, the three male gardeners have taken a few steps closer, as if coming to Sarah's aid. Owens looks at them.

"Wow, you're an intimidating bunch. Three blind mice."

"Everyone is blind," one of them says. Thinning gray hair but thick muscles. A retired superhero. "Some of us are more honest about it."

One of his compatriots says, "And some of us are more deluded."

Owens gives his sister one last, disappointed glance.

"Sarah, please. Come back."

She isn't even facing him, not that it matters.

"You should stop coming here, Mark. It's . . . dishonest of you to pretend to care when you're only here to talk me out of my life." She speaks slowly, choosing her words with care. Or painstakingly reciting a prewritten response her cult leaders have passed out to them in braille, *How to Talk to the Unbelievers*. "I think you should go." A breath. "And never come back."

He waits. The three men linger, arms crossed.

"Sarah," he tries, his voice more gentle. "Come on. You need to think this through."

"No, Mark. You need to go."

It feels like she's watching him as he leaves.

CHAPTER 8

The next morning, Owens hears Sarah's voice in his mind as he enters the grand lobby of Bio-Lux Technologies. This company represents all that she and her fellows despise. It's one of the main research sources for EyeTech, for which it frequently subcontracts. Not only vision tech, but also replacement limbs, with metal fingers as dexterous as any made from flesh and bone. Bionic sensors that will one day alert us if we've inhaled certain bacteria or viruses. Skin grafts, born from stem cells, that will restore suppleness and full feeling to burn victims (of whom there are many, post-Blinding). Sonic augmenters that aim to do for ears what vidders do for eyes, granting the sense of hearing even to people born deaf.

And the Holy Grail (or the atom bomb), the dream (or nightmare) of everyone: the ability to permanently and seamlessly fuse machine learning, the Internet, and heightened processing speeds to the human brain. The so-called Singularity. If science has found a way to beam visual data straight into our cerebral cortex, then implanting all sorts of other data—and, eventually, every fact known to humankind—shouldn't be that far off. The maps and weather were an early enhancement, the pop-up ads an annoyance, but more is coming.

So they say. Owens has a hard time imagining it.

Yet he can't suppress the voice in his head, Sarah arguing with him still. *This place is evil,* she'd be ranting. Even before The Blinding, she spoke that way. Horrific events only accelerated her conversion.

They're not just turning their backs on humanity, they're turning our backs on humanity. We have no say in what they're doing. We haven't voted on whether or not we should combine the human with the machine, but they're doing it anyway!

Owens would counter: *But we did vote, in a way.* With our wallets. We want this, we crave it. Even before The Blinding, we always needed the latest gadgets. The phones and the apps and the networks. Yes, please, sign me up and take my digital privacy with you. Then we needed sight, so yes, attach the machine to my skull, definitely. So of course we'll enthusiastically line up for whatever they come up with next. Credit cards embedded in our fingertips, remotes in our eyelids, God knows what. Every bad fashion trend you can imagine, times a million. Trying to fight it is like trying to stop the sun from rising in the east. One person refusing to play along won't stop it, nor will a hundred or even a hundred thousand acolytes of Reverend Miriam moving off to their little commune in the woods.

Not that Owens is entirely comfortable with this. Just a realist.

He looks around the grand lobby, shiny marble floors everywhere, a few chairs that look far more expensive than mere lobby chairs have any right to be, a twenty-foot-high ceiling and holograms playing news shows in the corner. Business is good.

Everyone walks very, very fast from the entrance to the elevators, like they can't fucking wait to start working. If Owens saw people walking that fast on the sidewalk, he'd assume they were fleeing a crime scene. How can someone like their job that much?

He and Peterson make snide but also envious comments. They don't often visit buildings like this, and when they do, they don't appreciate the reminder of the stark gap between this and their moldy police headquarters. This office no doubt offers free massage therapists, whereas police HQ has about three plumbers on call to address the various daily leaks.

They check in with a stern man at the front desk and are told to wait in one of those wonderful chairs. While they do—God, they're even more comfortable than they look—a 3D hologram projection regales them with facts about the company. Owens hates noise pollution like this, but he helplessly watches the diorama of a brain, an optical nerve, and an eye.

"Every day, Bio-Lux makes discoveries about the relationship between our minds and the world around us," the hologram infomercial boasts. "No fewer than twenty of our patents are included in EyeTech's Vidder 5.7. Research on everything from texture analysis, to the anti-glare function of ospreys' eyes, to the way snakes can detect heat through their eyes has allowed us to enhance vidders above and beyond our previous visual abilities."

The man from the front desk walks over, escorts them to an elevator. Hits a button, steps out, sends them on their way.

Thirty-two floors up, the doors open and a young woman greets them with a short smile, immediately stricken from her face. People are never sure how to greet cops on a visit like this.

She escorts them through a narrow hallway. The right half is all glass, affording them a view of a large research lab that stretches out below. Dozens of people work at computers, watch 3D projections, take notes on tablets. Serious money here.

At the end of the hall sits Dr. Leonard Pelzer's office. The assistant leaves and Pelzer walks around his desk, shakes hands. Wears the serious expression of a man not used to dealing with police detectives. Thin, mid-fifties, frail but with watchful eyes. He invites Owens and Peterson to sit in what appear to be the finest office guest chairs money can buy.

"We're all still in shock, honestly," he says, after some basic questions.

Owens asks, "How would you describe the relationship between Drs. Jensen and Leila?"

"They've both been primary investigators here, which means they spearhead different projects. PIs can be competitive."

"What was he working on?"

"We're always looking for ways to enhance the orbital interface in the brain. Getting our cerebral cortex to better understand the information and stimuli that our vidder sends it."

On the wall to Owens's right is a black-and-white still of that Buñuel film, the eyeball slicing. Taken before the actual slicing, thank goodness. He assumes it's a sick joke.

The window behind Pelzer offers a killer view of the city.

"EyeTech must pay most of the bills around here," Owens observes. "You do most of your work for them, right?"

EyeTech, led by its young genius Kai Ballantine, was the first company to create vidders that fulfilled their promise. Even before The Blinding, back when blindness was something that afflicted "only" 40 million people worldwide (Owens, like everyone else, had looked up that startlingly high stat), techies had been working on various ways to cure blindness. Electrodes on tongues, implants behind ears, heat gauges beneath skin. Many failures, each one supposedly bringing them closer to a workable solution. Myriad studies of bats, whales, shellfish, sharks. Attempts to re-create echolocation in human form. Then The Blinding came, kicking that kind of research into overdrive. Governments and those businesses that could still function and had access to capital got in on the cause.

EyeTech made it happen, and, with its initial success, became the single most powerful company on earth.

It created the physical vidders and also ran the software and networks that sent signals to them, all while maintaining the vast worldwide infrastructure that supported everything. It had a potential customer base of the entire planet. There was plenty of room to grow, either through continual updates and improvements to its damn-near-essential product, or through the still vast numbers of people who didn't have vidders. Last Owens heard, something like 5 percent of Americans were vidderless; many people, especially those who had already been blind before the disaster, chose to remain so (they all didn't move to communes like Sarah's; plenty lived the same lives they always had). But that still meant millions of Americans who wanted vidders were still suffering through life blind—and the numbers were even worse in most other countries.

Creation and distribution of the devices had been partly funded by the U.S. government, but eventually politicians tired of that largesse and pulled back. People who used to work the sorts of menial jobs that robots were gradually taking over found that they couldn't afford vidders and that their fellow voters were tired of paying higher taxes to help the economically disadvantaged catch up.

EyeTech, meanwhile, would have been broken up as a monopoly years ago if not for the fact that the fate of civilization pretty much rested in its hands.

Regulators tend not to want to create another apocalypse.

"Well, yes, EyeTech as well as the government," Pelzer explains. "That's how it works in science. We receive government funding, but yes, EyeTech invests in a lot of our ventures—our moon shots, if you will—knowing that everything we create will only make their products better. In fact, EyeTech's new vidder contains no fewer than twenty—"

"Yeah, we heard the informercial downstairs. I heard EyeTech's got some big new product coming out, right? All the latest upgrades and whatnot. Was Jensen involved in that?"

"Researchers like Dr. Jensen wouldn't work directly with EyeTech. That's what our account people do, but our scientists keep their noses to the grindstone, so to speak. And many of them, honestly . . . It's just a different skill set, the science part and the client-slash-government services part."

This bores Owens. He cuts to the interesting part.

"I'd rather you kept this between us," Owens says, "but Dr. Leila told us she couldn't see the attacker—that he appeared as a black blur, no matter what angle she looked from. Have you ever heard of a malfunction like that?"

Pelzer fidgets in his seat.

"I mean, I've heard people blame their vidders when they do or see something they shouldn't, sure. Who hasn't?"

Exactly.

"But for the record," Owens says, "and to put our minds at ease. You're a scientist, you specialize in vidders, you understand how these things work as well as anyone. Is it really possible for a person to black themselves out to another person, as a way of committing a crime undetected?"

"No." Headshake, sober look. "Of course not. They just don't work that way."

The two partners ride a glass elevator down to the ground floor. Glass elevators all the rage now, builders using more glass than ever before, everyone reveling in sight again. Owens had even heard of some fashion designer who held a runway show with nothing but transparent clothing, though it didn't catch on, thank goodness.

"Kind of amazing, when you really step back and think about it," Peterson says. "Who woulda thought we wouldn't need eyes?"

"We'd be pretty ugly without 'em. You'd be uglier, I mean."

Peterson lets that go. Then he admits, "I miss the way it was."

"Jesus, who doesn't?"

"No, I don't just mean the sighted days. I mean . . . after The Blinding, when cops were the only ones with vidders. Y'know?"

They look at each other. Peterson is toeing dangerous ground. Wondering if his partner will step with him or pull him back.

Owens keeps his face noncommittal.

"We could keep order better then," Peterson insists, sensing the need to explain himself. "We were in *charge*. These laws, this due-process bullshit . . . Like the Slade case, man. If we'd had X-ray all along, we coulda nailed them a lot sooner. I wouldn't have gotten nearly shot in the face. That case would have been so much easier and less risky, for both of us. Tell me I'm wrong."

Owens considers his reply carefully. The elevator seems to shrink. Peterson belatedly seems to realize he should have kept such thoughts to himself.

The elevator door opens.

"I don't miss those days, Jimmy."

* * *

From his office high above, Pelzer's heart rate has returned to normal as he watches the two cops leave the building. He picks up his phone, autodials a number.

"We have to talk. You're not going to believe it."

CHAPTER 9

They've done Owens the courtesy of reserving a conference room rather than an interrogation room, but his deposition for the Truth Commission feels like a grilling nonetheless.

He is reminded of why he put this off so long. He sits beside Winslow, his union-appointed counselor, whom he barely knows. On the other side are two black suite–clad attorneys; a fresh-faced, white assistant prosecutor named Hollis; and the main inquisitor, Jeffrey Huntington. He's an African American man whose shiny tie clip, perfect nails, and trim mustache suggest a painstaking attention to detail.

On the table between them is a small digital recorder.

Huntington enunciates for the mike. "This is Hearing 176–5-B regarding events that occurred during the week of June twelfth, seven years ago. Detective Owens, according to station logs, you were on foot patrol in southwestern beat 5 on June twelfth."

He gives Owens a look suggesting that although that wasn't a question, an answer is expected.

"That is correct."

So it begins, the torturous rehashing of a horrific week. A horrific month, a horrific year.

He hates this. Even before The Blinding, Owens had never been one to agree with the notion that the best way to heal from trauma is to discuss it, examine it, put it under a microscope. Prod that fucking wound over and over until all the pus has magically, therapeutically seeped out. No thanks. Call him stoic, but that degree of self-analysis seems like someone just *asking* to stay trapped in a doom loop, a never-ending cycle of suffering and self-reproach.

The Blinding is over. Let's just walk away.

Alas, that is not how the new President and his Truth Commission feel about it—or voters, apparently. Everyone wants to *figure out what happened.* Even though some things are clearly beyond figuring, beyond the limits of our comprehension.

What Owens really fears: they're just looking for someone to blame.

And yes, bad things happened during The Blinding. In addition to, of course, the fact that *no one could fucking see.* Worse, so many people used that as the cover they'd needed to indulge their id. Like a permanent cloak wrapped around the shoulders of some very bad people. Rapes went through the roof. Burglaries too, even for items that weren't much use to people who couldn't see (computer monitors and TVs—why? What the fuck were people thinking?). Vehicle theft, insane thrill rides that ended very badly indeed. Even the cars that had e-drivers, thieves sometimes disabled them on purpose. Suicide by car, a thousandfold.

Never in history had there been so many homicides by strangulation. Guns couldn't be trusted, and even knives were a risk. The tactile sensation of wrapping your fingers around someone's neck, of compressing those arteries and collapsing the windpipe, was apparently too much to resist.

Fires everywhere. Whole neighborhoods gone. In some parts of the world, entire cities.

And this Huntington bastard wants Owens to *talk* about it?

Question after question. Time seems to stop. The Blinding had felt that way too, at first.

Owens tries to maintain a disinterested tone of voice but he gets progressively more annoyed.

"I'd like to talk about the evening of June fifteenth," Huntington says maybe ninety minutes into the session, "in particular, the incident at Western Market."

Goddamn it. He knew this was coming.

"I gave a report about this, a long time ago."

"As you should understand, the Truth Commission is attempting to dig a little more deeply than some of those more . . . scattershot reports allow."

A fair point, but Owens doesn't like it. Reports at the time were all dictated, voice-activation software creating transcripts for posterity. A while ago, Owens had gone back and reviewed a few, the flashbacks hitting hard. Cops could barely talk in complete sentences at that time, it was all fragments and expletives. Half those reports sound like the person was unhinged, as in literally mentally ill.

They *were*. Everyone was. Reality had been torn apart and everyone was falling through the cracks, falling, falling.

Owens takes a breath. "What exactly would you like to know?"

"Why don't you just take me back there, starting at the moment you arrived at the Market."

Another breath. "Our orders were to protect the workers who were unloading the shipments and to contain the crowd and prevent them from stealing anything. Which was made difficult by our deteriorating vision. This is all just . . ." He shakes his head.

"'Contain the crowd.' So the crowd had already gathered before you were sent there? That isn't clear in your report."

"'Isn't clear.' Excellent choice of words. Nothing was goddamn clear, if you'll recall."

"Owens," Winslow says gently.

Huntington lets a tense few seconds pass. On the mistaken assumption that things will miraculously become less tense after a pause.

"Please answer the question."

"Yes. My partner at the time, Officer Morales, and I had been sent by Captain Fox, who passed away a few days later." Suicide, his police-issued revolver. One of dozens in this state alone. "A shipment of food and drinking water was being sent from the airport to the Market. It was supposed to be a secret, and the appropriate agencies were going to disperse it to the community through the appropriate channels, but word got out. I think one of the foremen at the airport warehouse admitted he couldn't see, so they needed to find another guy to handle it, and during that delay, I don't know, word spread."

The night in question was six weeks after The Blinding had reached their city, and Owens was one of several officers who had severely impaired vision at that point. Few had anything approaching normal sight.

Huntington asks, "So Western Market was . . . Was it surrounded? Where exactly were people gathered?"

Again, Owens wants to ask *Why. Why why why.* Bad things happened. People were starving. Terrified. They came because they'd heard there would be food. Such scenes had occurred the world over during various wars and disasters, and they often went badly. Now add blindness, or at least major visual impairments for most everyone at that point, and how can you sit at that desk and criticize us for making mistakes, being stressed, having flaws?

"Look, you're asking me about something that took place years ago—"

"Your other reports have always displayed impeccable memory."

"—during The Blinding, for God's sake. Do I have to remind you that details are hard to recall from that time?"

Memories, thoughts, facts. It was amazing how they all seemed to escape, once torn from any tether to visuals. Life had become a surreal dream. The people you loved weren't people anymore, they were voices, ghosts. Your home was nothing but hard surfaces that struck you at unexpected times. The sky vanished. Depth was an almost incomprehensible abstraction. You were reduced to your body, which itself had been reduced.

Also no screens, no text, unless you were fortunate enough to already know braille. No video. For years people had been worried about the effect of all those screens in our lives, and now they were gone. It was like everyone had lost not one sense, but two.

He would sit with Jeanie in his apartment and they would ask what the other had done all day and they'd both have the hardest time remembering. And that was in the beginning.

Some people got laryngitis from talking so much, everyone working the vocal cords overtime, as if all that aural stimuli might make up for a lost sense. Narrating their lives for each other, in hopes that made their lives more real.

That night went badly, he wants to say but doesn't dare. *It went very, very badly and I dream about it every night and even when I'm awake.*

I feel those hands on me, always.

It's when Huntington starts questioning him about the exact number of bodies that Owens says he needs a break.

After ten minutes in the men's room and pacing the hallway and conferring with Winslow, who doesn't appear to be doing much to earn the paycheck provided by Owens's union dues, they're back in their assigned seats.

The young assistant is missing, but Owens doesn't care.

"Let's just get this over with," he says.

"I'd like to move on to a separate incident. Two years ago, August twelfth, the death of Jeanette MacArthur."

A switch is thrown inside Owens. "Excuse me?"

Winslow says, "Whoa, Jeffrey, there was nothing about this in any of our correspondence."

"I'm sorry, but I only recently came upon something."

Owens asks him, "Can I ask about *your* wife, asshole?"

Winslow puts a hand on Owens's arm. "Let me handle this."

Owens shakes him off as Huntington says, "Again, I'm sorry if this didn't make it into my memos, but I have the right to ask anything, and a suspicious death involving an officer's—"

"'Suspicious'?" Owens burning.

If he could have looked at himself he would have seen a deranged smile, as if this were almost comical and he was trying to make sense of it. His expression seems to give Huntington pause, just for a moment.

"Yes, suspicious. And I don't know why it—"

Owens bolts from his seat. He steps around the table and Huntington rises in anticipation. Which only makes it easier for Owens to grab him by the collar and pin him against the wall.

Winslow shouting, "Owens, stand down!"

Huntington grasps at Owens's hands. Trying to pry them off. Scared. What he doesn't realize is that this flurry of motion and sudden violence is actually Owens holding himself back.

"What exactly do you want to ask about my wife?" Owens's voice strangely slow, even to himself. "Do you want to know what it was like to see her body hanging there? Would you like to know how cold her skin felt?"

Winslow again, "Detective Owens, stand down. *Now.*"

Owens releases Huntington. Smells the man's sweat, his own. Huntington holds out a finger. Wanting the last word. Then deciding maybe that's a tremendously bad idea.

Owens brushes past Winslow on his way out. "Write whatever the hell 'truth' you want, but leave Jeanie out of it. You need me to sign any forms about the Market riot, leave them in my fucking box."

Memories are indeed sharper now, impaled against our vision like tiny butterflies. He already knows he'll remember this moment for a long time.

CHAPTER 10

Hours after being released, Dr. Leila paces in her living room. At first she had assumed they were holding her for her own protection, as the murderer must still be out there somewhere. Then the detectives asked the wrong sorts of questions, and life became like a car headed off a cliff she couldn't steer away from.

That's when she realized they were holding her because they suspected her.

Nothing she told them seemed to dissuade them. Jesus, cops. Always looking for the easiest possible answer. She was the only witness, so they recast her as the killer. Great—excellent work, gentlemen. She'd called her lawyer, but they'd stonewalled him for as long as legally possible.

Habeas corpus laws had been changed during the days of The Blinding, back when there were states of emergency everywhere, cops saying they needed to put certain people away without taking the time to give official reasons. Vidders have been commonplace for years now, yet police have proven mighty reluctant to give back their new power. Still, she never really expected to be one of the victims of such overreach.

She had begun to fear they were truly going to charge her, that she'd never be free again, that the nightmare of the shooting would be overwhelmed by the nightmare of prison.

Finally her lawyer got her out, and now freedom, her apartment.

Freedom in a world that has a killer psychopath in it somewhere.

Prison or a psychopath. How her life has been reduced to this, she has no idea.

The killer had let her live, though. So she must be safe. Right? Because obviously killers subscribe to logic, behave predictably.

Her apartment is lonely, and small, yet it boasts no fewer than twelve mirrors. Her friends have teased her for this, hinting that she's vain. She's not. She likes reflections, and reflections of reflections of reflections. She arranged the mirrors precisely so, creating an Escher-like effect from nearly every angle. She likes that she can look in one direction, not just see in another, but in a direction her brain can't even immediately determine, an outward spiraling, like her mind's eye is falling into an endless void of sight. When she tries to explain this to people, they find it freaky, but to her it's comforting.

There is always more to be discovered, more to be understood. Something as mundane as the hallway in a one-bedroom apartment contains multitudes.

On her living room screen she watches the news. The host informs her, "EyeTech recently announced the successful implantation of ten thousand vidders in poverty-stricken regions of Bangladesh and Pakistan." A drop in the bucket, she knows. The gap between haves and have-nots is more of a chasm when the unfortunates can't even see.

Her phone rings. A colleague from Bio-Lux, one of the few she trusts.

"Yeah, they let me out," she explains. "Listen, you need to tell me everything you know about what Jensen was really working on."

Another shift in the books for Amira and she's greatly looking forward to a hot shower and bad on-screen entertainment. In the station's subterranean garage, she's only a few feet from her car when a voice she doesn't recognize calls out.

"Officer Quigley! Can I have a minute?"

He's half jogging over to her. Black, fortyish, dressed like an attorney. A prosecutor she doesn't know? He looks like he's had as bad a day as she has; his tie is askew and the top button is gone, just some tiny threads dangling there.

"Jeffrey Huntington," he says as he extends his hand and they shake. "I'm with Internal Affairs, working with the Truth Commission."

She already regrets shaking his hand. "I wasn't even on the force then."

"Of course, you're not under investigation. But there's some information I'm . . . having a difficult time getting from Mark Owens. I was hoping you might help."

She reaches for her car door, pulls it open.

"You guys just want to crucify all the cops who were busting their asses during The Blinding."

"No, I don't. And that's not what I want to talk about. It's his wife."

That stops her for a moment. "His wife? We have nothing to talk about."

She gets in, closes the door. Wishes her window were thicker, that it could block his voice.

What the fuck does he want to say about Jeanie? What does she have to do with anything? Amira wants to tell him off, but she's also alarmed by the fact that this stranger knows she's with Mark and seems to know her weak spot.

Her and Mark's relationship isn't exactly a secret, but they hide it at work. No good would come of flaunting it. They're in different divisions, with different ranks—only problems would ensue. He's close to a decade older than her, which hasn't felt as weird as maybe it should, though sometimes she wonders what that says about her, or him. They seldom cross paths at work, and when they do, they barely make eye contact, give each other a wide berth.

And also: calling it a *relationship* might be a stretch. They hooked up one night, shortly after meeting on the job. Then a few more times, spread across weeks. He hadn't seemed anxious to start something serious, and honestly neither had she, at first, but they fell into a sort of routine, spending one or two nights together most weeks but never really discussing what this meant. The two brief conversations about her moving in were the closest they'd come, and that last chat hadn't gone well. Maybe it was a sign that she should back off, that he wasn't worth the trouble.

And yet this IA attorney knows about them. It scares her, though she knows that's not rational. She turns on the engine.

"Officer Quigley, I'm not the bad guy here."

"Neither is Owens." She raises her voice to be heard through the window. "Whatever pissing fight you two are in, leave me out of it. Now step back, please."

She shifts to reverse so she can back out of the spot.

"Look up the records, Officer," he says as she eases back slowly enough for him to step away and keep from having his feet run over.

As she's shifting to drive and cutting with the wheel, he calls out, more loudly than before.

"She didn't kill herself."

Amira stops and makes eye contact with him for just a moment. Then she hits the gas too hard and nearly clips the back fender of the car she'd been parked next to. As she pulls away she checks the rearview and sees him standing there, shaking his head.

She grips the wheel harder so her hands won't shake.

CHAPTER 11

Owens is on his way out of the station when Peterson intercepts him.

"I heard about the hearing," Peterson says. "You all right?"

That was fast. "Heard what, that I snapped? That I'm falling apart?"

"I already knew that about you. C'mon, let's get a drink."

"I don't know, Jimmy. I'm not the best company right now."

"That wasn't a question. Buy me a drink. It's me and Cynthia's anniversary."

Something inside Owens snaps to attention. He nods, knowing he can't refuse.

Minutes later they're at Burke's, the sort of no-frills joint they both prefer. Years ago, according to legend, places like this ceased to exist. Real estate in the city was so sky-high that only classy, high-end places with obscene prices and wealthy clientele could survive. The Blinding put an end to that. As this and every other city slowly claws its way back to some semblance of normalcy, dark and sparsely decorated bars with four beers on tap and a small collection of liquor do just fine.

Peterson rants for a bit about the new President, whom he loathes, and his damn Truth Commissions. Easier to talk about that than the difficult personal matter that brought them here, but he finally gets to it when he's near the end of his first beer.

"I visited her this afternoon," he says. "She's looking good. They're taking care of her."

From the way Jimmy nods, Owens can tell he's talking himself into what he just said.

"That's good."

"Didn't know who I was at first, though. Took a little while. Some awkward chitchat."

"Sorry, man."

Peterson takes a swig. "I'm used to it."

It's been about four years since Peterson had his wife institutionalized.

She suffered a traumatic brain injury during a sudden riot toward the end of The Blinding. A panic had broken out in the streets near their apartment, later determined to be due to a false rumor about a man lighting things on fire. She'd picked up some food and was on her way home. Peterson hadn't been there, had been on the job, so he was able to piece only a few things together afterward. At some point she'd been knocked down, trampled. Maybe someone or something landed on her. She had a broken right arm and a fractured skull that the doctors struggled to treat since most of them couldn't see, couldn't operate their equipment as well as they should have.

Perhaps it was the sort of injury that would have doomed her in any era, but the fact that it happened when it did made everything worse.

Cynthia was in a coma for two weeks. When she awoke, she suffered from headaches, could barely talk. As she regained her voice, it was clear her mind wasn't right. She'd lost whole chunks of her memory.

Remembered marrying him but not meeting him. Remembered being pregnant but not miscarrying. Vividly remembered some parts of her childhood, couldn't recall a thing about college. It didn't make sense to Jimmy, why some memories she retained and others she didn't. The doctors shrugged, moved on to the next patient.

As far as Owens could tell, Jimmy did everything he could for her short of quitting his job. Arranged for a full-time nurse. Spent all his non-work hours at home fussing over her. But the memory problems worsened over time for reasons the doctors didn't understand.

Once upon a time, Jimmy had been more of a joker. His sense of humor more fun-loving, less bitter. That Jimmy was gone.

Owens remembers one of their conversations right before Jimmy put her in the institution. He had been wrestling with the dilemma for months, but her condition had deteriorated to the point she needed constant care, which he couldn't afford. Health care coverage for people injured during The Blinding was complicated and confusing, but apparently institutionalization was covered in a way home care wasn't, for cops' insurance plans, at least. The two partners didn't talk about this much, only when Peterson brought it up. Owens tried to show concern, but it felt too delicate a subject for him to bring up himself. He knew that Jimmy didn't want to be seen as someone who'd abandoned his wife or backed away from a challenge.

But the dilemma clearly agonized him, for months. He was hell to be around then. Started arguments with Owens and other cops over the smallest things, and woe be to any perp who talked back to him.

Finally he had her committed. Two weeks later he applied for a transfer to a joint city-federal task force aimed at shutting down the latest wave of opsin flooding the market. Volunteered to work undercover, for nine months. As if completely reinventing himself, shedding a past life. Owens didn't see or hear from him. When the task force was disbanded, Peterson returned to the Department, and though his mood still seemed dark, at least he was less of a walking incendiary device.

"It's strange," Petersons says now. He's nearly finished his beer and Owens has barely dented his. "To be erased from someone's memory. It's kind of like that part of you . . . just ceases to exist."

"You still exist, man."

"That part of me, though. The husband part. The once upon a time, the boyfriend part. Courting. All that shit. It's gone."

He wants to tell Jimmy he's wrong, but he's not sure that's the case. It's a new twist on the tree-falls-in-a-forest question. You reveal a part of yourself to a person, to just one person. A part you were afraid to reveal to anyone else. The act of revealing yourself changes you, maybe, but only in the other person's eyes and your own. And if the other person's eyes are gone, if her memory is gone, then that old self of yours might not exist anymore. Maybe Jimmy's right.

We change as we age, and those past versions of ourselves are shed as we make our way through life. Or they're scraped off by hardships we never saw coming. What's left underneath becomes our new skin, our new self. Parts that we once tried to hide, parts we were afraid to let out.

Or parts we were *smart* to hide. Parts we knew shouldn't come out. But now they're out, on full display, whether we like it or not. Our best selves are gone.

That old phrase *What doesn't kill you makes you stronger*? It occurs to Owens that he hasn't heard anyone voice that since before The Blinding.

"It's good, though," Peterson says. "I hadn't seen her in a while. You know, it just gets tougher. You make excuses. But today"—and there's that nod again—"I'm glad I went. Because it made clear that that part of me *is* gone. And it's okay. I've made my peace with it. I miss her, I miss the person she used to be, so goddamn much. But the person that she is now . . . She's in the right place. They're helping her. She's happy. And the person I used to be, way back when I met her? That dude doesn't need to exist anymore."

Owens feels he's above-average at knowing when someone is lying, but the toughest thing to pick up on is when someone is lying to himself.

Jimmy finishes his beer, his wedding ring glinting in the dim light.

An hour later, Owens sits in his parked car, glancing at a second-floor window across the street. He begged off after having only two beers to Peterson's four. The conversation had safely veered away from Cynthia and they moved on to other things, so it felt safe for him to call it a night early. Peterson tried to get him to stay, but Owens just wasn't in the mood, made excuses.

He gets a call. Peterson's face appears on the screen.

"Hello again."

"You left your bag at the bar, man. You need me to bring it home for you, or can I just take it to work tomorrow?"

"Tomorrow's fine, thanks."

"Hey, where are you?"

"Keeping watch on Dr. Leila."

Owens is staring at her window so he doesn't see Peterson's reaction, but there's a pause of a few seconds.

"Why? Even if we believe her story, she says the guy let her go. Why would he go after her again?"

"I don't know, Jimmy. Maybe I just needed to feel useful."

"You walked out on drinks with your partner for *that*?" Peterson sounds insulted, and should, Owens thinks, telling himself he's a shit friend. "Look, if you really think she should be watched, you could've had some uniform do that."

Peterson assures him that there's no need for them to watch her at all. No reason Owens needs to kill his night sitting in a parked car.

Owens wonders to himself if he's partly doing this to avoid Amira. He wonders if he all but ended their relationship by telling her not to move in. Wonders if giving away all of Jeanie's art changes anything. His sister hates him and his parents are gone. He's running out of people in his life, things to be thankful for, to enjoy, to give him reason to get up in the morning.

It was so hard for so long. To try one's best to stay positive, or at least not stay depressingly negative. To put things in perspective. To count one's blessings, even as the blessings were stripped away. Things got a bit easier, with time, with experience.

Then, weirdly, they got harder again. Except this time you were weaker, you had less in reserve, you had fewer resources, and the idea of staying positive just seemed too hard, too much work for no reward.

He doesn't want to talk to Peterson. But maybe being alone with his thoughts is worse.

"I'll come over and join you," Jimmy says. "I'll bring some Jameson, make it a party."

Owens is about to reply when he hears a gunshot.

"Fuck."

"What was that?" Peterson asks. He must have only barely heard it over the mike, to not know what it was.

Owens grabs his radio and reports shots fired, requests assistance.

"I'm on my way," Peterson says, and his face vanishes.

Owens exits the car, draws his gun, runs toward the building.

Inside, the lobby's clear but for a doorman who looks very alarmed indeed at Owens and his gun.

"Police!" Owens shouts, holding his badge with his other hand. "Did someone just come in here?"

The doorman opens his mouth, takes a second. "Not in the last ten minutes."

"Stay here. If anyone comes down to leave, don't get in their way but get a good look at them."

Both elevators are in use. He finds the stairs, leaps them three at a time.

He checks the second-floor hallway. Empty. Looks down the hall and sees that one of the doors is open. Door 231, Leila's.

He steps into the hallway, slowly. Across the hall, Door 228 opens and a twentyish white guy still wearing business attire steps out.

"Police! Get back in your apartment and lock the door!"

The guy gives him *Holy shit* eyes, obeys.

Owens stands outside Leila's open door. "Police! Dr. Leila, are you in there?"

No reply. But he hears a sound.

He rushes in. First through a small entryway, jackets hanging on his left. He throws open the door to his right, sees a closet, moves on.

He sees a man, nearly shoots him. It's himself, backward. No, forward. Christ, that's weird. Mirrors and mirrors, double and triple reflections of himself. He walks slowly and sees what he's become—frazzled white man, no longer young, decent shape but needs more sleep, bad hair, sweaty, automatic pistol in his hands. Self-portrait of paranoid cop.

And on the living room floor he sees Dr. Leila. On her back. The bullet hole in her forehead could not have been centered more perfectly. Like Jensen's. The killer had gotten *that* close.

Fibers of her carpet absorb the blood, the circle a red halo growing outward. He doesn't bother checking for a pulse.

Sound again, movement from another room. ·

He points his gun around the corner. Enters the bedroom. More fucking mirrors, and again he nearly shoots his reflection. Would be a doubly bad omen.

A window is open, and he just barely sees movement. Was that a black leg?

"Freeze!"

The leg does not freeze. The leg escapes. Owens runs through the bedroom and looks out the window. He sees, leaping from the fire escape, a black blur. A person-shaped darkness, like he or she has been etched out of Owens's world by some omniscient god wielding a stencil and an X-Acto knife.

"Police! Stop right there!"

He'd normally hold his gun with two hands, but he uses his right to adjust his vidder. Surely this is a malfunction. Surely this isn't right. Even though it's exactly like Dr. Leila had described it.

The figure lands on the alley floor. Seems to look up at Owens. Seems to point at him.

A gunshot. Glass shatters and Owens ducks. Two more shots from the alley.

Peterson's voice from the living room: "Police! Owens, you here?"

"In the bedroom!" Owens calls out. He stands up and watches as the black blur sprints down the alley. "We got a . . ." A what? What the hell is happening? "A man in the alley!"

Is it even a man? He's not sure. The blur doesn't stick to the outer boundaries of the person, it's blockier, projecting a couple inches or so outward in every direction. The person could have long hair or short, could even be wearing a hat, have breasts, be thin or stocky. Owens can't tell.

Peterson enters the room, crouched low. "You hit?"

"No."

Owens looks out the window, just in time to see the blur reach the corner of the alley and vanish out of sight. If it was ever *in* sight.

Owens climbs out of the window, onto the fire escape. Leaps down. Lands hard and his knees hurt but he ignores it. Runs. At the turn of the alley, he sees the figure, sprinting toward the next street.

Twelfth Avenue, a main road. A marquee glows twenty feet away—*Shit, a concert just got out.* Pedestrians everywhere.

A shocked man stops in front of Owens but weaves drunkenly. Owens pushes him out of his way, looks up the street, down. He doesn't see the blur.

He leaps onto the hood of a parked car for a better view. A few people gasp at the sight of his gun. He looks in every direction. He sees farther than he would have seen pre-Blinding, back when the evening's darkness would have drawn the borders of night closer around him, but it doesn't help. Nothing but normal city traffic on the road, all these damn pedestrians on the sidewalk, and no blur.

Peterson finally catches up, emerging from the alley. Looks up at Owens standing there on a car like some crazed street prophet.

"You lose him?" Peterson asks.

Owens never had him. He can't respond. He keeps looking for a few more seconds, hoping it's not in vain, that the blur has been hiding behind something and will step out eventually.

"Owens, what am I looking for?" Peterson annoyed.

Owens finally admits failure and climbs off the car. Stands next to his partner. Owens's eyes wide. Stunned.

"What did you see?" Peterson keeps asking. "What did you see?"

CHAPTER 12

Dr. Leila's apartment reincarnated as crime scene. Cops everywhere, dusting walls, taking videos and stills. Leila's eyes still open, which strikes Owens as even more tragic and ironic than usual, since she couldn't even see the person who shot her.

Carlyle approaches Owens, who lingers near the body, already having checked her pockets carefully, finding nothing. She was home, after all; she was supposed to be safe. Yet still Owens hovers over her, in shock.

"Owens," Carlyle says. Trying to sound patient. "Please."

"I know it's crazy, but . . . it was exactly like she said the other day."

"Come on. When we file the report, you actually want to go on the record saying you saw a black blur?"

Owens snaps from his fog and straightens his shoulders. He remembers the way Leila reacted when he and Peterson belittled her story. Now he's singing the same tune and he knows it sounds off to others, the way your recorded voice feels so foreign to your own ears.

"Someone is . . . messing with people's vidders, Captain. She was telling the truth."

He knows people are looking at him. Maybe they've all heard about his meltdown with Huntington. Maybe the stories are spreading that Owens has snapped. The fact that he has alcohol on his breath doesn't help, even though he technically wasn't on shift, was just staking the place out on his own time because he has nothing else to do.

He realizes he needs to make everyone else take this seriously.

"Captain, if they can mess with a cop's vidder, whose can't they do it to?"

Owens looks over at Peterson, who seems to have just exchanged glances with Carlyle. A glance that seems to say *I don't know what to think about my own partner anymore, sir.* Peterson wipes the expression from his face, but not quickly enough.

Two hours later, after checking off all the formalities and finally being told by Carlyle that they are no longer needed, Owens and Peterson leave the apartment building. Owens walks in a daze and Peterson strolls to his side and behind a couple steps, the way a cop knows to do if a subject is strung out or mentally unstable.

Owens stares at everything as if trying to find visual evidence of other errors. Is anything else blacked out, or out of place, or just funny somehow? The entire world before him transformed to a puzzle he needs to solve. His awareness so heightened now, his heart rate still way up, as every single moment might contain more discrepancies he needs to focus on, figure out, make right.

Is that car really parked there? Is that really its tag number? Is that person on the other side of the street really there?

He holds a hand in front of his face, wiggles his fingers, testing how his vidder interprets motion.

"You leaving your car here?" Peterson asks him.

"Yes. I need to walk."

The truth is, he's afraid to drive right now. Afraid something else in his vision will go wrong while he's hurtling thirty or forty miles an hour down the road. He could use the e-driver, sure, but even that he doesn't trust.

His world coming undone.

So instead he says good night to Peterson and walks through the city, slowly, staring at everything he sees, or thinks he sees. A couple holding hands—the woman notices his stare and looks away, muttering to her boyfriend. A young woman through an illuminated second-floor apartment window, her body a silhouette, long hair swaying. An airplane overhead, lights blinking on ascent. The intricate details of a sewer cap, an emblem he'd honestly never scrutinized before.

Detectives are supposed to be skeptical, to assume people are lying, but he's in a whole new stratum now. Doubting all that he sees. The entire *world* is lying to him. Or his own eyes are.

He's not sure which is worse.

PART TWO

CLOAKS

CHAPTER 13

The sun has just started to rise as Amira enters her small, cramped apartment. The lair of a woman who isn't home much and sleeps at odd hours. Sparse furniture, few decorations other than images of her parents.

She drops her heavy jacket on a chair. The chair topples.

That kind of night.

She bends down and picks everything up, sighing to herself. She helped on another dark-rape today, her third this month. She's seen the figures and knows that they're spiking again. Dark-rapes are when women alone are attacked from behind by someone wielding something hard enough to bash their vidder. A blackjack, a bat, a rock. One swing and usually she's unconscious; sometimes she's still awake, but the point is her vidder is busted and she's blinded. That's when they attack (it's nearly always a group of them), knowing that she won't be able to ID anyone afterward. Even though she's suffered horrifically, and may have had her eyes inches—or less—from her attackers, she won't see anything. The victim might well remember the voices of her attackers, but voices are hard to report. Police departments do not have an index of voices the way they do faces.

If the cops get lucky and find a suspect, sure, they can bring him in for a lineup and make him talk, and maybe, *maybe,* the victim will recognize his voice. It's happened, once or twice. But when they do catch the perp, it's almost always because they talked about it later or because an eyewitness to the crime comes forward. Much more commonly, the attacks occur in isolated locations, where the attackers are confident they'll be free of witnesses.

These are Amira's least favorite shifts.

The women shocked, inconsolable. The assholes getting away with it, most likely. She takes the women's statements and tries to console them and empathize, hating how little help she can truly provide. The victims are in no condition to give a statement and almost always they're still blind, their vidders permanently busted, and it takes a while to get a new one, so they're doubly traumatized, or maybe *continually* traumatized is the better phrase, because they're still living in the same darkness that precipitated their attack.

People are just evil, Amira's thinking.

Anyone who had lived through The Blinding knew all about our limitless potential for cruelty, yes, but by becoming a cop Amira had hoped she was joining a force for good. Had thought she would be part of a movement, a worldwide step in the right direction after years of madness.

Hasn't worked out that way.

Sometimes she fears she's made a terrible mistake.

And then to put a perfect bow on her day, that Internal Affairs hack Huntington tried fucking with her head as she was on her way home. Telling her that Jeanie hadn't killed herself. What was he trying to do? No, Amira had never pulled Jeanie's file—of course not; she had never felt compelled to do so. Because why would she? She felt haunted by the woman quite enough as it is. She didn't need to read about her suicide, too.

If Jeanie hadn't killed herself, then she was murdered. So Huntington was all but telling Amira that her on-again, off-again boyfriend was a killer—that she too was in danger. In which case, why didn't he just say it outright?

No, Jeanie was a suicide, *had* to be.

Huntington was after Owens, clearly. For something that happened during The Blinding. And he was making things up about

Jeanie, in hopes that he could win Amira over, or just to mess with her.

What she still doesn't understand is why.

After a sad reheated dinner, she empties her pockets, glances at her phone, remembers she got a call from her mother that she let go to voice mail. She hits play.

"Hey, *mija*, I hope you're being safe out there." She starts nearly every message with that. *Mamá* has never loved the fact that her daughter chose this profession. "I just wanted you to know, I saw Daniella the other day, and I really think you should drop by when you can. She just seems . . ." A weighty sigh. "More down than usual, you know?"

Daniella, Amira's older sister by two years, is in jail. She's been there for three years and might get out in seventeen if things break really, really well for her.

Which they never have before.

True, Amira hasn't visited Daniella as often as she should. She knows her parents stop by weekly, sometimes more, so the fact that she doesn't keep pace does not reflect well on her. Nor does, once again, her chosen occupation. As if *she's* the one who did something wrong.

"Okay, *Mamá*, okay," Amira says to herself once the recording ends. She dreads the visit already.

Daniella and Dante were twins, Amira always the third wheel. Locked out of the secret language the twins seemed to have, the weird telepathy, their ability to communicate in glances, sometimes even in barely audible exhalations. Amira hopelessly behind, not just younger but different, an Other in her own family.

Then one day Dante was gone and Daniella lost her mirror, her foil. Daniella was like the last tribesman on earth who spoke a dying language. The language survived in her, but with no one to share it with, did it matter? Did she matter? Losing Dante didn't bring the sisters closer together, just like it didn't save their parents' marriage.

As Amira enters her bedroom, the console turns on automatically, and a 3D hologram of a newscaster appears.

"Hi, Amira, you have one message."

"Play."

A new male face appears, young, white, impeccably groomed. Like a slightly cooler version of the newscaster.

"Good afternoon, Amira Quigley!" He is way too excited for her current frame of mind.

"My name is Ray Singleton and I work at EyeTech in New Product Development. This isn't a marketing call; it's actually great news. You've been chosen as one of only two hundred winners *worldwide* for our new beta product—"

"Fuck off."

Most models require the user to say *Turn off*, but she's personalized it to her preferred style. The screen goes blank.

She collapses onto her bed. Reconsiders.

"Wait. Resume."

The not-a-marketing-call guy reappears where he'd left off.

"—a product not expected to go on the market for another three months and at a price of five thousand dollars! If you're interested in being one of the first two hundred people *in the world* with a special enhancement to your vidder, and for absolutely free, please call at your earliest convenience."

The number automatically feeds into her phone. She won't call now, as most sensible businesses are closed. But if this isn't some scam and EyeTech really is offering her some "enhancement" for her vidder, she'd be crazy not to take one for free, or at least to hear them out.

She lies back down and closes her eyes, and her vidder cuts itself off, creating the darkness she needs for the next few hours.

CHAPTER 14

Midmorning—the quietest the police department ever gets. Any earlier and the late-nighters would still be here, filing reports, questioning subjects, racking up more unpaid overtime. Owens's shift doesn't start for hours but he barely slept, haunted by visions of killers he couldn't see.

At his computer, he digs up old files. A few unsolved, but most of them closed cases. A queasiness in his stomach. Hopes it's due to lack of sleep and too much coffee but suspects otherwise.

The oldest excuse in the book, Peterson had told Dr. Leila when they'd grilled her. Wrong choice of words—The Blinding wasn't that long ago, so it's hardly *old*—but the sentiment was dead-on: it's become the most common excuse cops hear. *I couldn't see anything, vidder glitch, sorry, I can't help you.* The people who used to wear "No Snitching" T-shirts and play dumb whenever the cops were trying to find witnesses to daylight killings now had new, gold-plated excuses. *Sorry, Officer, I know the guy was shot right outside my apartment, but I guess my vidder wasn't working right.* Chuckles, elbows to their friends' sides.

Peterson hadn't been lying. It *is* an easy excuse.

But Owens has a very bad feeling, as he looks up case after case, digging for the ones that might fit the profile. The new profile—one he hadn't dared admit existed until last night.

One case he remembers in particular. Takes him a while, but he finally finds what he's looking for. Reads through it again. Funny how an old story can seem so completely new once you view it through a different lens.

He slaps the table. A couple other cops look up from their desks like spooked groundhogs, don't bother asking what's up. Too busy with their own casework to care about another man's epiphany.

Epiphany, Jeanie once told him, came from the Greek *epiphaneia.* A manifestation or striking appearance. Sometimes referring to the sudden appearance of God.

Except even atheists can have them.

He digs up the addresses he'll need and stands to leave. His attention is drawn to one of the video screens someone has left on. The newscaster says, "In one week, EyeTech CEO Kai Ballantine will be unveiling the company's new product to investors. Rumor has it the latest vidder will allow wearers—get this—to alter their own appearance."

Owens stops, stares at the screen.

"Bullshit."

He is a man talking to a hologram. The other groundhogs don't notice, he hopes.

He waits, but that's all the reporter has at this point. EyeTech plays things famously close to the vest, at least until its big to-do before stockholders. The reporter and the anchor chitchat about rumors, industry gossip crossed with celebrity gossip about the company's handsome, young, and fabulously wealthy founder, Kai Ballantine. By the time they move on to some solar company's IPO, Owens is moving again, wondering how easy it might be to crash next week's stockholder event for the most powerful company on earth.

Police-community relations were hardly strong before The Blinding. Years of horrific shootings and stranglings, racial profiling, countless instances of abuse, the fallout from bad laws and worse enforcement, the legacy of cops' role in enforcing a status quo that was never fair or just and had only seemed to have worsened over the years, all that and more had taken a toll even back when vision was not a concern.

What had made everything even yet worse, though, was cops getting vidders before civilians.

Government spending had partly funded the R&D that led to the first vidders, and the government wanted essential workers fast-tracked for what was being called "New Vision." Doctors and hospital workers and all other medical staff, and anyone who worked in public safety, meaning cops and the military. Everyone on earth wanted vidders, immediately, but whereas civilians would use vidders to help themselves and their families first and foremost, cops would use them to help others.

That was the theory.

It didn't take long for stories to get around. That cops armed with vidders were hacking into civilians' ration accounts, hoarding food and water. That cops armed with vidders were moving their families into the choicest of the many abandoned properties, and even some that hadn't officially been abandoned yet. That cops were *making* those properties become *abandoned*, then taking them. That cops were using their vidders the way cops had always used their power: for themselves, and for those fortunate civilians who'd won (or paid for) their favor. That cops were eliminating competition, rounding up the various people they hadn't been able to lock up legally and instead putting them out of circulation by extralegal means.

Making people disappear at a time when no one else could even see it: *They haven't disappeared if they never appeared in the first place.* That cops had become a militia in their own right, secret police meets the Army meets the Eye of God, a fascist takeover that didn't need to happen under the cover of night because everyone else was still under cover of The Blinding.

So many people died during that time, often vanishing into the void. It's hard to look for someone when you can't see. So many accidents, suicides, but everything could be spun as *Maybe the government took them. Maybe the cops rubbed them out.* Everyone in uniform was under suspicion, a possible liquidator of enemies.

And yes, Owens has at times heard comments from other officers, has reason to believe some cops did break the law. He's not naïve. He's learned to steer clear of certain people and holds him-self to a higher standard. Still, the rumors of widespread corruption bother him, implicating him by association. He'd taken the job to help people, and then, at a time when people most needed help, he felt he'd been labeled an enemy.

He'd made mistakes then, of course, as had everyone. The Market riot haunts him—he dreams about it often and asks himself what he could have done differently. Hates himself for it. So many decisions he wishes he could take back. But every different path he imagines taking only leads him to a worse place.

Honestly, he hopes the Truth Commission finds every dirty cop and cuts them out like the cancer they are. But he worries they'll take him too, for the sin of being there at the wrong time, for not being perfect.

He remembers when he got his first vidder—the early models had been poor in quality, everything fuzzy, details hard to discern. Reading anything on paper was damn near impossible; reading on bright screens was doable if you pressed your nose up to it. Owens fell down stairs more times than he could count, nearly slipped down an open manhole, even put his hand through glass (four stitches, not nearly as bad as it could have been). In some ways, he maneuvered through the world worse with his first, glitchy vidder than he had when blind. Like the old saw about *a little knowledge,* they were dangerous.

But as Owens and his fellow officers acclimated, the vidders were updated and improved. Each new model brought them closer to what real vision had felt like. At one point Owens broke down cry-ing when he noticed tiny details in his vision: the way grass swayed in the breeze, the shine of his wife's hair, the countless shades of gray in the sky when the sun broke through after a late-day rainstorm.

Coming after weeks of madness and violence, even those old-model vidders were a godsend.

Vidders quickly hit the open market, though not quickly enough. They were overpriced due to the demand, making earlier debates about income inequality seem quaint.

For a time, either you were rich or you were blind.

Vidder theft became endemic, as research labs and the few stores that carried them had to hire armed guards, draw wide perimeters around their buildings. The devices themselves were worthless if you didn't also have the needed circuitry threaded through your skull, but thieves didn't realize that. Not only were stores and labs raided, but people were attacked, their vidders torn off. Sometimes they popped off easily, sometimes they came with viscera attached. Owens worked many a grisly crime scene.

Thieves got smarter, recruited former or current EyeTech employees, easily bribable government agents, scientists from rival tech firms. Different crime crews had their own in-house vidder installer, able to take a stolen vidder and successfully implant it on someone else in minutes.

EyeTech got wise, made its next models all but impossible to remove by third parties (people tried, though, to their owners' everlasting agony). It made all vidders trackable and linked to a federal government database, which meant more privacy concerns, but at least the thieves got caught.

Finally, after a few long months, vidders went down in price and taxpayers got government funding, and vidders finally reached a near-saturation point among all but the poorest, at least in what used to be called First World countries. But that still left plenty of others. EyeTech experimented with cheaper models so that more working-class people could afford them, but the idea of "only decent" vision was insulting to customers. Plus it damaged the brand, as they say. EyeTech went back to making only top-notch products and refusing to budge on price. For every commune of deliberate abstainers like Sarah, and for every conventionally blind person who chose to stay that way rather than add some odd tech contraption to their body, there were countless people who were blind not by choice but due to financial circumstance.

None of this helps EyeTech's image; people feel an odd mixture of reverence, skepticism, and fear about a company that's grown so powerful. And whatever this new product feature is that they're planning, Owens will want to learn all about it.

But before wealth, poverty.

He knocks on doors, searching for one Lance Sanderson, a man whose long-ago story about a murder had once seemed insane to Owens, but now less so. Owens had written him off as a liar, but now he needs to hear that story again.

Alas, these are the sorts of doors no one lives behind for long, and it's already been years since Lance lived here. This neighborhood, now dubbed the Embers, was cleared out during The Blinding after several fires gutted most of the buildings. Eventually the remaining structures became overrun with squatters. For a while certain government agencies were trying to get them to clear out, bankers attempting to reclaim titles and rehab old buildings to one day sell, until that proved to be not worth the effort. The people who live in the Embers live here beyond the reach of the law, pretty much; Owens and his associates only come here when they need to talk to someone for a case, and even then they need to really, really want to.

No one who answers any of the doors in the Embers recognizes Owens, and he doesn't recognize them. Which means they don't know he's the guy who put Lance away for manslaughter. None of them even know Lance, haven't heard of him.

He still feels edgy after last night. Weirdly mistrustful of his eyes, his vidder, the world around him. Wondering what might go black next, what strange hallucinations might be thrust upon him. But so far, all appears normal.

He drives to another neighborhood, knocks on more doors, tracking down Lance's past associates and friends.

On the other side of one of those half-opened doors, a skinny thirty-year-old with tattoos damn near everywhere south of his chin nods.

"Yeah, I know Lance. Knew him. What he do now?"

"Nothing. I just think he might know something that could help an investigation."

The painted man gazes slowly at Owens, his badge, his hangdog expression. The painted man gives off vibes of *reformed opsin addict*, his voice betraying every ounce of the struggle behind that *reformed*.

"Lance has come a long way, man. I mean, Detective."

"I'm glad to hear it. Sincerely. This is about something from a long time ago."

"Maybe a guy shouldn't be bothered about something from a long time ago. Maybe you should let him be."

Owens wishes he could say the truth, that he's afraid Lance has already dealt with more trouble than was merited and that maybe it was Owens's fault. But he can't admit that yet, out loud or even to himself.

"I'm not here to bring him more trouble. Just the opposite."

"I doubt he can help you. I haven't seen him in months, and no one else has either."

Owens doesn't like the sound of that.

"You mean . . . he's vanished? Someone messed with him?"

"No. The rumor I heard is that he's with Reverend Miriam now."

Owens tries not to visibly cringe at that name. Even if something inside him shrivels when he hears it.

Only an hour till his shift starts. He has another stop to make before Peterson joins him, so he drops by the Cortex Vortex.

Even in this strange new era, when the difference between day and night is all but meaningless, people still keep to mostly circadian schedules. Something about the effect of vitamin D, the feel of the sun on your skin, the dilation of even unseeing pupils. That said, sleazy bars and clubs continue to attract clientele at all hours, and at midafternoon like this the Cortex Vortex likely hosts a few of its saddest customers. Those most in need of escape.

Used to be a movie theater. The marque outside still claims it's called The Avalon, and in place of the movie title the movable letters spell out "CORTEX VORTEX," and then two lines below, "COME ENJOY." Unfortunate double meaning. This was a happening neighborhood once, long before Owens's time. Now it's just another part of the Embers.

Some of the dives are back now, like this place. Owens passes a few prone bodies on the sidewalk, homeless or strung out on opsin or both.

He approaches the ticket counter, a kid barely eighteen, his mohawk impressive in its height. Owens flashes his badge.

"I'll let myself in."

He walks through a maze of small rooms that were constructed with cheap walls in the old theater. Some of them only plywood, painted black. He hasn't worked Vice in years, yet he navigates his way through the labyrinth like he was here only yesterday. He's read articles about this phenomenon, how the layout of places you walked frequently during The Blinding have been burned into your muscle memory with such permanence. He could close his eyes and find his way through here, much as he wishes some of those memories could in fact be erased.

In most of the back rooms, as if safely away from prying cops (*dream on*), he sees a variation on the expected scene. A person, always male (*what the fuck is our problem?*) sits in a reclining chair that the owner of the place looted from dental offices during The Blinding. Extending from a large, old-school computer, a long metal arm has attached itself to the man's vidder. Owens can hear the computer whirring as the arm blasts electronic signals direct into the man's visual cortex.

Owens stops when he finds the man he's looking for. Not the guy in the chair, who's an overweight fortysomething with thinning hair, lying back with a huge smile on his face, his eyes open but eerily blank, like he's high, which he sort of is. His arms held out before him, at first he looks like a puppeteer dangling invisible marionettes, but after a moment Owens can see the sensual way his fingers move, and anyway Owens knows full well it's not puppets the man is caressing.

The man is seeing a beach maybe, or a hot tub, and with him are two or three gorgeous women, likely naked.

The man's mouth opens and his tongue sticks out, a mollusk searching obscenely for invisible food. Owens is tempted to slam the guy's jaw shut, teach him a lesson.

Instead he clears his throat. The customer is oblivious, but Blake Hinners, who had been crouched down working some controls on the console, looks up, confused.

"Unless he's French-kissing his favorite entree," Owens says, "you're fucked."

"Detective!" Hinners nearly leaps out of his seat. Late thirties, hair dyed orange and hanging long across his forehead to distract from the fact that it's grown so thin. An aging geek. "Oh, hey. We were just in the middle of, um—"

Hinners hits a button. The customer stops waggling his tongue. Closes his mouth, looks around in shock and confusion. His eyes seem alive again. Alive with disappointment.

"What happened?" the customer whines. "Where are my babes?"

Owens smiles at Hinners, whose shoulders slump in defeat. Owens grabs Hinners by the neck and starts walking him out of the room.

"Where are the titties? Hinners, I want my titties or my money back!"

Owens stops, releases Hinners, walks right up to the disappointed customer and holds his badge before him.

"Your vidder on again? You see that?"

"Um . . . Yes?"

"Get the hell out of here and be glad I'm not busting you, too."

He's up and he's gone. Then Owens closes the door behind him, points to the reclining chair and tells Hinners to sit.

Hinners blows hair out of his eyes as he collapses into the chair. "I thought they moved you off Vice. I already paid them off this month."

"I don't want to hear about it."

It's depressing to see this same scene again. More often, these days, people can perform this service on themselves from the comfort of their own homes. VR hookups have become more realistic than ever, so the people who can afford the latest gadgets get to indulge in their illicit virtual thrills without coming to a seedy joint like this. Most of those scenarios are illegal, too, but addicts know where to find them online. There are whole subcultures, Owens knows, who have become shut-ins, barely venturing out so they can instead indulge their darkest fantasies with their eyes shut, vidders plugged into the Net and its sundry games.

Schlubs like the man in the other room can't afford those setups, or don't know how to find them, so they patronize places like this. Hinners still has a large enough clientele, probably always will.

"You used to work at EyeTech, right?" Owens asks.

"In a past life."

"Before they found out about your little perversions."

"There's nothing perverted about this. People shouldn't be ashamed of their libidos. It's human nature, man."

Owens holds out a hand. One of the many great things about being out of Vice is not having to engage in these philosophical debates anymore.

"You have any friends at EyeTech still?"

"Maybe. Why?"

Owens takes a breath. Can't quite believe he's going to let another person, especially a civilian, know what he saw, but he's come this far. So he asks, "Have you ever seen a black blur? Like you're looking at someone, but instead of seeing them, they're all blacked out?"

A long pause as Hinners scrutinizes him. "Personally? No."

"But you've heard of it."

"Sure. Folks say someone gets censored from their vision. But most of what I hear is from people here in the Embers, you know? Either they're high, or they've just walked out of here and their vidders are a little fried, so they're having trouble interpreting what they see."

"Because something like that isn't possible, right?"

Hinners doesn't answer, just watches Owens carefully.

"Talk, or I shut this place down and you're looking at two-to-five for your third bust."

Hinners sighs. "Everyone I can think of who's ever said they saw a blur, they're all gone now."

"Gone, meaning dead?"

"Some, yeah. The others have gone over to The Darkness."

"Why?"

Hinners holds out his arms, exasperated. "Shit, man! People pay me good money to mess with their visuals, you know? They want their doors blown off, I blow 'em off. That's the deal. But you're strapped to a chair here, you're safe. Now, how would it feel to realize you can't trust your vidder when you're out in the world? You'd go nuts! People who can't hack it in the real world anymore, they need a safe place. Reverend Miriam provides that, I guess."

Owens shakes his head. He's already heard that name enough today.

Hinners says, "Look, I'm not a follower, obviously. I'm just telling you what I've heard. What I've seen."

"I need names. I need to find some of these people who say they saw black blurs."

"Why? They're all crazy."

Owens waits, wonders again if he's a fool to admit it to a civilian. He finally says, "I saw one too."

Hinners measures that response for a few beats. Waiting for a punch line that doesn't come. "And you weren't . . . No offense, but you weren't high?"

"I was not high. There was someone I couldn't see, and he was fleeing a murder scene."

Hinners exhales, leans forward, runs his fingers through his hair. "Fuck, man. You are seriously blinking me out here."

"Why?"

"Don't you get it? They do their shit down here, where only freaks and users will see it. That way they can deny it. But if a *cop* says he saw it, then it must be true."

"What are you talking about?"

"The feds, man! CIA, FBI, Homeland, military intelligence, some new shadow agency with no acronym yet, who the fuck knows?! They run their experiments here in the Embers. Testing out their vidder-control technology on poverty-stricken lab rats, knowing no one'll believe it."

Owens looks away, shaking his head. "I'm so tired of the conspiracy-theory bullshit. That The Blinding was a government plot so they could enslave us. That secret agents control what we see, or EyeTech does."

"That's really so hard for you to believe?"

"People tell those stories because they want someone to blame. Or the stories that, somewhere out there, there are people who can see without vidders. Only they don't realize it. Like some latent super-power. Come on."

"I get it. You're a skeptic. You only believe what you can see with your own two . . . oops."

Owens folds his arms. "Do you have any evidence for this other than street rumor?"

"Dude, that's the best evidence there is."

Hinners had been one of Owens's first big busts. He'd been a hot-shot developer at EyeTech but had been let go for reasons the company wouldn't disclose. His next stop had been at a place similar to this but in far more posh environs. Disguised amid offices for fertility consultants and plastic surgeons, Hinners's so-called oph-thalmology office had been complete with fake diplomas from top medical schools. Catering to the elites and working from his high-end contacts in Big Tech, he gave his customers thrill rides that he claimed were not actually illegal. Which might have been true for a little while, until the laws caught up, and things like virtual por-nography and virtual murder became every bit as illegal as the real thing.

"Based on what you know from EyeTech, how would it work?" Owens asks. "How can someone get into my vidder and manipulate what I see?"

"They don't have to physically get into it," Hinners says, yanking on one of the metal arms beside him. "Not like these things. They just alter the data that's being sent to it. Honestly, it wouldn't be *that* hard. They hack into the same GPS and radar data that your vidder uses to tell your brain what's happening around you, the same way they give you the ads and the weather and shit. And they use the GPS of the second person—the one they don't want you to see—so they know exactly what to black out."

"That's impossible. The guy was *running*."

"Doesn't matter. Look, even before The Blinding, what we saw wasn't totally accurate. The eyes have blind spots, and because we have two of 'em there are things that don't align, so the brain auto-corrects. And yes, in real time. Doing what these guys are doing, it's hard, yeah, absolutely. But impossible? No. The more programmers they have on this, the more possible it becomes."

"I'm crazy to be listening to this."

"No, you're crazy to think it's crazy. What you're talking about, for the right people, would be very doable if they had enough re-sources."

"'For the right people'?"

"Someone at EyeTech, or former EyeTech. Or connected people in the government. Or both." Hinners pauses, thinks of something. "And the more often they tried doing this, the better they'd get."

CHAPTER 15

For Amira, visiting her sister in jail always feels like some sort of penance she's paying for someone else's sins.

Even though she knows that her sister, and to varying degrees her other relatives, view Amira as at least partially at fault.

Daniella's problems started years ago when she got hooked on opsin. Her legal troubles, at least. She was plenty troubled before then.

Though opsin became known as the ultimate blindness-coping drug, it actually had been invented a few years before The Blinding, just the latest of the many variations on X that chemists enjoyed concocting. Opsin was particularly known for its visual hallucinations, the way every sound seemed to register as a color, a shift in one's field of vision. Every voice made your perspective quake and shimmy (and yes, Amira knows from experience: she took it once, years ago).

Then The Blinding hit and opsin's ability to conjure extremely vivid images transformed it from the latest party drug to a refuge for millions. People who desperately wanted to find a way out of this nightmare could finally do so, at least for a few hours. They took their pill and no, they couldn't see their apartment or their face in the mirror, but they at least could see *something*. Sometimes you saw the faces of your children, which you hadn't seen in months. The face of your spouse, who was finally more than the shape of their nose and the softness of their cheeks, the press of their lips. You could finally see their eyes again, see the way they absolutely *shined* when they smiled—that was the look you'd fallen in love with. And those who had lost people, sometimes the hallucinations brought back those departed faces, like they were there again. It was spectacular and crushing all at once.

Marijuana had been legalized years ago, but no event did more to persuade the public that maybe our antidrug laws were too harsh than the combination of The Blinding and opsin did. Everyone wanted it, or at least knew someone who was on it, and how could you judge them when all they wanted to do was see again, at least for a few hours?

Amira has learned not to wear her uniform when she visits her sister. No good comes of that. She did it once and the dirty looks she received were nothing compared to the way Daniella was treated afterward by her fellow inmates. *Never do that to me again,* her sister wrote her.

She wears her badge on a chain around her neck only to get past the first two security checkpoints, figuring the gold star gets her just a bit more consideration from the guards. But once she's past them, she tucks it inside her sweatshirt.

God, she hates coming here.

It's no worse than the city jails where she brings those she's arrested, but what breaks her heart is the knowledge that she'll be visiting here for years.

She remembers their old arguments. *What's wrong with me hooking people up with what they need?* Daniella would ask. *I'm helping people. Giving them something positive for a change.*

No, Amira would counter, you're taking their money because they're hooked on that feeling, and every time you do it you make it harder for them to accept the world as it is.

And the world as it is is fucked! Who says it's better for the people who go out in the world and play along? We have machines plugged into our heads, Amira. Machines! How can you blame people for wanting to take a dose and remember what it was like to really see?

The long hallways, the thick doors. The weird announcements. The stale air. The sad families. The impassive guards who look at her differently from the ones a few minutes ago did, when her badge was out.

The slumped shoulders of the other visitors, sitting in the sad little carrels, talking to their loved ones on the other side of the glass.

Amira is directed to carrel 4 and she sits there and waits. The seat is cold.

Two minutes later, Daniella appears. Amira still isn't used to the buzz cut even though it's been Daniella's look for nearly a year. In her memories, Daniella always has that long unruly mane.

"Hey, girl." Daniella's voice nearly deadpan. Like she's just crossing paths with someone she sees every day.

"How you holding up?"

"Another day. Ten zillion to go." The same dead stare Amira gets from perps all day. "What's up? *Mamá* and *Papá* tell you to come?"

"I just wanted to see you." Why wasn't she a better liar?

Daniella picks up on it, grins. "Sure. They tell you I looked bad? That I needed a rescue?"

She does look bad. Acne or some rash across her cheeks and her forehead. A certain pallor to her skin.

It still strikes Amira as strange how people can respond to the same tragedy so differently. When you're a kid you hear stories about people who suffer some calamity, and after that they're more religious or kinder or maybe a bit more paranoid, but always somehow stronger. In real life, though, there are an infinite number of ways we respond. What makes tragedies even yet more tragic is when family members go in different directions afterward.

Your brother dies senselessly and you become a cop, dedicated to helping people get through their own awful problems.

Your brother dies senselessly and you deal drugs, trying to cope by escaping into memories of our old reality.

In both cases, you stare at your sister and wonder how she can live with her decisions.

Amira says, "They told me you've been shutting off your vidder."

Vision strikes, they call it. When prisoners shut off or disconnect their vidders. Like a hunger strike but less fatal. More annoying. They don't fall into their single-file lines as well, they miss the turns into the cafeteria, they bump into others and wind up causing fights they claim they hadn't intended. When an entire wing does it, it becomes chaos, and sometimes succeeds in persuading the prison to change some policy or another. When it's just a random inmate or two, nothing changes except the strikers' lives get even yet worse.

"Yeah, sometimes. What of it?"

According to *Mamá*, Daniella's vidder was off for their last visit. *Mamá* had asked her, pleaded with her, to turn it on ("Don't you want to see my face, *mija*?"), but Daniella refused.

"If you were trying to prove some point, it didn't work."

"There was no point." Staring at the carrel wall. "Maybe that's my point."

Once vidders were invented, the pendulum of public opinion swung against opsin users. We could finally see again, sort of, so anyone who turned to a synthetic drug to conjure old visions had forfeited the right to our sympathy. Laws got tighter again. Plus, more stories appeared about people on opsin doing weird things. Catching themselves on fire, plunging off buildings. Either the hallucinations were confusing the users, making them think they were being chased by something, or the users were just so sky-high ecstatic that they did the unthinkable—thought they could fly, wondered if they were bulletproof or could stop trains with their mind, who knows.

Now anytime someone dies from an opsin binge, their dealer can be tried for murder.

A woman Daniella had sold to went on a binge and wound up climbing over a wall and sprinting across a highway. Daniella's lawyer tried to claim the woman had been suicidal, but he failed. Opsin hallucinations and drug-induced euphoria were surely to blame. Which meant the dealer was to blame.

Which is why twenty years is the best Daniella can hope for.

"Dani. There are ways to make things easier and ways to make things harder. What you're doing is definitely making it harder."

"If you're here to tell them to put me in the Psych Ward, please God, do not do that."

"I didn't say I was—"

"The last fucking thing I need is you trying to help, Amira. Stay out of it. Like usual."

That comment feels like a blow swung at Amira's stomach. She sharply inhales.

Why didn't you do more for your sister? they all asked Amira. *What's the point of you being a cop if you can't protect your own people?*

Meaning, why hadn't Amira put her finger on the scale. Why hadn't she talked to people at Vice, pointed them in a different direction. Why hadn't she tried to blackmail prosecutors, destroy evidence, find flaws in her sister's arrest, plant evidence that the dead woman really *had* been suicidal, that it wasn't the drug's fault and therefore wasn't the dealer's fault. To the family, Daniella was forever the charming one who made mistakes, but that's just her. The tragic twin, as if Amira hadn't lost a brother, too. Amira was the responsible one, the *cop*, for God's sake, and she should have used her pull to help her sister out.

Her parents still haven't forgiven Amira for being so *ethically pure* (her father had spat that phrase at her) that she'd sit on her hands and "let" her sister get put in jail.

"Is there something you'd like me to do?" she asks now.

"Couple years late for that."

She tries to imagine what it's like for Daniella. First The Blinding, hitting them both in their tender teen years. That horrible darkness, inescapable. Coinciding with losing Dante. Their parents constantly terrified something would happen to the girls, too, that they'd be set upon by roaming hordes or fall down an elevator shaft, and how can you be called paranoid when the worst has already happened to you? Then vidders bring New Vision and Daniella embarks on an off-and-on cycle of drugs, abusive boyfriends, and legal trouble.

Which means that for years now, Daniella has mostly seen only darkness or the inside of a prison. When Amira lets herself try to imagine that, she can't suppress a shudder.

Daniella's turning her vidder off is perfectly understandable in one sense. At the same time, it's often a sign that the next step is a suicide attempt.

And Daniella's never been the sort of person who *attempts* to do something but fails.

"I know this sounds crazy," Amira says, "but *Mamá* needs you. *Papá* needs you. Even here."

Daniella does that half laugh thing someone does when they're disgusted. "You're trying to guilt me? Seriously?"

Amira could indeed talk to people at the prison and use her pull to insist they put Daniella in the Psych Ward, keep a closer eye on her. If she does, Daniella will hate her. If she doesn't, Daniella might not make it.

"I'm just trying to remind you that there are people who care about you. People whose lives revolve around the days they've marked on their calendar to sit here and have you roll your eyes at them."

After a few seconds, Daniella nods. For a moment Amira thinks she sees tears in her sister's eyes, but Daniella's stubborn. She keeps staring at the wall until she's willed the tears away, and Amira wonders if she'd only been imaging it, or hoping for it. Tears would at least mean emotion, that there's something there Amira can grab hold of.

When Daniella makes eye contact again, that fleeting bit of emotion has passed and the room feels even colder than before.

She and Owens both have the night off, so they meet for dinner at a Thai place near his apartment. She brings a backpack with a change of clothes, just in case, though honestly she's not sure if she'll be spending the night.

As usual, he takes the seat facing the exit. He always needs to see the way out, she's noticed. And he seems edgy, off. Glancing around the restaurant at odd moments, not making eye contact as much as usual. If she didn't know better, she'd think he was on something.

"What's wrong?" she asks.

"Did you hear what happened to me a couple of nights ago?"

"A little bit." She's heard some rumors and had thought of calling him sooner. Then had decided, *No, let him come to you this time.* They haven't actually spoken since the morning he said they shouldn't move in together, other than a quick call to set up tonight's date.

He tells his story about chasing a murderer he couldn't see. She's heard stories like this before, from people she's arrested, people stoned out of their mind, usually on opsin. But coming from Mark?

"You don't believe me."

"I believe you."

Does she? It sounds impossible, and coming from just about anyone else, she'd write it off as bullshit. But why would he lie about this?

He finishes his drink and orders another as the waiter passes. She's barely touched hers.

"I don't understand how they did it, or who did it. I've been going through old files, trying to find every case where someone claimed they saw something similar."

"That sounds like a lot of files."

"It is."

She tries to help him make sense of things. She recaps, "The second victim was a witness to the first murder. They could have killed her that first time, but didn't. So why come back and kill her a few days later?"

"I've been wondering about that too. She'd said the killer chased her down, then seemed to taunt her when he had her cornered. Pressed the gun against her forehead but then said he had no reason to kill her if she couldn't see him. Yet a few days later, he comes back and kills her anyway."

"So he's crazy. He gets off on the chase."

"Or he worried afterwards. The first time, he thought he was safe from her ever IDing him, so he let her live. But then later he got nervous, decided he'd taken too big of a risk." He sipped his drink. "Or, yeah, maybe he just gets off on it. Wanted to do it again, went back to her because he knew she'd be all the more terrified."

"Or it's more than one person," she says.

He nods, and his expression shows that he doesn't want this to be true but fears it is. "After the first murder, the killer reports back to his accomplices about how he let her live, and they tell him he was stupid to do that, that she might have some way of identifying him. I don't know—his voice, his smell, something. Maybe they were afraid she'd figure it out eventually, so they tell him to go back and finish her off. Or someone else in the group does."

"Sounds complicated," she says, trying to shoot down the idea she herself had voiced. It's bad enough he may be seeing things; she doesn't want him imagining a conspiracy too.

"Yeah," he says after the waiter delivers his next drink. He sounds embarrassed, chastened, like he's realizing now how he sounds. "Maybe not."

After they've finished eating, she mentions the dilemma with her sister and asks him what he'd do.

"Do you think she's going to hurt herself?"

"Her whole life she's been hurting herself."

"You know what I mean."

She thinks for a moment, about the things no one ever wants to think about. "Yes. I do."

"Then make the call and get her in the Psych Ward. Tonight."

She's surprised, had figured maybe he'd tell her to back off, let her sister make her own decisions. But then she realizes, of course, that this is a man who lost someone to suicide. The fact that Amira may be in a position to prevent another suicide makes this situation, to him, a no-brainer. She feels guilty for having missed this.

Assuming, of course, that Jeanie really was a suicide.

She hates herself for wondering that.

* * *

Back at his apartment, she notices two paintings are missing from the living room. When she asks, he explains that he's donating Jeanie's work to the museum. Curators have been coming by in shifts, and there's still more to move, plus an old storage shed of Jeanie's across town.

She feels guilty again. "You didn't have to do that."

"It was time."

With that he pours himself a bourbon on the rocks, asks if she wants one. She says yes.

It was time. Three words and he leaves it at that.

She's never fallen for talkative men, men who are in touch with their feelings. She is drawn to those with tough shells, spiky armor. This is a curse, she realizes. Maybe it's from having a super-chatty mother and a mostly silent, macho father, and she's repeating her family's dynamics. Or maybe she's a masochist. An unpleasant thought and a less pleasant reality.

Mark is handsome and she likes his dark sense of humor, but he can be annoyingly closed off. Every now and then he seems to open up, and those brief glimpses of vulnerability become so addicting to her, she'd gladly walk miles just to get another peek.

She had hoped that moving in with him might get him to loosen up. Now that he's closed the door on that idea, she's been wondering if it's a sign she should leave him.

Yet she remembers how fragile he seemed the night he'd nearly shot Peterson. How desperately he needed her there, even if he hadn't admitted it. She thinks of all the times his face seems to go blank and she knows he is thinking about what he did during The Blinding, haunted by those weeks on the job in a time of madness. She knows he is broken and she still thinks she can fix him.

Anyone would tell her this is not a healthy way to view a relationship.

What most troubles her, and this she knows is petty but she can't help it, is the fear that, when his face goes blank like that, he's really thinking of Jeanie.

He probably is.

He doesn't bring her up as often as he used to. So this decision to divest himself of her old artwork suggests maybe he's taken what Amira said to heart. Maybe he's ready to move on.

Or maybe Amira made the mistake of being his first true relationship after the love of his life killed herself. Maybe there's no way she can be more than The Rebound Lover.

She thinks about telling him what Huntington told her—*Jeanie didn't kill herself*—but she can't bring herself to do it. She's afraid of what he might say. If it's not true, the last thing she wants to do is bring Jeanie up and get him obsessing over her again. Huntington must have been wrong, or trying to mess with Amira for reasons she doesn't understand.

He hands her a drink. "I don't mean to be unromantic," he says as he sits next to her on the sofa. "But if you were going to call someone at the prison about Daniella, maybe you should do it now."

"You're right," she says. She takes out her phone and he stands up, walks to the bedroom to give her privacy.

She winds up being on the phone for nearly an hour, shuttled from one functionary to the next. It's night, but there are always people working at the prison, and she finally gets the right people on the phone and makes her case. Her badge makes them take her more seriously than perhaps they might otherwise. The last person she speaks to gives Amira her word that Daniella will be kept safe.

When she hangs up she feels gutted. She stands, pours herself another drink, and calls out that it's done.

"You did the right thing," he says.

"The right thing feels pretty horrible."

"That's how it works sometimes."

He has faraway eyes again. Thinking of Jeanie, no doubt.

"Here's to feeling horrible," she says with a frown, raising her glass.

* * *

She lies beside him in his bed afterward, drunker than she'd meant to get. Somehow they'd salvaged a night that had way too many serious conversations. Alcohol sure helps, but she doesn't like the crutch it's become.

He drank more than normal, like he's chasing away the stress from his strange murder case. She wonders if he'd had too much to drink the night he supposedly saw the black blur, too—hadn't he said he'd been at a bar with Peterson beforehand? Could that have contributed to what he saw?

She sleeps, wakes in the middle of night, tosses and turns.

Realizes Mark is talking in his sleep. Apologizing.

"I'm sorry. I'm so sorry."

He's never done this before. She puts a hand on his shoulder and gently shakes him, hoping to rouse him just enough to free him from his nightmare.

"Mark. Shh."

The room is dark, but of course she can see his face perfectly, and his eyes are open now. Open and blank.

"I killed her. Oh Jesus, I killed her."

His face scrunches into a grimace and she pulls her hand from him. Then his eyes close again. His breathing slows down and he's out.

She sits up, waiting for something more. Telling herself she didn't really just hear what she heard.

I killed her. What the hell?

He was having a nightmare, that's all. She tells herself this. She's drunk, and so is he. He wasn't making sense, and she can't make sense of anything anyway.

What she also can't do: lie back down and fall asleep after hearing that.

She gets up, goes to the bathroom. Stalling. Thinking.

Looks at herself in the mirror for a long while.

Then she quietly collects her clothes from the floor. Gets dressed in the living room, leaves him a note, makes something up. She'll catch a cab, sleep in her own bed, wake up and try to figure out what to do next. Figure out what's going on with him, and what Huntington was really trying to tell her.

CHAPTER 16

The next few days pass far less eventfully than the previous week for Owens.

He and Peterson get another case, because there's always another case. He keeps digging through old records hoping to find connections to the black blur, and he keeps trying to track down Lance—a man he once put away—and a few other people he thinks might shed light on this, but comes up empty.

All the while, his vision seems normal. No glitches. No more black blurs. He can almost tell himself he imagined it, but he knows he didn't.

The lobby of the Four Seasons is aglitter with jewelry and expensive haircuts and the sort of supposedly casual blazers and T-shirts and jeans that cost more than Owens's entire wardrobe. He's been here only a few times, usually to interview a witness, some rich member of the upper stratosphere who just happened to be at the wrong place, wrong time and see something one day. Today he walks through the lobby, with Peterson, slowly, just to soak it in.

So this is what it's like to be rich. Imagine seeing scenes like this all the time.

All around them, 3D holograms glow just above their heads. "EyeTech Industries," they announce, and "CleerVu" and "New Vision for All."

Men and women queue up to two large, uniformed security guards outside the presentation hall to flash their special invitations. EyeTech's headquarters is only a few miles outside the city, but the company seems to enjoy the spectacle of holding its shareholder meetings downtown, with all the ritzy dazzle of an old-school Hollywood red-carpet opening night.

When Owens and Peterson reach the threshold, they flash their badges.

"We forgot our invitations," Peterson says, and smiles.

To even make it into the building, they'd had to pass a number of Sight Is a Right protesters chanting their various slogans. Owens mostly agrees with their argument—it's fucked that some people are still blind because they can't afford vidders—yet still he finds himself annoyed by the sorts of people who hold placards and scream at passersby. He wants the progress without the work, and he knows that's wrong, and lazy, but at the same time he can't imagine standing at an intersection and shouting at the world.

Now that he and Peterson are in the big room, they sit in the back row like wannabe truants. Easily a thousand people in here, the air alive with gossip and expectation.

"This is a waste of time," Peterson grouses halfway through the first speaker, some CFO or CIO (Owens has forgotten already) who seems to think that a few bad jokes and cool shoes make his speech interesting.

"Just be patient."

"I didn't know business meetings had opening acts."

Apparently they do, they come to learn, as well as second and third acts.

As they sit there, Owens notices that Peterson isn't wearing his wedding ring. Interesting. Something about his last visit to Cynthia finally made him do it. Owens opens his mouth to comment, then thinks better of it.

Finally, after they've been sitting for forty minutes and it feels like the rest of the crowd, too, is growing restless, the mighty Kai Ballantine is introduced.

The first thing Owens notices is he's short. *Good, he's not perfect.* They must always film or photograph him next to smaller people, or on a stand, Owens figures, as he'd assumed he was half a foot taller. From back here he looks tiny, of course, but two enormous screens on either side of the stage convey what Owens already knows: Ballantine is youthful, attractive, energetic. With a Black father and a mother who is the daughter of Chinese immigrants, he has the multiethnic look of a model, like someone chosen by a marketing department's focus groups to appeal to as many demographics as possible. He turned thirty sometime this year, prompting many editorials about the passage of time, as well as celebrity gossip about who he's dating and will he ever settle down. He wears the apparent tech uniform of bespoke blazer, jeans, sneakers, button-up and tie, as ties have become the latest retro craze among the digital cognoscenti.

During the long, long applause, Owens asks, "How do you think it feels to be worth that much money?"

"Sexually satisfied. He must get it all the time."

"Invented the company when he was sixteen. What were you doing at sixteen?"

"Torturing animals."

The State of the Union–level applause finally dies down maybe a full two minutes after Ballantine took the stage. He's already pointed to a few people in the crowd, even blew a fucking kiss. Owens feels like he's surrounded by all the people he hated in high school.

The second that Ballantine begins talking, 3D holo-logos for EyeTech appear around him.

The first ten minutes are as boring as everything else, even if Owens must admit to a vague, animalistic jolt at simply seeing someone so famous this close. Strange how something inside us insists on being near the powerful.

Finally Ballantine gets to the reason Owens bothered to come.

"So with great pride, we're unveiling our newest product, something that will revolutionize not only how we perceive our world, but how we blaze our unique paths through it."

The holograms begin to morph, changing from the EyeTech logos to different words. *Black, White, Lesbian, Bi, Disabled.* They hover in the air, then morph without warning into slurs: *Dyke, Wop, Lard-Ass, Raghead, Retard.*

Owens almost doubts his vision, but a few gasps and chatter from the crowd tell him he's not alone.

"We live in a cruel world," Ballantine says as the holograms continue morphing behind him like bathroom graffiti writ large. "We like to think we're better than our forebears, but we still rely on bias and prejudice to make certain decisions. It happens without us realizing it. We may not be proud of it, but the statistics don't lie. Even the best of us fall victim to hidden biases that we can only begin to comprehend. I'm happy to announce, we at EyeTech believe that way of thinking will soon be gone."

All the slurs fade and are replaced by "CleerVu."

"Our vidders receive a barrage of data every millisecond—radar, GPS, color patterns, texture data, glare factors. CleerVu will allow vidders, for the first time, to *transmit* signals as well. We'll be able to inform others about our appearance, and will even be able to alter that perceived appearance as we see fit."

"What the fuck?" Peterson whispers. He's not the only one whispering. Chatter in the crowd, some headshakes, some nods.

"People no longer need to feel that their existence is defined by how they look or what they look like. Your skin tone, your weight, the bone structure of your face. What if none of that mattered? What if you could strip away all those labels and categories and just . . . be you? What if you could be, simply, the core *you*?"

The rest of the presentation is a whirlwind of eye holograms, artistic renderings of the brain, way too much information about myelinated nerves, and arrows moving back and forth to explain how the new software works. No trade secrets are revealed, but Ballantine assures everyone this is "a game-changer." Tired buzz phrases like "first to market" and "breakthrough innovation" and "one-of-a-kind user experience" echo over the speakers.

He wraps up with, "I'd be happy to open it up to questions from shareholders."

Hands everywhere. An audience comprised of the smartest kids in the room.

A Black woman near the front, her voice amplified by a mike handed to her by a lackey in a yellow EyeTech T-shirt, asks, "Mr. Ballantine, with all due respect, why on earth do you assume that people who aren't white would want to look white?"

Ballantine's smile isn't going anywhere. "I don't, not at all, but thank you so much for bringing that up. In no way is EyeTech trying to tell people how they *should* appear. The whole point, after all, is about eliminating bias, and being free of others' assumptions and expectations. That wouldn't work if we were imposing our own." As he says this, holograms beside him show people of one race morphing into another, over and over, seeming to disprove his point.

A few more people question him along these lines, talk about cultural appropriation, sensitivity, social norms. Ballantine assures people that his own experience of being mixed race and born blind, of not having sight until he himself invented vidders, of not perceiving race in a visual sense until later in life, has given him perhaps a unique perspective on these issues, one that he hopes can help society, but Owens doesn't follow everything, his mind trying to trace how this new product could impact his own work and his current case.

Eventually an older white woman with gray hair gives voice to the very question Owens has been pondering: "But if anyone could look like anyone, wouldn't that be chaos?"

"If we hadn't gotten a few things right, maybe it would have been." A cocky chuckle. "With CleerVu, when you see someone, even though their appearance may be radically different than it used to be, you will still *know* who they are. The visual data connecting to your vidder will still convey the person's identity. So tomorrow I could choose to change my hair or melanin levels, widen or narrow my nose, maybe add to the pectorals, ha-ha, overall completely change my appearance, but anyone who sees me will still know it's *me*. That's a key part of our innovation, that identity will remain the same, albeit disentangled from all the labels and descriptors we often link to it."

Owens whispers to Peterson, "Bullshit. We're talking to him."

"Question one of the richest men in the world? Here?"

"Might be our only chance."

"This won't be a good look, Mark."

Two white detectives trying to squeeze a conversation out of the world's favorite multiracial wunderkind. He's right, Owens knows. But if anyone on earth has some of the answers they're looking for, it's Ballantine. And they'll never get this close to him again.

After the big show ends, the titillated crowd slowly makes its way out of the ballroom, half of them on their phones to tell people the big news and buy more stock.

Owens and Peterson linger by the back wall and watch as Ballantine is surrounded by a scrum of shareholders, shaking hands, posing for pix, and slowly moving toward an exit in the front. Security guards form a loose perimeter around the great man.

Owens and Peterson make their way toward the guards, who sense the approach of other alphas and seem to inflate their chests in response.

"Chill out, boys," Owens tells them, flashing his badge.

Ballantine hasn't noticed them yet, still smiling with his adoring fans. Within the cordon of security guards is a second cordon of PR handlers, three young women and one man in slightly less hip blazer-and-EyeTech-T-shirt combos, all clutching tablets like flotation devices and gently telling some of the stockholders that they've now exceeded their allowed thirty seconds with the CEO.

One of the PR handlers, a thin young woman with a dark ponytail and eyes that dart from person to person with an expression not far from anger, notices Owens's conspicuous lack of a lanyard. She shakes her head with the sort of hard-nosed authority he would find impressive in a cop that young, even as it annoys him.

"I'm sorry, gentlemen, no more questions."

Owens holds up his badge, trying to do it in a way that others won't see, but he knows that's not possible. "But we're really big fans."

Ballantine has noticed them now; the other conversations have quieted at the sight of the badge. Previously genuine smiles suddenly seem a bit false on confused faces. Someone beside Owens steps back and holds up a phone for a picture.

"Mr. Ballantine, I'm Detective Mark Owens. I know you're very busy, but I was hoping we could step into another room to ask you a few quick questions."

The PR flacks have found a small conference room, where four of them now sit along with the CEO, Owens, and Peterson. Ballantine is still smiling—his cheek muscles surely hurt by now, Owens thinks—and Owens gets the sense the powerful man is only letting them question him because he's genuinely curious to hear what these knuckle-draggers think of his great technology, as if the interview is just another user test.

"I apologize for keeping you," Owens says, "but we can be brief."

The ponytailed handler says, "Any questions can be forwarded to—"

"This CleerVu thing," Owens interrupts, still looking at the CEO. "If people can disguise their appearance, investigating crime would get awfully difficult, wouldn't it?"

Another handler, a pale, freckled woman who multitasks on her tablet as she speaks, sighs. "He should just talk to Legal."

But Ballantine maintains his confident smile. "I knew there would be some concerns from law enforcement, but, wow, I didn't think it would be this immediate." Another little chuckle, as canned as the one from onstage. "As I explained, there are numerous safeguards built into the system."

"But if this new thing gives people the ability to alter what others see, there must be a way for someone—a hacker, or even an employee of yours—to make alterations that other people can't correct. Right?"

"No, no, it's not—"

"Like say, for example, completely censoring yourself from other people's vision. Wouldn't that be possible?"

Ballantine's expression reads *I haven't been interrupted in so long that I don't even remember how to handle it.* The PR flacks all freeze, Pharisees in a temple where someone has blasphemed. Soon they'll all be looking for the nearest stones.

Owens wonders whether that expression on Ballantine's perfect, possibly even surgically enhanced face might be due less to the interruption and more to the mention of censoring people from view.

The smile is finally gone, in other words.

"No, it would not."

"What if I told you that I've had people telling me they've seen that?"

The PR handlers are shaking their heads, annoyed in unison.

"Detective," Ballantine says, and allows for a withering pause, "people always blame their vidders. I'd assume a cop would know that."

"Yeah, well, my opinion about that changed dramatically when it happened to me."

"How?"

Owens realizes he shouldn't be discussing this with civilians, let alone so many, let alone one person famous and the others skilled at manipulating public opinion for their own ends. Yet he says, "Last week, I followed someone across three blocks, and from every conceivable angle he was blacked out. Even when he was running. So forgive me if I'm not inclined to write that off as some technical glitch."

Ballantine leans back a bit and swivels in his chair. Owens notices that the man has no visible birthmarks or blemishes anywhere. It unnerves him. It also makes him wonder if Ballantine is using the CleerVu feature even now, perfecting his own appearance.

"Things like that are rare," Ballantine says, "but they do happen from time to time. The thing is, it isn't the vidder that's at fault—it's the person's brain."

"My brain?"

"I know nothing about what happened to you personally, but assuming you dragged me here so you could get my opinion about how these things work, then yes. Your brain. Look, even before The Blinding, vision was always part eyes and part brain—any number of things can get in the way of our being able to process the signals. Environmental factors. Or stress. I don't suppose you were stressed at the time? You do seem the type."

Now Owens is the one who's annoyed. Also he realizes Peterson hasn't said a word, that this has become his show alone. He fears this case looks more to Peterson like a crusade, a fool's gambit. He glances at his partner, who seems to be watching him warily.

"You're saying I was too *stressed* to see the guy?"

Peterson finally speaks: "And would you feel confident explaining this under oath, Mr. Ballantine?"

The second PR handler slams down her tablet and says, "This conversation is over."

Yet Ballantine is smiling again, entertained by the threat. "You want to subpoena me about what someone else claims he saw? There some new police powers I don't know about?"

Owens shoots Peterson a look—the threat was a bad move, all but ending the conversation. Ballantine stands up, and everyone else does too.

"I think what my partner is saying," Owens says, trying to salvage things, "is that I know that someone manipulated my vidder. And I'm certainly not saying that your company did it, but I do say that someone at EyeTech probably knows how it can be done, especially if you're about to roll out some new vidder-manipulation technology."

He extends a business card to Ballantine, who takes it. One of the PR handlers offers to take it from the great man, who shouldn't be troubled by such trivial matters, but Ballantine pockets it.

"If your department really wants to pursue this, Detectives, then, as Jessica here said, you can contact our legal department. Now, if you'll excuse me, I'm late for some interviews."

Ballantine strides toward the door, as do all the less important people who do his bidding. Owens and Peterson watch them go, Owens trying to sound sincere as he thanks them for their time.

Once the detectives are alone in the room, Peterson says, "Arrogant little prick."

Owens had been expecting worse. He wonders if Peterson is only saying that to empathize with him, because clearly Owens made a mistake in forcing that little interview.

"How long do you think it'll take," Owens asks, "for him to lean on someone who leans on someone who makes Carlyle discipline us for daring to talk to him?"

"You saw them texting. I'd say it's happened already."

CHAPTER 17

The waiting room at the EyeTech customer service office is everything Amira's office at headquarters is not: spacious, clean, recently painted, supplied with great coffee, staffed by happy people. She's here during her off hours, out of uniform, blending in like a civilian.

She never *feels* like a civilian, and she wonders if she ever will, even if she quits. Will she ever quit? Did she just think that? She hadn't actually been considering it, but she's been imagining it, which maybe is a first step toward considering it.

The job grinds away at her, scraping bits and pieces away, and she's afraid of what will be left behind.

She's doubting everything these days. Her decision to get Daniella into the Psych Ward. Whether to stick with this soul-crushing job. Whether she believes that Mark really saw some weird black blur flee a murder scene. Whether she should even be with Mark or should run the hell away from him.

I killed her, he'd said in his sleep. Maybe he'd just been having a nightmare. Maybe he hadn't even been talking about Jeanie.

It's been nearly a week since that night and they haven't gotten together since. A few calls and texts, but that's it, their schedules not aligned. But, she admits, she's been putting it off on purpose.

She has an idea, possibly a crazy one, that might help her figure out what Mark had meant. And maybe help her preserve their relationship, if that's what she wants.

Assuming it works.

* * *

She follows the young assistant into the exam room. Sits in the comfy chair and leans into the large magnifying glass and speculum. A freshly painted logo for CleerVu stares at her from the wall on her right.

The EyeTech technician, a young Asian woman, enters. White lab coat, loud sneakers, nose ring, cool hair.

Small talk, then on with the exam. Amira leans forward and the technician does the same, like they're looking at each through all these lenses and machines, when really their eyes aren't doing much of anything. But the technician is indeed examining Amira's eyes, assessing different elements not only of her eyes and sockets but the shape of her face in general, making measurements, entering data.

"Okay, you can lean back," the technician says.

"I haven't been in one of those in forever."

"You wore glasses as a kid?"

"Yeah, nearsighted. I didn't think anyone used these anymore."

The technician adjusts some controls on a monitor screen.

EyeTech made its big announcement about CleerVu only yesterday. It had placed calls to the lucky few who'd get first dibs even earlier, but hadn't explained what exactly the new enhancements were until Ballantine gave his big reveal to shareholders.

"Our eyes might not work the way they used to," the technician explains, "but that doesn't mean they've no use whatsoever. Now we get to the good part: have you given much thought to the new appearances you'd like?"

"You're sure it's not permanent? It can be switched back and forth?"

A smile, a snap of the fingers. "Just like that, whenever you want."

"But, hypothetically speaking, I can't change appearances so I can, say, walk into a bank and take all their money?"

The technician laughs. Amira wonders if the woman had checked her file, noticed what she'd put down under "OCCUPATION," and thinks this is some poorly orchestrated sting.

"No, it doesn't work that way. Your appearance will be different, but people will still know who you are. If they need to access their memories later to describe you to the police, say, their memories will be of how you truly appear."

Interesting. She's not sure she buys that, but if it's true, at least it means that the world isn't about to undergo an epidemic of criminality. Another one, that is.

"It really works that way?"

"It really does."

"In theory, though. Right? Since this is only a beta test, that means there could be some glitches?"

A tight smile. "We don't think of it that way. We're constantly iterating and enhancing our product, yes, so it's always being improved, which means, by definition, the earliest models are not a hundred percent flawless. But at the same time, we'd never install something that isn't ready for users."

Users. Amira lingers on that word, all its negative connotations. We are a world of users now.

"But, back to my question: have you thought about the new appearances you'd like to try?"

The new Me I want to beta-test, Amira thinks. She pauses, considering.

Is she really going to do this? Is she crazy?

She asks, "What if I want to look like a specific person?"

"The official policy is that users are not allowed to mimic the appearance of another living person. There are legalities there."

"Sure. But what if the person is deceased?"

Hours later, another shift in the books. Long day, longer night. On her drive home, all she can think about is taking a hot shower and drinking a cold beer.

After her shower, she stands in front of her mirror, the half-empty beer on the counter. The receptors in her brain convey the information that her eyes, if they worked, would be interpreting: tiny globules of steam cling to the mirror, obscuring her reflection. So she reaches out and, with a hand towel, wipes her reflection into existence.

How do you assess your own appearance? So many people are vain, overconfident. They take what nature gave them and leverage it into something more, something beyond what they deserve. She's known so many men who think they're better-looking than they are, convinced of their appeal. They talk their way into jobs they're not qualified for, women they don't deserve. Some women are like that, too, sure, but not nearly as many.

Why are some people so deluded?

And why is she the opposite, so unsure of herself, always feeling inferior? She's worked her way onto better shifts and more interesting beats, she's not a terrible cop, yet she wishes she asserted herself more. And when it comes to relationships, she's rarely lacked for male attention, but she seems to attract some serious oddballs. She stares at herself, and as usual she wonders what she's done wrong to find herself in her situation, with a man who still seems to be in love with a woman who's been dead two years.

She wishes she liked her reflection more. She hates her nose, her nonexistent chin, her unmanageable hair, her freckles. She knows many men fetishize Latinas—she's half Latina, through her mother, and can thank her Irish father for the freckles—but it's only seemed to half work for her: she attracts the randoms, never the good ones. Mark seemed the exception, but now she's not so sure.

She reaches up for her vidder and remembers the technician's instructions.

The vision before her changes. More accurately, her brain's interpretation of the vision changes.

Gone is her wet, short, normally curly hair. Gone are the brown eyes and freckles.

The hair she sees is long, almost jet black, and straight. Not *too* straight. Just enough body and wave to make it interesting. Not just interesting—perfect. Like the crystal blue eyes.

Is it a little too perfect?

Maybe. Maybe this isn't really how Jeanie MacArthur looked. Maybe she wasn't quite this gorgeous, and this is only Amira's insecure projection of how much better-looking she imagines Jeanie to have been. Those piercing ice-blue eyes. That cute little nose. That open, slightly vulnerable space between eyes and brow. She's seen plenty of pictures of Jeanie, of course (far more than she wishes), so she knows very well what Jeanie should look like.

But this is the first time she's seen Jeanie staring back at her from the mirror. *Someone else* in a mirror. Amira feels a shiver—her body saying, *This is not natural*, like the uncanny valley times a thousand—but she maintains eye contact with herself. No, not with herself—with her reflection.

Her false reflection. The projection of all her insecurities. A martyr she cannot supplant.

"Jeanie. Why can't I decide if I hate you or pity you?"

CHAPTER 18

Captain Carlyle stands at a podium before thirty uniformed and plainclothes cops. Owens, Peterson, Amira, Khouri, among many others.

Carlyle had indeed chewed out Owens and Peterson for their impromptu questioning of Kai Ballantine a few days ago. The commissioner herself had been notified about the interview (from whom, Owens has no idea), and had called Carlyle to ask him what the hell two of his detectives were doing by cornering a celebrity like that. Owens had tried to explain his reasoning, his suspicion about this new CleerVu thing and what it could mean for his case, but Carlyle had rolled his eyes and informed him very clearly that such concerns were far above his pay grade, as was Ballantine and any other executive at EyeTech, so stay the hell away from them.

Owens also had noticed, during that uncomfortable meeting, that Peterson barely spoke. Didn't exactly have Owens's back on this. He worries Peterson doesn't believe him about the black blurs, that Owens has been making himself an island.

Today, Carlyle greets them all and hits a button. A 3D hologram of the city appears behind him.

They're here to go over their roles for the National Day of Mourning, next week. President Myers himself has decided to visit the city, for electoral reasons, no doubt, and to give a speech after attending services at a downtown cathedral or maybe visiting a hospital. Hosting a presidential visit of any kind is a big enough pain in the ass, but factor in the Day of Mourning, everyone's emotions rubbed raw, PTSD spiking everywhere, the inevitable protesters and rise in suicides and likelihood of crazed gunmen deciding now is the perfect time to execute their grand plans, and it all adds up to a day everyone wishes they could call in sick. On top of that, the President's Truth Commission has hardly endeared him to police departments anywhere.

"The Secret Service will have control over everything," Carlyle informs them. "Which means, yes, everyone here gets to be a glorified bodyguard and traffic cop."

Some sighing and eye-rolling from the audience.

"The powers that be will not share the exact details with us until the night before, so as to reduce the chances that the itinerary leaks and some asshole can plan accordingly. As of now, all I know is the President will be at the Central Plaza sometime between nine and noon, giving his talk there before moving on to whomever he decides to grace with his presence afterwards."

Owens steals a glance at Amira. As is their style, they don't sit near each other and try not to make eye contact. Sometimes avoiding such eye contact is hard, sometimes it isn't.

He looks her way twice, but she doesn't look back. He wonders if she's still angry at him for his not wanting her to move in, but their last night together had seemed normal. He had been afraid before that he'd blown their relationship, but maybe he hadn't.

Carlyle details assignments, who will be where when. Nothing interesting, and every cop basically spaces out once they know what they're personally doing. Owens thinks, *What a great day to commit a crime, with half the police force on crowd control for a politician few of us like.*

"Any questions?"

Khouri dispenses with hand raising and asks, "What did the Secret Service say about Slade's gun shipments?"

"I informed them that we'd rounded up a major haul of firearms and mentioned the possibility it could be related to the visit, but they didn't seem interested. Which I guess means they haven't heard any credible threats, so they don't feel it's related. And neither do I. But Khouri, Owens, Peterson: if the feds do call asking for more information about that, I expect you to be the courteous and polite sonsabitches I know you to be."

No more questions. Class dismissed.

Owens and Peterson are sitting at their desks when Owens's notices a blink on his monitor. Someone in Technical Forensics has sent him a file: Jensen's phone records.

He tells Peterson as he opens the file.

"Send it to me," Peterson says. "I don't mind; I already have a headache."

"No, I got it."

Click, drag. He scrolls through phone numbers, cross-referencing them with a city map so he can see where Jensen's phone physically was when he made each call. Most are in the city, and Owens will have to spend time checking who the calls were placed to, but this is just a quick glance to see if there's anything interesting geographically.

There's something interesting.

Every call Jensen made during the last week of his life was made when he was within the city, except for three calls on two different days. The map veers far to the west for those calls, the last of which was made three days before his death. An out-of-the-way location that Owens himself knows better than he wishes he did.

He wonders aloud, "Why would a scientist like Jensen go to the Inner Sight commune?"

Needing some air, Owens walks through the city.

Thinking, someone kills a scientist while manipulating the victim's vidder (or their own?) so the lone witness can't report on the killer. Later he kills the witness too (just for kicks, or because he decided later the witness had indeed seen something, or heard something, or smelled something—or because there's more than one killer and they disagreed about letting her live?). Both of the dead scientists worked for a research company that works with Eye-Tech, which is launching a new visual-manipulation "feature." One of the scientists visited the Inner Sight commune recently.

Owens doesn't want to go to the commune to look into this, though he'll probably need to eventually. Peterson is looking up whose numbers Jensen called while at the commune. The conversations were five minutes, twenty minutes, and one minute. But why was Jensen even there? Owens remembers the new building he'd seen at the commune the last time he'd visited; Sarah had said it was some kind of a research center. Could Jensen have been helping with it somehow? He can't remember if Sarah said anything else about it, or if that's when he'd started the argument that ended their conversation.

So he walks, hoping to get the blood flowing, make sense of things.

He stops when he sees her.

Only sees her for a second, so quick he might have doubted it, except you can't doubt your wife's face, even if you haven't seen her in two years.

Jeanie.

Then her face vanishes in the crowd. The light changes and pedestrians are crossing back and forth, and she'd been a block away. *Wait, which way did she go?*

There. He sees her again, from behind this time. That familiar long hair, her body the right height, the hair the correct length.

Wait, no: it's Amira.

He touches his vidder with his right hand, his other temple with his left. Cradling his skull as if he can press sanity back into it.

She looks like Jeanie but he knows it's Amira. Or at least he thinks it is. How can this be?

Jeanie's dead, Mark. You know she's dead. You buried her.

His heart is pounding and he wants to scream.

What in the hell is happening to him?

In the days and weeks after she died, he saw Jeanie constantly.

He'd never realized how full the city was of brunettes her height, the same body type, with the same hair length. So, so many times he'd thought he saw her crossing the street, ducking into a cab, chatting on her phone. Her ghost everywhere, haunting him.

Then she would stop on the sidewalk and he'd focus and he'd realize, *No, that's not her. You didn't see her.*

You will never see her again.

She'd been buried in an open casket. He remembers kissing her cold forehead. He understands, in a dry, cognitive sense, that Jeanie is dead and will never be back.

That didn't stop him from seeing her over and over and over again.

But this, now. This is different. *He saw her. Her face.* No doubt, no question.

He knows it's not her. Some part of him knows it's actually Amira. How? And why? Why would he think he sees his wife but also think it's his girlfriend? What kind of sick fuck has he become?

There! He sees her again. She's outside that bakery. Talking on her phone. That's the way Jeanie's lips moved when she spoke. That's the shift in her eyebrows when she's surprised, a split second before she smiles.

What the fuck is happening?

She's more than a block away. He steps into the street so he can cross diagonally, intercept her. His heart is pounding and he nearly feels dizzy. He would fear he's having a panic attack but knows he isn't, because he's had those before and this is different.

A car honks. Brakes squeal. He holds out his badge to shut the driver up and tries to focus on the top of Jeanie's head.

Another car from the other direction honks, doesn't brake in time. It hits him in the back of the knees. Not hard enough to break anything, but he topples backward. Catches himself before his head can hit the hood of the car. Turns around, finally crosses the street. People are staring but he doesn't care.

She's gone. The car distracted him and the sidewalks are aswarm with faces that aren't hers. He runs down the street, first with his badge out to clear a path. Runs past the bakery, stops, turns back and makes sure she hasn't ducked in there, but he doesn't see her. Runs back out, looks this way and that, doesn't see her.

You're making a fool of yourself. Stop.

Badge back in pocket. He knows better. Knows it couldn't have been her.

Hands on his knees, catches his breath. Looks up, finds himself staring at his own reflection in a storefront window.

It's them. Whoever redacted the killer from my vidder, they just implanted Jeanie there.

They're trying to drive him mad. Make him look like a fool, get him fired, maybe. Or just break him. He's been living with a knife handle sticking out of his chest for two years, and he thought he'd healed well enough, but they've twisted the handle.

He hates himself for falling for their trick. Hates how much it hurts. Hates that there are tears in his eyes.

But wait, no. *Think.* His mind is so confused and outpaced by the quickly spinning world that he missed the more obvious cause. That new EyeTech feature they were boasting about—being able to alter your appearance to look like someone else, while people would still somehow know it's you.

Could it be that . . . Amira is making herself look like Jeanie? But why would she do that?

He reaches into his pocket and grabs his phone. He could call Amira right now, ask where she is, what she's doing.

But he's afraid. He realizes he doesn't want to know, not right yet. Even though he knows it's irrational and impossible, a tiny part of him still wants to believe. Because it *looked just like her.* He wants to believe it could be Jeanie, somehow. And that tiny deluded part of him makes his fingers release his phone.

He walks over to a bench and leans down, elbows on knees. Hides his face. Tries to breathe slowly. At least with his eyes shut no one can fuck with him.

He misses her so, so much.

* * *

The day they met.

Someone wants to do a ride-along, he'd been told. Not many people did them, usually just journalists or mystery writers who wanted a glimpse of the city's seedy underbelly. Ride-alongs were discontinued during The Blinding, of course, the city too unsafe even in the early days of vidders.

Way back when he'd met Jeanie, though, no one knew The Blinding was coming. Owens was in his early twenties, almost a rookie still, forced to take the ride-along because no one else wanted to.

She'd shown up wearing all black, as ride-alongs sometimes did. Thinking it helped them blend into the night or something. Her long dark hair dyed red at the bottom inch, a black knit cap atop her head, badass black boots. He wanted to make a joke about her looking like an apprentice cat burglar or aspiring ninja but held his tongue.

She asked him a lot of questions about the job as he drove her through the city. Finally, tired of talking, he tried asking her a question.

"So how does one become an artist?"

"How does one become a cop?"

"First one becomes a Marine and does a couple tours. Then one comes back after a few years and isn't sure what to do with oneself." He thought for a moment. "One might waste a year or two wallowing, or maybe one might find gainful employment but still be unsatisfied with it. Because one might miss that feeling of service, of helping other people. Or maybe one might be drinking too much and just need a change. In any case, one eventually decides being a cop might be the closest thing to what one thinks of as normal."

She looked at him then, wondering which of those biographies was in fact his. Wondering if maybe all of them were.

Or maybe she was startled he'd said so much, expecting her police escort to be taciturn, quiet. Honestly, *he'd* startled himself by opening up like that. He was attracted to her from the start and unsure of himself in her presence.

"Your turn," he said.

"I don't know how one *becomes* an artist. I'd argue it's more just who you are. Or if you're asking how I actually make a living at it, that involves the usual stuff. Luck, talent, timing, hard work, connections. Some combination of all that."

"Can I see some of your work in museums?"

"You can." A few years older than him, she was not yet thirty but was already well on her way to becoming the closest thing to a rock star a visual artist could get. "Go to many?"

"It's been a while." Not since he was a kid, in fact. "So I hear you specifically requested a ride-along with Vice?"

"I did. Does that reflect poorly on me?"

"Just means you have weird taste."

"So say many art critics."

He would learn later that she'd arranged the ride-along mainly out of her own distrust of cops. She wanted to push against her biases, see the other side. She had already worked on a photographic series on nightwalkers, women who plied their trade on some of the most dangerous streets in the city. When he later heard about this, he'd been surprised and impressed to learn she'd taken such pictures, as doing so was not without risk. She'd also ridden with truckers throughout the country, to see for herself what happened at truck stops, to photograph the poor girls, sometimes as young as twelve, who were farmed out to the drivers.

Having already seen the world from the women's perspective, she'd wanted to see how the arm of government worked. She was here to judge him, basically.

He didn't know her motives yet that first day, but he always felt some element of surveillance when joined by a ride-along. That was the irony. Cops were allowed to perform surveillance, to watch people and be on guard for lawbreakers—a power some of them abused, certainly—but then the civilians wanted to watch the cops in return, because cops couldn't be trusted. Even before The

Blinding, the world seemed sick with this lack of trust, everyone needing to be watched by everyone else, oversight on the overseers, phones recording everyone, mutual outrage online, gotcha videos, an endless loop of spies.

Often the fates had it that his ride-alongs coincided with dull shifts. But not that time.

He'd been slowly driving through what had been dubbed Payers Way, the unofficial name of a two-block stretch of Ayers Way known as a popular spot for turning tricks. At four in the afternoon, all was quiet. Owens was hoping Jeanie would tire of the dullness and would call it a day before night came and things changed, but at the same time she gave off a vibe that she'd be sticking out the full twelve hours.

He'd nearly reached the end of Payers Way when a body dropped through the sky and landed ten feet in front of them.

Jeanie screamed "Jesus!" and he hit the brakes hard. Turned on his flashing lights, stopped in the middle of the road.

Happened so fast he'd need to review the dashcam to be certain, but it seemed like the woman had been thrown through the third-floor window of the brick building to their left. She lay in a heap, shards of glass everywhere. He stepped closer to her, soles crackling on the glass, looked down at her. Eyes shut. Blood on her forehead. A broken nose. Her left arm bent the wrong way. A flimsy green dress that matched her green hair. Maybe sixteen.

Owens crouched down, found a pulse. He called it in on his radio.

Looked up and saw a male face peek out of a shattered third-floor window, eyes widen, vanish.

He recognized the guy. Not a pimp but a regular john, one he'd busted once before.

Jeanie had already stepped out of the car but he told her to get back inside while he grabbed his mike, called it in to the station, then ran into the building. Drew his weapon and headed for the stairs.

While he was gone, ultimately catching the son of a bitch, he'd miss a few things. Jeanie would tell him about it later, and the dash-cam would back her up.

She ignored his advice about getting back into the car and instead walked up to the woman, saw she was really a girl. Jeanie bent down on one knee. Checked her pulse even though Owens already had, because he hadn't told her if she was alive or not, had only barked police code into his radio, which Jeanie hadn't understood.

She felt the pulse. Started talking to the girl, whoever she was. Her eyes were shut and she started moaning, low and animalistic. Jeanie told her help was coming and she would be okay. Unfortunately this was hardly the first time she'd needed to comfort an injured victim like this.

Jeanie heard screams from inside the building and wondered if Owens had caught the guy. Then again, this was a building in which screams were not uncommon, she knew from experience.

The girl's forehead wound was bleeding a lot, her hair thick with red already. Jeanie had recently trained in first aid and she figured the squad car must have some gear, so she went back to the car, checked the glove box, popped the trunk. Realizing that she'd signed paperwork explicitly stating she would not do any of this, but unable to resist.

Found a first aid kit in the trunk. Pulled it out, walked back toward the girl.

Saw a man there, trying to get her to her feet.

Jeanie had photographed enough prostitutes to know that pimps did not in fact have a stereotypical appearance but could look like anyone. Some wore garish dress, sure, but just as many wore suits or regular attire and found ways to blend in. This man was short but powerfully built, wearing jeans and a tan jacket, running shoes. He could have been a marketing account manager, a soccer dad.

"What are you doing?" Jeanie called out to him.

"Mind your fucking business." He was tugging on the fallen girl's right arm, trying to wrap it around his neck so he could lift her.

"An ambulance is coming."

"Fuck that. She's mine and they ain't taking her."

If Jeanie had been slow to understand what was happening, *She's mine* made it clear. This son of a bitch felt that he owned her, and he would take care of her himself so he could farm her out again once she recovered.

He had pulled her up high enough now that even if Jeanie shouted, "Put her down!" and the guy complied, he might literally drop her. The girl likely already had a concussion or worse, maybe a spinal injury.

Jeanie froze for a moment, realizing she had to get the girl away from him without making him drop her.

She ran and grabbed the girl's other arm, so that she was dangling between them. The girl's unconscious head hung low, and she was still moaning.

Jeanie still couldn't believe people could be so evil.

"*Let go*," she demanded.

"Fuck you and beat it before I knock you out like her!"

Jeanie was gripping the girl with her left arm, so with her right she pulled pepper spray out of her pocket and blasted him point blank.

He screamed and let the girl go.

Jeanie had closed her eyes, in case any discharge came her way. She hoped it wouldn't hurt the girl, who was even closer, but her head was hanging low and seemingly out of harm's way. Jeanie pulled her a few feet away from the man. She dropped the canister and put a hand at the back of the girl's skull, like she'd done with friends' babies when holding them, and she thought of that, how this broken and mistreated young woman had been a baby once, someone's child, and not very long ago at all. Jeanie laid her down as gently as she could.

The man was still screaming. He'd fallen to his knees, but now he was struggling to his feet again. Clawing at his eyes.

Jeanie stood up, walked over, and kicked him in the face. Kickboxing classes coming in handy now.

He flipped over and lay flat on the ground, so she kicked him in the ribs. She was still kicking him when cops pulled her away and clamped cuffs on her.

That was a hard one for them to live down, both of them.

Jeanie, because she was initially charged with battery, though the charges were quickly dropped. Owens, because it had happened with his ride-along, and all the other cops ridiculed him for allowing her to go ballistic like that. *How can you police a beat when you can't even police your own squad car?*

Somehow her lawyers were able to keep it out of the news. She hadn't been a *huge* star in the art world yet, so it might not have made a splash anyway. Years later, when she became truly famous, the story escaped and just added to her legend.

Only a few days after the ride-along, she called him at his desk.

"There is no way you're ever doing another ride-along in this city," he told her. He would be proven wrong, after they married.

"I wasn't calling for that. I wanted to see if you wanted to get dinner sometime. Unless you're still working the night shift, in which case, maybe coffee?"

He laughed to cover his shock. "I got disciplined because of you. And you think I'll let you keep using me as research?"

"Oh, you know you liked it." She was right: he had watched the dashcam footage of her beating the pimp several times. The whole office had—they fucking loved it. He'd had to warn everyone not to post it online. "And I'm not asking you to dinner for research, I'm asking for fun."

"So, a date?"

"If you're into labels."

He hadn't seen this coming. That's how Jeanie was, though, and he'd soon learn to roll with her unpredictable tides and storms. For a while, at least.

"You'll leave the pepper spray at home?"

"A lady has to protect herself. What if you make a move I don't approve of?"

"No pepper spray, but you can still wear those shit-kicking boots."

"Deal."

Owens isn't sure how long he sits there with his eyes shut. Long enough for Peterson to wonder if and when he's returning to the station, probably.

He lifts his head, dares to open his eyes. Tells himself maybe he just imagined it, maybe *they* aren't really toying with him. Maybe Amira isn't messing with him for some unknown reason. Maybe he's just going crazy.

He calls Peterson, who answers with, "Where'd you run off to?"

"Sorry, I'll be back in ten. I just had a thought, though. When you were on that opsin task force, did you guys ever trace any of the drug to the communes?"

A pause. "You mean Reverend Miriam's people? No. Come to think of it, that's damn near the only place in the state we *didn't* find any. Why?"

"Just wondering. It's probably nothing."

As if on cue, he hears a voice: "Seek Inner Sight, my friends! Reject the false visions of our material world!"

He stands up. The voice is close.

"I gotta run," he tells Peterson, then kills the call.

He walks down the street and around the corner, to a quieter side street. There on the sidewalk between two busy restaurants he sees the familiar face. In an unfamiliar getup. Owens has seen the getup many times before, of course, but never on this particular person.

Lance is much thinner than Owens remembers, like he's gone vegan or survived cancer. Head shaved, downright vicious tattoos climbing up his neck. They are otherwise obscured by his flowing brown robe. Looks like a former gangbanger turned monk, which is exactly what he is.

Vidderless, too, like the rest of Reverend Miriam's followers.

Owens stops a few feet away. Lance seems to sense Owens's presence, and he extends a pamphlet to him.

"Are you ready for the truth?" Lance asks.

Owens lets the pamphlet dangle. "Does this mean you go by Brother Lance now?"

Lance's face clouds. "I recognize your voice. But . . . from a bleak time."

"This explains why I couldn't find you anywhere. I heard you got out after twelve months. I also heard that you'd come to this, but I didn't quite believe it."

The Lance he knew was evil through and through. The murder Owens charged him with was simply the best case they had, the lowest-hanging fruit. On higher boughs were pimping, running an underage prostitution ring, several assaults. In none of those cases had they gathered enough evidence or managed to find a witness willing to testify. The murder case, albeit not perfect, had seemed their best bet. The fact that Lance only served a year burns.

"I did my time," Lance says. "Leave me alone."

"We need to talk about what happened to your friend Ollie."

"Why? You still think I killed him?"

Owens doesn't dare answer. "Remind me what you saw that day."

"You're a government devil. You use the vidders to control the rest of us. I see that now."

"I don't control anything, man. If I did, you'd still be in prison for what you did to those girls."

Lance starts walking away. In search of a better perch to spread his creed, distribute his little tracts. He makes his way swiftly and surely, with the disconcertingly certain pace and posture of those who have gone over to The Darkness, as if they can somehow still see.

Owens follows, puts a hand on Lance's shoulder, spins him around.

"Let me go!"

Owens keeps his voice down. "I've seen what you saw. You hear me? I've seen it too."

Lance's face goes from angry to confused to . . . frightened.
"The black marks."

"Yeah. I saw one flee a murder scene."

Lance's face goes back to angry. "You . . . You didn't believe me."

Owens releases him and steps back.

"I . . . I may have been wrong then."

Lance stands there another moment, then he leans over, catches his hands at his knees, as if Owens just gut-punched him. The tiny pamphlets crinkling from the pressure.

Okay, yes, the case had always troubled Owens. They get a call about a shooting, they show up in a seedy apartment that Lance was rumored to use for housing his girls. They find the body of Ollie Rice, one of Lance's "business partners," shot in the head, point-blank, by a .45. They find Lance slumped in a chair, big bruise on his forehead, fresh blood. They find a .45 on the floor, missing one bullet. Tests would later show both he and Ollie had BAL's indicating shit-faced drunk.

Easy case: the two pimps had a drunken argument, Ollie hit Lance in the head with a gun, Lance then wrestled control of said gun and shot Ollie in the head before passing out.

And Lance's side of the story? Sheer lunacy: he'd claimed someone else entered the apartment, someone he couldn't see. A black blur. Vidder malfunction. Sorriest excuse out there. The black blur, he said, attacked them. It shot Ollie and knocked Lance out.

In Owens's and Peterson's opinion, Lance had been crazy fortunate to get only a year for manslaughter. But also this: why didn't the gun have any prints on it? They figured Lance wiped it down, then dropped it before passing out. Still, weird.

And this: why didn't the gun have any of Lance's DNA on it, from him being hit in the head? Could he have been struck by some other object, which was no longer in the room? In which case, who had fled with that object?

Like Peterson, Owens chose not to obsess over minor incongruities. Sometimes things didn't add up right but you trusted that God just fudged his arithmetic sometimes. Owens was glad one asshole was dead and the other would do time for it. Combo Special #1, cops called it.

Now Lance's story makes a bit more sense.

The street prophet slowly regains his posture. "They put me in prison. For a year."

"Your story seemed crazy then. But . . . I think I made a mistake. I'm sorry."

Lance laughs. A horrified kind of laugh.

"A *mistake*? That's . . ." Shakes his head. Blind eyes darting all about as if hoping to conjure invisible witnesses. "When you *ruin* someone's *life,* you don't call that a fucking *mistake!*"

Lance knows a thing or two about ruining lives, Owens remembers. He thinks of the girls, the many who were too terrified to testify in other cases. He wonders where they are now, if they're still alive. He's already told Lance he was sorry once. That's all he gets.

"Maybe it was all for the best, huh? It appears you've been rehabilitated, and now you're in with the true believers. You've discovered all that's right about mankind."

Lance's shoulders sag. "It's not that easy. For some of us, maybe. But for the rest . . . it's a constant struggle."

Owens waits for a moment, then says, "I need to meet with Reverend Miriam."

Lance recoils, like Owens asked him to donate a kidney. "She doesn't just 'meet with' people. Only her followers. You need to become an acolyte first, then go through weeks of purification and—"

"Free manual labor, right? Transfer all your savings to her spiritual rescue fund? Quite a racket she's got."

"Reverend Miriam is an amazing person. She's done so much for me."

"Well, I've always wanted to meet her. And I need you to get me to her."

"Why . . . *Why* would I ever want to help you?"

Owens steps closer, and even though his shoes didn't scuff, he knows Lance feels it.

"Because somewhere out here is a person who fucked with your vidder and killed your friend right in front of you. They've killed other people too, and they're going to do it again." He pauses to let this sink in. "Unless I find them."

Lance's sightless eyes seem to peer through Owens's skull. Then the pimp turned street prophet shakes his head.

"Bullshit," Lance says. "You're trying to pull something. Pull *me* into something. I don't know what it is, but, hell no. Stay away from me, and stay away from Reverend Miriam. She may preach peace, you fucking pig, but we don't always follow her advice."

With that, Lance turns, opens his retractable cane, and taps it before himself as he makes his way, his steps appearing less certain as he reaches the first corner and turns out of sight.

CHAPTER 19

The Museum of Modern and Contemporary Art was not looted during The Blinding, which made it luckier than most. Some of its front windows were destroyed, but armed, robotic SecuriGuards—vanguard of the future, Owens and other cops had been warned—managed to dissuade anyone from trying to break in and make out with priceless works that they couldn't even see.

Tonight, three days after Owens tracked down Lance, the wide first-floor gallery is hosting a gala cocktail party, a fundraiser for the city's elite. Many rich old ladies in attendance, all of them dressed a tad more seductively than Owens thinks appropriate for women of their age; money lets you get away with it, apparently. Interspersed among the wealthy elderly are some of the young and hip, artists themselves, maybe, or successful tech business folk who like to feel artistic by donating money at events like these.

Cathedral ceiling soars overhead, Modernist mobiles dangle. The walls in this room are normally bare, Owens remembers, but today he sees several of the paintings and collages that used to reside in his apartment. The museum moved fast.

He feels uncomfortable in his jacket and tie. He occasionally dresses this way at work, but here its lack of style marks him. The wrong pattern or the wrong cut or the wrong lapels or, surely, something wrong. Some whole category of wrong he doesn't even know exists, but they all do. He wills this to end quickly.

He'd known this event was coming. The anniversary of her death, and also the anniversary (five years earlier) of when the museum added a collection of her work. That was partly why he finally decided the time had come to tell Maxine he wanted to donate her remaining pieces. They could add the announcement about the new donation to tonight's already-scheduled proceedings, and then it would be done and he could try to move on. In theory.

Beside him, Amira is better dressed for the occasion, in a colorful red-and-white dress with a beat-up black denim jacket, just the right combination of formal and fuck-you. He knows this must be awkward for her, and he feels bad for inviting her. But he feared that not inviting her would have been worse. She'd surprised him by accepting.

"You're a saint for coming."

"I wanted to be here."

Either she is a fabulous liar or a wonderful person. Possibly both.

He thinks about the other day, when he thought he saw Jeanie but felt it was Amira. This is what Ballantine had been talking about at that shareholder meeting. CleerVu: the ability to look different than before but still have people intuitively know that it's you. He wants to confirm with her that this is what happened, and somehow she has this new functionality in her vidder already. If so, did she really do that on purpose?

But he fears the answer. And, worse, he fears that if he's wrong, and he asks her that, she'll think he's either crazy or an asshole or both. *You think I want to look like your dead wife? Why would I do that?*

Yeah, why would she do that?

So he keeps the questions inside for now, where they hurt less. Or so he hopes.

A waiter walks by bearing drinks, and she relieves him of two. Hands one to Owens, then takes him by the forearm. "C'mon, let's mingle with the artistes."

The invitation claimed that the speeches would start at seven but of course things are running late. Artists. Or maybe that's the idea—get the rich folks drunk first so they'll open their wallets by the time the speeches come. His job provides plenty of challenges but he's thankful it doesn't involve asking people for money.

He's never been particularly skilled at small talk. And artist crowds, Jesus, they're the worst. He knows there are levels upon levels in every conversation, yet he's usually stumbling through the ground-floor level of literalness, unclear what any of the rest even means. Jeanie would always tell him to relax, that artists and critics are just colossally insecure, so they invent their jargon and strange social customs and unwieldy hierarchies to cloak those insecurities. All the sideways looks and cultural references merely the protective layer of porcupines. Without those sharp quills, they're just little rodents.

Still, his face is starting to hurt from all the fake smiling when he and Amira bump into a couple he hasn't thought about in a long while.

"Mark. How are you?"

Ursula, prematurely and defiantly white hair combed in a swoop across half her face, wears a dress made from what appear to be found objects: rubber from old car tires, weird strips of plastic, pieces of dulled sea glass, even part of a street sign. Beside her is her lifelong yet seemingly asexual partner, Ash, a thin man dressed in standard-issue all black. Last time Owens saw him, he still had some hair.

"Doing all right," Owens says. "Amira, this is Ursula and Ash. He shared a studio with Jeanie."

They shake, stiffly. Ash always struck Owens as in dire need of a surgeon to remove the metal pole that ran from ass to skull.

"Nice to meet you," Ash says to Amira. Lying, surely. He turns to Owens. "How's detecting these days?"

"Chasing more people than I'm catching. How's the painting going?" He never knows how to ask. Once he asked a painter if he ever literally watched paint dry. Didn't go over well.

Ash doesn't answer. Instead, he theatrically addresses his next comment to Ursula. "Detective Owens here liked to threaten me with jail time when Jeanie wasn't in the room."

Owens mirrors the trick, telling Amira, "Ash here liked to offer

Jeanie drugs to, quote, *help her art.* He still owes me for the fact I never busted him for dealing."

"And how should I repay that favor? What sins have you committed that I can pardon in return? Anything to confess?"

Owens can't keep up with the witty ripostes, so he just raises his glass in a mock toast. "I'm sure you'll come up with something."

"He's been clean for two years," Ursula snaps at Owens. Her voice calm but her eyes livid.

"Congratulations. Good seeing you both."

Owens walks away, gently steering Amira with him.

Two miles away, Kai Ballantine is leaving his office earlier than usual.

Workaholism has skyrocketed thanks to vidders. With the difference between day and night all but meaningless, legion are those who work insane hours, borderline living at their offices. The youngest generation faces the worst of it, all the pressures of keeping the economy going with none of the benefits, no time to see the kids off to bed, or even have kids. Birth rates dropping, everyone blaming one societal ill or another.

So Ballantine has done his part to make EyeTech the greatest company to work for, which shouldn't be hard, since it's the wealthiest one on earth. Every perk you can imagine. Chefs from a dozen cuisines in the free cafeteria, exotic coffee drinks on every floor, yoga rooms, nap rooms (almost never used), masseuses (frequently used), and alcohol in all the fridges (not indulged in as often as one would think). All Kai does is work, and he expects the same from his staff, and they meet his expectations. Whether it's out of peer pressure or love or fear, he doesn't know and doesn't care.

He's talking on the phone to the COO, Seema, who manages to stay on top of every important issue while Kai tries to stay laser-focused on only two or three at a time. She reminds him of tomorrow's most important calls, the crisis in Indonesia, the latest decision they need to make about government censors in China. Half the world's dictators have made clear to him that they want—no: *insist* on—ways to censor their citizens' vidders. Restrict what they see and how they see it. Turn the entire physical world into text they can erase or obscure at will.

"Chairman Zao is threatening to shut down our factories in Guangdong again," Seema says.

"He's smart—being difficult right as we release the new product."

"Have you heard his speech yet?"

"Saw the bullet points."

As he approaches his red sports car, the single acknowledgment of his insane wealth (not counting the houses, which he does his best not to flaunt by never inviting anyone but young women and *sometimes* young men to them), its doors automatically open.

Seema says, "He's calling CleerVu a capitalist abomination."

"Hey, he used to say that about us in general. And it'll only help sales. His people fear him, but they still love to buy what he hates. It's like a dysfunctional parent-kid dynamic."

"Sure, but if he outright bans it, they can't buy it."

"He won't go there."

"Maybe not, but read between the lines. He's angry because he thinks that if we have the ability with CleerVu to let people alter their appearance, then surely we have the ability to meet all his wonderful censorship needs."

"You know my answer on that."

"I understand. I'm only saying that CleerVu will make it much harder to keep walking that tightrope."

The tightrope of letting people see the world around them, while also appeasing the many world leaders who aren't into the whole *transparency* thing. Of course, it helps when you have zillions of dollars because your product is borderline essential to human functioning. Kai's weathered plenty of storms, chitchatted with leaders of every political and governmental inclination, so this problem seems no worse than several others he's navigated.

"Our tightrope skills remain impeccable," he tells Seema, opening a door and tossing his bag into the passenger seat.

"I'm just worried we've tipped our hand. Made it too strong."

They've had this argument before. He still hasn't won her over.

"There is nothing wrong, ever, with having a superior product." One of his slogans. "Period."

"But people are going to be expecting more. The wrong people, expecting the wrong things."

"We don't do value judgments." Another slogan.

The debate continues as he lets the e-driver take command. Leaning back into the comfortable leather seat, he's so engaged in the conversation that he doesn't notice he's being followed.

Amira finds herself alone during the interminable cocktail party phase of the evening as Owens searches for the restroom. She'd never thought she'd so look forward to hearing some art curator give a speech, but she wants this over with. She feels awkward in her dress—she wears flats to minimize her height, but she still feels like an ungainly Amazon among all these precious *artistes* and their patrons.

She hadn't wanted to come, no, but she knew it was an important night for Mark.

And also, yes, she wants to watch him. Wants to see how he reacts to everything. If he seems to act guilty.

She still can't tell if it makes her a horrible person to be suspicious of her own boyfriend like this. Or, if it makes her deluded to be with a man who might possibly be a killer. Maybe she's both.

She tries not to look too obviously stranded as she wanders between groups of people when she sees, a few feet away, Ursula. She, too, seems to be without her date for a moment, and not locked in conversation, so Amira makes a move.

"Hello again," she says, and Ursula looks up at her with an unreadable expression.

"Hi."

"So, did you know her well?"

"Not really. We met a few times at shows and some parties. Big groups, you know."

"She sounds like she was . . . a special person."

"She was."

"What Ash said a moment ago . . . about Mark wanting to confess anything. What do you think he meant by that?"

Ursula seems to assess Amira for a moment. Realizing that this is not small talk, that Amira is asking in a work capacity. "You two, you're a . . . you're a thing, right?"

"We are." Were they? Still, it felt good to say it out loud. Even to this freak show.

"And I take it you're a cop."

"You're two for two."

Ursula tips back her drink and finishes it. It had been half full a second ago.

"I don't really know what Ash meant. There's a lot of shared history there that I'm not privy to."

"Ash said he shared a studio with her. Were they still sharing it when . . . when it happened?"

"Yes, we were," says Ash, who has reappeared at Ursula's side. "Whyever do you ask?"

Amira's thrown for a moment. She hadn't liked this guy from the start and had been hoping to get information from Ursula.

But she's come this far, so she says, "That must have been very difficult."

Mark will be out of the restroom at any moment, she knows. Guys always take just a second.

"It was." He keeps his eyes locked on Amira. "It was also very, very difficult to get your colleagues to give a damn."

"What do you mean?"

He gives a bitter laugh and looks away. Sips his drink. Seems to be considering whether he wants to continue this conversation.

"Jeanie was a lot of things: smart, difficult, exasperating, energetic, imaginative." He lowers his voice. "But hanging herself? Please."

She has to spell it out. "You don't think she did it?"

"I was helping her plan a major show. She'd had a down period, yes, as we all did, but she was still bringing new ideas *every day*. She had passion for what she was doing, a purpose. And then, suddenly?" He throws up a hand like he's tossing something away. "She just decides to end everything? No. It doesn't work that way. But I couldn't get anyone at your *department* to take me seriously."

Over his shoulder, on the other side of the crowd, she sees Mark looking for her. She needs to end this convo, quick.

Yet she wants to hear more. And she doesn't agree with what Ash said. Sometimes it *does* work that way. Sometimes people who've made the decision to end everything experience a sudden euphoria, relieved that they've given themselves permission to cross that line. Their loved ones are all the more shocked when it happens, so many people insisting, *But I thought they were finally doing better.*

Or maybe she's just saying this because she wants it to be true.

"Is there anything you could tell me that we should look into?"

He shakes his head. She realizes he has tears in his eyes. Ursula puts a hand on his elbow and tells him they should go.

"Watch your step with that one," he says, then they turn and head into the crowd.

When Mark finds her, she makes herself smile. He doesn't seem to have noticed who she was talking to.

Owens has been toggling between wishing he wasn't drinking tonight and wishing he were already drunk.

Finally the speeches begin. Most people stand, but some of the older attendees sit in the few chairs that have been provided for them as Maxine thanks them all for coming. She stands halfway up the grand marble staircase, a mike in her hand. Beside her is a large 3D projection, a silent documentary showing Jeanie painting in her studio, Jeanie hosting an art show, Jeanie teaching a class of little kids, and then images of her artwork.

As always, even when he knows it's coming, the sight of her makes him catch his breath. Especially after that weird vision of her downtown. It hurts all the more.

He is torturing himself, he fears, by being here. Amira—at his side, holding his hand—is torturing herself too. Or maybe he's torturing her.

The guilt compounds everything.

At first he doesn't even hear Maxine, has no clue what she's saying. Just watches Jeanie assembling some of her collages, talking to high school students, touring urban neighborhoods. The footage he's seen before hits him with painful nostalgia. The footage he's never seen before feels even worse, to be reminded that this person he loved so dearly had sides to herself he never knew. It doesn't seem fair. If she can't be here anymore, at least he should be allowed to travel through time and watch her, see all the moments he wasn't there for, know her more fully.

He finally tunes in to what Maxine is saying.

"The Blinding was both a curse and a strange gift to visual artists, none more so than Jeanie MacArthur. After the invention of the first vidders, her groundbreaking work with three-dimensional forms and the wonderfully vibrant texture of her pieces ushered in a new way for us to understand our changed reality."

Christ, his eyes are watering now. The alcohol was a mistake. Amira notices; she releases his hand and moves hers to his arm, squeezing it gently.

"Not content to merely sit back and observe the world, Jeanie was an active participant. She collaborated with scientific researchers, philosophers, and even law enforcement in her quest to understand vision and how we relate to the world around us."

The holograms show Jeanie talking to a lab coat–wearing scientist, debating with professors in some lecture hall, then walking a beat beside a younger, healthier, uniformed Owens. Neither of them wearing vidders yet. No idea what was in store.

"Despite her breakthroughs, which helped us all, Jeanie ultimately could not accept New Vision. She felt she couldn't see the world as she needed to in order to continue as an artist."

The hologram shows some of her final pieces, the dark ones, the ones it hurt anyone to look at, but especially him.

Especially after.

He feels sick to his stomach. He turns and Amira's hand falls from his shoulder as he walks away.

Maxine is still talking, but he weaves through the crowd. He honestly doesn't know if people are staring or not, because he tries to focus every brain cell on the door in the distance, fixate on that small space and let everything else blur, the faces around him, their eyes.

"Mark, wait," he hears Amira say, when he's passed everyone and is close to the door and her voice won't disturb the others.

He turns to face her. Maxine is talking about Owens's wonderful donation to the museum. Soon people will be applauding, looking for him.

"I need to take a walk."

"I'm coming too," Amira says.

"No, please. I just . . . I need to be alone."

He hates himself for the look in her eyes as he turns to leave.

Ballantine disables the e-driver and takes the wheel. Loves the control. Loves how *he made this possible.*

Traveling fifty-five miles an hour on the urban throughway, stimuli assaulting him from all angles. Yet his brain understands it. He sees that SUV turning, opening up a small lane, which he accelerates to fill. This is amazing. Have people forgotten how amazing this is? To navigate through the universe at breakneck speed, to exhibit full command of the ever-changing reality around us? The stock price and ubiquity of his product assures him that people do indeed appreciate his achievements, but at the same time, he wonders.

The throughway begins to clog, so he hits an exit, opting for side roads. E-driver may be disabled, but not his nav, so it recommends a route. On the screen it looks like the blood red trail left by a bleeding wanderer through an urban labyrinth.

He casually turns the wheel this way and that, taking some of the small roads faster than perhaps he should. He's been pulled over a few times in the past, the experience riskier for him than for tech wizards of bygone days due to his skin color. When it's happened, he's kept his hands on the wheel, his voice polite. He's had a couple scary moments, but once they realize who they've pulled over, everything changes. *Mind if I get a selfie, sir? Try to keep your speed down next time, thanks, sir, no ticket. Sweet car, by the way!*

Then he sees it in his rearview mirror.

A black blur.

What?

Not a person-sized blur like that cop had described. This one looks big enough for an entire car to fit inside.

"Oh my God."

He tries to understand this. Adjusts his vidder, which does nothing. He nearly clips a corner during a turn, so he switches back to e-driver and tries to focus on what's behind him. He turns around, as if the problem might be with his rearview mirror and not his vision.

Someone is following him and he can't see who it is.

Someone is driving a car and has completely redacted it from Kai's vision.

The e-driver takes a right turn. Still facing backward, Ballantine starts to feel carsick. Or maybe that's fear.

The blur takes the turn too, still following. It's only three car-lengths back.

He faces forward again, regains control of the wheel and hits the accelerator.

Opens the glove box and blindly searches for that cop's business card he stashed there last week.

CHAPTER 20

Owens walks through the city, trying to rein in his emotions. He wasn't always such a mess, was he?

His phone buzzes. At first he doesn't want to answer, doesn't want to see Amira's name and face, doesn't want to feel yet more guilt for abandoning her at an event that she no doubt hadn't even wanted to attend.

He takes it out of his pocket, sees to his annoyance that the number is blocked. That is very, very hard to do these days.

He answers with, "Owens."

"Detective, this is Kai Ballantine."

Owens can hear the man's fear.

"What can I do for you, Mr. Ballantine?"

"I'm being followed, on Martin Street. By someone I can't see!"

Owens stops. "What do you mean?"

"A black blur, like you said! It's following me!"

Owens tries to remember where he'd parked. "Where are you exactly?"

Ballantine speeds along an access road beneath the throughway. To his left is the river, to his right old factories. Other cars pass, heading in the opposite direction. Do they see the blur too? He can't tell. He hasn't seen anyone pointing, anyone tapping their friend on the shoulder, *Hey, what the fuck is that?* But he's driving too fast to gauge any other driver's reaction, and he hasn't passed many pedestrians in this part of town.

At a momentary lull in traffic, he makes a sharp left. Cuts across the lane, nearly spinning out of control. But the car's got some serious wheels and low suspension and it handles like a dream. He makes it across and onto another side road.

He's still on the phone with Owens, set to speaker, and he's been narrating his journey best he can, in hopes the cop will catch up and bring the fucking cavalry.

Ballantine prides himself on his great sense of direction, but that talent eludes him now, and he realizes as he races up a hill that he's pulled into a dead end—the road simply becomes a large, old construction site that looks like it hasn't hosted any actual construction in years. He spins around again, but he's cornered. Abandoned factories on three sides, potholed concrete square in the middle, like he's in some postapocalyptic Coliseum.

Instead of lions, though, in comes the black blur.

"Shit!"

He drives around the outer perimeter, as fast as he can without losing control. Hits a deep pothole and sees a designer hubcap escaping to the rear left.

The black blur heads straight toward him. Ballantine turns hard to the right, fleeing, hoping he can draw the blur into the center of the site so that he can then race around it and get out of here, back to the main road again.

Pop, pop, pop!

The passenger window explodes. He ducks. Feels something come in contact with his jacket. Holds his breath, all his muscles clenched.

Owens turns off the throughway and floors his accelerator and nearly goes airborne at the top of the hill, into the upside-down U of abandoned factories.

He sees it then, the black blur. The size and rough shape of a sedan.

How the hell are they doing this?

He hears gunshots as the blur and a red sports car drive toward each other, like they're playing chicken. They don't collide, but something shatters.

Owens turns right and hits the brakes hard. His window down, he reaches outside with his gun and aims at the moving darkness. Fires twice, three times, four. Windows shatter, metal gives way. He knows he hit it, maybe every time, but has no idea where or how badly.

The blur keeps driving, slower this time, and Owens hits the gas to give chase.

It's headed back out the only road. Owens looks to the other side and sees the sports car, no longer in motion. Sees the top of what must be Ballantine's head, and it's leaning down. Sees lots of shattered glass.

Shit.

More gunfire. Parting shots, sent Owens's way. He ducks, hears a lone ping against the side of his car. Checks himself for injuries, but he's good, he thinks.

Looks up in time to see the blur disappearing from view. He must have hit it badly enough that the driver has decided to retreat, for now, at least.

He wants to give chase, but knows better. And he needs to check on Ballantine. He picks up his radio.

"It's heading back onto Riverview, going south."

Dispatch asks, "Make and model . . . ? Detective, make and model?"

"Negative, I couldn't . . . It has some bullet holes in it, okay? And probably some shattered windows."

They ask him again but he cuts them off, tells them he's leaving his vehicle to check a possible gunshot victim. He steps out, holding his gun with both hands.

Even amid the mess and litter and potholes, he notices two shell casings as he approaches the car. He sees bullet holes in the driver's-side door, and the windshield has been shot out, nothing but a jagged edge at the top and bottom like the jaw of an attacking shark.

Steps closer.

"Police! Mr. Ballantine, are you hurt?"

The young mogul slowly lifts his head, hands raised as if under arrest. Eyes wide.

"Are you hurt?"

Ballantine shakes his head, mute.

Owens checks him, sees no blood. He circles the car, smells for a punctured lithium battery, but they got lucky. The engine's off, everything all quiet but for the hum of distant traffic.

He holsters his weapon. And now is when he realizes his heart is trying to escape his chest, sweat all over his body.

"Jesus Christ," Ballantine says, breathing hard, nearly hyperventilating. "That was . . ."

Owens opens the driver's-side door, getting a full visual. Still no blood, but tiny diamonds of windshield stick to Ballantine's close-cropped hair.

"Yeah," Owens says. "But it's gone now. You're okay. You're safe. Just try to breathe."

He waits a moment for Ballantine to catch his breath. He lets nearly a minute pass, he thinks, but time is weird right now.

Then he can't help asking, "So do you believe me now?"

"I'm sorry," Ballantine says. "I . . . I never thought this could happen."

Owens tells him to sit tight, then he jogs back to his car, reports Ballantine's condition, and asks for an ambulance anyway. Asks Dispatch if they've caught the perp, but no.

He walks back to Ballantine. His adrenaline cools into a hardened anger.

"Okay, no more bullshit. Who's doing it?"

"I don't know." Like it's the stupidest question in the world.

"Mr. Ballantine. You could have called 911, but you called me directly. Why? Because you knew I was the only one who'd believe you?"

"I don't know. I just . . ."

He sounds like someone who can't remember the last time he said "I don't know," and he just said it twice.

"Please explain this much: how is he doing it?"

"Look, I . . . None of this I know for a definitive fact. But I've heard rumors." He's still trying to slow his breathing. Talk in digestible gulps.

"Rumors about black blurs?"

"Yes and no." He motions to his open door. "Mind if I get out?"

Owens backs up and the entrepreneur stands shakily on his feet. "Wow."

"Your adrenaline's gonna go through the roof for the next few minutes. You might feel okay now, but all kinds of muscles are going to be sore tomorrow. Want to sit in my car?"

"No, thanks." He surveys the damage to his fine ride, then turns and leans against it.

"You were saying?"

"Okay. Rumor is, there was this start-up. Working for the government. On this very feature."

"'Feature'?"

"Enhancement. How to disguise yourself from vidders. And when I say *government*, I don't mean through ordinary channels. I'm talking intelligence agencies, classified projects. Bids that don't exist."

"Go on."

"This company, Obscura Technologies. They made the key breakthrough. Figured a few things out, about the optic nerve and the cerebral cortex. Ways to manipulate one into confusing the other. How to trigger the mental glitch that makes this kind of vid-altering possible."

"What 'key breakthrough'?" The last thing he wants is another stockholder presentation, but he needs to understand.

"Look, what our new CleerVu does . . . It lets you change how you look to other people, period. They still *know* who you are, intuitively. You can't use it to disguise yourself as someone else so you can commit crimes, I swear. We thought of that, obviously, and programmed against it. Come on, give us some credit. I can't make myself look like you, then walk into a bank and hold it up, and have you take the fall. That's just not how it works."

Owens thinks about that weird Jeanie/Amira moment a few days ago. It took him a while to get through the confusion, to figure out what was really happening. Honestly, he's still not entirely sure what happened. This CleerVu nonsense isn't as perfect as Ballantine seems to think it is. But . . . Owens did know that it was Amira, eventually. So maybe the damn thing does work. Mostly.

"And in the bank robbery scenario," Ballantine continues, "cameras would have captured the real you anyway. Footage would have revealed the truth. We can prove that, to any government regulator in any country. I'm not worried about that. What this Obscura did, though, and this is all according to rumor, but what *they* did was figure out how to tap into people's vidders, and from there, their brains."

Owens still doesn't follow, but he's not sure it matters. What he wants to know is, "So then what happened?"

"Some senator found out about the project and cut the funding. Then the lead scientist, who was suddenly broke and under a gag order . . . He killed himself."

"And his company?"

"It's like it never existed. You can't even find old records anywhere."

"Then how does anyone know about it?"

"Exactly! That's why I always figured it was an urban legend. Used to be, paranoid types would talk about jackbooted agents in black helicopters. Now it's black blurs and government agencies that don't exist." Ballantine shrugged. "So, you tell me what to believe."

"Yet here your company comes along, with an eerily similar product to Obscura's."

Ballantine shakes his head. "Obscura made their discovery, fine, but we made ours, independently. Now, maybe the CIA or someone wanted to use Obscura's information so they could send black blurs all over the planet assassinating people, but we want to use the technology for *good*. That's why CleerVu comes with unbreakable safeguards. Whoever's doing this, they're . . . They're preventing our brains from processing who they really are. CleerVu does *not* do that."

"You expect me to believe that whoever's doing this doesn't work for EyeTech, and it's just a wild coincidence that they'd start doing this right when you launch your new product? And that they'd go after you?"

"Whoever's doing this is not related to my company."

Said with all the confidence and outrage of a wealthy parent who can't believe his straight-A, varsity letterman son also happens to be a date rapist.

Owens posits, "Unless it's someone so inside your company that he knows how to break those unbreakable safeguards."

Ballantine shakes his head again.

"Then why would they want to kill you?"

Ballantine laughs. "Plenty of people want to kill me."

Owens thinks for a moment. "You must have bodyguards."

"Sure, when I travel. At home, only sometimes. They're annoying."

Owens tries to make sense of this. Tries to figure out whether the killer could be a business competitor, someone who wants to make EyeTech look bad, or someone who just wants to terrorize the world by making people doubt their vidders forever.

A long silence.

"I wish I believed more of your story," Owens says.

"So do I. But ultimately, I don't really care what you think."

More silence.

Then Ballantine asks, "Did you know I was born blind?"

"I may have read that somewhere."

"But I never fit in with the blind community. People said I was in denial, or stubborn, because I wanted to make sight real for us. I was at MIT when I was thirteen. Their first blind student in years. When The Blinding hit, I'd already been working on an early-model vidder, and had made decent progress. Then suddenly people started throwing money at me." He shakes his head like he still can't believe his life story. "All I've ever tried to do is help people, and for the most part they're thankful. But then you have these . . . these *freaks* who insist it's evil, that I'm somehow corroding their soul. What's so wrong about wanting to understand the world as it is?"

Owens opens his mouth to answer but is interrupted by a gunshot.

He grabs Ballantine's shoulder and pulls him to the ground with him. A second shot, and this time he can tell where it came from. He looks up, to his left, and sees a black blur on the roof of one of the factory buildings. From this position Owens and Ballantine are exposed, on the wrong side of the car, nowhere to hide, so he aims and returns fire but already the blur is gone.

The car had driven off, then come back a different way. Or it had pulled over nearby, let one blur out to serve as a sniper. In which case there's more than one of them.

He looks down at Ballantine and sees the awkward way in which he's lying there. His head at a funny angle.

Owens pulls on his shoulder and Ballantine's head turns toward Owens, his right eye replaced by a red hole. Only now does Owens see the blood spattered all over the car behind them.

No.

Even though he knows he's too late, he drags Ballantine with him as he crawls around to the other side of the car, in case the blur is still up there. He readies himself to lean out into the open and take another shot.

Time passes. Owens checks the roof again, waiting for more fire, which never comes. He exhales for what seems like the first time in a long while, then looks down at another person he couldn't save.

Later, this wasteland thrums with squad cars, ambulances that are sadly unnecessary, a fire truck. A news helicopter hovers overhead like the world's most annoying gnat. Cops everywhere, looking for shell casings.

Carlyle and Peterson question Owens, Khouri hanging in the background. Owens wears plastic gloves, which he'd put on once he was confident the shooter was gone and it was safe to check the car, Ballantine's body.

He realizes he keeps staring into space and blanking out as they question him. Keeps needing to return to the world. Someone tells him he's in shock and he denies it, inhales deeply, straightens his shoulders, *All is functioning normally, thank you.* Knowing he's wrong but trying anyway.

"The *whole car* was blacked out?" Carlyle in disbelief.

"Yes, sir."

"And there were no other witnesses?"

"How the hell do I know? Have someone ask around! You think I'm making this up?"

Carlyle stares at him for a long moment. Peterson behind him, brow wrinkled with concern. Finally the captain steps away, and Peterson walks over, claps Owens's shoulder *hard.* As if trying to snap him back to normalcy, if such a thing exists anymore.

Carlyle quietly confers with Khouri.

"Ballantine's nav was on, so you can reconstruct his route," he says. "Find every security camera that he drove past. See if it looks like anyone was following him."

"And if there wasn't?"

Khouri is tired of seeing these men fuck up left and right. The veterans from The Blinding. Tired of the corners they cut, tired of the slack that their superiors cut them. As if they're allowed to get away with it because once upon a time they saved the world or something. They didn't. They were the ones with the unfortunate timing to wear a badge during all the turmoil, yes, and she sympathizes, but the hard truth is, many of them are damaged as a result. Some of them did unspeakable things that they're still trying to hide—she's sure of it—that the Truth Commission is belatedly bringing to light. For the Department to keep letting broken—and worse—cops like these wear a badge is a gigantic risk. Tantamount to malpractice. Putting civilians' lives in danger.

Owens was a fair and patient mentor to her, once. Gave her a hard time, sure, but delivered sound advice. Yet even then she had thought, *This man just ain't right.*

Something had once come loose that cannot be re-screwed. The threads are gone.

Carlyle hasn't answered her. He's watching Owens, who stands thirty feet away, talking with Peterson. Really Peterson is talking, Owens staring blankly beside him. Looks like a goddamn zombie, and surely Carlyle sees it.

"Captain?" she repeats. "What if I find nothing?"

"Then you'll tell me and we'll go from there."

Carlyle walks off to confer with some techs. Khouri stays where she is and keeps watching Owens and Peterson, thick as thieves. Wishes that weren't the phrase that pops into her mind, but it is. Something is very wrong here.

She watches as Owens makes a face, reaches into his pocket. His phone buzzing.

He checks the screen. Takes the call.

"Dr. Pelzer, what can I do for you?" she hears him say as he looks up at his partner. "Yes, sir. We'll be there tomorrow."

CHAPTER 21

The murder of Kai Ballantine kicks this case into a new stratosphere.

That night, Owens is briefed (lectured, more like it) by the Department's chief information officer and several of her underlings. He's warned that his apartment may be staked out by reporters who indefatigably cover celebrity murders, as if to make up for all the homicides they ignore. The CIO warns Owens how sophisticated some of the reporters have become, especially the tech-obsessed paparazzi. He should expect that his phone and email will be hacked, his social media histories scoured for anything he'd ever posted that might possibly be construed as evidence he'd always hated EyeTech and had been plotting Ballantine's murder.

Carlyle walks up to him right after the CIO leaves.

"She told you to talk to no one, right?"

"Of course."

"And say nothing about these black blurs, to anyone," Carlyle says. "Understood?"

The last thing the captain wants getting out are stories that some invisible serial killer is on the loose. Or that everyone's vidders are compromised. If someone can kill one of the most famous men alive, he can kill anyone. That sort of thing inspires panic, mobs, chaos. The Blinding gave the Department its fill of chaos, thank you very much.

Yet what Owens feels is precisely panic. It's hours since the shooting and his heart rate hasn't returned to normal and he hasn't eaten and isn't hungry and his nerves and muscles are so fired up he feels he could jump fifteen feet high.

"Understood?" Carlyle repeats.

I don't understand a goddamn thing that's happening.

"Yes, Captain."

He makes it home long after midnight.

No press, not at first. But an hour after he gets home, and showers and pours a stiff drink, the calls start. All of them unrecognized numbers. All of them reporters who got his number somehow, leaving messages, questions. Then texts. Then a call from the doorman downstairs, saying he has a visitor. *Lots* of visitors.

Owens apologizes to the doorman, whose job he's made far more difficult. Apologizes and says, *No, no visitors, don't even let them in the lobby.*

Closes his blinds so no one can photograph him, Mark Owens, the detective who was there with Kai Ballantine when the wunderkind was killed. Wonders how long until the headlines recast him as the detective who probably killed Kai Ballantine, then made up some crazy story about black blurs to cover himself.

It's no doubt happening already.

The next morning, making it through the gauntlet of reporters outside his building and ignoring their questions without snapping at any of them requires all his self-control and more. He misses the days of sunglasses, wishes he could use the dark lenses to hide his face. Knows he looks tired, bedraggled. Imagines it reads *suspicious, guilty.*

They holler at him, *People want to know!*

No shit, he thinks. *I want to know, too.* But he has no answers.

He fears someone will ask, *Is it true you saw the shooter only as a black blur?* No one does, fortunately. That news isn't out, at least not yet. He wonders how long it will take one of them to discover it, which cop will crack first.

How long till his fear goes viral, and panic once again descends on the city.

Owens and Peterson sit for the third time in the office of Dr. Pelzer, a man who has now lost not one but two of his employees to murder. They were back again a few days ago, after Dr. Leila's murder, to see if by chance Pelzer had uncovered any signs of interoffice intrigue that might have inspired homicide. If the doctor/businessman had seemed skittish during their first visit, the second time he seemed wan, like the mere act of pondering what had happened was too much for him and he might pass out.

Today he looks every bit as pale, plus nauseated. His hair appears thinner than a couple days ago, which doesn't seem possible.

He had called Owens to say he'd found something he could only discuss in person. So the detectives once again make themselves comfortable in his expensive chairs as he gets down to it.

"You had asked me what Dr. Jensen had been working on. The truth is, I wasn't entirely sure. Our PIs have a lot of latitude to pursue their own research. And he in particular was known for pursuing certain projects for quite a while before letting anyone know exactly what he'd been up to."

Nice job to have, Owens thinks.

"After you left," Pelzer continues, "I was checking into his files and . . . they're gone."

Owens doesn't follow. "Gone, how?"

"His work space was cleared out, and his files were all deleted."

"When did you figure this out?" Owens says.

"Three days ago."

Peterson asks, "Three days ago, and you didn't tell us till now?"

"I'm sorry. I'd . . . assumed it was an internal problem, something competitive among our staff. Or maybe another company had sent in a spy. That sort of thing happens, you know—corporate espionage. We don't always involve the police in such matters."

Owens and Peterson exchange a glance, then Owens turns his full fire on Pelzer. "Two of your staff have been *murdered*, and you didn't want to involve the police?"

"I realize in hindsight it was the wrong decision." He folds his hands on his desk. "But again, you have to understand, the things we do here . . . Many millions of dollars are at stake when it comes to these projects, and I couldn't just let two men I didn't know into our proprietary matters just because—"

"Just because we're cops investigating your employees' murders?" Peterson looks ready to strangle him, and Owens feels the same way. "You condescending asshole."

Pelzer sounds defeated as he mutters, "I did consult with our lawyers, and they adv—"

"Oh, it must be okay, then," Peterson mocks.

"Look, I've called you here today, all right? The point is, the reason I called . . ." He sighs. "Well, I need you to promise to be discreet about this. What I'm about to tell you, it's very—"

"Do we need to remind you that there are laws about obstruction of justice?" Owens asks.

Pelzer holds out his palms. "Okay. I had our IT people dig through our system to unearth deleted files from an old network, and they found this." He hands them a tablet. When they touch the screen, diagrams and words appear. Might as well be in Greek.

"What are we looking at?" Owens asks.

"It appears to me that Dr. Jensen was trying to cure blindness. Without vidders."

Owens looks away from the gobbledygook and at Pelzer. "I thought that was impossible."

"Well, yes. Everyone thinks that. The *vidders* are our cure for blindness. But Jensen apparently thought he could find a way around them. A way to cure people without devices, so that we could return to our wonderful old vision." He says this with a fanciful air, the tone of someone who clearly feels that life is better now, because his bottom line certainly is. "But when I sat down and reviewed his research . . . Well, there's no guaranteeing anything, but . . . it seems he made significant progress. His ideas—there's no way to tell without further study, of course, but . . . they could work." He pauses. "They could possibly let us see the old way again."

Owens and Peterson take this in. It's like hearing someone say that a pill currently in development might let people grow wings and fly.

"Do you honestly believe that?" Owens asks.

"As I said, it's early, so it's still theoretical and unproven." He holds up his hands again. "But, judging from the science, it appears possible. At the very least, it's worth running some of these tests he'd proposed."

"And you think someone wanted to *kill* him over this?" Peterson doesn't seem to buy it.

The good doctor calmly folds his hands on his desk, full lecture mode. "Detectives, in the years since vidders were invented, do you know how many peer-reviewed studies have attempted to find biological cures for blindness?"

"No clue," Peterson says.

"Zero. Because there's no money in it. Maybe initially, for the surgery or the vaccine or whatever it would be. But after that, when we can all see again, without devices? Think of the economic havoc that would wreak. The vidder industry would be crushed, as would several other segments of the tech industry. Not just tech: without vidders, all sorts of companies wouldn't be able to advertise in our brains anymore. It would be enormously disruptive for the entire economy."

Owens thinks aloud. "EyeTech sure wouldn't like it."

"No," Pelzer agrees. "But they're merely the largest company that would be harmed. There are plenty of others: advertising, marketing, PR, communications, media, every good or service that gets advertised to us through our vidders . . . We'd be talking a complete remaking of our economy, after all we've already been through to put the pieces back together."

Owens scrolls through the tablet again, as if he might understand any of the scientific jargon or the diagrams of brains and nerve cells.

"The week before Jensen died," Owens remembers, "he visited the Inner Sight commune. Any idea why he might have gone there?"

It doesn't take Pelzer more than a second. "If you were trying to cure blindness, where would you find better guinea pigs?"

Back at the station, Owens places a call from his cell, pacing in the hallway. Not wanting to use his department phone, not wanting to be overheard.

She answers, and she's not happy to hear him. She's even less happy to hear what he asks.

"I wouldn't ask you this if it weren't important."

He tries to visualize her.

The first few times he visited her, she was living in a group dorm. She's told him that she and her fiancé (what was his name again?) have moved into their own house since then, but he hasn't seen it. His visits have never lasted long enough before they start bickering and she tells him to leave. He imagines she's sitting on a plain wooden chair, handcrafted either by herself or her fiancé or one of the other members of their commune or whatever the fuck they call it. He imagines their room dark and spartan. Maybe it has extra windows, which they leave open, so they can hear the birds and the squirrels and the wind in the trees. Or maybe they have no windows at all, since why would they need them?

"I am not going to bother Reverend Miriam," his sister says. "What, you want to talk her into kicking me out because you're so concerned about your unborn nephew?"

Standing, he leans his forehead into the window. Staring at his city.

"No, that's not why I— Nephew? It's a boy?"

"Yes. We found out yesterday."

At least they have an obstetrician. A blind obstetrician? The thought terrifies him.

"Congratulations. Don't name him after me."

He can hear her smile. "Don't worry, we wouldn't."

He feels bad calling, but all roads seem to be leading his investigation to Reverend Miriam's little utopia in the woods.

"When's the due date?"

She tells him, and he startles.

"Whoa. That's Dad's birthday."

"I know. Weird, huh?"

"Yeah."

He stands there and they listen to each other listening to each other. For a while. He wonders if she, with her more focused hearing, can detect things in the silence he can't.

"Sarah, do you . . . Do you still see in your memories? I mean, is it like real vision in your mind?"

Long pause.

"It's hard to explain, but . . . yes. I can see your face when I hear your voice. Or when I think about you. And I can see Mom's and Dad's. But I'm sure that, over time . . . they're changing."

He has a picture of the four of them in his bedroom, the last good one taken before The Blinding. Before his parents were trapped in a burning apartment building the firefighters couldn't get to through a mob. Before Sarah blamed him for the fact that the firefighters couldn't get there, or blamed him for the police not clearing the area in time, or blamed him for the fact that, unlike her, he didn't insist on blaming someone for every misfortune, and was therefore suspect.

"The other day, I thought I saw Jeanie. Looked so much like her. I realized later I was wrong, but . . . at that moment, I could have sworn it was her. Then I realized, I'd been tricked. It was actually Amira." He swallows, knowing she can't understand. "I know how terrible that sounds."

"Oh, Mark."

He puts one hand on the window.

"It makes me . . . question what's in my own mind, you know? My own memories. The things I've seen. The . . . the person I am."

"I'm sorry, Mark."

"I worry sometimes that . . . That if I hadn't been so much of a wreck after The Blinding . . . If Jeanie hadn't been with me, if she'd been with someone else, someone less fucked up . . . she'd still be alive."

She tells him he's wrong, but he knows he isn't.

CHAPTER 22

Amira sits at a bar drinking alone. Not because she is depressed, although maybe she is. She's working.

Tonight she is bait.

She knows a guy who knows one of the bartenders and placed a call with him that afternoon. Told him a tall brunette in a black dress with a red necklace would appear at the bar and order "one of your finest bourbon and gingers," and that the bartender should then serve this woman ginger ale and a wedge of lime and mix in a splash of tonic but no alcohol of any kind. Told him he'd get a very fat tip for doing this, and that she'd be having two or maybe three rounds of said drink. Told him to keep this to himself.

She's sitting here because three recent rape victims had been drinking either here or at a place across the street before they were attacked, so the cops figure a regular is haunting the area and communicating with a crew. Every time, the victim was a woman walking on the street alone between the hours of midnight and three. Every time, someone smashed her vidder from behind and got her into an alley or a vacant building and attacked her with two accomplices.

Amira has never had an assignment like this, but she volunteered for it. She's tired of meeting with the victims afterward, tired of taking down those horrible reports. Tired of feeling powerless, a mere transcriptionist of evil.

She wants to take a swing at evil for a change.

Two other cops, male and female, are drinking nonalcoholic beer in a nearby booth. A fourth sits in a parked car trying not to fall asleep.

Also: Amira does not look like herself.

She's got her Jeanie appearance back on. Finding that she rather likes it.

The other cops blinked out at first when she showed up in her Bait Outfit. *Whoa, what the fuck?* Some had heard of the new CleerVu thing, others hadn't. They all said that yes, they knew it was Amira, they cognitively understood it was her, but she didn't look like herself at all. None of these officers know Owens or ever met Jeanie, so to them Amira just looks like some random other woman.

The men, she could tell, are more than just surprised or confused. Jeanie's a stunner, basically. Amira's noticed how they act differently around her. Almost deferential. She's still the junior officer, but she wields a power she hadn't possessed before.

It feels wrong. This whole CleerVu thing is only making her—and will only make everyone else—that much more pessimistic about mankind, how superficial we are. How transparent. Even now, looks are so goddamn important. We know this, those of us who can turn heads and those who can't, we've read the articles, the studies about who does well in interviews and who gets promoted, who owns the room, yes, we understand, but only when someone who once looked one way becomes transformed and everything changes will they truly fathom the differences.

It's so odd, she thinks, that even when everyone is technically blind, appearance dictates so much. That attraction or repulsion and everything in between can be so reliant on the shape of your eyes, the size of your nose. Maybe CleerVu will become a sensation, everyone trying to look like their idealized self. Deleting moles, extra chins, jowls, gray hair. Perfecting themselves, projecting perfect avatars and hiding the real them, forever. Some people might go out of their way to make new friends, people who had never seen the old them, so they can bury that less attractive self behind 1s and 0s for eternity.

Partly Amira thinks that looking like Jeanie gives her more confidence. A disguise, cosplay, a superpower. But it also makes her more depressed, to realize what she's always missed out on for being Merely Ordinary.

So here she is, Amira as Jeanie.

Feeling powerful but with the worst case of impostor syndrome imaginable.

She's been drinking fake bourbon and gingers for ninety minutes and is learning that it's a boring thing to do, pretending to drink alone at a bar.

A man decides he will help.

Late thirties, maybe, some gray at the temples, dress shirt. Works in finance, perhaps. He's walked a few blocks in the wrong direction after work.

He chats her up. She says her name is Jeanie. Why not. He looks her up and down.

She puts up with him. Passes the time. She's merely bait and isn't supposed to be scanning the room too obviously for the potential perps—that's what the other undercovers are doing. So chatting with this pickup artist is better than her staring off into space and looking suspicious.

He's a stockbroker (shocker!) and divorced (ditto!). Amira's nails haven't been as finely manicured as his since high school, maybe. No, not even then.

His name is Gary. He asks about her and she makes shit up. Not leading him on but not telling him to go away, at least not yet.

They talk about sports. He brings it up, and Amira is a big fan, so at least she can banter without much effort.

She makes eye contact with Douglas, one of the undercovers, who sits in a booth chatting with Peloni, another undercover and his pretend girlfriend for the evening. Douglas rolls his eyes at Amira, quick.

Gary the stockbroker insists on buying her another round. Proposes shots but no, "Jeanie" will stick with another bourbon and ginger.

The bartender serves them and Amira sips it and yep, the bartender got confused, this has real booze in it. Oh well, one round won't dull her senses too much.

More time passes. They can talk sports only so long. The stockbroker starts talking instead about how drop-dead gorgeous Amira/Jeanie is. Scoots a little closer to her on his stool.

He's not too bad-looking, but he's annoying, and she doesn't even feel complimented, since he can't see the real her. This whole situation just too weird.

She sees Douglas at his table scratching at his wrist. The signal for *Let's go already.*

Gary the stockbroker invites her home to his place for a nightcap. Actually uses the word *nightcap.*

"That's real sweet of you, but I'm going to have to pass."

He looks surprised. A little insulted.

"O-kay. Early-morning plans tomorrow or something?"

It's past midnight.

"Yes. Very early."

"Well, maybe another time. Maybe another round here before we go?"

Jesus, he just will not take a hint. She needs to scare him off, now.

"It won't work between us, Gary. I'm a con artist. I come here to take men for everything they're worth, and, no offense, you don't look like you have enough to be worth my time. And you're cramping my style. So I need you to pick your drink up and finish it somewhere else. And if you tell a single person what I just told you? That bartender there, who's with me on this, he and some buddies will beat the living hell out of you."

He's staring and staring and waiting for her to break out her *Just kidding!* smile.

God, it feels good to hold a blank stare this long.

"So run along, Gary. Run like your life depends on it."

Gary looks down and reaches for his drink, misses it, reaches again, grabs it, and leaves.

Finally she lets herself smile, real small.

Two minutes later she settles up and makes like she's one degree before shit-faced, swaying her way to the exit.

She walks a block through a quiet city. Her vision works as well in the dead of night as it would if this were high noon, yet still it feels different. More garbage cans on the sidewalk, more rats on the street (no creatures but humans were affected by The Blinding, weirdly). She sees more of the sorts of people who don't like to be seen in the daytime.

She walks a second block. A predetermined route. She'll double back and walk this again if she needs to, fake like she's lost her car or something.

A third block. A fourth.

Of course, they won't catch anyone tonight. It will require many attempts, nights, weeks maybe, and even then, they could very well come up empty. The gang might have shifted to another neighborhood by now.

She concentrates not on the abandoned street in front of her but on sound, smell, feel. These assholes jump drunk women, victims whose senses are dulled and whose heads are in the clouds, who have momentarily forgotten all their worries. Whereas Amira feels all her other senses turned up to 11, waiting waiting waiting for anything out of the ordinary.

She's nearly at the end of her predetermined route when she hears the steps. *Barely* hears them—he's wearing sneakers.

She's surprised, too: pay dirt on their first night? That *never* happens. Her heart starts to pound.

She doesn't smell him, no cologne or BO or fresh soap; he's smart.

Knowing that he'll be aiming high, for her vidder, she spins around and lowers herself and swings with her right hand. She'd been clutching the hilt of a telescopic baton against her inner arm. As she swings she lets the full length spring out and she drives it into the side of his knee.

He screams. He hadn't been running but he'd been moving fast, and his momentum carries him into her even as she's ruined his leg. His body folds over hers, as she's still in a squatting position. His weight on her right shoulder. She does squats four times a week and this dude isn't even that heavy. She powers up and throws him down, nearly a body slam.

"Police!" the other undercovers are yelling.

She looks up and sees this motherfucker's two accomplices; they'd been holding back, waiting for him to disable the prey. Douglas and Peloni are charging after them. Peloni ran track in high school, even has some medals on her desk, and Amira sees her tackle one of them from behind, textbook-perfect. Douglas chases the other one around a corner.

Amira looks down at the attacker. He's rolled onto his stomach and is trying to push himself up.

She jabs him in the kidneys and he howls again. Pulls his hands behind his back, grabs the cuffs from the outer pocket of her purse and clamps them on.

Goddamn, that felt good.

On the ground behind him she sees the blackjack he'd been carrying, the one he'd been planning to slam into her vidder.

She takes a close look at his face, the right side of it, at least, staring up at her from the sidewalk. Not the tough-looking twentysomething like they'd assumed but older, maybe even forty, wrinkles around his eyes. Someone who just blends in to real life, concealing his secret identity, making him all the more terrifying.

"You're under arrest. If you even try to get up, I'll shoot you in the other knee."

Takes her gun out, chases after Douglas and the other perps. Feeling more comfortable in her own skin than she has in a long while.

CHAPTER 23

Late morning, Owens hosting Amira again.

She'd called on a high after her shift ended. Busted a crew of predators. She was nearing twenty-four hours without sleep but was too hyped to lie down, apparently, and wanted to know if he was interested in breakfast somewhere.

Ten minutes after breakfast they're back at his place. Old habit. And she looks good. He sees from her eyes that she's tired, yet there's a glow there: excitement, pride. She wants to celebrate, and he's only too happy to indulge her.

They've barely made it a few steps into the apartment before they're kissing, and this feels good, he's missed her. He wishes he weren't such a wreck, wishes he hadn't pushed her away. Maybe he can salvage things after all.

In the bedroom things get weird.

He's not sure why. Maybe she's tired after all. Or he's not as into it as he should be. It's the hour, midmorning, their bodies too confused. Perhaps they're too sober, which would be a sad statement. They still have their underwear on, but it's that awkward going-through-the-motions thing, lying on the bed beside each other, each waiting for the other to escalate, and he knows from experience that she's going to complain about her jaw getting sore soon, she's a clencher when she sleeps, can only take so much kissing.

She rolls away, stands, heads toward the doorway.

"Maybe we need to mix things up a little," she says.

True, he supposes their tastes do run rather vanilla, but he'd always been fine with that. "What do you mean?"

"Give me a second."

She steps into the bathroom. He can perceive based on a certain glow that the morning sun is shining directly on his white curtains. Once upon a time, he'd used a sleep mask when he was on night shifts and had to sleep all day. No longer necessary.

Another woman steps into the room and he nearly leaps off the bed.

"Hey there, stranger," says Amira's voice. And yes, it's Amira, he understands that, but at the same time she has blond hair, shoulder-length, blue eyes.

What. The. Fuck.

She's giving him a come-hither look for a few seconds. Then she breaks into a smile. "I can switch back if you want. I just thought . . . it'd be fun. Role-playing, almost."

"How the hell are you doing that?" He is slightly horrified and slightly turned on. The fact that such a combination can exist makes him feel a bit sick, too, ashamed of himself. We are such strange creatures.

"CleerVu. I got a beta test package for free. Lucky me. Or lucky us?"

The woman who does not look like Amira but sounds and smells like her steps forward, puts a hand on his cheek.

She notes his hesitation. "So maybe it's not true that gentlemen prefer blondes?"

"I just . . . thought I was hooking up with *you.*"

She laughs bitterly. "Which is why you weren't that into it."

"You're the one who was yawning."

She sits in his lap and kisses him. He feels like he's cheating on her as he kisses her back.

Eventually he breaks it off and puts his hands on this stranger's cheeks.

"Amira. Go back to you. Please."

He moves his hands and she touches something on her vidder, then she looks like herself again.

He's about to tell her that if he's done anything to make her feel that she wasn't enough, then he's sorry, but he's still figuring out how to say this when she speaks.

"If you want, I could look like . . . her."

It takes him a moment to understand what she's saying.

"Jesus Christ," he's barely able to say. He slides her off his lap and he stands up, takes a few steps away from her. Feels like he's been punched in the stomach. Turns to face her again. "Why would you think that?"

She shakes her head as if realizing what a mistake she's made.

"And a few days ago . . . That was you, walking around downtown. Looking like her. Why?"

He's been wanting to ask her this for days but has been afraid of the answer. Afraid she'd take it the wrong way if he was mistaken. *You looked at me and thought I was her?* But now, after what she's said, he has no choice.

"I don't know," and she looks away. "I think I just . . . wanted to see what it was like. To look like someone else."

"But *her*?"

"I know it was stupid. Maybe I was . . . wondering how you'd react."

". . . *What?*"

"You've been acting differently, Mark. For a while. I was wondering if it was . . . the anniversary of her death. You giving away her art. You—"

"You wanted me to do that."

"Don't put that on me. I never told you to give it away."

He waits for a moment, and nods. "I wanted to do it, yes. It's time. And if I've been acting weird, it's because some weird goddamn shit has been happening to me. Seeing you look like Jeanie sure didn't help."

She opens her mouth but nothing comes out. Like there's something else she wants to say but is afraid to. He can't imagine this can get any worse.

"What?" he asks.

"Some IA guy came up to me a little while ago and started asking questions about you. Huntington. He said—"

"Jesus. Don't talk to him."

"I didn't." They look at each other for a moment and he fears that she's lying to him. Or that there's still more she isn't telling him. He shouldn't have cut her off.

"I just . . ." he tries to explain. "I hate how they're trying to dredge up all this old shit. Nobody's proud of what happened those days, but, my God . . . I was doing the best I could."

He realizes as he says this that he spoke while pacing away from her again, breaking eye contact. Wonders if that's his tell, if it looks to her like *he's* lying or withholding.

Which he is.

"You know," she says after a pause, "you guys get awful touchy whenever that time comes up."

"You don't . . . you don't know what it was like then."

"Oh, life was so easy for me? I was blind too, Mark. You aren't the only one who lost people then."

"I know. I'm sorry." He knows about her brother, the impact it had on her sister. There's barely a soul who wasn't affected by some tragedy. "I meant, what it was like to . . . to have people expecting you to help them, when you could barely do a thing for yourself."

"You're right, I don't know." She leans back against the wall. "So why don't you tell me about it?"

He laughs, sort of. Looks away again and realizes how that appears. So he faces her again, forcing himself to, as if challenging her now. She meets his gaze. Amira has never been one to avoid a challenge.

"So, what, just . . ." He's not sure what to say next. "Just tell you all about it? Now?"

"Yes."

"Okay." He nods. Stalling to prep himself. "What do you want to know?"

"Whatever it is that makes you freeze up now and then. Whatever it is that Huntington's hounding you about."

He's never told her about what happened at Western Market. She's never asked, yet surely she's heard rumors.

Those rumors, he realizes, are precisely why she hasn't asked.

He's going to be late for work if they really get into this now. He could use that as an excuse. Say he's in a rush, no time. It would be such an obvious cop-out.

"Huntington wanted to talk to me about what happened at what used to be the Western Market. By the 12th Street canal."

"My family used to shop there."

"Yeah." He sits on the bed. He wonders how long she's wanted to ask him about this. How much she'd put together from workplace gossip, archival records. "It had been empty two weeks when finally a shipment from some distributor was coming in. Food, water, the works. The store had kept it quiet because they were afraid of a riot, but somehow word got out. They wanted ten cops there, a show of force. This was early June, when some people could still see. The rest of us just were in denial, you know, hazy smudges and all, trying to stumble along, praying it'd get better."

That sensation so strange and awful, like driving drunk, convinced you're strong enough to master your failing senses but knowing deep down you're wrong, that you're putting yourself and others at risk. "Half the cops had quit or run off or Christ only knows, but I was trying . . ."

Thickness in his throat, stopping him.

"I know." Her voice both gentle and tough.

"There was a huge crowd before we even got there. Couldn't really see 'em, but you can *hear* that many people. You can feel them. And we'd heard rumors a couple street crews were going to be there, try to steal the food so they could resell it. They'd done that before and we were told to be ready for them, but . . . Our sergeant, Ross, I'm pretty sure she had the best vision at that point, and . . . Remember how strong our sense of touch was? You could just brush up against something and know exactly what it was?"

She takes his hand.

"Yes."

He shakes his head and issues a laugh that sounds strange even to himself. Demonic. Laughing to keep from crying. It doesn't work.

"I felt hands on me," and he takes his hand back from hers, runs his right fingers along his left forearm to demonstrate, "and my partner yelled *Gun,* and someone else, too, and then I heard shots."

He avoids her eyes by staring out in front of him, at a wall that's been blank since he donated all the artwork.

"I couldn't . . . I couldn't even see where they were coming from. They sounded like they were coming from my right, and close. And then . . . people just surged into us. Then another shot and I . . . I fired back."

"I probably would have done the same."

"Twenty people died."

"I know."

She can't know it all.

"The shooting came from all over. But right after I pulled the trigger, that one second when I could feel so many hands on me, right before they backed off—these fingers brushed up against my wrist." He caresses his forearm again. Crying. "They were so *small.* Like, a kid's. Jesus, who'd bring a kid to something like that?"

He shakes his head and he's crying harder now and she leans forward to wrap her arms around his shoulders.

"I shouldn't have even been there. Shouldn't have pulled my gun . . . on people I couldn't even see."

He wonders again if she'd already known about the kids. They're in the record. Had she always known but been afraid to discuss it, or had she never looked it up and this is new information for her? If this is new, he wonders if is he forever different to her, if *he's* the one who's morphed before *her* eyes.

CHAPTER 24

Been a bad week for Jonathan Naylor, aka Nayles. First the bust where his boss gets shot and killed by a cop, then the charges going from gunrunning to fucking treason. His attorney's been telling him the treason will be dropped, it's a ploy, an attempt to goad them into a plea deal, but still. He's always believed the maxim that you make your own luck, that you're your own man, but suddenly all his life is shit and he's become a mere pawn in a game he doesn't understand.

And now an even worse morning, or at least an unexpected one. He's summoned from his cell, told his presence is requested by city police. The same son of a bitch detective who put him away, Owens, wants to talk to him again.

The prison screws take him down a long hallway. Add handcuffs and ankle shackles to his prison wardrobe.

Then marshals appear, escort him onto a bus with the other convicts who have important appointments with judges or cops or executioners.

The long ride downtown, staring through windows so covered with bars that he gets a headache trying to discern what he's seeing.

In prison, he heard the amateur, weight-room attorneys telling him how, back in the early days of vidders, every prisoner had his vidder taken away. The idea being it made prisoners more compliant. Easier for the screws to fuck with. Took a couple years before some criminal justice attorneys took it to the Supreme Court, which ruled that sight was a right that couldn't be forfeited even if you had committed murder or rape. Nayles wonders why he'd never heard this. But he's not the type to follow the news, or to care about those more fucked than he is. He's just glad he got to keep his vidder. Prison is hell but adding blindness to it would be too much to bear.

Bus ride ends, he's escorted through the bowels of the downtown police headquarters. Marshals hand him like a baton to two uniformed cops. His shackles and chains jingling like a satanic Santa Claus. Everything your parents warned you about. Naughty, not nice. They make you look and sound criminal so they can then point at you and tell people, *See? A criminal.*

"Why am I here?" he asks the cops as they lead him down another hallway.

"How the hell would we know? Someone wants to question you, I guess."

"Why now?"

What new topic could they possibly want to grill him about? He's been interrogated already, told them to fuck themselves in as many ways as the English language permits plus some new ones he coined. Clever retorts being pretty much the only thing they can't take away from him.

Unless he really does get the chair.

The cops stop at the door to an interrogation room, unlock it, push him in. Small table, a chair on one side, two chairs on the other. Two-way mirror.

"I want my lawyer here."

"I'm sure one of our finest public defenders is on his way."

"Fuck that, I have an actual attorney, and—"

They close the heavy door behind him, leaving him alone and annoyed.

Down in the basement-level garage, three uniforms finish loading dozens of crates into a white tractor trailer marked "POLICE."

"They found *all* of this at Slade's club?" one of them asks. "Guy must have been trying to take over the world."

Another cop reads the manifest from a tablet. "Why are we moving this from the station, anyway?"

"Beats me. We're just the muscle, right?"

Footsteps and they turn. Approaching is a short white man with a dark buzz cut. The blue suit screams *Lawyer,* but the badge dangling from his pocket clarifies, *Fed.*

"The FBI will take it from here, gentlemen." He pats the side of the truck. "Thanks for the muscle."

Nayles imagines the interrogation room never even had a clock in it back in the sighted days, all the better to make people stew. He knows the time thanks to the clock at the bottom bar in his vidder's display, and he can't help noticing he's been sitting here a goddamn hour already.

"This is bullshit," he announces as loudly as he can without actually screaming. The walls are probably soundproof, all the better to hide the beatings. "I gotta use the can, all right? Somebody take me back to my nice warm cell."

Finally the door opens.

His first thought is that his vidder's on the blink. Or some unfunny cop prank, an attempt at intimidation.

Because the person who enters is concealed from his vision, as if wrapped in midnight. Darkness moving. Closing the door behind it.

"Who the hell are you?" Nayles asks.

Nayles can discern the rough shape of two legs, two arms, a head. That's it. The black blur stands there another few seconds.

Then the figure raises one of its arms, pointing it at Nayles.

"What in the—"

And he's just starting to think that the finger the blur is pointing is awfully fat and long when he hears the beginning of a sound, a sound that no doubt became louder as all the sonic waves blitzed through his auditory canal and struck his eardrum, but his brain is unable to receive those messages from his vestibular nerves and auditory nerves, unable to process what the sounds mean, because half of his brain is no longer in his skull.

CHAPTER 25

Captain Carlyle has a very large family, and it seems to Khouri that every member is represented on his office walls. She sees shots of family reunions—several skin tones and many generations of Carlyles wearing matching T-shirts while standing around a few grills—photos of graduations, weddings, police academy inductions, amateur baseball teams. As a woman, she's afraid to put up a single picture of a family member lest she be labeled soft and sentimental, yet here the captain has visually documented the hundred or so people most closely related to him. She resents the double standard, but at the same time she mentally tips her cap to a man who cares about his people that much.

"What did you find?" he asks her.

"Nothing. All the cameras Ballantine drove past that night were malfunctioning."

He leans back in his seat, not liking the news. "Come on. *All* of them?"

"Every single one, Captain."

Downed or broken cameras are not uncommon, but they aren't usually all in the same area like that.

He seems to ponder this a moment, then asks, "You get reports from any other witnesses? Anyone on the road that night say they saw something funny, a black blur instead of a car?"

"No one."

She lets him work through the ramifications. It's not hard.

Owens made it all up. There was no black blur in the shape of a car. Unless you were so paranoid that you believed someone hacked all those cameras, made them all go blank at the right time. And unless you thought everyone else on the road that day somehow just didn't notice, like Owens did, that a car was blacked out.

Maybe it really happened like Owens said and *maybe* the person found a way to black himself out only to Owens or only to the people he wanted to deceive, but Khouri by nature distrusts any sentence with one *maybe* in it, let alone two.

"You work with him more closely than I do," he says. "How's he seemed to you lately?"

He's inviting her to toe the thin blue line.

"He's seemed like Owens." Thinking, *I too can equivocate with the best of them, sir.*

"Meaning?"

"What, other than this? And other than him nearly killing Peterson because he thought it was a good idea to shoot a man even though his vidder was busted?"

In other words, *Ask yourself that goddamn question and don't you dare put* me *on the spot.*

"Okay," he says. "I'll talk to him."

Someone pounds on the door. Khouri turns and sees a young male officer, out of breath, opening the door without having been invited to.

"What?" Carlyle asks.

"We got a 1–7." Code for homicide. "Inside the station."

Owens notices the commotion later than most. Earbuds in to block out the noise, he's been absorbed in online searches for Obscura, the company Ballantine told him about in the last moment of his life. A company that may or may not have actually existed.

Once again, he can't believe he's doing this, chasing the kinds of ghost stories he's long ridiculed as paranoid delusions. Most of the sites he finds are clearly the product of diseased minds. Every time he thinks he's found something interesting—a website with a leaked transcript from a congressional hearing into government surveillance programs, biographical information on past Obscura researchers who eventually met suspicious ends in car crashes, fires, hunting accidents—that same site includes a link to some fire-breathing rant about New World Orders, Zionist conspirators running the banks, sects of sovereign citizens uniting to fight our oppressors, future followers of Reverend Miriam spreading their madness online as they prepare to renounce all technology, et cetera.

He's heard all this before, usually from people in the back seat of a squad car. Roughly half the people he arrests subscribe to some skewed belief system or another, desperately using those narratives to arrange the chaos of life into a tidy story that explains their predicaments.

Sure, it's not that you chose to commit a crime, it's that you were manipulated by forces larger than yourself. Your thoughts are not your own, they were implanted by powers against your will. Schizophrenia writ large, spread online, disseminated to the bored and similarly afflicted. A nation of the delusional, and *No, we can't help it, Your Honor.*

Eventually he hears "1–7" penetrate the music in his earbuds. He pulls them out and looks up, asks what's happening.

"Somebody got shot in one of the interrogation rooms," a uniform tells him, hurrying past.

Jesus. "One of *us*?"

"No, a perp. Goes by Nayles."

His legs propel him out of his chair. How did Nayles get shot in an interrogation room? What cop would do that? And why was a man Owens locked up brought back to the station without Owens being notified?

He's pondering all these questions and more when Peterson walks up to him.

"Jimmy, what happened?"

"One shot to the head, I'm hearing. Less than half an hour ago."

"Why was he even here? You call him in?"

"No. Figured you did."

"I didn't. I haven't worked that case in days. The prosecutors have it."

They stare at each other for a moment, half expecting the other to explain. But there is no explanation, at least not yet.

They head to the interrogation room, but halfway down the hall their path is blocked by Khouri.

"Sorry, guys. That's enough."

"We're the ones who arrested him," Owens says. "I need to see the room."

She shakes her head. She looks nervous but she stays in the center of the hallway. "Sorry. Carlyle put Williams and Lin on it. He doesn't want anyone else in the room."

Behind her stand three uniforms, young but big. Chosen for their size, no doubt. Their faces betray the sense that they didn't ask for this assignment and don't want it, but they want to disobey a captain's orders even less.

"Khouri, what the hell?" Peterson snaps as he and Owens understand. "You're telling me Carlyle specifically doesn't want either of us to even see the room?"

They're staring daggers at the junior detective, who's younger and smaller but working to muster the strength to give those daggers right back. "Do you think I'm enjoying this, Jimmy?"

"I think me and Owens are enjoying it a hell of a lot less. So it's someone else's case now?"

"It's a murder so it's a new case and stop putting me in the middle, goddamn it."

Peterson shakes his head. Unsure whether she's actually against them on this or just doing what she's been told. Either way, he's not liking it. "I'm not the one who put you there, kid."

Owens takes one last glance down the hall, at the open door to the interrogation room. Sees techs he recognizes, sees Detective Lin taking notes. Lin, a smart and thorough investigator, looks up and notices Owens, turns away without a nod.

Owens realizes something large and heavy has been set in motion, and he's a small breakable object in its way.

Owens and Peterson confer by their desks. Standing there, too hyped up to sit down. Someone has killed one of their subjects, here in headquarters, and they've been cut out of their own case. A case they thought was closed, violently reopened.

Then they compare notes on what they've most recently learned about Ballantine. EyeTech has a world-class PR team, of course, and an even better legal team, so the company is giving the Department the runaround. Making it difficult for searches of Ballantine's office or his many homes, not even giving them access to Ballantine's executives or underlings. Delaying, stonewalling, making necessary the acquisition of warrants. Which they'll get, of course, and quickly, but even that short passage of time is enough for files to be deleted, servers to be moved, stories to be rehearsed, evidence to vanish, international flights to be booked.

"Why would the same person want Jensen, Leila, and Ballantine dead?" Owens asks. "It's something to do with EyeTech, has to be. We need to get into those offices."

"Ballantine," Peterson says, shaking his head. "It's crazy."

"Someone knocking off two researchers from the same company, fine, I see the connection. But to move up to the CEO of fucking EyeTech? I mean, who's next, the President?"

Peterson scoots his chair closer, lowers his voice. "Mark. You're absolutely a hundred-percent positive that—"

"Yes." Underscored, in bold. "Jesus, don't tell me you're doubting me too."

"I'm not. It's just . . . It's awfully goddamn weird, all right? You said yourself when we questioned Leila, it's the easiest excuse in the—"

"I'm telling you what I saw, Jimmy."

"An entire car blacked out? There's no way maybe you were just stressed and—"

"Stressed and what, snapped? Hallucinated?" Loud enough that heads turn. "Went crazy? When have I acted like that before? That's more *your* style, man."

Peterson's face goes cold. "The hell's that supposed to mean?"

"Nothing." Owens shakes his head. Feels like an asshole.

"No, it meant something."

"I'm sorry, forget it." Both of them thinking about Peterson's volcanic rage back when he'd had his wife committed. All the arrests that were rougher than they needed to be. The times Owens signed his name to statements that were less than true, out of respect for what Jimmy was dealing with.

"You haven't exactly been a Boy Scout since Jeanie passed," Peterson says.

"I know. I'm sorry."

They've both been through a lot, each suffering different wounds. It was years ago, so why haven't they healed? Why aren't they *better*, and what would that even mean?

Peterson shakes his head at him, then sits heavily in his seat, swiveling toward his monitors. Owens fears he's losing allies by the hour.

Another hour later he's still at his desk when he sees two unfamiliar suits emerge from Carlyle's office, the captain right behind them. The two suits walk straight to Owens while Carlyle lingers by his door.

"Detective Owens? I'm Special Agent Vincent Magnus, with the FBI. This is my partner, Joe O'Dell."

Owens stands and shakes their hands. The prominent widow's peak atop Magnus feels like a dark arrow pointing at Owens, or maybe that's just the way the fed is eying him. He's Owens's height, thick, a former wrestler or football player. O'Dell is more slight, but judging from the cords in his neck, it's all muscle. Light gray hair, combed perfectly, not a one out of place.

"We'd like to have a talk at the Bureau field office," O'Dell says.

Alarms blare in Owens's skull.

"I can talk just fine here. What about?"

"The murders of Madeleine Leila and Kai Ballantine."

"The black blurs," Owens says, folding his arms.

"If you say so." O'Dell smirks.

Owens eyes him. "I do say so."

"We'd also like to chat about Mr. Naylor," O'Dell says.

Magnus makes a show of looking around, all the cops hovering, eavesdropping. "I think we should talk in private."

"Like I said, I can talk here. And you want to talk about Nayles, what, an hour after he was shot? You got here awfully fast."

"We were already on our way here, actually," O'Dell says. "I only wish we'd been a little faster."

Owens realizes the full weight of it now. It should have been clear earlier, but he didn't want to admit it. They suspect him. That he's made up the stories about black blurs, and that he just shot Nayles.

As it hits him, Magnus takes a half step closer and lowers his voice. "Detective. Let's not make this any more awkward than it has to be. Leave your badge and firearm on your desk."

"You've got to be kidding me."

The world seems to spin on Owens. Then movement to his left, Peterson coming to his partner's defense.

"This is absolute bullshit," Peterson announces, backing Owens despite their earlier argument. He's a dervish of energy, willing to be the berserker so Owens can save face, like a manager getting tossed so his star player can stay in the game. Peterson looks over the feds' shoulders, sees Carlyle standing against a wall. "Captain, this is crazy! You can't let them come in here and—"

"Take the rest of the day off, Detective Peterson," Carlyle commands. "*Now.*"

Owens can feel the breath leave Peterson's body. Feels it in his own chest too.

"It's all right, Jimmy," Owens says, not wanting to share his troubles. He says to the feds, "Okay, boys. This sounds fun."

He places his gun on his desk, but not the badge. "I'm hanging on to this, thanks, unless my captain objects. There a suspension I don't know about?"

"That's fine," Carlyle says.

Owens notices now that IA attorney Huntington is here too, at the other end of the room. As still as a perched hawk studying the terrain for rodents. Owens opens his mouth to say something to the IA bastard, decides it's not worth it.

Sensing his distraction, O'Dell puts a hand on Owens's shoulder. Not roughly, but Owens turns to face him.

"Don't do that," Owens warns.

O'Dell takes his hand away and accepts the stare-down for a few seconds.

Owens turns to move and follow Magnus, then stops when he notices something. Still standing uncomfortably close to O'Dell, he asks, "We've met?"

"I don't think so," O'Dell says.

Owens trying to remember.

He feels dizzy again, askew, like the building is being tipped to the side by some celestial finger. Maybe this is how everyone feels as they're being led off to be arrested. Maybe he's been surrounded by people with vertigo all his career and never appreciated their plight until now.

But no. He's seen O'Dell before.

Somewhere.

He mentally flips through visual files as they walk down a hallway he's walked for years, but it's never felt this long. Magnus in front, Owens in the middle. They distrust him so much they're boxing him in as they go. He notices that Huntington falls in line behind them.

O'Dell's perfect hair, he thinks. He can see O'Dell's hair becoming unperfect, uncombed, can see it bobbing on the man's forehead.

Why is this image in my mind? Where does it come from?

Elevator doors at the end of the hallway. Before that comes the men's room.

"I need to use the restroom."

"Me too, actually," O'Dell says. Forced casual. *We know you're just stalling, asshole, but we don't mind, we have all the time in the world.* Owens has done the same dance with perps for years.

They walk into the men's room. Owens sidles up to a urinal and O'Dell chooses the one right beside him, even though five others are available. *Get used to violations of etiquette, personal space, manhood.* Magnus lingers behind Owens. At first Owens thinks Magnus is going into a stall, but no, Magnus is simply standing behind him. *Don't get any ideas.*

Huntington hasn't joined them and must be standing in the hall, guarding the door.

A long mirror sits head level, so guys can see what they look like when they piss; God only knows why someone thought that was a good idea. While Owens does his business, he glances at O'Dell's reflection, tries not be obvious about it.

Sees the reflection of the perfect hair, the perfect part on the mirror-reversed side. And it clicks.

His visual memory: the hair in O'Dell's face. O'Dell running. The part seems on the wrong side because Owens saw it only in reflections before, never actually saw O'Dell's face head-on.

Reflections in windows.

In the alley, on the street.

That celestial finger nudges the building *hard.* Owens nearly sways to the side as he understands it.

The alley outside Dr. Leila's apartment. Owens chasing the black blur. As they ran, the blur passed by an alley window, a few of them. A parked car, which also had windows.

The reflections hadn't been blacked out.

Whoever had hacked into Owens's vidder to black out the killer hadn't been smart enough or agile enough to black out every reflective surface the killer had run past. Owens had seen the killer without realizing it until now.

The killer is standing next to me, with his dick out.

O'Dell was the black blur.

This is an epiphany and a lightning bolt or maybe he's crazy, maybe it's the stress of being arrested and his life coming apart.

The synapses in his mind are flooded, fresh connections appearing in ways they shouldn't, beginnings and endings of different stories tied together incorrectly, resulting in chaos, madness, an arrested cop making a horrible mistake.

Owens coughs. Half strategy and half involuntary, his body rebelling against all this stress. He's finished pissing and has carefully returned himself into his underwear but hasn't zipped up yet, doesn't want to reveal that he's done. He coughs again, violently. The third time, he reaches over and grabs O'Dell's head and slams it forward into the mirror.

Through the fragments of broken mirror Owens sees O'Dell falling, sees himself lunge back with his right elbow out. His elbow glances off Magnus, not a direct blow, as Magnus saw him coming and is already backing up and reaching for his weapon. Owens turns and launches himself at the fed. They wrestle, each trying to get a firm grasp of Magnus's gun. The stall door swings open as they topple inside.

Magnus would have fallen but the side wall of the stall holds him up. Owens throws a punch square into his nose. His head bounces off the stall wall and offers itself to Owens's next punch, and the third. The gun hits the floor.

Owens turns, sees O'Dell climbing to his feet, reaching into his jacket pocket. Owens kicks him in the face, then the stomach.

The only conscious person in the room now, Owens grabs Magnus's gun off the floor. Runs toward the bathroom door, which opens as Huntington begins to enter, gun drawn, arms locked forward. With all the noise in here, any halfway decent cop should have had enough time to barge in and aim at Owens and fire, but Huntington is an IA suit and likely hasn't done anything like this in years, if ever. Owens kicks the door shut, closing it on Huntington's arms. Owens swats the gun away with his free hand. He pulls open the door again and Huntington stumbles in. Owens pistol-whips him and the suit hits the floor.

Owens steps into the hallway. It's empty. Pockets Magnus's gun and runs down the stairwell. Passes a few cops and nods at them—

nothing to see here. Hardly anyone knows he's supposed to be arrested. He's just Mark Owens, detective in a hurry.

The station is loaded with cameras. He probably has less than a minute before someone stops him. He takes out his cell and calls Amira.

She opens with, "Are you okay?" That and her tone tell him she already knows about the feds visiting; Peterson must have called her.

"Are you at the station? Meet me at your car, now."

He keeps his head down as he makes his way to her usual parking spot in the subterranean garage.

His less-than-a-minute is almost up when he sees her approaching. "I need your car."

"What's going on?"

"One of the feds who came for me, Agent Joe O'Dell, I recognized him. If O'Dell's really his name. He was the black blur."

"What?"

"I recognized him, from the alley outside Dr. Leila's." He looks over her shoulder, turns as he talks, fearing that they'll come for him any second now.

"But you said you couldn't see his—"

"In the alley, he ran by a window and I saw his reflection! I didn't realize it till now."

"Mark, are you sure—"

"He can't really be a fed. Or if he is, there's something they're covering up." His hands are shaking. He knows he sounds crazy, looks it. At least he remembered to zip up his fly and button his pants. "I got a tip that the CIA worked with a company called Obscura Technologies on vidder-manipulation technology, a few years back. Find out who they are."

She holds up two palms. "Maybe we should just take a minute and think this out."

"I don't have a minute! Amira. You need to trust me. Or arrest me."

For the first time, he is perfectly still. They stare at each other for a heavy moment. She's a good cop, tough but fair, and if she wants to draw her gun on him right now, she can.

But it's her left hand that moves, into her pants pocket. She hands Owens her keys.

"You stole my keys. I didn't see you."

"Find out who O'Dell is."

"Mark, they'll track you. Your phone, your vidder."

He'd thought of that too. He pulls out his phone and drops it on the ground. Then he reaches up to his temple. He starts to rotate the vidder, unscrewing it.

"Mark, please don't."

It takes another moment, and Owens is reaching for the side of the car with his other hand as he does it, but finally the vidder detaches.

The darkness takes him. He can't see. No fuzzy gray pixelations like when Slade hit him the other night; this time it's pure black, instantaneous and impenetrable.

He drops the vidder on the ground and hears it land. His hands his guides, he opens the car door and carefully pulls himself inside. Closes the door behind him, presses the ignition button after a brief search for it. Hits the gas and takes what feels like his first breath since he was sitting at his desk with Peterson.

He tells the car, "Driver, Fifth and McDonough."

Turns his head so he's facing to the left, where he thinks Amira might still be standing. Wonders if she is shaking her head, if she's watching him go, or if she's already left.

He grips the wheel to steady himself as the car pulls back. Barely moving but still the roller-coaster sensation kicks in, to have his body jerked around without seeing where he's going.

The car drives over something as it pulls forward, either his phone or his vidder, the crunch faint but decisive, irreversible.

PART THREE

THE DARKNESS

CHAPTER 26

He tries to tell himself he's not really blind, that he knows this city so well he should be able to imagine every inch of the drive, see it in his mind.

He tries to do exactly that.

Imagine this awning, that storefront. The frankfurter guy whose cart is always set up at the corner of—yep, there it is, he can smell it. The bad retro metal blaring out of the Death Trap Tavern, no matter the hour. Later a street musician, dude on acoustic guitar covering folk hits easy to murder with a few chords, only he's in a different place every day and Owens feels that vertigo effect again, becoming less sure of his exact whereabouts. But no, he knows this street. Feels those same bumps from the succession of potholes the city will never, ever fix. Knows they're right before the intersection with State Street, an interminably long light, surrounded by office towers, and the professional classes walk by griping about work and bad dates while they grip their to-go coffees, okay, he can hear them now, he knows where he is, he can do this.

Good God, he forgot how mentally exhausting this was. The strain of trying to imagine a mental map that aligns with the world around you, the stress of getting it wrong, which he did over and over again during those awful days. He'd never slept so hard in his life, each night collapsing into bed.

"Think, Mark. Fucking *think*."

The car's newscaster begins her spiel, "In local news, all subways and downtown buses will be disabled on Tuesday morning in preparation for the President's visit for the National Day of Mourning. President Myers spoke to reporters briefly today, saying that former Secretary of State Harbin and any other former cabinet member will be arrested if she does not honor her subpoena to testify before the Truth Commission next week. Several former off—"

"News off," he says. "New destination: St. Mary's Cathedral, on Seventh."

Car horns in multiple octaves. Curses in at least two languages. The beeps of pedestrian signals, the unexpected laughter of children.

The car swerves right and turns when he doesn't expect it, no doubt to avoid traffic at a light, and then an equally sudden left, and just like that he has no idea where he is.

The darkness envelops him. It is a blindfold fused to his soul. He's breathing too fast, nearly hyperventilating. Heart rate going up. All that mental energy to reconstruct the world was his way of trying to stay sane, meditation through geospacing, and now that he can't do it anymore, the fear that had been lingering at the pit of his stomach opens up into full-on terror. He's falling falling falling into a darkness he can't claw his way out of and shit he's breathing even faster now. He doesn't know his coordinates in the world anymore and it hardly matters, he is a fucking atom cast about the universe, shrinking with every breath. The world, the country, the city, this very street is so vast and incomprehensible, he is meaningless within it.

"Shit, shit, shit."

Saying it over and over will slow down his exhalations, he hopes. Stave off a panic attack. *Calm down, calm down.* Old lessons in deep breathing from The Blindness return to him, *Breathe slow, hold it in, now exhale.*

Not being able to see the turns coming makes his stomach flutter and his neck hurt, a kind of carsickness he also remembers from The Blinding. The memory of which makes him feel even sicker, and everything feels compounded, flashback upon flashback.

A siren. A sound that soothes him more often than not, but not now. He fumbles about for the CB controls.

Dispatch talks to cops, cops talk back. He doesn't hear anything about himself yet.

The siren fades. It's not for him. He thinks.

"Calm down. Calm down. Calm. The fuck. Down."

Another red light and this street is quieter, so peaceful he can hear a jet overhead, as if the world is holding its breath and reminding him of all that transpires above him, his own tininess.

"And out of darkness we came to a new understanding, my friends, not their so-called 'New Vision' but a *true* vision!"

Owens doesn't recognize this voice in particular, but he's probably heard it before.

The intersection just south of St. Mary's Cathedral has become one of the favored locations for the acolytes of Reverend Miriam. They pop up in random spots across the city, unpredictable as some annoying rash, but there always seems to be one here. He's not sure if it's because the local Catholics are too kind to kick the false prophets away, or if the panhandlers choose this area to spite the church.

He tells the car, "Park wherever you can."

The car pulls to a curb on the right. Which, Owens belatedly realizes, means he'll need to open his door on the traffic side and hope no one hits him, since the computer and miscellaneous cop equipment makes sliding across to the shotgun seat impossible.

He rolls his window down first, leans his head out the window, concentrates on sound.

Doesn't hear a car coming, so he gets out quickly, traces his fingers along the top of the car, then around back to the trunk, then he steps over the curb and onto the sidewalk.

He's safe. He's actually feeling proud of himself for successfully navigating *six feet* of space. And he still hasn't lost contact with the car yet.

He hears the street preacher continuing with his rant, maybe twenty feet away. On the same side of the road, thank goodness.

Owens leans close to the car to conceal what he's doing as he takes the stolen gun out of his pocket. He thinks, mentally adjusts some scales. Then he opens the passenger door, stashes the gun in the glove box, locks the car, puts the keys in his pocket.

He turns around, stands tall, and hesitantly walks forward. Had he planned this in advance, he would have had a cane, and he's remembering how vital an appendage that was during The Blinding. Without one, this is so much worse.

On his fourth step, his knee strikes something. A car alarm starts blaring.

"Goddamn it." He reaches for the parked car he's walked into, steadies himself, tries to read its roof with his hands so he can better orient himself. He steps away from it now, two steps, and tries to walk straight on the sidewalk. Holds out two palms, hoping that will show other pedestrians that he can't see so that they'll do the work of avoiding him.

The street preacher has gone silent, distracted by the alarm. He no doubt hears Owens's shoes scuffing toward him. Two blind men, perhaps aiming their heads at each other, aware of the other's presence.

The preacher starts up again.

"You must ask yourselves: why did we decide to stop trusting our own eyes, our own hearts, our own minds? Why did we decide to let someone else come in and put these visions in our heads? Why do we think so low of ourselves that we decide *that's* the answer, that other people know more than we do, that we must simply follow them like lemmings?"

Owens focuses on that voice, a beacon in his darkness, lighthouse in his storm. He steps closer, closer. His right hand touches something cold. Think. An old streetlight. Useless these days but the city never took them down. He walks past it, toward the voice.

"Was it really The Blinding that did this, or was it something else? Did The Blinding only accelerate an illness that was already festering in our hearts?"

Someone moves past, bumping Owens in the left shoulder. He pivots but holds his ground. Hands ball into fists instinctively, but nothing else happens. Just a pedestrian in a hurry, like Owens would normally be, not even noticing the blind man.

He takes two more steps, bumps into something again with his knee. Feels around—it isn't tall, stops at his waist. The bench for a bus, he thinks. He wonders if someone is sitting at the other end, staring at him.

He's made it maybe ten feet and his entire body is damp with sweat.

Slowly he circumnavigates around the bench, not tripping on any-one's feet. The preacher stops when Owens finally gets close enough for them to talk.

"Help me, please."

"What do you seek, my brother?"

"Inner Sight."

Two warm hands grasp his shoulders. Hold him steady as if the preacher is staring into his eyes, which of course he can't.

Can he?

Owens doubts everything right now. He can smell the man's breath—minty, a happy surprise. The people he'd met at the com-mune never seemed big on hygiene. He *feels* the breath too, feels the man himself as he inhales and exhales, both of their shoulders seem-ing to rise in unison, like they've briefly become a single organism.

Then the preacher's hands move and start to trace Owens's shoul-ders to his neck, up his face, his cheekbones, the softness at his tem-ples. His bare, vidderless temples.

"You've taken the first step, my brother!"

"I can't see a damned thing."

A pause, the tiny wet crackle of a cheek, and Owens knows the preacher is smiling.

"You will, my brother. You will."

* * *

The preacher introduces himself as Brother Augustine. Owens claims his name is Dave Johnson, and they shake hands awkwardly, Owens's reach uncertain but Augustine's confident and firm.

Augustine may be blind, but he knows these streets. He tells Owens he can take him to "the station," and he guides him there, walking slowly but seeming to navigate the sidewalk and the flow of pedestrians without trouble. He uses a cane with his other hand, Owens can hear. A few times Augustine tightens his grip on Owens's arm and they stop, then Owens feels the breeze of a passerby, then they continue again. Augustine had somehow intuited the approaching pedestrian, knew when to stop. A few times he tugs Owens a bit more this way or that way, like he has radar.

Still, Owens nearly trips over depressions in the sidewalk, or what might have been a fallen broom or tree limb or a sleeping bum's legs. Augustine holds his right arm, which means Owens's left shoulder occasionally bumps into kiosks or light poles or God knows what.

He remembers again, from before, not only how vital a cane can be but also how he could never hold things with both his hands. Hold something in one hand, use a cane with the other, sure. But carrying something with two hands meant not being able to hold a cane, which made the world unnavigable. One of his arms is held by Augustine, but his other hand is empty and useless.

They turn right and reach a busier street. More than once, other pedestrians glance off Owens.

"Excuse me," Owens says the first time. Or, "Sorry."

Eventually someone collides with him so hard that he uses his cop voice and snaps, "Watch it."

The other person doesn't reply, already gone, escaped into Owens's past, the darkness, gone forever. People disappear so easily.

Augustine sounds like he's smiling again as he says, "It gets easier, my friend."

"If you say so."

He's not sure if he can take this much longer. He wants to scream.

Wants to grab the next pedestrian who bumps into him and holler into his or her face, make them understand how hard this is, what he's sacrificed.

He's made a mistake. He can't do this.

No, no. Calm down. Slow breaths.

He tries to surrender himself to Augustine's guidance. They still walk slowly, yet Owens is amazed by the sureness of the other man's steps.

"I want to meet Reverend Miriam."

"You won't just meet her, my brother. You will see her."

An eternity later, or maybe only five minutes, but also both.

Owens hears dogs barking at each other. Passing teens swear profusely and also employ a few non-swear words. Pop music erupts from a car radio like fluorescent light, immediately dimmed.

His shoes have crunched on fast food wrappers or chip bags or other trash. He let himself get turned around again, all his brain cells focused on not falling or colliding with someone, but he still has a decent idea of the general neighborhood. He smells body odor, wet dogs, garbage.

Augustine tells him to stop for a moment. Owens hears a door open, and Augustine guides him inside.

"Where are we?"

"It used to be a bus station, my brother. And it still is, but just for us."

The door closes behind them and yes, this does smell like a bus station. He hasn't traveled by bus in years, but he's had to visit stations plenty, looking for witnesses, interviewing station attendants, *Have you seen this missing girl?* He smells insufficient cleaning products, old urine.

He's remembering the downside of having a heightened olfactory sense.

Augustine tells him to stop, turn to his right, sit. Owens reaches behind himself to be sure of the chair, then lowers himself into it.

Wow. It has never felt so good to sit down. All remains darkness, but at least the world has stopped hurtling past him. If he can just sit here in this unseen chair for the rest of his life, he will be okay.

He doesn't realize how loudly he's exhaled until Augustine tells him, "You did fine."

"Thanks." He can't help but crack a smile at himself. He's not used to being so vulnerable, let alone exposing that vulnerability to a stranger.

"How many come here?"

"Some days, none. Some days, six or more. Our message is spreading."

"What do we do now?"

"We wait. You're lucky, the bus will be by in an hour or so."

Augustine asks if he needs anything to drink, or to use the facilities. Another challenge Owens hadn't thought through properly. He says, "No, thanks." Simply sitting still while the great world spins without him feels like a blessing enough.

They sit in silence and he hears coughing, some whispers. There are at least two others in the room, he thinks, maybe more. It is so, so strange for him not even to know what they look like. As a detective, it's his job to be observant, to notice things. To detect. And he can't, at least not in the way he's been trained. He thinks of the times he's spoken to witnesses who hadn't seen assailants but had overheard them, the huge disadvantage they have compared to actual eyewitnesses. An eyewitness can look at lineups, scan through digital databases of mug shots and surveillance video, in search of that face they saw, that telltale configuration of eyes and cheekbone and hair, the cut of the mouth. The ones who only *heard* the perp, though? Only a handful of times has Owens ever closed a case by getting a suspect to say something out loud so the witness could recognize their voice from before. Despite everything we've been through, despite these devices on our temples, we are still such visual creatures.

There's a reason *earwitness* isn't a word.

* * *

He hears at least one more acolyte (is that what he is now?) join them in the bus station as they wait. Later, one of them changes her mind, says she can't do this, and leaves. Augustine, to his credit, makes no effort to talk her into staying. Apparently, despite their incessant proselytizing, they'll only take the willing.

Finally, after what seems like longer than an hour, during which time Owens hears police sirens no fewer than four times (and clenches and holds his breath and then relaxes as the siren fades, each time), the door is opened and Brother Augustine tells them that the bus has arrived.

He stands and, arms extended, hesitantly tries to retrace his steps back out of the waiting room. He walks toward the sound of the outside world, the feel of the cool air through the open door. Someone, Augustine probably, gently takes his shoulder once he's at the threshold and guides him.

More hands, and a new voice, telling him the number of steps to the bus. He walks on, counts the steps, until another set of hands positions him so he can climb into the bus.

Using his hands as guides, he walks halfway down (or what he assumes is halfway, since he can't tell exactly how long this bus is) before choosing a row and sitting down. He scoots all the way to the window, reaches for it, feels around. Is it open? It suddenly feels very important that it be open. He remembers this from before— the reassurance of breeze, moving air. The thought of being in an overwarm bus, of not having air blow in his face once they start moving, disturbs him. He'd never thought he was claustrophobic before, but the closing off of one sense has ratcheted up the feeling that walls are closing around him. The window is shut. He feels around for a latch, turns it, tries to pull the window up, fails, tries again, finally figures it out.

Cool air on his face. He drinks it deeply.

Someone sits down beside him. Their knees don't touch but he feels the seat sag from her weight. How had he known she was a woman?

"This is the rightest thing I've ever done," she says. Elderly, but not frail.

He realizes he should say something. "Absolutely."

"I feel . . . closer to my husband already."

Moments later, Augustine announces that if anyone has any second thoughts, they may now exit.

Silence holds them in place.

Fifteen minutes into the drive, after they've left the stop-and-go of the city streets and pulled onto the highway, they finally seem to be moving at a decent speed.

No one has spoken since they left, but now a recorded voice thanks them for taking this important step. Owens wonders how he knows it's recorded, that there's a hologram video playing, that this isn't an actual live person. The audio is crisp, no fuzz or static, yet somehow he knows the speaker isn't actually there with them.

The voice tells them, with somewhat overdone solemnity, that they will now hear from Reverend Miriam.

Owens knows what she looks like. Miriam has seemed to shy away from attention of late, but Owens has seen video from some of her early talks. Back when she needed to work harder to recruit her acolytes, before word spread and her followers learned how to find her. It's been a few years now, but at the time Miriam had gray hair shorn monk-short. Always clad in a gray tunic, something she herself had sewn out of found rags, or so the legend (and celebrity profiles) had it. She was tall, thin, lean, like some farmer who worked with her hands all day. Owens remembers her piercing blue eyes, how they always stared to the side when she was on camera, focused on nothing, but conveying vast reservoirs of energy nonetheless.

Miriam begins by thanking them for taking this important step. Thanking them for recognizing the truth of their shared situation, for rejecting falsehood, lies, deceit.

"You heard the words, that you were blind and then you saw, that out of the dark you had been brought to the light. But you knew in your heart it was wrong. You tried to accept what so many others have, but finally you admitted: 'No. This is a false prophet. This is not the world we have been promised.'"

Owens feels how still everyone has become, focused on every word.

"I am here to tell you not to be afraid. Because you are right to have felt that way. You are right to mistrust these visions. You are right to reject what the government has handed you, what the corporations have sold you. You want to tear that offending disc from your head, but you're afraid. You remember The Blinding and its darkness. The fear. I am here to tell you: in The Blinding, you were alone. But now, my children, *now* . . . you are not alone."

By the time Miriam's speech has ended, and the infomercial has taught them more about the commune's short history, the bus has left the highway.

Owens realizes anew how far he is from home, the city whose streets he's memorized. Out here is wilderness, a world his brain hasn't mapped. Here be monsters. If his plan fails, he'll be like an astronaut detached from the space station, drifting forever outward, no identifiable planets or stars to orient himself.

His heart rate spikes again. *Please let this not have been a terrible mistake.*

He tries to calm himself with a vision. The first face he thinks of is Amira's.

The bus slows down. He hears the driver—someone with vision, obviously—say something to the security guard. He hears the sound of a barrier being lifted, then the bus pulls forward.

One by one they get off the bus, clumsily. He hears other people say *Excuse me* and *Sorry* just like he had on the sidewalk. He waits until the sounds cease and he's fairly sure he's the last one aboard, then he carefully stands, lets his hands guide his way along the chair backs, then he's at the front row, and he turns to the side and finds the metal railing and carefully steps off. The last step is always extra high on buses and it feels like a weird leap of faith when he lets his foot reach out into nothingness, and then he's outside.

Augustine announces, "Brothers and sisters, we have reached but the beginning of your journey. I know some of you still wear the devices of false sight. In order to gain admittance, I have to ask that you remove them now."

Owens listens and hears sleeves rustle, cloth pulled gently against elbows. Some arthritic joints crack softly like twigs underfoot. One by one, those who had still been wearing vidders are removing them.

He hears a soft gasp. Someone reacting to their new darkness. Regret. Or resolve.

Also tears, from a different direction. Soft but insistent.

Now a beeping sound, some electronic device with which Owens isn't familiar. Coming from roughly where Augustine had been standing.

The brother says, "One of you is not ready."

A few seconds later, the person who had been crying, a young man, maybe even a teenager, says, "I'm sorry. I . . . thought I could do it, but . . ."

Footsteps. Augustine walking. Sleeves again, then the barely perceptible sound of a touch. A hand on someone's shoulder, Owens guesses. Like before.

The kid is crying harder now.

"It's all right." Augustine's voice gentle, empathetic, calm. Not unlike how Owens himself has sounded when coaxing a would-be-suicide from the ledge. "Don't despair. The bus will take you back. When you're ready, we'll be here."

A weird sound, like the kid is trying to reply but is crying too hard. Another sound—what is it? Hair, maybe. The kid has long hair and he's nodding. The whisper of locks against some synthetic jacket, or maybe leather.

Then footsteps as the kid walks away. The footsteps grow harder and echo as he ascends the bus.

"Good, everyone," Augustine says, walking to Owens's left as he speaks. "Now, to stay together, turn to your left. Reach out with your right hand and place it on the shoulder of the person in front of you."

They become a human chain. Owens tries not to think about felons chain-linked to each other, fails. At the same time there is a beauty to this; he can't deny it. They are each of them lost, alone, but together they attain a purpose. They literally have each other's backs. They will be fine, so long as they stick together and follow their strange leader.

The indoctrination is working already.

"And we'll walk, slowly. Right foot. Left foot."

Like an ungainly caterpillar, they begin.

Owens assumes they came in the same entrance he's always used to visit his sister, unless there's some other one for insiders. If this was the usual entrance, then he should know what's before him. He should be able to reconstruct it in his mind. He tries to, but the steps he takes don't seem to converge with his mental picture. The memory isn't clear enough. It's like the first time you jog or walk along a stretch of road that you've driven a thousand times—it becomes completely different. You'd never noticed certain rises and dips in the terrain, you'd no concept of how truly far from each other certain landmarks were when you were zooming blithely by at 35 or 60 mph. That's vision, he realizes: the ability to coast through the world without truly experiencing it. The assumption that you have mastered a realm that's so much more complex than you have dared to imagine.

Their feet now fall in unison. What had started as a cacophony of footfalls has solidified into a near-military cadence.

Then another repetitive sound: digging. That and the loamy dankness in the air informs him that they're walking past one of the gardens. He wonders if Sarah could be out there, if she can spot him.

Then he catches his breath and realizes no, of course not, she can't see either. How did he forget, even for a millisecond?

Still, he wonders if she could be there, just a few feet away, kneeling in the damp earth. Wonders if she might be raising her head, if she's smelled him, or if some other sense, something indescribable, has alerted her to his presence.

He wants this to be true, even if it frightens him.

CHAPTER 27

Jimmy Peterson's head is a bit too crowded these days. He's already on his fifth and sixth OTC painkillers of the day because he's trying not to drink in the daytime, but the headaches keep coming, and he needs to find some way to keep things straight. He'll have an ulcer in a week, sure, but for now he's good.

Night has fallen and he's walking toward his car in the station's basement garage when he hears someone call his name. Turns and sees Khouri chasing him down.

"Jimmy! You okay?"

"No. Of course I am not okay. How in the hell could I possibly be okay?"

She stops a safe distance from him. He wonders if she's scared of him. He wonders if she should be.

"You believe this?" she asks, trying to go all camaraderie on him, like they're in this together. "Owens finally snapped."

"No," Peterson says. "I *don't* believe it. And I think you're crazy to."

She folds her arms. "Don't give me shit for doing my job. I'm sorry I couldn't let you two in that room, but Carlyle said—"

"Sure, great, keep doing what you think is your job." He salutes her. "Throw a cop in jail."

"*I* didn't arrest him, I just kept him from contaminating a crime scene."

"'Contamin—?'" He can't even finish the word. He shakes his head.

"Maybe if you weren't so close to him, you'd see this for what it is."

She's tough, he'll give her that. She's never challenged him like this before, even if she is standing a safe distance away.

"What, Khouri? What should I see?"

"Come on, Jimmy! He's been losing it, you know that. He nearly shot you at Slade's, and now he's making up stories about black blobs. We're lucky he didn't take us down with him!"

"Is that a threat?"

Now she backs up a step.

"What?"

"You think I had something to do with Nayles, too? Am I next? Should I be on the run from the feds, too?"

She hadn't expected this reaction, he sees.

"No. Jimmy. I'm on your side here. I'm trying to help you."

"My side? How? What exactly are you trying to help me do?"

"Trying to help you see that your partner's gone full psych-case, all right? He's lost it. You haven't done anything wrong, I know that, Carlyle knows that. And I know I'm not a full detective yet, and I wasn't a cop in the dark old days so my opinion doesn't carry for shit around here, but nonetheless? Between you and me? The more you get involved in trying to *help* your very problematic partner, the more risk you're putting on yourself."

He considers this, then says, "What makes you think I'm trying to help him?"

"Call me psychic, but I have a feeling you weren't planning to head home and watch the game and go to sleep. I have a feeling you're going to go out looking for him. And I'm telling you now, as your friend: that would not be a good idea."

That sounds like a threat.

He opens his door. "I didn't realize we were friends, kid. That's sweet. You have a good night."

He takes at least some satisfaction in knowing that he and Owens have trained her well, because, yes, she does know exactly what he's doing next.

* * *

Amira stands at the entrance to Owens's apartment, her path blocked by a male uniform she's seen around but doesn't know. He's apologetic but won't let her through.

Over the uniform's shoulder she sees the feds, O'Dell and Magnus, searching the living room. Owens's warning about O'Dell rings in her head. What he told her sounds insane, but he clearly believes it: O'Dell was the black blur who killed Dr. Leila, the one Owens chased down an alley. Amira doesn't understand how that can be true, or why, or how Owens could even think it.

She isn't even sure what she should be hoping for. That Owens is confused, borderline deranged, or that he truly is the victim of some conspiracy involving federal agents? That a murderer is standing in his living room right now, checking under the cushions of a sofa on which she and Owens have made love?

She thinks of that moment less than a day ago, when he'd told her about the Market shooting. She had brought up Huntington because she had intended to finally tell Owens what he'd said about Jeanie not killing herself, but the conversation got derailed, and Owens seemed so broken and vulnerable. Despite all the chaos around him, and despite the fear she'd felt that other night when, half asleep, she'd heard him mutter *I killed her,* Amira still found it impossible to believe he'd hurt Jeanie. But she realizes now what a mistake it was not to have finally asked him, not to have put that question to him and demanded that he answer, to see his reaction, despite the consequences it might have had for their relationship. Then at least she'd know.

She sees that Huntington is here too, sitting at the kitchen table, working on a laptop. It's not technically Amira's apartment, but it feels halfway like it is, and seeing these men in a space that Owens had shared with her feels like a violation. It makes her feel even worse than when she'd seen the look in Owens's eyes as he took off his vidder.

This is real. It's actually happening.

Happening *again*. She thinks of her sister, the phone call from her mother about Daniella's arrest, the murder charge. The sense that someone you love has fallen to a place where you can't reach them anymore, that no matter how hard you want to pull them up, you can't.

For years she's told her parents there was nothing she could have done to keep the charges off Daniella. But she *could* have done things, if she'd been willing to sacrifice her ethics, and maybe her job. Her reason for getting up in the morning.

Still, she believes she made the right decision. And she lives with its awful consequences every day.

If she helps Mark now, she wonders if she'll have switched sides, betrayed those ethics. Why? For a handsome man? Is she crazy? A dumbstruck woman in love, blinded by the need for her man? Is she just like all those many sad women she's encountered on the job and silently judged, the domestic abuse cases who defend the boyfriends and husbands who put them in the ER?

She'd had another chance, in that moment in the police garage. She could have made Mark stay, could have not handed him her keys. She'd made her choice, even if she had felt rushed, unprepared.

But no, she shouldn't have felt rushed. That's no excuse. For days now she's been trying to figure out what's going on with him, if there's more that she can't see. She's been afraid to make a decision, and in her fear she made a decision by default.

She tries to push her doubts away for now. She calls out to Huntington, "Any half-intelligent cop should know a frame when he sees one."

Huntington looks up from his laptop. He stands, grimacing like he has the worst headache of his life.

"You want to know how to use the coffeemaker while you're here?" she goads him. "Where to find the bagels?"

Huntington walks up to her and motions for the uniform to give them some space. O'Dell and Magnus stop their search, watch from the background.

"Officer Quigley, please," Huntington says, so polite she hates him more. "Where is he?"

"How should I know?"

She wonders how well Huntington knows these feds. If O'Dell really is a killer, would that be news to Huntington? Is the IA guy a hapless pawn, or is he a part of this?

"I understand he stole your squad car today?" he asks.

She wishes she could talk to Huntington without the feds in earshot, get a better sense of where he stands. For now, though, she goes full confrontational.

"He borrowed it. Why, are you looking for someone else to frame? I'm next? You can look wherever you want, you're not going to find anything on me. And I'd be stunned if you found anything on Owens."

"Officer Quigley, two people have been killed on his watch in the last two weeks, both times with no witnesses. He assaulted me in a hearing, nearly shot his partner during an arrest, and now he calls a prisoner into an interrogation room, for no apparent reason, and minutes later that prisoner is found dead. *Then* he attacks two FBI agents and myself so he can flee. Oh, and he recently gave away millions of dollars' worth of art. Now, are you, a police officer, going to tell me you didn't find anything suspicious about his behavior?"

She's noticed how weird the apartment looks with the walls bare. Some of the paint is discolored from where the artwork had been removed, leaving nail marks like tiny bullet holes. She'd never liked seeing Jeanie's work everywhere. She'd always looked forward to the day he'd take some of it, or all of it, down. Yet not seeing it here, she realizes the soul has been cast out of the place.

"The art, seriously? You're trying to tie *that* in to your case?"

"I'm sorry if you're so close to him that you've lost perspective. He's your blind spot. But it's obvious to everyone else that he's not right, and I'd hate to see him take you down too."

She puts a finger in his chest. "You've had a vendetta against him because he wouldn't play along with your Truth Commission. This is all some elaborate way to pay him back for that, isn't it? Anyone who won't bow and scrape and take the blame for what happened back then, you'll make them pay the price."

He gently moves her finger away. "There is no vendetta."

Behind him, the feds have stopped their search and are paying close attention to her. She makes eye contact with O'Dell and holds it. He has tape on his eyebrow and a bruise on his right cheekbone.

The elevator dings behind her. She hears the uniform say, "Sir, I'm sorry, you can't come in—"

"Save it, rookie," Peterson barks. Amira steps to the side as Peterson steers his bulk through the entrance.

Amira can't help but notice the way Huntington literally leads with his chest, inflating it like a fucking rooster to try to block Peterson. "This is a joint IA and federal investigation, Detective. Not a city matter."

"Well, let me know if you need any real cops to help out."

"What I need is for you to leave, both of you." Huntington turns to Amira. "If you have a key to this place, I need you to turn it over to us."

"I'm not aware of any law saying I need to do that."

"I can file a subpoena."

"Then do it, you're a paperwork guy."

Huntington's shoulders shift, like he's tired of the macho shit, even disappointed in her. He motions to the kitchenette and says, "Could you and I speak privately for a moment?"

She looks at Peterson, who shrugs. As the feds continue their search, now focused on the desk and computer in the corner of the living room, Amira folds her arms and steps closer to Huntington.

He lowers his voice and says, "I tried to warn you. You never looked into the files on his wife, did you?"

"This is exactly what I mean. You have a vendetta, going back years."

"If I were you, I would look at those files very, very carefully."

She hadn't heard Peterson coming over, but his massive hand is on her shoulder.

"Amira, let's go. Fuck these guys."

She lets him steer her out to the hallway, where he hits the elevator button.

"He's trying to sell you that old Jeanie story, huh? Motherfucker."

Peterson has good ears, she's thinking. She asks, "What is that about?"

She hadn't asked Peterson about Jeanie's death before, figuring he'd go right to Owens and warn him, *Your girlfriend thinks you're maybe a murderer.* But now finally seems like an acceptable time.

"Old stories," he says. "Old bullshit."

The elevator doors open and he steps in first. She follows. Once the doors close, she demands, "What old stories?"

He holds up his palms. "That he killed her. You needed me to say it out loud?"

The elevator's descent feels faster than normal. She'd expected what he's saying, yet still it jars her.

"There were rumors about that? Really?" The fact that it's not just some cruel hint dropped by Huntington makes this worse.

He looks at her with wider-than-usual eyes. "Just rumors, okay? Spread by assholes."

"Was her death . . . investigated? To make sure it was really suicide?"

"Yes, it was. Chen handled it." She vaguely knows the name, an older detective who retired not long ago and moved to the mountains. "She hung herself, Amira. No dirty play involved."

She nods, wishing that felt more reassuring than it does.

"Now, you tell me," he continues. "There's a lot of crazy shit going on, but you're the only one who knows what it's like to lie in that guy's arms. Does he strike you as someone who'd kill his wife? Or do you think maybe something really goddamn weird is going on?"

What he doesn't say, but she realizes with a nauseated feeling, is that both possibilities could be true.

CHAPTER 28

When Owens wakes in the middle of the night, it's so dark he can't see a thing.

Then he realizes: he literally cannot see anything.

His entire body jerks and he pulls himself into a sitting position. From sleep to full-on panic like *that*. His heart racing. Until finally he remembers the previous day, and what he did to himself, and where he is.

He hears other people breathing. They had retired to a large dorm room, more like a barracks based on the way sound traveled. Augustine had passed them off to an older woman named Sister Lucy, who spoke soothingly, as if to children. She'd explained that there were half a dozen acolytes who had bused in from the city that day, and that they were joining three others who had come a day earlier.

Owens leans back, gradually, into the hard bed. Someone who had been snoring chokes a bit, then coughs, then breathes more quietly. In the distance he hears a rooster, which he knows from past trips to rural areas do not crow merely at dawn but whenever they feel like it. So he has no clue what time it is.

It's so odd not to know, to have no way of knowing. At least during The Blinding he had a digital assistant he could ask for the time, the weather. He's always lived a regimented life, taking advantage of every spare minute, calculating how much more sleep he's going to get whenever he rolls over at night. Now he doesn't know if it's midnight or six in the morning, and he feels that sense of helplessness all over again.

Hoping he can fall back asleep, he closes his eyes, not that it matters.

They had eaten the night before in some sort of dining hall. It felt large, the clink of silverware and glasses coming from far off on either side. He wasn't sure how many such dining halls they had: was this the only one? If so, did all the residents eat here together, or just the new recruits? Does Sarah eat in her house or here? Maybe she might hear his voice—do they eat in shifts? He didn't feel ready to meet with her, not yet.

It occurred to him that he'd had no clear idea how many people lived here. Could have been a hundred, could have been several times that. He'd never ventured too deeply into the property and wasn't sure how large it was. If Augustine had been telling the truth about how many newcomers they got each day, they could have thousands by now.

He had feared initially that the new acolytes were going to be asked to introduce themselves, but it turned out the newcomers didn't have to say anything. At least not yet. As time went on he began to gather that they were being sequestered from the long-timers.

Sister Lucy and a few others had helped them with their food at first. They sat on a cold bench in a room with central heating (no fireplaces, thank goodness, as he didn't trust them around flames, although he knew that would insult Sarah). They guided his fingers to a spoon, to the bowl of soup, to a crusty hunk of bread, a mug of water, its ridges suggesting that it was handmade. This too brought back bad memories of The Blinding: the awkward grasping, the common slips between cup and lip. The knowledge that he occasionally left stains on his shirts, embarrassing even though he knew no one could see them anyway.

Some of the people here smelled very bad indeed, as if hygiene was another affectation to leave behind.

While they ate, Sister Lucy switched from explaining the basics of care and feeding to delving into far weightier matters.

"First they gave the devices to the police and the Army," she had said. Her voice so calm, not quite as eerie as a monotone, but close. "To subdue the masses, arrest the agitators, and cart away those who did not agree. Then they gave them to the government officials, to write new laws that would bind us, and then to the business leaders, to set up a new society that would profit from us, construct the labyrinths that would forever restrict our movements, even our thoughts. Then, they implanted their devices onto us, in-side us, and all we could see was the horrible world they'd created. A false world."

Her voice was soothing despite the dark news she imparted. The utter calmness transporting, like a drug. He felt completely at her mercy.

Hell, they didn't need to drug the food. The entire experience cast a spell.

When they'd finished eating, they'd been handed wet cloths to clean the table, which again felt odd, to be in charge of cleaning something they couldn't see. Sister Lucy told them that eventually they'd do their own dishes, but not yet. She led them to the bar-racks, where one by one they fumbled about in the restrooms, then found their assigned beds. They didn't seem to be divided by gender in this room, which struck him as reckless, but it went with their egalitarian vibe, their belief that they were all united, that they had somehow left the world of sin and violence behind.

So here he is, some unknown number of hours later. He lies and listens to an owl and waits for sleep to take him.

They're awakened by what sound like chimes. They're as soothing an alarm as he's ever heard. It takes him a while to realize what they must be—one of the brothers or sisters walking while lightly hitting a triangle, the high notes rousing everyone.

He doesn't have a toothbrush or deodorant and sure as hell isn't going to try shaving. No matter, because just like last night no one offers him a shower. People use the bathroom, and then they're led outside again, toward the dining hall. Before bed last night they were given canes; holding his is both a sad reminder of the state to which he's returned and a profound relief, making it easier to get around.

It's cold out, surprisingly bitter (how early is it? Again, no clue—he hears birds calling, but he's a city boy and doesn't know how normal that is, what time they wake). He imagines his breath would be visible before him. Tiny clouds he can't see. He remembers how all the people here, when he visited his sister, wore cloaks that they themselves had sewn. He wonders how long it is until they'll be so clad, if that attire is something they must earn over time.

He's maneuvered to be the last in line, though he's not sure if he's succeeded. He hears Sister Lucy calmly welcoming people ahead of him—she must be standing by the door to the dining hall, helping people up the steps. When it's his turn, and he feels her hand grasping his forearm to guide him, he turns his face toward her and says, "I need to talk to Reverend Miriam."

"You will, my brother. But there is much to learn before then."

She's trying to guide him up the steps and past her, but he stops, his body a wall.

"This can't wait. Tell her Dr. Jensen would like an audience with her, today. Do you understand?"

Silence for a few seconds.

"I'm not sure that I do. But I'll tell her."

CHAPTER 29

The funny thing about eyewitness testimony, a public defender once told Amira, is that it's simultaneously flawed and deeply respected.

"It is a false god," she'd explained.

This was years ago, Amira still a rookie, and angry that a kid had just received a sentence for a murder she was pretty sure he hadn't committed. The kid came from a bad family in a rough neighborhood, but he had a good heart. Over the year Amira had known him, before he was arrested, he'd offered up information on a number of scary dealers, helping investigators build cases. Then one day he's picked up for a murder in a part of town he never visited, all because some rich lady ID'd him in a lineup.

"Jurors love eyewitnesses," the disgruntled public defender explained to Amira, in a bar, after the verdict. "Even though it's bullshit. Jurors find forensics confusing, DNA evidence makes them feel stupid, and he-said/she-said testimony makes them want to throw up their hands or just play favorites. An eye wit, though, will close a case every time. No matter how many times I cite them studies proving how fallible visual memory is, no matter how many stats I recite about how often eye wits are actually wrong, and prone to racial bias, and half a dozen other things . . . All those stats and actual *facts* just give them headaches. It's so much easier for them to get caught up with the drama of a person on the stand pointing out with their skinny finger and saying, *Him*. Then it's *Let the record show the witness is pointing to the defendant* and boom, case closed. Doesn't matter if the defendant is a different race and the witness doesn't know anyone personally who looks like that and maybe is mistaking one face for another, doesn't matter how bad they are at telling apart faces that are so different from theirs. Does. Not. Matter. You say you saw someone—even if it was months ago! A year ago! Even if it happened in two seconds and you'd barely been paying attention!—bam, I have lost my case."

"Almost makes you wish we had recorders in these things," Amira had said, tapping her vidder. "Let the debate end, just rewind and watch the footage."

"And so the police officer recommends a police state," the public defender had said, lifting a glass to her lips. "What a shock."

"But wouldn't it do more good than harm?"

The public defender had laughed. "Isn't that funny, how backwards that phrase even sounds? No one *ever* says 'more good than harm.' Human beings, girl, we are *always* doing more harm than good. That will be on this species' headstone. *Did more harm than good.*"

That conversation would work its way into Amira's long-term memory, maybe because she'd been a rookie then, and everything during her first year had seared itself into her brain with a painful clarity. And maybe because she'd liked that public defender, despite the fact that in the ensuing years they would often find themselves on opposite sides of cases, and would talk less, and drift apart. And maybe because of how disquieting the thought was, the incredible fallibility of our vision, and therefore of our memories. Something happens, but then it's gone. If you want it back, we say that you are *remembering* it, but really you're daydreaming it. You're imagining it. You are pretending that something is happening even though it isn't. Pretty much the definition of daydreaming. You are taking a historical event, something that once occurred in the real world, and wrapping it in the gauzy haze of fiction. The next time you *remember* it, you are wrapping another layer of fiction around it, impressing your imaginings upon its delicate surface. Convincing yourself that it's real, being so sure of yourself that you will one day swear to its veracity on the stand, before a judge and a Bible and the laws of this nation.

Even though you'll be wrong.

Because certainty isn't the same as truth. It just means you're really, really deluded.

She doesn't want to be thinking of the public defender right now but she knows why she is. She wants Owens to be wrong, wrong about what he said to her. That the very FBI agent who tried to arrest him is in fact the black blur that Owens claims he saw kill someone.

Claims. So she's doubting him already.

But if Owens *is* wrong, that means either he's created a royal mess for himself or, worse, that he's done something horrible and is now erecting a crazy narrative around it to justify what he's done. And she's at risk of being dragged in too.

She does some online research on Obscura Technologies, the company he asked her to look into. Not fully sure why. She stumbles down one rabbit hole after another. Layer upon layer of digital paranoia. She can't tell if the company ever even existed or is just an online folktale. She's wasting time.

She finds the names of some of the supposed founders. Looks up their names in various police databases, doesn't find any police records. Or death records. Cross-references the names against a few nationwide databases, finds a few, some minor criminal records, not even sure if these are the right people or just folks with the same name.

She's getting nowhere.

But wait, no. This is interesting.

One of the three founders does indeed have a record. A death report.

Killed himself two years ago. Threw himself off the Steve Jobs Bridge.

The file is short, but what she sees is enough to turn her stomach.

* * *

She digs up the personnel records of Albert Chen, the detective whom Peterson said investigated Jeanie's case. Hopefully he can set her straight; the case was only two years ago and he likely remembers it well since it involved a cop's wife. He's retired with a full pension, moved out of state, but she sees a phone number for his new place.

She calls, reaches Chen's wife. His widow. He died of cancer four months ago.

Amira feels horrible as she apologizes and the widow's voice sounds hollow as she says goodbye and hangs up.

Later she makes her way down to Records, a large windowless section in the rear of the building's second floor. Like the Evidence Room, this place went to hell during The Blinding. Electronic files were corrupted, paper records destroyed by fires and water leaks. The official record pockmarked with black holes. So cops, like everyone else, have grown inured to the fact that important information won't be there when they need it, though it's always worth checking.

The Records clerk is an older woman, early fifties, gray hair in a bun. Incompetent, or punished for something, to be working here with so many years' experience?

They don't know each other but Amira grins and makes nice as she requests the death records for Jeanie MacArthur.

She could have done this before, she knows. *Should* have done it before. As soon as Huntington warned her. But she'd been afraid. Afraid, first of all, that if she requested the report, it would have gotten back to Owens somehow, and he'd want to know why she was snooping around. There was no non-awkward way to explain to your lover that you were just double-checking that they weren't a murderer.

She'd also been afraid of what she'd find. It felt better trying to peer into Owens's soul than to try to look up the official report, see it all spelled out in black and white.

The clerk taps some keys, regards a screen Amira can't see. Amira hopes this lady doesn't know her, doesn't know her connection to Owens and his connection to Jeanie. She tells herself she's paranoid for even fearing it.

"Be a minute," the clerk says. She slinks off to a back room.

Amira wonders what Peterson is doing now, if he has some better plan to figure out how to clear Owens's name. Or if he's just in a bar drinking somewhere. At least he's a detective, with probably a better plan for how to proceed. She's only a beat cop, not entirely sure what she can even do, what information she could find, how to find it, what to do if she does, whom to tell.

The Records clerk returns with an apologetic look on her face.

"Sorry, no such file." Figures, with Amira's luck. "I checked under her name and her SSN—nothing. Sorry, girl, but you know how bad the systems were then."

Does Huntington have the file? she wonders. Why would he tell her to read a file that doesn't exist?

"Can you see if it's in the records of the investigating detective? He's retired now. Albert Chen." She tells the clerk the date of the incident.

Another ten minutes as the clerk digs thorough the archives in the back. Returns with a thick stack representing Chen's activities during that time. Amira thanks her, heads upstairs, reads a lot.

Nothing whatsoever about the death of Jeanie MacArthur. She reads a couple months before and after, just in case it was misfiled. Nothing. She can't decide if this is more suspicious or annoying.

Back to Records. Returns the file.

"Anything else?" The clerk so obviously has nothing better to do.

"How about the files for Detective Mark Owens from that same date?"

The clerk raises an eyebrow. "Owens. The one who's on the run."

"Yeah."

It's possible someone else has that file now, Amira knows, but she wants to check. More minutes pass. The clerk returns with another fat file.

Amira signs it out, thereby creating a traceable record that she accessed Mark's file. Something that could come back to haunt her, she knows. She's taking risks she won't be able to justify later.

Back at her desk, she reads quickly. Three other cops sit at their desks and she worries one of them will drop by, chitchat, ask what she's looking at.

She learns that Mark took bereavement leave for a month, then returned to duty. She goes backward, to the date of Jeanie's death, and there's her case file.

But the case file shouldn't be here. It wasn't Owens's case, yet it got filed with him. A random mistake, because it was his wife?

A coded flash in the file connects to her computer and she sees the images. Shit, Jeanie MacArthur's corpse. The rope still cinched around her neck.

Amira's never asked him if he was the one who found her, but she figured.

Another image of Jeanie's corpse, this time lying on a gurney, the swollen blue neck so different from the chalky pallor everywhere else.

She wonders if this is all in Mark's file because he requested it, read through it, misfiled it. Did he look at all these pictures, read all these findings?

Then she sees why it wasn't filed with Detective Chen: he's not recorded anywhere as the investigating detective.

Peterson is. That's odd, and isn't what he said yesterday.

She reads through more notes, find's the mortician's report, checks stomach and blood analyses. Then she understands.

"Wait a minute. Wait a minute," she says under her breath.

Rereads, feeling dizzy. Surely she's missing something.

Looks through the rest of the file, which is not voluminous. Which is, in fact, way too short. Which also doesn't make sense.

Two other cops laugh about something and she looks up, worried she's been found out. She feels warm under her uniform, sweat rolling down her back.

Huntington was right. Jeanie didn't kill herself.

CHAPTER 30

An audience with Reverend Miriam takes less time than he'd feared.

After a long morning and longer afternoon filled with history lessons, instruction on how to conduct various forms of manual labor without vision, and not-so-subtle hints that it would be best for them to cut off all ties with their friends and family (so he silently gives his sister credit for at least continuing to talk to him), he's eating his second dinner at the commune. The food is announced before the plate is slid in front of him ("chickpeas and curry with brown rice," vegan like yesterday) so at least he knows what to expect before he takes a bite. Tastes better than he'd expected and he wonders if that's due to heightened taste buds, or if they cook better for the newbies. Or if maybe they just eat well here.

Dinner is conducted in silence except for requests to pass condiments. The salt shaker has a braille S and the pepper a braille P. The polite thing to do, he's told, is to gently tap the shoulder of the person next to you before talking. Other than these requests, silence.

It reminds him of the time, many years ago, that his father took him on a weekend retreat to a Catholic monastery. His father had been raised Catholic, like dozens of past generations, but had lapsed. Owens and Sarah had been raised atheist, or agnostic, or whatever the proper term is for the parents not believing and not wanting to bother their kids about it. But after Owens's father had a health scare in his late forties, he began reconnecting with his faith, and tried to get Owens to do the same. You can't really reconnect with something to which you'd never been connected in the first place, Owens pointed out, but his father tried anyway. His father started taking an annual pilgrimage to a monastery in the mountains, and one day, in the summer after graduating high school, Owens was informed that he would be coming too.

He'd been perplexed at first—it sounded like a joke. Hang out at a monastery for two days? During the summer, when there were beach outings to be had and girls to be flirting with? When he realized his father wasn't joking, he'd been angry, tried to refuse. His mother had to intervene, took his side and tried to talk her husband out of it, but Dad somehow won. She told Mark to capitulate, that it was only one weekend out of his life. Think of it as a form of male bonding, she'd told him. Which would have made sense if they'd been going on a fishing weekend or to a basketball tournament or even on a grueling hike. But monks?

He barely spoke to his father for the week beforehand, stewing in resentment.

Then, at the retreat, the damnedest thing happened. He didn't hate it.

Which wasn't the same as saying he actually enjoyed it, he would hasten to add when trying to explain this experience to friends. All the Bible reading wore thin after an hour or so. Even if some of the passages were surprisingly interesting, in a violently epic sort of way (why had no one told him how many wars and slayings and adulterers that book contained?). The yard work, tending to the monastery's extensive grounds, was no worse than what Owens had been doing for spending money the last few summers anyway.

But what he mostly enjoyed were the meals, which were conducted in complete silence. A dozen or so people at a table, half of them monks and half of them guests like him and his father. Head nods or headshakes sufficed when it came to passing around the bread or the other dishes, when offering to pour water.

At first he'd felt overly self-conscious about the sound of his chewing, and he could even hear the elderly stomach growls of the monk sitting beside him. Once he got used to it, though, he found the experience relaxing, almost meditative. No pressure for chitchat, no need for fake politeness or worry about whether he'd pleased his parents or fear that his tempestuous sister would take offense at something he'd said. It made him wish his own family would dine in silence more often. In truth, they hadn't been eating together much in years, as his sports schedules often intervened, as did his mother's occasional nighttime hours at the hospital, and then his social butterfly of a sister, eating at this friend's or that, away so often that it took him longer than it should have for him to realize how hard she was hitting the drugs.

He didn't have many one-on-one interactions with the clergy during that retreat, but he recalls one of them.

Owens was helping cut down invasive shrubs on the outer edge of the property, with his father and one younger monk, and his father had walked back to use the bathroom.

"Is this as terrible as you feared?" the monk asked. Owens doesn't remember his name anymore, only the fact that he was in his twenties and therefore far younger than his fellow brothers. He wore a black T-shirt and had sinewy arms—a regular landscaper, apparently.

"What do you mean?"

The monk smiled. "Your father mentioned he was afraid you wouldn't come."

Embarrassed, Owens had shrugged, made some excuse.

"We aren't such weirdos here." The monk smiled. "Well, not all of us."

He had more of a sense of humor than the others, seemed more identifiably human. Owens asked how long he'd been at the monastery.

"Five years now."

"There don't seem to be many others your age," Owens said as he lopped off the base of a privet.

"It's true. Fewer young men are making the choice I did."

"Does that . . . worry you?" He started digging out the plant's roots.

"Do I worry that religion is dying out? That there are fewer believers with every generation, and there are so many more exciting things young men could be doing with their time?"

Owens stopped digging. "Yeah."

"I do, yes." The young monk's shovel was stuck in the ground, and he leaned his chin atop the handle. "But then I remember all the obstacles and hurdles that our faith has endured, the wars and the dictators who tried to wipe it from the earth. If those didn't succeed, I don't think a wave of indifference will either."

They returned to their digging.

The young monk asked, "I don't suppose you've ever considered a life of service?"

"Not this kind. I've thought about the military, though."

"They always need chaplains."

"I guess."

"But you'd rather fire a gun than hold the Good Book."

"I'm just not sure this is right for me, is all. I just . . ."

"Go on, tell me." The monk smiled. "No judgment."

"I have a hard time believing in something that you can't see, that you can't confirm. That you can't find actual evidence for."

"That's exactly what faith is. The belief in things unseen."

Owens shrugged, feeling awkward, and also guilty for telling a man of the cloth that he wasn't fully with the program.

"We do not look at the things which are seen, but at the things which are unseen," the monk said, and it took a moment for Owens to realize his sudden change in cadence meant he was quoting Scripture. "For the things which are seen are temporal, but the things which are not seen are eternal."

That was it as far as any hard sell. Owens's father returned from the bathroom a moment later, and they resumed their digging, mostly in silence.

Owens wonders how many of those monks might still be alive today. All the elderly ones, he's sure, have passed. But there were a few who were middle-aged then, and of course there was that one young outlier. He wonders how they tolerated The Blinding. Knows that some of the most devout people snapped, refuted their creeds when confronted with such horror; not everyone is cut out to be Job. Giant holes were torn into the spiritual canopy of the world, leaving room for new belief systems to germinate, new congregations to arise, of which Reverend Miriam's little cultivation is just one example.

Still, many people's beliefs only became stronger. Their faith was tested, and they passed. Even though Owens never found religion, he thinks about those monks now and hopes they made it. Hopes that they, in their monastery tucked deep in the woods, were not visited with the violence that broke out so many places. Hopes they overcame the trials and emerged stronger, maybe even risked their safety by helping others, doing the Lord's work to relieve suffering. He doesn't know. He's wondered about it from time to time and thought about looking up the monastery to see if it still exists, but he never has, afraid of the answer.

Sitting at the table after he's finished dinner and is awaiting the chimes that inform them when one activity has ended and another is set to begin, he receives a tap on his shoulder.

"Follow me, please," Sister Lucy says.

Which is easier said than done, of course, but he's learning. He stands slowly, turns completely around so he's facing her, he thinks. Then hears her feet shuffle off, and concentrates on walking at that same pace. Even with his cane, he bumps into someone and they both issue apologies, the other voice sounding particularly embarrassed, so he too must be an acolyte.

"Two steps down," Sister Lucy tells him.

He hears an external door open and he shuffles until his feet reach the threshold, then he takes the two steps, one hand out to catch himself in case he falls.

Cold air on his cheeks and fingers, ravens calling. Are they ravens? Actually, he has no idea. But they sound angry, aggrieved, and he imagines them, large and black, perched on stripped branches overhead.

He tries his best to keep following Sister Lucy, but he feels even more alone than before.

Minutes later he is truly alone—or at least, he thinks he is. Doesn't hear anyone else breathing. Doesn't feel another's heartbeat through the uncomfortable wooden bench on which he sits. Would he be able to, though? Did he become that perceptive during The Blinding? Would Sarah know for certain if she were alone?

This feeling is so alien to him, the cop who always chooses a seat with a view of the main door, who always makes a mental note of the exits. For all he knows, he's sitting in a dungeon. There could be a spike-lined pit three steps before him and he wouldn't realize it until it was too late.

He smells wood, fresh and clean, like the building is newly constructed. Built by the blind? It seems hard to believe, but this group keeps impressing him with their competence and ambition. Despite his years of criticism, it's impossible not to credit what they've accomplished.

Footsteps. More than one person.

A door opens. The footsteps closer now. He's guessing three people, but it could be more. He stands instinctively.

A voice he recognizes says, "You're not Dr. Jensen."

"How do you know that?"

A mild snort, an almost-laugh. Reverend Miriam says, "Well, you certainly don't sound like him."

"But you said that before I'd said anything."

He hears Miriam smile. A crack of the lips. "There are other ways, my son."

Silence. Maybe Miriam expects Owens to marvel at this.

"Shall I escort him out, Reverend?" asks a new voice. Maybe one of the "deacons," as they call themselves, the chosen who help run the place.

In normal conditions, Owens would tell off whoever said that. But he is on their turf and they do seem bewilderingly accomplished at navigating this world blind, so Owens says nothing.

"He's asked to speak with me," Reverend Miriam says, "so he can speak with me."

"Alone," Owens insists. He realizes his face is tensed into a death-stare he would like to aim at whichever deacon spoke earlier, even though he can't do that. Funny how innate his reactions have become, even when they serve no purpose.

Another pause. Tension lingers and Owens wonders if they have some nonverbal, nonvisual way of communicating. Some wavelength indiscernible to him.

"It's all right," Miriam says. "You can leave us."

Owens hears the deacon and at least one other person exit through the same door, he thinks. He isn't entirely sure whether it's just him and Miriam now or if another deacon is silently watching from some threshold.

"Yes, my son?" Miriam asks now that they're maybe alone. "What is it you'd like to discuss?"

"I'm a friend of Dr. Jensen's. I know he came here a few times recently."

"And do you always check up on your friends' movements, Mr. . . . ?"

"I do after they've been murdered."

Miriam takes this in for a moment. Owens wishes he could see her expression.

A ruffle of a sleeve. Maybe Miriam is making a sign of the cross, if they do that here. Maybe she's drawing a weapon, or beckoning a guard.

"I'm very sorry to hear that. That's horrible." Her reaction sounds genuine, if odd, given her flat diction. "But it is a dark world, and so many people remain misguided."

"I hate that I can't see your face right now. I hate that I can't look in your eyes while you talk."

"That's a lot of hate. You seem to be a very angry man. I can understand that. But I had nothing to do with your friend's death."

"Why was he coming here?"

"He wanted to discuss Inner Sight."

"A scientist wanted to discuss Inner Sight?"

"You find that so shocking."

"Yes. It's a myth that you push on poor, pathetic people."

Miriam sighs. Her first sign of impatience, the first hint she won't suffer fools forever. "I know people think that. But I'm not often confronted with it like this. Why are you so angry at me, my son?"

"I'm not your son. I had parents; they died in The Blinding. My sister couldn't handle it, so she gave up her life and came here. Other people may just laugh at you, but I take you more seriously."

"Dr. Jensen came to me because he said he could restore sight without using those horrible devices. He went on and on about rays and retinas, things a humble soul like myself doesn't care to understand. I'm just a woman who works with her hands."

"But not always. Not before."

Then she chuckles. "True. I used to be what they call a digital project manager, working on wireless systems, apps, 'the Internet of things.' Unknowingly laying the groundwork for their sordid designs."

"So what happened after you met Dr. Jensen?"

"He seemed a decent fellow. He was motivated by what he thought were good intentions. But he assumed I would want to work with him, that the people here would volunteer for his experiments. He was wrong."

"Because you don't want your people to see. If we could all see again like before, your little fiefdom would have no reason to exist. You want these people to stay blind and be your little slaves."

"No." Bordering on angry. *Good. She can be riled.* "I want them to seek the vision that lies in themselves." She says this slowly, like reciting bullet points, a corporate mission statement. "Vision of greater things than the commerce and sin the world surrounds them with. The Blinding, terrible as it was, served a purpose. It allowed us to step back from a deceitful, materialist, immoral world. If someone like Dr. Jensen does indeed find a way to restore vision, that would not be a 'medical miracle,' as he dared call it to me. It would be a spiritual disaster."

The floor creaks to Owens's left.

They're not alone.

"The Blinding was so terrible that people have forgotten how bad things were right *before* The Blinding. Today's inequalities didn't come from The Blinding—they were already entrenched. Constant wars, rampant poverty, racism and sectarianism dividing society into smaller and smaller groups that the elite could control. Environmental catastrophe, even before all The Blinding's fires." She pauses. "Restoring vision, even if it were possible, would only reset us on that awful path. But we believe there is a better way."

Owens wonders how close the others are. He raises his hands slightly as if to ward off a blow. Which he wouldn't see coming anyway.

"What better way? Staying out here suffering in The Darkness while they donate their life savings to you? How much money have you leeched off them? How many homes have you sold from under their feet?"

"I'm sorry to hear you believe those stories."

Another creak of floorboards. Someone is lingering only a few feet away. Maybe there are more of them. Maybe he's surrounded.

Maybe that's why Miriam sounds so confident as she says, "I think it would be best if you returned to the world you so clearly prefer."

A hand on Owens's left forearm. Gripping him, trying to pull him. Owens angrily shakes the hand off and pushes back at someone he can't see. Then more hands grasp his shoulders from behind.

"Get your hands off me," Owens snaps, turning toward them.

"Please stay calm," Miriam says.

Owens moves to the side a step, and the back of his right foot strikes something or someone. He turns again and something very hard hits him in the side of the head.

He's on the floor, his body partly numb. Unsure if this is a second later or if more time has passed. Blinking despite the darkness, as if he could somehow concentrate his way out of this, burn a hole of vision into the world through sheer anger.

He hears Miriam saying, "Remove the unbeliever, please," as another blow comes and he loses consciousness.

CHAPTER 31

It's late when Jeffrey Huntington finally makes his way into his apartment.

He lives in a narrow row house just south of downtown, a long enough walk and through unsavory enough neighborhoods that he doesn't head into work on foot as much as he should. Getting older, needs more exercise. He'd once expected to become one of those obnoxiously healthy middle-aged men who walked or even biked to their offices, but it hasn't worked out that way. He usually works till late at night, when the only people out on the street are the sorts his colleagues will be processing soon.

Except few cops truly think of him as their *colleague*. To them, he's an enemy.

When he was younger, new to the force, he'd never imagined he'd one day work Internal Affairs. He, like his fellow officers, thought of IA staff as traitors, heretics, cowards. What kind of person chooses to become a cop, then later chooses to investigate cops from the inside? Who would make that choice?

He hadn't made it, actually. He'd been assigned here after a reorganization, mainly because he'd proven his legal chops and strong stomach on a dicey case that had involved going after a crooked prosecutor. He hadn't wanted the job, but it was a promotion, and his superiors all but blackmailed him into it, telling him he'd get the worst imaginable beat if he stayed on the regular force.

His initial aversion to working IA faded, more quickly than he ever would have imagined, the more he realized just how many truly heinous cops worked in the Department.

He'd encountered his share of bad apples and done his part to remove them. But he's had to go up against *so many* that he's begun to accept the fact that the orchard itself is bad, the very soil poisoned. In his worst moments, he fears that means that even *he's* bad, and he's fighting a losing battle against a system that's corrupting him too.

The Owens case bothers him. Not because he doubts himself—Owens is clearly unhinged and needs to be warehoused, fast—but because he knows Owens has so many allies. Amira Quigley, obviously, as they're an item, but also Jimmy Peterson. Owens's big partner worries Huntington; he didn't like seeing Peterson show up at Owens's apartment like that and has passed word about it to their superior, Captain Carlyle, in hopes of some discipline or at least a warning, a reminder not to interfere in an IA investigation. It makes him wonder what else Peterson or Quigley might do to cause trouble.

He's thinking this as he opens the door into his apartment. It's a sad bachelor's pad, only three pieces of furniture in the main room, two chairs and a long sofa, not counting the liquor cabinet.

Step inside, drop briefcase on side table, walk up to kitchenette, remove small-of-back holster and gun, place on counter.

Only at the end of that routine does he look up and realize someone's sitting in his living room.

On the sofa is a black blur.

Huntington freezes. His other senses belatedly warn him: a hint of cologne or maybe skin lotion. The faint sound of breathing. The hair at the back of his neck standing on end.

This cannot be possible, yet it's what his brain tells him he's seeing. He's so stunned and confused that he doesn't even realize yet that this might mean Owens isn't so crazy.

But he's not thinking of Owens or his various cases. His thoughts are solely about himself and how much danger he's in.

"Hello," a voice says. Barely above a whisper.

Huntington's gun sits on the counter, three steps behind him. The black blur reads his thoughts, and Huntington hears a faint click of a safety being flicked off.

"If you make a move for that gun, I assure you, you won't make it in time."

His bedroom door is closed, which, he realizes, isn't how he left it. Now it opens, and out of the bedroom walks a second black blur.

Followed by a third.

"Whoever you are, you're making a mistake," he says, forcing some authority into his voice. "I'm police."

"We know who you are, Detective Huntington," the second blur says. He (and Huntington is confident it's a *he*; he has a sense of the gender, and the height—6 feet—but that's it) reaches for a bottle of bourbon from Huntington's shelf. When he touches the bottle, the bottle too becomes blacked out. Even the liquid that cascades from it as he pours seems blacked out, and as the bourbon hits the glass, that too goes dark.

The blur stops pouring and the glass reappears on the counter as if by magic. He puts the bottle down, then it too reappears. Next he picks up the glass, which goes black again, and based on his movement it seems that he's drinking it.

After a few seconds, the arm moves down and the blur says, "It's amazing technology, isn't it?"

"Who are you?"

The first blur stays on the sofa. The third has walked over a bit to Huntington's left. He knows the first one is holding a gun from the sound of the safety, but it's impossible to tell if the others are too. The blackness extends beyond the narrow confines of human shapes to a hazy bit of space just beyond. Huntington doesn't discern fingertips, just a wide darkness at the end of their arms. He wonders if that vagueness is deliberate, for the express purpose of concealing weapons.

The second blur, with the bourbon, pours another glass. Steps closer. The arm extends, and, though it takes an extra moment for Huntington to interpret the signals with this other person shrouded in darkness, and no facial expression to read, he realizes the man is offering him the second glass.

"No, thank you. I said, 'Who are you'?"

"It must be quite the mind-fuck to not be able to see us," a different one says. The one who'd been offering Huntington the glass steps back, apparently realizing he won't take it. "Would bother anyone. But you especially, huh?"

"What do you mean?" *Just keep them talking,* he thinks. The longer they chat, the better his odds of figuring out an escape.

"IA guys like you. On loan to the Truth Commission. Your whole mantra is to shed light on what happened during The Blinding, right? All that bullshit. So it must drive you mad to face something you can't shed light on."

IA guys? Wait—the only people who talk like that are cops.

"It's not bullshit," he says, his mind working double overtime, trying to understand while hoping to prolong the conversation. "Citizens deserve to know what went on when they couldn't see. What laws might have been broken by the people who were supposed to be protecting them."

"All the Truth Commission will really do is tear this country apart. Turn citizens against us. Maybe some cops bent some rules back then, but we held the damn society together. And prissy little weaklings like you want to tear it down because you don't have the stomach for what we had to do then."

"And what we have to do now," another one says.

Huntington shifts his gaze from one to the other to other, quickly, as if he might get his vidder to overcome whatever trickery they're using and he'll finally see one of their faces, but it doesn't work.

"So which one of you is Owens?" he asks.

Laughter. "He's not with us. But we appreciate the distraction you created. Honestly, we hadn't planned on killing you quite yet—it'll be easier to wipe out all you Truth Commission assholes later—but this will be easy to pin on him. So, we figured, why wait?"

Huntington isn't even sure which one of them shoots him.

CHAPTER 32

Owens has the dream again, the one that comes and goes and ruins whatever day he's waking into.

"I killed her, I killed her."

Kneeling on the floor of Jeanie's studio, stunned at what he'd done.

"I killed her. I killed her."

Even after two years, he thinks about all the ways he could have changed things. The nights he could have listened to her more. The mornings he could have started differently. The tone of voice he could have modulated. The small acts he didn't feel capable of making, or even willing to attempt.

When Jeanie talked to him about her problems, it always felt to him that she was complaining. He only realized after she was gone that she was asking to be heard, and maybe be helped, but at the time he hadn't felt capable of either. His job was nearly killing him, sometimes literally. At home he was exhausted, medicating with booze, sleeping terribly. And then to hear her, an artist—someone who was financially supported by others' largesse and could more or less do whatever she wanted with her time, someone who did not hold other people's lives in her hands—to hear her talk about how difficult her art had become just about broke him.

"I just feel like . . . I can't see," she said one night.

She'd said this before and usually he'd murmur something vaguely sympathetic, but this time he wasn't able to.

"What does that even mean? You can see again, we all can." He'd had maybe two drinks at that point, was working on his third. Had gotten home from work an hour ago, to the apartment where she was staring at two vexing canvases she'd recently brought over from her studio. They'd both been drinking too much at the time, but she was sober that night.

"But it doesn't feel real." She spoke to him while staring at the canvases. "The nuance isn't there. The . . . life."

He'd shaken his head.

They'd been bickering more lately. The Blinding had broken many couples, yet it had bound them together. Not having children to protect and watch over had made things slightly easier. Whenever either of them had been nearing a breakdown, they'd been helped to stay afloat by the other. So why was it now, after vidders had returned life to some semblance of normal, that they were arguing so much? Maybe they were too different after all, their careers from separate universes, their expectations and visions never aligned.

She said, "I just feel like work has become . . . impossible. And pointless. I don't think I can do it anymore."

"Jeanie . . . I'm sorry, but yes, you can do it." He knew he sounded dismissive, rude, but he couldn't stop himself in time.

"You make it sound so easy, Mark. It's not."

"It's a hell of a lot easier than some other things. I mean, Jesus, today I arrested a teenager who killed his parents. And two nights ago someone shot a fourth grader in the head." He motioned to her canvases. "And *you're* complaining about *this* bullshit?"

"Excuse me?"

He'd never said anything like that before. He'd always encouraged her to keep pushing, reminding her that her best work often came after periods of despair. He'd always served as the anchor on her tempestuous seas. Tonight, though, he couldn't muster the strength.

"I know it's been hard for you, but, fuck, it's hard for everyone.

At least you get to do something you supposedly love. No one dies if you fuck up."

"Jesus Christ, Mark."

"Sorry, I'm just not in the headspace to hear about how hard it is for you to sit in a room and do whatever the hell you want while the world is still burning around us and I'm stuck holding a busted fire hose."

"Yeah, you're such a martyr."

"At least I don't bring you my complaints after every shift."

"Well, maybe you should! Maybe you need to not be all bottled up all the time. Maybe talking about what you're dealing with every day might be a very good idea!"

He shook his head. Hated how the conversation had turned to him and his alleged problems, when she was the one who'd started this.

"Or maybe *you*," he said, grabbing his keys, "need to snap out of your funk and either do the work or don't do the work, but stop all this debating about whether you *can*. You *talk* about your work about ten times more than you do it these days. So pretend you have no choice, Jeanie. Just pretend you have no choice and do the fucking work."

He knew she was staring at him in shock, so before he'd have to deal with the fallout, he told her he was taking a walk to clear his head.

When he returned to the apartment an hour later, she was gone. She'd left a curt note telling him she'd be at her studio working and would spend the night there. She'd done that before when on binges of productivity, working herself to exhaustion, but this time was different, he knew. She was avoiding him. Maybe leaving him. He'd been an asshole and he knew it, but he didn't want to apologize. She'd been moping for too long; she needed a metaphorical kick in the ass to get herself going again.

That's what he told himself.

He didn't know that he would never speak to her again. That another full day would pass with no messages from her, no return texts. He traced her phone to her studio, figured she was just working, in a zone, not wanting to be disturbed. She'd taken his tough love to heart. But he worried. Maybe it was something else.

He called, again and again. *Just text back that you're okay.* Nothing.

Finally he visited her studio, during a work shift, after nearly forty-eight hours had passed. And that's when he saw what she'd done. What he'd done.

CHAPTER 33

Owens wakes from the dream to roosters, the clucking of squirrels, a massive headache.

He feels a stabbing in his neck as he tries to orient himself. He'd been half lying, half sitting, his head leaning against something hard and cold. He shivers and as he tries to sit up he realizes his hands aren't working right. They're bound in front of him, wrists crossed. He struggles a bit, but the binding—rope and not a zip tie, he's pretty sure—is secure.

"Hello?" he asks. No reply.

He's on some sort of upholstered bench. There's another one in front of him. He stands up and hits his head against a ceiling, metal. He swears, shuffles to the side. Trying to get his bearings. Where is he? His steps don't exactly echo, but they tell him he's in an enclosed space. The animals outside feel close.

Deep breath. Smells old industrial plastic, the ghost of exhaust. He's on a parked bus.

He slowly walks forward, wondering if there's any way he could open the door blind. Bus drivers control the door, but he doesn't even know what that control looks like, let alone feels like. Is it a button? A handle? He's nearly reached the front, he thinks, when he hears the door open.

Confident footsteps, bounding up the stairs right up to him.

He asks, "Who's there?

"Shh. Cool off, cop. They'll hear."

Lance. The former drug-dealing pimp turned acolyte of Reverend Miriam.

"What's going on?" Owens asks.

"Look, I'm not supposed to be here." Funny how even the blind use the term *look* like that. "I heard you'd caused a ruckus and they were going to send you back. Driver's gonna be here in a few minutes. You want to go back to the city, or not?"

"Not yet."

"Here, I'll let you out."

"They tied up my hands."

He feels Lance's hands on his chest, then on his wrists.

"I can cut this off." Owens hears a knife unsheathed. Tenses his arms, pulls back.

"Don't."

"What, you're afraid I'll slice open a vein or something?"

"Yes, exactly."

"Stay tied up if you want, then." A mocking laugh. "You sighted don't get it. After a while without a vidder, you'd be amazed at how well you can get by."

"Fine, do it." He offers up his wrists. "Careful": a command, a request, a sign of his helplessness.

Owens feels a tug and hears the sawing as Lance cuts the ropes one at a time. Feels the ropes fall off, waits a moment for Lance to pull back the knife before he finally moves his hands, free. He flexes his fingers, lets the blood flow again.

A small part of him is still bracing to be stabbed at any moment.

"Why are you helping me?"

"I'm sort of wondering that myself." A pause. "You said you were going to find who killed my friend. You mean that?"

"Yes."

"Then I'm giving you a chance to do what you say. I got put away for that. You find the son of a bitch that really did it and . . . It won't make us square, but . . . maybe it'll help my nightmares go away."

"I'm going to find them." Though, in truth, he's not much closer than he was the last time he talked to Lance.

"What were you doing bothering the Reverend?"

"I thought she might have information on a murder. And maybe I still think it, but she's not talking."

"The black blurs? Why would she have anything to do with that? She's a good person."

"No offense to your dear leader, but I had to check it out. Now I want to get back to the real world, but not on this bus. And with a vidder."

"I thought you said the vidders are how they go after you."

He stops for a moment, thinking. Now that this long quest to get an audience with Miriam is over, he's desperate to see again. Exhausted by blindness. But Lance is right—to have a vidder right now is to be at their mercy. Whoever *they* are.

"I've been thinking," Lance says. "What they did to me, and what they did to you too. If they can make themselves go dark to kill someone right in front of you, what else can they do? Can they make us hallucinate, see crazy shit?"

Owens has wondered this too. Blake Hinners had said the more times they manipulated vidders, the better they'd get. Iterating their way toward complete control. If they can make him see black blurs, and if vidders can now manipulate appearances, how does he know they can't do even more? Make him see people who aren't there, change what he sees, trick him into walking off a cliff or something. He doesn't understand the science of it, but betting that anything is beyond their abilities would not be a wise move.

These are the kind of mind-control fears he had always written off as the ravings of antigovernment lunatics. But the lunatics' hunches have been confirmed lately.

"There's another way. Where can I get a phone?"

Amira should be sleeping but she's not. She's tried every conceivable position, used three different pillows, and her white noise machine is useless. She actually did manage to get some sleep here and there, but then she dreamed of Jeanie's dead body, of Mark in handcuffs.

Her phone rings. Not yet eight in the morning, a time she'd normally still be sleeping off a shift. She grabs the phone from the bedside table, her head still on the pillow.

She doesn't recognize the number.

"Quigley."

"I wake you up, sweetie?"

She sits bolt upright. "Mark! Are you all right?"

"I'm fine. You believe what they're saying about me?"

"Of course not." Maybe. "Where are you?"

"Let me tell you later."

"You don't trust me?"

"I do. But I don't trust that someone isn't listening. Call me back from a burner. Somewhere outside."

She agrees, hangs up. Writes the number down on a scrap of paper, throws on some clothes and a baseball cap. Reaches into her closet, the old dresser there, the bottom drawer, where she keeps old electronics and other junk, and takes out one of her burners. Advice from one of her first mentors: own an extra phone, something that can't be traced, just in case.

A voice in the back of her head screams: *You're assisting a fugitive.* Her boyfriend is in a world of trouble, maybe deservingly. She didn't bail her sister out when Daniella got in a bind, but she's doing it for Mark. Still not sure which decision is right.

She leaves her real phone in the apartment, then heads out. Hallway, elevator, lobby, sidewalk. Gives herself a block, makes sure no one is following her or loitering too close by.

Technically, she knows she can be tracked by her vidder, but she's not on the run, and she knows the Department wouldn't be able to get a warrant to track her.

But if she aids and abets Owens, then eventually they *will* be able to do that.

She calls and he picks up on the first ring.

"Yes?" he asks.

"It's me, and I'm alone." Technically, she's broken the law just by calling him back.

"I'm sorry to put this on you. But I need you to go to a place called Cortex Vortex on Fourth and ask for a guy named Hinners. He owes me a favor. I need him to get me a black-market vidder."

Possession of a black-market vidder would get her fired, or worse.

"Mark, are you really sure that's a good idea?"

"It's the least bad idea I've been able to figure out."

There's more she wants to ask him, and more she wants to tell him, but she knows this isn't the time. Not yet.

She'll put it to him in person. Then she'll know, from how he reacts. She tells herself this. Believes that she'll finally be able to answer the questions when she sees him again.

He tells her, "And I need you to pull all the files on the Leila and Nayles murders."

Another bad idea. But she's gone this far. Or has she? She could still hang up. Tell him no, tell him to turn himself in. That he's only making it worse.

She considers this, for a full two seconds. She imagines Daniella in her cell, the vacant stare. The thought of Daniella turning off her vidder, withdrawing ever further from a world that proved to be too much for her.

She tells him she'll do whatever he needs, and it feels a bit like the sidewalk is opening, that she's slipping into something that won't let her out.

CHAPTER 34

It's come to this: Owens on a stakeout, blind. Using the security guard rent-a-cop as his eyes.

They crouch on the small hill that, if Owens remembers correctly, sits about two hundred yards beyond the guard post. A different guard is on duty at the moment; Owens was able to bribe this one away when his shift ended, offering him promises to put in a good word with the force if the kid does what he says.

Owens waits there in his own private darkness while the kid security guard, whose name is Marshall, watches the post.

"There's a car coming," Marshall says. "Sedan, I think."

Two seconds later and Owens can hear it approach.

"Squad car?"

"No. A silver hatchback."

"That's her. Anyone following?"

The kid takes a couple seconds to double-check. "No."

Owens has little choice but to trust what Marshall says. He has no reason to think the excited kid is anything less than honest, but he hopes this isn't a mistake.

"She's talking to the other guard," Marshall recaps. She's far enough away that Owens can't hear her voice, though he wishes he could. It feels like it's been weeks.

"They let her through." Five seconds pass. "She's headed to Sarah Owens's place."

"Let's go."

They stand and walk, Owens with a hand on Marshall's shoulder. Twice he steps into depressions in the ground and nearly stumbles. Then the kid stops.

"Wait. Another car's coming."

"Let's go, faster."

It takes only a second for Amira to fully take in Sarah's spartan dwelling. A small, undecorated parlor, walls gray and bare. Small windows open for the cross breeze but not the view, obviously.

Sarah and her fiancé, Kendrick, stand in front of Amira. Kendrick is an inch or two shorter than Sarah, with the same bad haircut, the same short length as those of other acolytes Amira has seen on street corners. She's never been here before and feels distinctly uncomfortable. These people are just *odd*, and they outnumber her.

Amira holds a small box in the crook of her elbow. Inside it is the black-market vidder she managed to buy off Hinners.

"I've heard a lot about you," Amira tells Sarah, which isn't true. Mark hasn't gone into much detail about his family, only that his parents died in a fire and that his sister lives here. Neither of which are subjects he enjoys discussing. "Good things, of course."

"I find that hard to believe," Sarah says. She had invited Amira in, but she seems something less than friendly. "What brings you here?"

Amira hears the sound of another car pulling up. She walks over to the small front window and sees a sedan, with Magnus and O'Dell. *Shit.*

She had taken a circuitous route, had told no one she was coming. Even left her phone at home. They'd tracked her vidder, must have. Which they shouldn't be able to do without a warrant.

Kendrick detects their presence and says, "Someone else is here."

Amira puts the box on the floor. She removes her gun from her small-of-the-back holster, feeds a round into the chamber.

"What's going on?" Sarah asks. She heard the gun.

Amira stashes her gun back into the holster. She turns and sees that Sarah has reached for Kendrick's hand.

"Stay inside," Amira tells them.

Magnus and O'Dell are emerging from their car as Amira steps out to meet them.

Owens and Marshall sneak in through Sarah's back door. Crouching low so they can't be seen through the small windows, they enter the front parlor.

"Who's there?" Sarah asks.

"Hey, Sis," he whispers. "Got a package for me by any chance?"

"Mark? What's going on?"

Owens asks the kid if he sees a box or bag anywhere, and Marshall says yes.

"That's the vidder for me. Pick it up."

He hears Marshall walk toward the box, then hears Kendrick step in his way.

"We don't believe in those."

"We can debate your philosophy after we're safe," Owens tells him.

"Mark," Sarah says, and he can hear her gritted teeth. "How many times do I have to say it? This is my house, and I won't have that here."

"Sarah, there are two men out there and they're wearing vidders too, and they're going to use them to kill all of us." He wishes he could look her in the eye, convey the dire importance here. "I can help us, but only if I'm fighting on a level playing field. I'm begging you, this once."

Owens hears footsteps again, Marshall saying, "Thank you."

"The rest of you should get in a back room and stay low," Owens says as Marshall hands him the vidder. Owens affixes it to his temple. "New ones take a couple minutes. You're still my eyes, kid."

They can hear through the open window that the conversation outside is getting heated.

"You have no jurisdiction in the communes," Amira tells the feds.

"Officer," O'Dell says, "you tell us where Owens is now, or we arrest you for aiding and abetting."

"Any guns drawn out there?" Owens asks Marshall in a whisper.

"No, but the two men are packing. Shoulder holsters, jackets are open. She has a gun in her rear holster, too."

"Let's go. Train your gun on the younger one."

Amira had been standing perpendicular to the door, so she sees it open as the young security guard steps out, his weapon pointing at the feds. Owens is right behind him, a hand on the guard's shoulder.

"Freeze!" the guard yells. "Put your hands in the air!"

He does not sound very convincing. His voice shakes.

The agents hold their palms out, not terribly high. Unnerved by the gun, certainly, but it's clear to the real professionals here that this kid is in over his head.

"You're pointing your gun at federal agents," O'Dell tells him.

"You need to put that down, now," Magnus says.

"Don't listen to them," Owens barks with every bit as much authority as the two agents.

"Whoa," the kid whines, "this is above my pay grade, man. They're *feds*?"

Amira takes a hesitant step toward Owens. "Mark, maybe we should all talk this out."

"They're *not* feds, they're murderers," he tells the guard. "Keep your gun on them."

"Don't listen to him," O'Dell commands. "This man is a fugitive and he's trying to pull you in with him. If you don't put that gun down now, you're aiding a fugitive and *you'll* be going to jail with him."

"They're lying," Owens insists. Then addressing the 'feds,' says, "Both of you, lie on the ground with your hands behind your heads."

"You're not in charge here," O'Dell says.

Magnus tries a reasoning-with-you tone: "Owens, are you trying to get your girlfriend sent to jail, too? And this guy? You need to calm down and realize you're making this worse not just for you but for other people, too."

"O'Dell shot Dr. Leila in her apartment and ran through the alley," Owens counters. "He blurred his appearance to me, but he didn't think of reflections. He ran by a few windows, and I saw him in them."

Amira sees it: O'Dell is betrayed by his reaction. He glances quickly at his partner, surprised.

Then he puts his game face back on. "I don't know what you're talking about."

She is tense and scared but also feels an undeniable relief, a warm sensation trickling out to her fingers: Owens isn't crazy.

Behind Owens and the young security guard, Sarah steps out of her house, disobeying the one order Amira gave her.

"Mark, what's happening?

Distracted, Marshall turns halfway to get a look at her.

O'Dell takes advantage of that one tiny moment. Draws his weapon and fires at Marshall, who takes it in the chest. He spins halfway around as he falls.

Amira draws her weapon too, and because O'Dell has shifted his aim toward her now, she shoots him twice without hesitation, center mass, like she's been trained.

Magnus ducks behind his car and fires a shot their way as he retreats. The round doesn't hit her, and, she hopes, doesn't hit anyone else.

Then chaos.

Sarah retreats inside, the door slamming shut behind her but popping open again because she'd swung it too hard. Amira follows, moving backward so she can keep her gun pointed toward the car Magnus hid behind. She ducks into the house's doorway for cover, shooting at the car twice before pulling back to think.

* * *

Owens drops to the ground, blindly searching the fallen commune guard's body, trying to find his gun. Thanks to his contraband vidder he can see a dark fuzz now, grainy and gray. Two lighter forms in the center: his hands. Vision returning, slowly.

His hands find clothing, warm wetness. Marshall's skin. A forearm. Then hands. The gun.

He grabs it and turns to face Magnus's car, but he can't see that far yet.

Hears another shot, from behind him. Then the sound of a body falling. A groan of pain. From a man.

A footstep to his left. He turns and points his gun and is about to pull the trigger when Amira shouts, "Hold your fire, Mark!"

He hears Amira step out of the house, proceeding cautiously. She holds Owens back with one hand, then walks past him. He hears her kick a gun away.

Finally the pixelations resolve themselves and like *that* Owens again has vision. *Hallelujah and praise Kai Ballantine, may he rest in peace.*

He sees Magnus lying on his back, dark red soaking his left shoulder. It was his gun Amira kicked out of reach.

Owens also sees the fallen O'Dell, only a few feet away. He's choking, near death. Owens reaches down and grabs the so-called fed's gun. Amira's rounds had hit O'Dell square in the chest. Blood on his chin. Owens crouches beside him.

"Who else is involved in this? Who are your inside guys, the tech people?"

O'Dell's face contorted with pain, and something else. Like he's actually trying to smile.

"You'll find out . . . tomorrow."

The struggle ceases and his body slackens. His sightless eyes stare at the dark sky and stop moving.

Owens checks O'Dell's pockets, finds his phone. He gets up and approaches Magnus, who sits on the ground now, leaning against his car, his teeth gritted in pain. Amira stands a few feet away, gun still pointed at him.

"Talk," Owens tells him.

"Fuck you both! Quigley, you've let this nut drag you down with him. You just killed a federal officer."

"Stop trying to play us!" she shouts back at him. "I saw his face when Owens called him out about the reflections. You hadn't thought of that."

"I don't know . . . what you're talking about."

"You almost got away with it," Owens tells him. "What did O'Dell mean about tomorrow? The more you talk now, the better it'll go for you. I'm tired of cleaning up your bodies."

"I'm not dirty, goddamn it!" Magnus spits as he says that. He's in pain and really, really mad. "O'Dell . . . Fuck, we've only been partners two months. If he was into something . . . *I don't fucking know about it.*"

More movement and Owens sees, slightly out of focus due to the distance, a crowd of commune dwellers. They've emerged from their homes, lingering in a large semicircle. In their midst stands Reverend Miriam, flanked by four deacons.

"This man needs medical attention," Owens calls out.

"From a doctor who can *see*, please," Magnus clarifies.

Sarah has left the house again. She walks toward Mark. She knows the way from the sound of his voice but doesn't realize Marshall's body is lying in her path. She steps on his knee and she recoils, jumps back. Slowly, hesitantly, she finds a new path toward her brother.

"What are you doing, Mark? What's happening?"

He remembers how sure-footed she's always been here, sees how uncertain she is now. He's done this, brought the confusion and danger of the sighted world from which she'd tried to escape.

"I'm sorry, Sarah. For all of this."

"You're safe now," Amira tells her. Owens wishes that were true.

And wishes that he had a clue as to how he'll explain any of this to Sarah.

So he dodges her question for now and looks down at Magnus. He asks, "If you want us to give you the benefit of the doubt, start telling us everything you know about your partner."

PART FOUR

OBSCURA

CHAPTER 35

At Central Plaza downtown, workers busily toil through the night, erecting a large stage and speakers. The homeless have already been kicked out of the park, the food stalls told to move elsewhere. Big day tomorrow: the President is coming.

The six streets that enter the Plaza have all been barricaded. To-morrow large screens will rise on three sides, partly so names of the lost can be projected there and partly so that no disgruntled citizen in a nearby skyscraper will have a clear shot at the President during his big speech.

Cops everywhere. Squad cars and trucks and wagons. Soon heli-copters will join the fun. The nearest subway stops have been closed, the trash cans removed.

One of the construction workers, crouched low on the newly con-structed wooden steps leading to the stage, finishes with his nail gun and looks up. Sees, walking down the street, the shape of a person he cannot quite make out. Like a black blur.

It turns a corner and is gone.

The worker adjusts his vidder and shakes his head.

Adrenaline still coursing through their veins, Owens and Amira stand by her car, the driver's door open. They've pulled the car's computer out, and it hangs before them on a long arm.

"I don't have much time," Owens says, motioning to his new

vidder. "I'm going to have to take this off before they figure out how to track me with it."

"They can track me, too," Amira realizes. "If they know I'm with you."

Before he can even explain what he's trying to look for on her computer, she steps in his way.

"Mark, wait. We need to talk."

"All I know is, someone killed Dr. Jensen because he was trying to cure blindness, which would make vidders worthless. He was here to try to recruit subjects, but Reverend Miriam turned him down."

"So someone with EyeTech killed him, to protect vidders?"

"Maybe. Or someone in intelligence. Ballantine told me the CIA commissioned research on this through that company, Obscura Technologies."

"Yeah, but all I could find on them was the report from when the owner jumped off the Steve Jobs Bridge. Don't you remember?"

He doesn't understand. "Why would I remember?"

She folds her arms. Watching him very carefully. "You and Peterson were the investigators."

"What?"

"Enough bullshit, Mark! I've put myself on the line enough here—I just shot a *fed*. What the hell is going on?"

He takes a breath, holds up both hands. "I've investigated some bridge suicides, but none there. When was this?"

"Two years ago. November thirteenth."

He thinks. So confused. Plenty of little jobs and cases you forget, but suicide by bridge he'd remember. Wouldn't he?

"I did not investigate that, I swear. I'd never even heard of Obscura until Ballantine mentioned it the other day."

She's staring him down. He's not sure if she trusts him anymore. She seems to be deciding this herself.

"And Jeanie," she says. "The death report on Jeanie."

A sick feeling in his stomach. He feels something coming, is dizzy already. His voice comes out smaller: "What about Jeanie?"

"You never read it?"

He can only shake his head no. Why would he have read it? He was there.

"Mark."

Finally he manages to speak. "I didn't need to read it. I found her. Why?"

She had been staring at him, as if afraid of finding something there, but now her eyes soften. "There were way too many sedatives in her system. Already metabolized. They'd hit her stomach two or three hours before her death."

She pauses, lets him process this.

"She never could have hung herself, Mark. She would have been unconscious by then. But it got filed as suicide anyway."

The dizziness spreads. Stomach, head, fingertips. He makes fists to ward it off. Paces as if he can hold himself in place, stop the earth from turning.

She continues, "That's why Huntington was after you: he looked into it years later and knew it was all wrong. You know who signed off on the report?"

He can only shake his head.

"Jimmy Peterson," she says.

It's like someone's punching him in the stomach again, and again, and again.

"You really never saw the lab report?"

"*No.*" His voice a whisper. "Jimmy . . . he said he'd review it for me. He told me about it. He . . ." He finally accepts it. "He lied to me about it. He didn't say anything about sedatives. Are you sure? Could he have just . . . missed something?"

"No." She recites the numbers, and he knows she's right. "Huntington must have figured Jimmy filed it as a suicide to cover for you. Or that maybe you forged Jimmy's signature, and *you* were the one who somehow buried the tox reports."

The sick feeling only gets worse. He has to close his mouth for a moment, concentrate on breathing through his nose.

"I didn't know anything about this, Amira," he finally says, "Jimmy was not . . . *covering* for me."

"I've been breaking this down every possible way, and there are only two options based on that car-crash of a file. Either Mark Owens killed her and covered it up . . . or Jimmy Peterson did."

He looks up at the black sky. "Maybe he . . ." He's grasping, he knows this. "Maybe he only *thought* I did it, so he covered it up to have my back? But really, someone else . . . killed her?" It's hard to squeeze out those last two words.

"Mark, has he acted like he thinks you killed your wife?"

How has he not seen this before? His partner was his blind spot.

"There's more." She speaks slowly now, aware that she's overwhelming him. "I asked him about Jeanie's death yesterday. He defended you and claimed some other detective had investigated it, a guy who retired later and died of cancer. Someone he knew I wouldn't be able to question. So he lied about that, to cover his tracks and keep me off his trail." She takes a breath. "He didn't want me to figure out that he'd been the one."

No other explanation makes sense. If Jeanie was that sedated, someone else had to have hung her. If there had been some other killer, Jimmy would have launched an investigation to find them, would have told Mark about the toxicology reports.

After a pause, she voices what he's thinking: "I think it was Jimmy who did that to her. I just don't know why."

They talk it through for another ten minutes, comparing notes, figuring out where their memories align.

In the last twenty-four hours, she's looked into whatever files on Peterson she could without tripping any alarms. He'd been on a joint task force with the FBI a few years ago, and apparently one of the task force leads had been Agent O'Dell. Didn't necessarily mean anything, but the other day, when the feds had come to arrest Owens, Peterson and O'Dell had acted like they didn't know each other.

The night Dr. Leila was killed by a black blur, Owens recalls, Jimmy had done his best to keep Owens away from her, stay at the bar with him and drink the night away. All to make it easier for his accomplices to kill her. They didn't want Owens to be near her apartment; maybe Jimmy tried to tell O'Dell to abort, but O'Dell figured he could do it anyway, that if he was redacted from view, it wouldn't matter if Owens was nearby.

And Amira tells him the police records show that Owens was the one who'd requested Nayles be brought to the station the other day, but Jimmy could have made that happen too, could have used Owens's police code so that the digital bread crumbs led back to Owens, not him. And why Nayles? Something about that case, moving all those weapons.

Jimmy had made all along like he didn't quite believe Owens about the black blurs. Hadn't defended him the way a partner should. At the time, Owens thought that was just because *no one* believed the black blurs were real, but no—it was because Jimmy *knew* they were real but needed to marginalize Owens, needed to prevent anyone else from truly investigating that angle.

Jesus Christ, he realizes. Whatever Jimmy's into, it's more than just Jeanie. It's the black blurs too.

And then the console hooked up to Amira's car rings. Peterson's calling her.

Owens steps toward the car.

"No, don't answer it," Amira tells him.

He ignores her and hits a button. A 2D hologram of Peterson's face appears.

"Amira, you okay? What's going on?"

Peterson's expression changes when he realizes it's Owens he's looking at.

"Hey, Jimmy." Owens's voice hollowed out. The shock of so many revelations.

"Mark! She found you, thank God! Where are you?"

Peterson will know the answer to that in seconds if Owens prolongs this.

He tries to say something, but his voice just isn't there. He tries again. "Tell me about Jeanie, partner."

"What? What about her?"

Owens steps so close to the hologram of Peterson's face that their noses practically touch.

"Why, Jimmy?"

"I don't . . . I don't know what you're talking about, Mark."

"She'd learned something you didn't want her to know, hadn't she? Something about vision, about what you're doing now."

All that research that obsessed her at the end. Trying to understand how vidders work, learn all the scientific details about New Vision, digging up academic reports and interviewing programmers, shadowing experts in her futile quest to make peace with the way we see now. He'd feared it was driving her crazy, and he'd kept telling her to let it go, just accept it, but she'd refused.

Had *she* figured out what Jimmy was up to, two years ago?

"Mark, man, we can talk about this when you get back. We need to hurry before the feds shoot you on sight for being a fugitive. Buddy, where are you?"

A few seconds tick past as Owens thinks through the possibilities. His mind in a very dark place, finding new corners and passageways, connections. He needs to kill this call before Peterson traces them.

"You miss it, you told me. You miss being able to see what other people can't. You miss having that power over everyone else. The power we used to have."

Peterson holds up a hand. Seeming to tell Mark to slow down. "You're very confused, Mark. You're dealing with a lot right now. Let's just meet and talk things out."

Owens turns off his vidder. Detaches it. The darkness returns.

"I'm seeing things a lot more clearly now."

He reaches out and it takes him a moment to find the right button, but he presses it.

Amira watches as Peterson's face disappears.

* * *

In the control room of the reborn Obscura Technologies, Peterson realizes the call's gone dead.

"Fuck."

He shakes his head and looks again at the hive of computers and monitors surrounding him, at the 2D and 3D holograms everywhere, including a large one of Central Plaza downtown. Feeds from body cams, street cams, helicopter cams. Hacked audio from squad cars.

Five techs man the computers, patch code. In another room, six more do the same thing. Some of them cops, some ex-cops, some ex-EyeTech. Beside Peterson stands Major Foyle, the highest-ranking city officer involved in this alliance.

"I had a lock on Owens," one of the techs says, "but he just turned his vidder off."

"Get a track on Quigley," Peterson says. "She's with him."

"Yes, sir. Should just take a few minutes."

Fucking Owens. A while back, Peterson had maintained hope that Mark would understand what they were doing, the need for it. Control, order. Get this country moving in the right direction again. Everyone was still recovering from The Blinding, mourning not just those who'd died but their lost sense, their old way of seeing the world. To have lived through that, to understand so profoundly how everything can fall apart, how civilization can be torn from its moorings . . . That never goes away.

Maybe in another generation or two. When survivors of The Blinding are old and gray, sitting in the corner muttering to themselves about how kids nowadays don't realize how good they have it.

Peterson was there. He had it as bad as anyone. Worse.

Watching what happened to Cynthia, the way she struggled through her injury, the way she failed to make sense of their new world. His heart broke every day. They tried their best to endure, so many times, so many ways. They couldn't. The Cynthia he'd known and loved was gone forever, lost in those damaged brain cells, the parts of her that had been squeezed by her fractured skull, swollen beyond repair. We humans are capable of such extraordinary acts of grace, but at the same time we're trapped by our bodies, limited by them. She would never be the same.

He felt empty for so long. Thought about swallowing his gun. Thought about taking his rage out on others. Okay, he *did* take his rage out on others. But it never helped.

If he could change anything in this sick world, he would have been home that day, would have kept her safe. From a fucking *mob* that broke out over an untrue rumor. Next thing you know, chaos, riots, trampling.

His job was to stop madness like that. To keep things calm and under control. He hadn't been able to do that when it mattered most.

He would never let that happen again.

It has now been years since the worst of The Blinding, yet still so much seems damaged, broken beyond repair. The only way to make things right is with courage, strength, power.

Someone needs to be in control.

Everyone seemed so euphoric when we got vidders, but over time the collective hangover sank in, the realization of how much had been destroyed and how hard it would be to rebuild. The economy has been stuck for years, government can't provide enough services, people feel their lives are going backward. The black hole of The Blinding still sucking at them like the swirl of a drain.

Strange how Owens can't see it Peterson's way. Like Peterson, he blames himself for all that didn't go right during The Blinding, for not being able to save more lives and prevent the chaos that they couldn't even see. Hates himself for the shooting at Western Market, among other catastrophes, as if they'd had any real choice back then. Owens has been treading water, barely, for years. His head just above the surface. Peterson's done all he could to try to send him a lifeline—hell, Peterson was the one who introduced him to Amira.

Which, yeah, Peterson did partly out of guilt for the fact that he was the one who'd killed Jeanie.

That hadn't been fun. That had been horrible.

Not the first person he'd killed, no, of course not. He'd snapped a few necks during The Blinding. And yes, before Jeanie there had even been a few times when he'd stone-killed premeditated, taking down people whom he'd never been able to get enough evidence on but who needed to go. One of the things people don't want to think about, don't like to imagine their sworn officers doing, but at the same time: yes, they do want these things done. They do want order upheld. They do want the bad people put away, warehoused, taken out of circulation. There are laws, yes, but they don't always work. Because there are lawyers. There is money. There is graft, corruption, greed, all of it, everywhere, what the hell can one lone cop do about it?

Turns out, he can do something.

He can hatch a plan. Start a movement. Talk some buddies into it.

What if there is a way? What if I told you that during an opsin-dealing investigation I busted a creepy old guy at EyeTech for some sick sexual stuff—he'd deal to young women, party with them, then tinker with their vidders while they were out cold. Then later from his apartment he found ways to hack into their vidders, mess with their vision—the women thought they were having opsin flashbacks, but really he was fucking with them. What if I told you he showed me how it worked? What if I told you what else it could do, with some more research and some funding and a lot of guinea pigs?

Starts as a few furtive conversations, only with people he trusts, the ones he knows in advance will agree. Then some anonymous chat sites for angry cops. He starts a group, quickly gathers followers. Some of them way smarter than him. Some of them with serious political connections or tech skills or both. Takes that group offline before it gets too large and gets noticed by the wrong people. Finds ways to connect in the real world.

What started as an off-the-books way to rub out the kinds of felons they were never able to nail legitimately—and a way to procure the occasional bonanza in drug money or gun money—becomes larger. Maybe a way to take even more power for themselves, to aim higher.

So he and his fellows start other online groups, not quite in the same vein but to seed the ground with similar opinions. Creating and germinating and supporting the sorts of groups that will come to their aid when the chips are down. Something this big will only work if a certain percentage of the population agrees with them, after all.

Then, Jeanie.

Annoying, bipolar Jeanie. Trying to channel her sadness over New Vision and vidders by learning everything about them: meeting with scientists, vision experts, radar techs, philosophers, geospatial programmers, hackers. As if, in learning all about these devices that she felt both enthralled by and a victim of, she might find the secret of her unhappiness. She might find out why she and Owens weren't working anymore, why her art wasn't working anymore. As if it was all the vidders' fault.

So Jeanie's research and fact-finding and police ride-alongs and long interviews with techies eventually led her to one of Peterson's guys. An EyeTech researcher, since laid off, whom Peterson had been supporting with some money he skimmed from pimps and dealers across town, a researcher Peterson fucking *owned* because Peterson had so much evidence of assorted shit the guy had gotten into, but Peterson would hold that back, would keep the guy's record clean, so long as the guy finished his research, perfected the product.

The beta tests downtown. Always in the worst neighborhoods, like the Embers. Always among the sorts of lowlife trash no one would miss and no one would believe when the survivors said they'd seen black blurs killing people.

Yeah, sure you did. Classic bullshit alibi.

A few of those cases even landed on Peterson's and Owens's desks. Peterson barely able to contain his glee as he saw the way Owens and the other cops laughed at the very idea of black blurs.

And yet. Those investigations gave Peterson plenty of opportunities to drop hints to Owens, to probe his feelings about this. About their role as police. About the society they saw—yes, truly saw—crumbling around them.

Mark, I wanted you to be a part of this. But you're a hopeless case, man. If Jeanie had been someone else, you would have seen the logic.

When the new President won and implemented his plans for a Truth Commission, that accelerated the time line. They needed to move fast, before most of them wound up in jail for shit they'd done years ago. *Citizens want to lock us up despite all the hell we went through back then?* Their plans became even more ambitious than before, aimed straight for the White House, at removing the sorts of people who only want to look backward, and installing someone who understands the importance of moving forward.

In the right hands, this power can remake the world. They can show people the kind of society they needed to feel better about themselves. What politicians and media used to call *optics,* they can do that all the time. Frame the world the right way. Because despite what the Truth Commission thinks, people don't really want to know about society's dirty underbelly, don't really want to know about all the shit that their protectors have to wade through to keep them safe.

With this new power, people like Peterson could keep citizens safe *and* keep their eyes away from what they didn't need to see. Rules being bent or broken but for the right reasons, great, let's not even engage in these annoying debates anymore because you don't even need to know those trade-offs are happening; we'll hide them from you. We'll hide plenty from you. You always wanted it that way but were afraid to admit it. Now you can live in privileged innocence, forever, and see only what we want you to see.

And the ones who didn't want to go along with them, who wanted to fight it? They could be removed, by black blurs.

Peterson and his friends would get filthy rich in the process, of course. They'd get to do what they wanted without anyone ever realizing they were behind this, yeah. But that wasn't the point.

Well, it was only partly the point.

Because if they could erect a better society, impose order on chaos, clean up this filthy city, this dirty country? Then they deserved a few rewards along the way.

"If Owens is smart," Major Foyle says in the control room, "he'll find his way back into the city without a vidder."

"He doesn't know where we are," Peterson says. The plan has come so far over the last few months. He's recruited so many more cops than he'd expected—so many that he actually worries there are *too* many, that there might be leaks. But they've made it this far, to the day they will step out of the shadows. Not just cops but also feds, prosecutors, a few judges, even three fucking *senators*.

At times he's feared it's spiraling out of his control, that the more it grows the less it becomes his. But overall it's a good thing, a wonderful thing. They have systems in place. Org structures, chains of command. Employees, for chrissake. This entire building.

"He's figured out you're involved," Foyle notes. "He could track you here."

Peterson folds his arms. If this son of a bitch thinks he can toss Peterson aside right as *his* plan comes to fruition, he is goddamn deluded, no matter how many stripes he has on his sleeve.

"No, he can't. He'd need a warrant to track me, and he can't get that as a fugitive. He'd need departmental resources, which he also doesn't have. And we're less than six hours from game time, so don't even think of trying to get me onto the sidelines."

He hates how close this has come to falling apart. O'Dell nearly ruined years of work by rushing things, deciding to take out Dr. Jensen when he learned of the scientist's experiments—not just killing him, but doing it in front of a witness whom he inexplicably let live. Then O'Dell had talked the others into targeting Ballantine, out of fear that the young tech exec would manage to marshal his company's resources against them. Taking out junkies in the Embers was one thing, but going after model citizens brought too much heat.

After today, though, all the risks will have been worth it. Peterson turns and focuses his attention on one of the monitors—Central Plaza lit up at night, the stage, the empty podium where the President will soon give his speech.

"Don't worry, Major. We still have a few tricks up our sleeves."

CHAPTER 36

Owens and Amira have been standing at her parked car for a while now.

Owens blind again, the vidder in his hands. Amira standing behind him, her eyes large. A hand on his shoulder.

"Jimmy. How did I not see it?"

"Neither of us did."

He thinks for a moment. "Before Jeanie died, she was doing all kinds of research on New Vision. She told me she needed to understand it, how it really worked and what the other possibilities were. I was worried . . . it was only feeding her depression. But she said she needed to do it, that the only way she could continue her art . . . was if she understood vidders better." He shakes his head, realizing he'll never have all the answers. "Maybe she met someone who clued her in to what was going on, even then. Maybe she learned something that led her to Jimmy."

As horrifying as it is to realize she'd been murdered, it makes more sense to him than suicide had. Sure, she'd had an artist's temperament, but he'd never imagined she would hurt herself. Her art gave her life meaning. She was endlessly questioning and searching and grappling with things, and all that uncertainty could bring her low, but at the same time she had a mission, a purpose, a drive that animated her. Even when she struggled with it. As bad as that struggle could be sometimes, the idea that she had simply given up had never made sense to him. It was easier to blame himself, to think *he'd* somehow made her do it, pushed her into it. Which, he only begins to realize now, was giving himself far too much credit, as if he were the one responsible for her decisions.

He does not feel absolved of being a bad husband and saying the wrong thing too many times. And this will all take time to figure out, realign in his memories.

What he does know is that, somehow, she must have brushed up against something dangerous and Jimmy decided she'd become a problem he had to be rid of.

What else was Jimmy involved in? Owens thinks back, to all those examples of perps claiming they'd seen black blurs committing crimes. Peterson and his allies must have been experimenting with their new abilities, just like Hinners had said, perfecting the technology. Peterson would have known which parts of town his allies could hit, which people to go after without raising a major alarm. Only taking out drug dealers and pimps, never a civilian with powerful friends, keeping the story out of the media. A street cop who'd worked Vice for years, Jimmy probably had a list of people they could eliminate without risk of the story getting out too soon.

Too soon. Meaning they didn't think it was too soon anymore. They had moved on to two scientists, wealthy civilians who had lawyers and employers and important friends, people they couldn't hide this from. Why? It made sense only if this was a new phase for them, if they'd decided they were ready for their little secret to get out.

They were on to bigger things.

He thinks back to past conversations he and Jimmy had. Over the years but more recently, too.

He thinks about Jimmy's wife, the way Jimmy had finally taken off his wedding ring after his last visit to her facility. Like he knew he was about to take a big step, do something he couldn't come back from. Like he was a new person now, different.

Jimmy had even said it: the old him didn't exist anymore.

"What do you think he's doing next?" Amira asks.

Owens realizes he had all but predicted it the other day: they'd taken out two scientists, then progressed to the richest man in the world, so who was next, the President?

Sure, why not.

"Get a map of who O'Dell's been calling the last two weeks," he says.

Amira hooks O'Dell's phone to the car computer, and a 3D hologram of the city appears. Cops used to not be able to access other people's phones like this, but more than a few laws had changed post-Blinding.

"There needs to be a central hub. Someplace they can broadcast the data to people's vidders."

Amira uses her fingers to scroll through the city map.

Lots of calls, all over the city. She zooms and scrolls, zooms and scrolls. Considers places, rules them out.

Owens impatient. "What do you see?"

"Give me a minute."

"Hurry. They're trying to track you."

There it is, has to be. A bunch of calls from Hanley Street, by the southside wharf. Lots of empty buildings, she knows from walking that beat a couple of years ago. One of the only viable businesses down there, other than a few shipping companies, is a midsized office building for one of the main telecom companies.

Several calls to a building half a block from the telecom. They could be hacking in from there. Accessing the network while working in a quiet part of town. Hiding in plain sight.

"I've got it." She tells him the address. Hopes she's right.

Truth is, they have no other option. They spend a few more minutes of Amira reading out addresses and the two of them mutually ruling them out. The building by the wharf is their best bet, by far.

Foot scuffs, several. Owens turns around.

So does Amira, and she sees that behind them, Reverend Miriam and half a dozen deacons have gathered.

"You have brought murder to our door," the spiritual leader declares.

"I'm sorry, and I wish I could have done this another way," Owens says. "But I've heard you say, Reverend"—he's never wanted to address her by that term before, feeling it unearned, but now's the time for flattery—"that there are puppet masters pulling the strings, right? This is your chance to pull back the curtain."

The curtain is being pulled tight at the headquarters for Obscura.

The building is indeed located by the wharf, a conveniently empty postindustrial neighborhood that also happens to be where several layers of cables and circuitry run, the perfect place to pirate signals. From the outside, the building that holds Obscura (no sign with the company name anywhere) looks like just another brick warehouse in need of some touching up. Inside, though, the two floors are full of programmers and gadgetry and, maybe, the first step in a revolution.

Like an old-school dot-com crossed with a police state, Peterson likes to think.

In the back of the building is a freight loading area. Peterson and Foyle watch as a dozen men, all in police SWAT uniforms, remove firearms from the boxes of guns they'd requisitioned from Slade's place a couple weeks ago. They load weapons, check and double-check, review their plans.

"First line's in position already," Peterson tells Foyle. "After the President goes down, we move the crowd out."

The SWAT cops psych each other up. Pep-talk speech, chants, nods. *Let's roll.*

Peterson and Foyle stand back while the others climb into two police squad cars that headquarters is just starting to realize are missing, plus a black unmarked and the same police tractor trailer that brought all those firearms here from the station a few days ago.

One of the senators' assistants calls from an untraceable phone. Peterson answers and gives the signal, "Skies are perfectly clear."

"Very good." Hangs up.

Peterson still can't quite believe this is happening.

CHAPTER 37

Back on the bus, Owens and Amira trace his journey to the commune in reverse.

No human being at the wheel, the bus using e-driver, as the only other sighted person at the commune was the security guard who lost his life to this. Owens hates how they left his body there. Hopes he'll be back soon to handle things properly. Hopes this isn't a doomed mission.

He and Amira sit in the second row. Behind them, more than a dozen deacons are spread out, men and women.

Kendrick had led the way, walking up to Owens and saying they were ready. Owens doesn't know if their participation is sanctioned by Reverend Miriam or if they're risking expulsion in offering their aid. Doesn't know if his sister talked Kendrick into this, and then the rest of them, or what. Didn't really have time to figure any of this out.

Owens told them his plan, which isn't all that complicated.

So here they are. Owens and Amira sit beside each other, vidders in their laps. Took them off and deactivated them so they couldn't be tracked. They'll put them back on later, right before they've arrived, but for now they sit in darkness, holding hands.

"Thank you," he tells her. "For coming for me."

"Of course."

"I know it must have looked like I'd lost it."

He hears her smile. "You never had it to begin with."

"Yeah."

Silence feels even emptier in the dark.

"But seriously. I know you didn't have to. I know you had to cross some lines. I'm still hoping it'll shake out at the end."

"If they fire me, they fire me. Maybe I'm not right for this job anyway."

"Don't say that."

He squeezes her hand. He both wishes he could look her in the eye and feels relief that he can't. He's afraid of that intimacy right now. He knows he doesn't deserve it, doesn't deserve her.

"Listen. I just wanted to say . . . I know I haven't been good for you. I know I'm still a train wreck. Maybe I . . . made the mistake of thinking that being with you could save me. But sometimes I just haven't felt worth saving." He swallows. "I know that's put you in an awful position. And I'm sorry."

He feels her pull his hand with her second hand, holding it there, rubbing the top of it.

He continues, "I'm sorry I've made you feel like you aren't enough. Because you are."

"You aren't as terrible a person as you think you are, Mark."

More silence. Maybe he's supposed to say *Yeah*, but he doesn't.

He should have seen it with Jimmy. Worse, he had enabled it. He remembers all those times he fudged the truth in reports, found ways to justify his partner's too-aggressive behavior. All the warning signs he failed to heed. He had allowed Jimmy to go bad on his watch, had enabled Jimmy's anger to fester into something worse, because he hadn't wanted to admit what he saw.

"No one's been their best self, for a while," she says. "But we have to figure out how to forgive ourselves and keep going."

He feels her lean her head on his shoulder. He hadn't expected that and he just sits there, staring at the blackness. He relaxes his shoulder a bit, accepting her weight, and they slowly lean into each other, their breaths slower now.

He doesn't know what this means for them, if there is a *them* anymore. He just knows that he loves the weight of her right now, and though he's lost track of how long they've been on the bus and how far they have to go, he finds himself hoping they won't arrive too soon, that they can sit here a while just like this, not saying anything, not seeing anything, just feeling that the other is there.

CHAPTER 38

Sunrise. Captain Carlyle has already been awake four hours and has been on the street for three and a half. Squeezed in just enough sleep to be alert and functional on what promises to be a bitch of a day.

Presidential visits are nightmares. Such visits coinciding with a holiday on which everyone's nerves are rubbed raw? So much worse.

Hundreds of people have already gathered in Central Plaza, a green square with more dirt than grass and a few insignificant trees, flanked by skyscrapers. The onlookers have all been shunted to this section or that depending on the color of the invitation they've been lucky enough to procure. The video footage will make this seem like a happy assembly of a random assortment of Americans, when really it's just movers and shakers, donors to the President's reelection committee, young politicians hoping to get even better access to the great man at some cocktail party tonight.

Before them is the stage, and between the stage and the barricades Carlyle is but one of dozens of cops and Secret Service agents.

His phone buzzes him. It's been buzzing him off and on ever since he woke up, and this is one of the few times he checks it. Anyone important would be communicating via police radio.

Amira Quigley. He hesitates, then takes the call.

Turns out it's Owens using her phone.

Once one of his best detectives, now apparently a lunatic. The last thing Carlyle needs: a potentially dirty cop, a suspect in several murders and a goddamn fugitive. Carlyle has already had his own job threatened by some self-aggrandizing FBI agents who have pull with the mayor, and let's just say he's afraid the feds might be willing to follow through on their threats this time.

Owens is the last thing Carlyle needs to be thinking about.

Worse, the man is ranting.

He's telling the captain that no, he's not psycho, but actually his partner Peterson is dirty, that *Peterson* is the one—he killed Owens's wife years ago and apparently other people too, and one of the feds who tried to arrest Owens the other day was the supposed black blur who killed one of those scientists, as well as unknown others in the Embers—this thing is big, we need to stop it, it's spiraled into some kind of plot involving dirty cops and feds.

"I'm talking to a dirty cop," Carlyle snaps.

"Captain, you have to listen to me. I'm not a part of it. I just figured this out, me and Amira Quigley. Jimmy wants to go back to the days when we were the only ones with vidders. The black blurs, they're *real*. They want to be able to tap into what people can and can't see. I should have figured this out sooner, but it sounded so crazy."

"Yes, it does sound crazy." Carlyle takes the phone from his ear, yells at a nearby cop, tells him to instruct an onlooker in the crowd to back away from the rope that he's leaning on. *People are so stupid.* "It sounds like the very definition of crazy."

"O'Dell said something's going to happen today. And his partner, Magnus—I don't think he's dirty too, but he just told us O'Dell had gone out of his way to get himself posted to the security detail for the President's speech today. Captain, I think they're going to do something at the Plaza."

"Owens, if you want to be part of the solution, turn yourself in. In the meantime, I have a hell of a big job to do."

The tractor trailer loaded with cops bent on killing the President drives through town. Approaches one checkpoint, gets waved on by a cop who has no clue, just knows that they're on the list.

Approaches another checkpoint, gets waved on by a cop who's actually in on this.

The loaded truck enters what is currently the most secure area in the country.

In the Obscura control room, Peterson kind of wishes he were at the Plaza to see this happen himself but also realizes how important his presence is here. This is where the technological magic happens, and although he doesn't understand how exactly the magic works (that's for the tech nerds), he's here to wave his wand and make sure everyone does their job.

He sees helicopter footage of the truck passing the second checkpoint.

"Excellent. They're in."

The tech in front of him clicks and drags. "We're a go. Going dark in five, four, three . . ."

A local town councilwoman whose husband died saving their children from a burning skyscraper during The Blinding is giving a speech so sad, Carlyle feels woozy in his stomach even though he isn't really listening. Her tone of voice is enough. He's facing the crowd, and just seeing everyone's expressions makes him depressed.

He stands at the periphery of the crowd, watching for any odd movements, any sign that someone might have somehow secreted a weapon through the many concentric circles of metal detectors and security checkpoints. Also making sure his officers are doing their jobs while projecting the proper solemnity and respect, which is borderline impossible.

He speaks words of encouragement into a collar mike.

"All right, folks. President's up in thirty, more or less."

Then he notices, at the edge of the Plaza, driving down a blocked street that's only supposed to be open to police traffic, a large black blur. Very large. The approximate size of a tractor trailer. It was in motion, but now it stops.

He stares in disbelief. Reaches up to adjust his vidder. Which doesn't help.

"Anyone see what just drove up to the southwest corner?"

Thirty yards away, Khouri had been facing the other direction, but now she turns and sees it. More precisely, she doesn't see it.

"Negative, Captain." Her throat's already gone dry. This cannot be happening. "It's . . . blacked out."

Something weirder happens. It looks like the blur is molting, growing boils and then shedding itself. No, Khouri realizes, what's happening is that other smaller black blurs are moving away from the larger one. That's a truck, it has to be, but it's blocked from her vision somehow, and right now many, many person-sized blurs are emerging from the truck. They walk in pairs, splitting up with military precision as they approach the crowd.

CHAPTER 39

From outside it looks to Amira like just another old warehouse converted into a tech start-up. Brick walls, new windows, two stories. A quiet neighborhood, no traffic. Tall antennas stand on the roof, a taller one looms in the distance.

The commune's smelly bus pulls up at the nearest intersection, a block away. Owens and Amira are wearing their vidders again, having put them back on just a minute ago. Waited as long as they could, not wanting to do it too early and give headquarters or Peterson a chance to trace them.

"You seeing okay?" she asks him.

"Still fuzzy, but good enough."

"Same here. I hate how long it can take."

Owens instructs the e-driver to move up another thirty yards, closer to the building. It's an old bus and the e-driver is wonky, but it works. He'd been worried about even using an e-driver, in case Obscura had somehow coded a system of alerts to let it know if and when anyone entered its address into their e-driver's instructions, but they've made it this far.

"There's a loading dock in back," Amira says, pointing.

"Okay. You take that, I'll get the front door."

He stands up and addresses the men and women on board.

"Time to convert the heretics."

* * *

Khouri doesn't understand what she's not seeing.

Carlyle's in the same predicament, as are the dozens of cops staring out at the crowd and wondering why chunks of their vision have gone black.

Carlyle notices even more black blurs: not only are some emerging from what must be a giant truck that's redacted from his vision, but other black blurs appear. People in the crowd, who must have had VIP passes to get this far, have suddenly gone black, as if they've been stricken from his vision. He'd think he was slowly going blind again if not for the fact that Khouri and some others tell him they see the same thing.

Suddenly he wishes he could be talking to Owens again. Or could replay their conversation, hear some of the points he'd barely been listening to. Peterson and dirty cops and some feds? Planning an assassination at the Plaza? It didn't make sense a few minutes ago and doesn't make sense now, but he's seeing it, or not seeing it; the point is, this is what Owens was talking about. Black blurs are everywhere and they're quickly converging on the stage.

He hears Khouri over his earpiece: "What's going on, Captain?"

Over his mike he asks his next four lieutenants if they see black blurs too or can they actually see the people who have been redacted from his own vision. Three of them say they can't. One isn't even responding.

He issues an order to everyone: "I don't know how they're doing it, but whatever those are in Areas 1, 2, and 3, stop them, now!"

The crowd, most of which hasn't yet noticed the black blurs coming from behind, bursts into applause, because the President has finally been announced and is walking up to the podium behind Carlyle. Probably smiling at the crowd and waving.

Whoever these black blurs really are, Carlyle realizes that they've timed this almost perfectly. But only almost. They didn't factor in how a politician would slowly wave to the crowd and shake hands for a while before isolating himself at the podium. Or so Carlyle hopes. He's yelling alerts to the Secret Service, telling them to get the POTUS the hell out of here, now.

All those black blurs who suddenly appeared in the crowd, maybe they're not VIPs at all. *Dirty cops and some feds,* Owens had said. Jesus, some of these are Carlyle's people. That's how they got through the security perimeter before erasing themselves from view.

He gives more orders over his mike, wondering all the while if the wrong people are listening.

The employee parking lot behind Obscura Technologies is blocked by a large metal gate. No attendant, just a keypad and scanner that controls the door.

It turns out the gate isn't strong enough to repel a speeding bus.

The e-driver had refused Amira's spoken commands. She finally has to turn off the e-driver and get behind the wheel herself (safe to do now that she can see again). She floors the accelerator. The gate flies off its hinges. Cracks appear on the right side of the bus's windshield, but the vehicle speeds on unimpeded.

She slows to a stop barely one foot before she would have slammed into a row of parked cars. Maneuvers her way through the lot toward the back loading dock.

"All right, people, here we go!"

She gives her blind assistants the rough measurements of the parking lot, tells them how much space they have to work with. Not even sure if they'll be able to use this information or not. She still doesn't understand how much help blind acolytes could possibly be, but Owens said they were better than nothing.

Not exactly true: if she's brought these people to their death, that's far worse than nothing. She hopes this isn't a colossal mistake.

She pulls the handle to open the bus door and out the deacons pour. Seven men, three women. All clutching staffs.

Outside the bus, the acolytes start proselytizing to an audience of zero, as if they're at any other street corner. As if there are any pedestrians around.

"Seek Inner Sight, my friends!"

"Do not fall for their wicked illusions!"

Amira jumps out of the bus and hopes they're a good enough distraction as she hustles toward the building's back door.

In the Obscura control room, Peterson had been watching 3D holograms displaying the scene at the Plaza, but now he notices another monitor. A commune bus. Robed, blind men and women, screaming right outside.

"What the hell?"

One of the techs sees it too, then speaks the obvious: "Wait. That's happening *here*."

"Get them out of there!" Peterson snaps. He knows something happened to O'Dell last night—he and his partner went to the commune to catch Owens, and they haven't been heard from since. Which means Owens was at the commune. And now the commune is here. Which means Owens and Amira are here, too. Do they have anyone else? Is half the Department about to storm the building?

Pulse racing, he checks more monitors. Doesn't see any squad cars. No helicopters. Plus they've been monitoring the police frequencies and haven't heard anything about this. Owens and Amira have only the blind as allies.

He realizes no one has responded to his commands. He looks at one of the techs, a twentysomething named Jones, who actually started out in the Police Department's IT unit before being fired for inappropriately looking up information on attractive civilian women and trying to blackmail them. Peterson personally recruited him for this job.

As an ex-cop, though, Jones should know how to handle a weapon.

"Go out and get them the hell away from here," Peterson tells him. He would send more, but he can't spare the manpower. He needs all these techs at their controls, now especially.

"Sir?" one of the seated techs says as Jones checks his weapon and heads out the door. "All are in position. Time to go from dark to gone."

"Do it," Peterson says. "Let's see if this works."

"Going to gone in five, four, three . . ."

Five Secret Service agents rush in from the edge of the stage. They've heard Carlyle's alert but hadn't needed to, because they too see what the captain and Khouri and so many others are now seeing. Mysterious black blurs massing around the perimeter and even snaking through the crowd toward the stage.

Three of the agents pull down on the President's shoulders, interrupting him while he'd still been waving at the crowd. The other two aim their weapons into the crowd, which goes from cheers to shrieks like *that*.

"Get down!" one of the agents yells at the blurs, whatever they are. "Get down now!"

As if to obey, the blurs vanish.

They're gone.

The other two agents stare as their colleagues hustle the POTUS offstage. Carlyle stares from his position twenty feet away. Khouri stares as well.

All of them wonder if maybe the blurs weren't there at all. Wonder if maybe this was just some weird mass vidder glitch. If maybe all has now returned to normal.

Unless.

Everyone in the crowd is in flux, people ducking because the Secret Service agents and several cops are pointing weapons at them, people turning to flee what they fear is about to become a mob, people trapped against other people because everyone is trying to move at the same time and there's nowhere to go.

Then Khouri notices something funny. Despite all those bodies being pressed together, there are little pockets of space here and there.

Empty spaces. Person-sized empty spaces.

Then, *gunshots*. Automatic weapons.

The stage is shredded with bullets. The Secret Service agents are down, several cops are down. Carlyle finds cover behind a metal bollard barely thick enough. Khouri crouches low, relatively safe because no one seems to be firing at the side yet.

She and Carlyle figure it out then. The black blurs may have disappeared, but they're still there. Whoever those people were, they went from redacted to invisible. Whoever is manipulating everyone's vidders just took a big step forward with their tech wizardry. They've figured out how to make people disappear completely, make other people see through them, not even realize they're there.

Invisible assassins are firing at the stage and Khouri doesn't know how to fire back. She aims her gun but doesn't pull the trigger. Firing into a crowd of civilians would be terrible enough with a discernible target, but she has none.

Some of the other cops who'd been lining the front point with their weapons, also looking for targets and not seeing any.

One by one, they fall.

CHAPTER 40

In the Obscura parking lot, the robed evangelists wander randomly around the building as they preach to no one. Some approach the front door but mostly they wander in vague circles.

An Obscura employee in white shirt, black slacks, an ID badge, and a holstered sidearm walks out the front door.

"This is private property!" he yells. "You need to leave, now!

"Telecom devil!" a deacon replies.

"You must seek the truth!" another says.

The tech walks closer to the bus, takes a pistol out of his pocket, and aims it at the first deacon who mouthed off.

"I said get the fuck out of here!"

"He's pointing a gun," one of the deacons says. Not alarmed. Just calmly stating a fact. It makes the tech think, *How the hell does he know? How could he hear that?*

It makes *him* the alarmed one.

Four deacons slowly encircle the tech.

"You can't see," he states the obvious. It *should* be obvious, right? "How would you know . . . ?"

"Your voice," one of them says. "Your tone. The smell of metal."

Another adds, "The smell of your fear."

The tech feels like he's been dropped into some weird nightmare from a Catholic school past he doesn't actually have.

"You have three seconds to get—"

Before he can finish his threat, another deacon, who'd been standing to his side, wields his staff as a weapon. Expertly knocks the gun out of the tech's hand.

A deacon on the other side of the tech strikes him in the stomach with the butt of his staff, doubling him over.

Two whacks to the skull and the tech is out.

Owens opens the door to Obscura's lobby, his hands in his cloak. Two deacons trail close behind. A beefy security guard stands not behind but in front of a large desk. He'd been watching the inexplicable fight through the window and was about to abandon his post to help out, but now these three newcomers block his path.

"This is private property."

Owens brandishes the gun he swiped from O'Dell. The two deacons hold their staffs at the ready.

"Police!" Owens shouts. "Hands in the air, now!"

The guard is frozen for a moment. Then he smiles.

"I *am* police, asshole. Damn near everyone in this building is police."

In the control room, a seated tech gets the news he's been waiting for. He zooms in on a map and tells Peterson, "I just got a lock on Owens's vidder."

"Where is he?" Though he fears he knows the answer.

"He's . . ." The map looks very familiar. "Oh, shit."

The guard, Owens, and the two deacons maintain their standoff.

Owens demands, "I said put your fucking hands in the air, now!"

The guard who claims to be a cop keeps his composure impressively despite having a gun in his face.

"You're very disturbed, Detective Owens," the man says. "People have been worried about you. I think you need to sit down and rest a minute."

Owens steps forward.

"Don't make me do this. Put your hands up. Now."

The guard twitches for his pistol. He doesn't have a chance with a gun aimed at him. Maybe he doesn't truly believe this is happening. Maybe he doesn't think Owens will really do it, shoot a man who claims to be a fellow officer.

Owens doesn't hesitate. Squeezes the trigger. The guard goes down.

He kicks the man' gun away. Tries the entry door, but it's locked. Fires at the knob, twice, and kicks at the door.

"Oh my God," one of the deacons is muttering to another. They heard the body fall, hear that the guard isn't talking or breathing. They are realizing what they signed up for.

Owens tells them to wait here.

He peers past the open door. Sees a long, wide hallway. Marble floors gleaming. Doors every few feet, all of them closed. Each portal potentially providing a bit of cover.

He proceeds slowly. Listening. Which door? He sees no signs. Hears voices but can't tell where they're coming from.

A figure appears at the end of the hallway. A tall man, dark hair. Armed, gun raised.

Owens flattens himself into one of the doorways as the man fires. The shooter fires twice more, a third time. Pause.

Owens leans out, fires twice. The man falls.

Owens steps out hesitantly, then races forward. As he's about to pass another door, it opens. He sees another man, another gun.

Owens fires, but something doesn't compute. He hears bullets strike metal. The gunman vanishes. Not because he's fallen but because he's not there. He wasn't there at all.

Owens keeps aiming at where the man had been.

The second gunman hadn't existed, he realizes. It's what he's been most worried about: if they know you're coming for them, they'll find other ways to manipulate your vidder. They're doing it right now. Maybe the first gunman had been real, then they'd started hacking into him. Happening that fast.

He steps forward, even more hesitantly than before. Fear amping up higher.

"Police!" he screams. "We're shutting you down! Come out with your hands up!"

Most likely a waste of breath. He doesn't know how many of them there are, how heavily they're armed. And if they can play with what he sees, he's fucked.

He feels motion from behind. Feels it or hears it? He's not sure, but he spins around. Through the front door—the same one he'd blasted his way through—steps another gunman. Real or not?

The gunman starts to lift his gun. Owens fires twice. This gunman too vanishes, like the last one.

And in that one instant, in walks Amira. Right where the nonexistent gunman had been.

She's hit in the chest by Owens's bullets. She falls.

Everything is eerily silent. Owens lowers his gun as he walks toward her, stunned.

His mouth opens but he can't even talk. His voice gone.

Oh my God oh my God oh my God.

She's lying on the ground, blood darkening her shirt. Not even coughing. Not even blood on her lips. There's one twitch, a spasm of the legs, and then she's still.

Owens hears only a buzzing. The very sound of the cognitive dissonance in his addled brain.

He steps toward her. Vidders aren't affected by tears, so he sees her clearly even as his eyes fill. He drops his gun.

He never should have come here. They tricked him, made him shoot his own girlfriend. He thought he could outsmart them and he was wrong. And she's the one who's been punished for it.

He finds his voice. "Oh my God. Amira . . ."

He's still processing this when Petersons enter the hallway. Gun aimed at Owens.

"Hey, partner," the son of a bitch says.

Owens turns. Unnecessarily wipes away the tears; old habit.

"You want to blame me for that one, too?" Peterson asks. "Fine, I'll take it. Been covering for your mistakes a while now."

Peterson takes another step and kicks Owens's gun away.

Owens feels dizzy. A sickening sensation he remembers all too well. No matter how hard you try to suppress something, it's always there. And when it comes back a second time it laughs at you for thinking you could escape it.

"I felt bad about Jeanie, Mark. It wasn't supposed to happen like that. She was trying to learn about how to manipulate vidders, for her 'art.' Stumbled upon some sensitive information. I wish it hadn't gone down that way."

Owens makes himself stop looking at Amira.

"The other guys wanted to frame you for it," Peterson says, "but I didn't see any reason to go that far. I did you a favor, man, marking it a suicide. Otherwise you might've been locked up."

Owens shakes his head. "How many cops are in on this?"

"Enough. The rest will join in when they see what we're doing."

"And what is it you think you're doing?"

"This isn't about hit jobs, Mark. Now that we have the technology down, think of the possibilities! We can give people what they want to see: a peaceful, perfect world. Hide the dirty parts from them. Cops have always been the ones that are supposed to trick people into thinking the world's a perfectly safe place, or at least keep the shadows away from them."

"Because you'll be the shadows? You're crazy, all of you."

"No, Mark, you're crazy not to be on board. Jesus, don't you get it? They're coming for us! The Truth Commission, the fucking President and his army of lawyers like Huntington. They're gonna take us all down, unless we do something to stop them. They all want to blame us for what went down during The Blinding. Okay, so some cops did well for themselves back then, so some of us managed to turn a little profit out of the chaos, so what? Other people would've done the same if they'd been in that position."

"I didn't fucking profit. What did you do, steal some property? Sell opsin on the side?"

"I'm as human as anybody else. But come on, man, what did you think was gonna happen after your deposition? You think they'd just let you walk for what happened at Western Market?"

"Don't you fucking compare what happened that night to the shit you've been up to! That was a mistake, Jesus, it was an awful mistake that I live with every day, but it's not the same as you deliberately taking—"

"Save it, man! Tell it to the judge. No wait, you won't have to, because *we're* taking out the fucking Truth Commission so guys like you don't have to see the inside of a cell."

Owens shakes his head. "Don't make it sound noble. You just want to get what you want and control people."

Peterson shrugs. "That too."

"You set me up. And Slade—he was just a drug dealer. You needed a way to arm your little militia under the radar, so you made like he was a gunrunner. But *you* were."

"And even though nobody at EyeTech would work with us, we got enough of their disgruntled former employees to do what we needed. Want to see the control room? Amazing stuff, not that I understand how most of it works. And they're getting better at it, Mark. They'll be creating whole new worlds soon, virtual reality times a million. Places where people will be able to hide, escape, relax."

"While you do whatever the hell you want in the real world."

"Now you're getting it."

Then Peterson seems to notice something at the edge of his field of vision.

Peterson turns and beholds a dozen deacons running toward him. Silently. They look insane. Blind eyes wide, teeth bared, faces gaunt and thin. Starved zombies desperate for flesh. Running toward him with staffs. Eerily gliding, noiseless.

The lack of sound should be a tip-off, but the sighted have always put more stock in vision than the other senses. Peterson points his gun at them and fires.

No one falls. They keep coming.

"What the hell?"

He fires again and again and again, but still they charge. One runs into him. Through him. Not a zombie—a ghost.

He's just realizing what's happening when Owens tackles him from behind. With his gun in his hand he can't brace himself. His head hits the ground hard.

The deacons weren't there at all. This time Peterson was the one seeing things. The manipulations can work both ways, depending on who's at the controls. The deacons or some other ally of Owens must have broken into the control room, taken over, told Obscura to target Peterson's vidder. But that's the least of Peterson's worries right now.

The two partners roll on the ground, grappling, searching for leverage, an advantage of any kind.

In the control room, the very aggrieved techs sit at their desks with wooden staffs pressed up to their necks. The room has been overrun with staff-wielding deacons, including Kendrick.

On one of the monitors, Owens and Peterson fight, but of course the deacons can't see what's on a 2D monitor, can't perceive any rumblings or vibrations. They can only hear the struggle over the speakers.

"Good," Kendrick tells the tech whom he'd been about to strangle if he didn't do what Kendrick told him. "Now shut it down—all of it."

Owens and Peterson wrestle with each other, rolling over. Owens on top, he drives a punch into his partner's face.

Then he sees that they've rolled close to Amira's body. It distracts him. Literally sucks the breath out of him. Bad timing. Peterson slips a hand out to the side, to throw a punch.

As he does, Owens sees his arm pass through Amira.

She's not really there, Owens realizes. She'd only been inserted into his vision. He hadn't really shot her.

Owens's eyes are wide, but the joy doesn't last because Peterson clocks him.

Chaos at Central Plaza.

Secret Service agents and cops are gunned down by invisible attackers. Civilians scatter in whichever direction they think offers safety, or whichever direction they can get to first, or wherever they see a friend go. But no place is better than any other.

Near the stage, Carlyle is still crouched behind a stone bollard.

"Does anyone have a visual?" Khouri barks into her mike. She continues to stand at the side, hears the gunshots and sees where they're hitting, but still has no clue where the invisible shooters are. As the crowd escapes, the shooters have plenty of empty space to hide in.

And just like that, they appear.

The gunshots pause for a moment. Carlyle, still crouching behind the bollard, dares to take a look, and he sees the shooters standing in the open. Cops in SWAT gear, their guns smoking. They're looking down at themselves, seeming to realize that something has gone wrong.

"Those are not cops!" Carlyle shouts into his mike. "Take them down, now!"

From their cover all over the Plaza, the embattled cops and agents finally return fire. Ecstatic to have a visual target. The attackers had been confident in their invisibility, not needing to hide behind anything. But now they're exposed, standing in the middle of an abandoned plaza.

They start dropping.

It ends with surprising speed. They all wear vests, so the non-dirty cops have to aim for the head. More than a few of them take a few rounds in the chest, fall, keep firing, until they're shot again, and again. Blood everywhere. At least the crowd has dispersed, the innocents now far away.

Khouri notices that some of her colleagues hold their fire, unwilling or unable to fire on people wearing the uniform. Even though they're clearly saboteurs, turncoats. More than a few of the SWAT-clad men and women who'd been blurs a moment ago manage to escape, fleeing from the Plaza and into the side roads.

Carlyle slowly walks out into the Plaza, keeping low. Khouri and a few other cops do the same. Kick away guns, scan the perimeter, double- and triple-check that there are no other shooters. Cops surround the tractor trailer, demand that anyone left inside come out. Over the radio they hear calls for the bomb squad, just in case.

Helicopters still fly overhead. Security cameras silently take note from awnings and street poles.

Owens and Peterson wrestle on the ground, hands at each other's throats. Peterson gains the edge, rolling over Owens and pinning him with his greater bulk.

Yet Owens frees a hand and smashes Peterson's vidder with his fist. Might have broken a bone in his hand, but he can see from Peterson's eyes that it worked.

Peterson reciprocates. A meaty fist clubs Owens in the side of the head, twice in case the first one didn't work.

Owens's vision flickers. First he sees nothing but pixels in different shades of gray, then all goes black. Again. Like at Slade's club.

The two blind cops break free of each other and back up a few steps. Both breathing heavily.

They slowly circle each other like blind, bloodied boxers.

Both know there are two pistols on the floor, somewhere. Each realizing the other could be about to step on one.

"Come on, Mark. Admit you're on the wrong side. Maybe we can let you back in."

Owens doesn't realize it, never will, but his foot has just missed stepping on one of the pistols. By less than an inch. Then he moves on, the gun farther away with each step.

"Keep talking," he says.

They circle some more. Slowly. Waiting. Hoping.

Peterson wins. His right foot glances against something solid. It doesn't make a sound. He puts his foot back on it, gently, to make sure it's there. Yep, that's a gun. He can't let Owens know he's found it yet.

Peterson slowly bends down. Tries not to grunt, which he tends to do when he squats like this. Wonders if his clothes make any audible sound as he does so, if his tendons creak, will his aging ligaments betray him.

He reaches for the gun.

His fingers close around the handle. He slowly raises himself back to full height. Exhales deeply, which is probably a giveaway, but at this point he's won.

Moves his head, pointing the gun blind, seeking a target. He just needs Owens to talk.

Owens knows. From the way Peterson changed his gait, from that exhalation. Peterson has a gun now, he must. Owens can't say a word or he'll be giving the bastard an aural target.

Peterson says, "She was still alive when I put the noose around her."

Owens wills his face to stone. Must. Stay. Silent.

"So drugged out she didn't realize what I was doing. Even gave me a big sloppy kiss."

"Motherfucker—" Owens can't resist saying.

He makes himself stop, but it's too late, he's given himself away.

The next thing he hears is that tiny wet crack, lips parting, the sound of Peterson smiling now that he knows where Owens is. He can't hear Peterson moving his arm and aiming but he knows that's happening, knows he's lost.

"Keep breathing, Mark."

A gunshot.

A second.

Time is weird without vision, especially in moments of silence and extreme stress. It could be two seconds, maybe ten. It feels an eternity. Owens sees nothing, hears nothing. Doesn't smell gunfire yet. Feels nothing but his injuries, the sweat all over his body, his aching head, the slight shake of his limbs from the adrenaline.

He hears a body hit the floor. Feels the force of it landing.

Peterson's a big guy.

Amira's voice: "Mark!"

He touches his chest to double-check. Sweat but nothing that feels like blood. Nothing that feels worse than the punches he's absorbed. No bullet wounds.

Footsteps coming toward him.

"Amira? That really you?"

"It's me." Her voice closer than he'd expected. "It's over."

He feels a hand on his shoulder. Her hand.

He reaches out, takes her face in both his hands. Feels her there, knows it's her.

In the background he hears more footsteps. Amira assures him it's the deacons—real ones, not holograms. Walking slowly, staffs at the ready, not realizing that the danger has passed. She tells him she's already zip-tied the Obscura staff.

He feels her pulling him toward her. Their chests meet; he turns his head to the side so his chin can clear her shoulder. Somehow she feels even taller when he can't see. They fit together so well. They breathe like that for a while, neither letting go.

"Are you hurt?" a man asks. Kendrick, Owens thinks. Thank goodness he's still alive; his sister never would have forgiven him had anything happened to Kendrick.

"We're good," Amira says.

She and Owens step back. She finds his vidder on the ground. Peterson had hit it so hard that it detached. She carefully picks it up.

CHAPTER 41

News reports will attempt to make sense of what happened at the Plaza. A coup attempt by a rogue faction of police officers, FBI agents, even a few members of Congress. The political alignments not always intuitive, even confusing at first, except for this: they all had done something during The Blinding that they needed to keep hidden.

Investigators and journalists will sift through conflicting statements, so many people who still aren't sure what it is they just saw. The indisputable fact that someone had figured out how to manipulate vidders, hide in plain sight, spread chaos to disguise their true plans.

The chaos has been dispelled, but not the doubts. If these madmen can do that, what will the next madmen do?

The President will later give a speech letting everyone know he is alive and well. He'll thank the selfless officers and Secret Service agents who gave their lives defending him. He'll vow to bring all the perpetrators to justice and initiate proceedings into anyone associated with the coup attempt. Yet another Truth Commission will be needed. He will insist that the police and federal authorities can be trusted (they aren't *all* corrupt, right?), and, just as important, he will assure people that they can continue to trust what they see.

Reverend Miriam will also give a statement, reminding people that "no one can manipulate what is truly in our hearts and minds." Her following will grow.

* * *

On the other side of town, at the Museum of Modern and Contemporary Art, the few patrons who have managed not to be scared home by the news alerts about the nearby violence walk through a new gallery of Jeanie's work. A sign at the gallery's entrance reads "Forever Clear, Forever Obscured: The Visions of Jeanie MacArthur."

At the gallery entrance, beside two long paragraphs detailing her life and work, a hologram of Jeanie welcomes visitors. It was recorded not for this showing, of course, but for a documentary a fellow artist had been working on, six months before Jeanie's death. Her murder. The documentary came out a year after her murder and went on to win an award. Owens had never watched it.

Jeanie's long hair blows in the wind of another time. She reaches up for her vidder. Removes it.

"Some of my best-known work I did blind," the hologram of Jeanie from years ago says. "I just . . . have to take this off sometimes. Need to stop using it as a crutch. Trust what's inside me. Trust my own visions."

One day, not long from now, Owens will return to the museum. He will not run out in tears like at that cocktail party. He will wander through the exhibit and will actually stand there while his long-dead wife hovers before his eyes and seems to address him.

"Sometimes that leads to something incredibly ugly, you know?" the hologram of Jeanie will say. "But just as often I find a beauty there, a clarity I wouldn't have otherwise had. You have to risk one to discover the other."

But right now, in the Obscura hallway, only a few feet from his fallen partner, Owens feels the vidder that Amira has placed in the palm of his hands. His eyes are blank, but if he could see, he'd be staring down at the vidder.

He holds it in front of himself, unsure what to do with it.

ACKNOWLEDGEMENTS

This is a work of speculative fiction. Although the idea of blindness—especially mass, worldwide, near-instantaneous blindness—is treated as a strong negative by most of the characters, it's not my intention to aim scorn or disrespect at the millions of blind people in our world today. As always, my characters' opinions on various subjects are not stand-ins for my own.

In writing about the experience of navigating the world blind, and understanding the relationship between vision and cognition, I found *Touching the Rock* by John M. Hull and *The Mind's Eye* by Oliver Sachs to be particularly helpful. To appreciate the consequences of new surveillance technology on law enforcement, I recommend Jon Fasman's *We See It All: Liberty and Justice in an Age of Perpetual Surveillance*.

Big thanks to: my family and friends, especially during this rough pandemic time; my agent, Susan Golomb, and her colleagues at Writer's House; my editor, Kelley Ragland, and the team at Minotaur; Michael Koryta, who was a very early reader, and whose enthusiastic reminder about this project propelled me in a new and better direction; the many booksellers and librarians who have passed my work on to readers; and, of course, readers like you.